TROUBLE

ALSO BY J.L. BERG

Twist of Fate

By The Bay Series

The Choices I've Made

The Scars I Bare

The Lies I've Told

The Mistakes I've Made

TROUBLE

THE CREED LEGACY
BOOK TWO

J.L. BERG

Trouble
Paperback Edition

Love N. Books Press
An Imprint of Wolfpack Publishing
1707 E. Diana Street
Tampa, FL 33610

www.lovenbookspress.com

Edited by My Brother's Editor

Paperback ISBN 979-8-89567-765-0
Ebook ISBN 979-8-89567-764-3
LCCN

For Persie, our missing piece.

NOTE FROM THE AUTHOR

Due to the sensitive nature of some scenes, I believe it is my responsibility as an author to inform my readers of any content that might be potentially triggering.

- Bullying (brief)
- Homelessness (mentioned, brief)
- Poverty (mentioned, brief)
- Revenge pornography
- Emotional abuse/neglect
- Talk of past trauma
- Alcohol consumption
- Chronic illness (mentioned, brief)

TROUBLE

PROLOGUE

Presley

AUGUST

I'm never drinking again.

My skull feels like it's being used in a drum line. I'm pretty sure I'm sweating some sort of alcohol—*god, is that tequila?*—out of my pores, and my stomach is both growling and queasy at the same time.

I crack an eyelid open and try to wipe away the remnants of last night's mascara while simultaneously blocking out the sun.

Jesus, that's bright.

What did I do last night to earn this hellish hangover?

Or maybe the right question is what didn't I do?

As a bartender, I should know better than this. I really should. But when your thirtieth birthday trip gets shot to hell because your ex-boyfriend decides to fuck you over—and I mean *really* fuck you over—normal rules don't apply.

This was supposed to be a romantic weekend for two. I'd planned it months ago. Non-refundable, of course.

So instead of sightseeing and dinners out on the strip, I spent my time getting wasted by the pool, trying to forget all about Jace and his stupid...

A deep groan pierces the silence.

Oh god, I didn't.

I peek over to the other side of the bed.

Oh god, I did.

I let out a high-pitched shriek, pulling the sheets up to my eyeballs. Am I naked? "What the fuck?"

I must have one hell of a hangover, because it's only then that I notice my surroundings. My eyes widen. This is definitely not the hotel room I started my trip in.

Believe me, I would have remembered.

Compared to the standard queen I checked into a few days earlier, this room might as well be a palace. It's like the kind of suite you see in movies reserved for high rollers. I once saw this movie where the casino offered some hotshot poker player a suite just like this. That's how nice it is. There are floor-to-ceiling windows, a full bar, and a large sitting area. The bed is so massive, no wonder I didn't notice my mystery man sleeping next to me.

Speaking of...

God, I can't even remember the last time I had a one-night stand. This is so embarrassing. I glance over, and although most of his body is hidden underneath the sheets, I do get an eyeful of defined pecs and ripped biceps.

Okay, Mystery Man isn't looking too bad so far.

My eyes move upward until I'm staring into a set of familiar green eyes. Oh my god...

"Hollis?"

"Hey, Pres." His voice sounds different in person, and

I feel a shiver run down my spine as I hear my name roll off his tongue.

"I'd say long time no see, but we seem to have already reacquainted ourselves." He clears his throat.

I'll say...

I haven't seen Hollis Beck since high school. Until two months ago, I hadn't spoken to him in twelve years. But that's all we've done—talked and sent a ton of texts. This is the first time I've seen him as an adult.

And what a fine adult he's turned out to be.

My cheeks pinken. How could they not? I'm hungover and in bed with my brother's best friend from high school. "Yeah," I nervously chew my bottom lip and pull the sheet tighter against my body. I realize then that I am not, in fact, naked—just nearly. I'm stripped down to a lace bra and panties. "Do you remember what we..." I blush again.

Jesus.

"No, all I remember is our phone call the day before yesterday. When I found out you were here by yourself—"

"You flew out to surprise me," I say, finishing his sentence.

He nods with a sheepish smile. Hollis Beck has always been good-looking. When he moved to Malibu, every girl in school wanted to date him. Now, he's just stupid hot. His auburn-brown curls are longer than I remember and contrast perfectly with his soft green eyes.

"I do remember that."

Now that he mentioned it, that part of my birthday is returning. He called me and said he had something delivered to the hotel for my birthday, and I needed to go down to the lobby to collect it. I expected to find flowers or a box of chocolates. Instead, I see Hollis standing in the lobby with a small suitcase and a huge grin. I couldn't believe he had dropped everything to fly all the way from Nashville to be with me on my birthday. "But everything after we left the hotel is sort of blurry. I remember walking around Vegas and maybe having drinks at a bar?"

His lips part in a silent gasp, and I see his eyes go alarmingly wide. Does he remember something? Is there a spider? I wait for him to say something, but he doesn't. He just stares intensely at my...*boobs*? No, those are hidden under the sheet.

I look down and realize I'm still clutching the sheet with my—

Now, it's my turn to gasp.

Because resting on my hand is a slim gold band.

"Oh, no, no, no," I start chanting like it will somehow do something. Like the foreign piece of jewelry on my finger will vanish if I simply will it away with enough words.

My eyes dart across the bed in hopes that I'm just jumping to conclusions. Maybe I just bought myself a present?

But Hollis is already holding out his left hand, staring at the matching gold band on his own ring finger.

"What the fuck did we do?"

"I think we got married."

Chapter One

PRESLEY

JUNE—TWO MONTHS EARLIER...

He's late. Again.

It's fifteen after. His shift started at seven sharp, and this is the second time this week he's been late.

I can practically hear my older brother judging me, saying something like, "This is why you shouldn't date coworkers, Presley."

Unfortunately, Cash might be right on this one. To make matters worse, Jace isn't even my coworker.

He's my employee.

I've been working at Creeds, my family's bar, ever since I turned eighteen. About a year ago, after trying to prove myself for over a decade, my dad finally decided to hand over the reins.

One of my first decisions as boss was hiring my new boyfriend, Jace.

Yeah, I know. It was a bad idea, but he needed a job. At first, he was the model employee. He was eager to learn, always willing to help, and the customers loved him.

But that was then.

I don't know why I check my watch again. It's still fifteen minutes past seven, and normally I wouldn't be this annoyed. It's a Wednesday, and Creeds isn't usually too busy this time of the week. But without him here, I'm the only one here to man the bar, so naturally, we're slammed.

I swear, every Manic Fanatic in the state walked through our doors in the last hour, and we're now packed with people, all wanting to catch a glimpse of the place where Zander Tate, lead guitarist for Manic at Midnight, started out.

"Is it true Zander used to play here?" the redhead in front of me asks as I mix her Malibu and Coke. She's barely a day over twenty-one—believe me, I checked—and her hopeful gaze roams the crowd like Zander himself will manifest any second and whisk her away.

It takes every ounce of willpower not to roll my eyes. Zander never comes here anymore. He can't—not when celebrity-themed tour buses like the one that's parked outside stop by on the regular.

"Oh, I wouldn't really know," I lie. I'm not in the mood to chit-chat, especially when there is a line behind her that nearly reaches the door.

"You do know he worked here, right?" she says in a condescending tone. "He's friends with the owner—the new guy who's covering for Evans. Hendrix? Do you know him?"

I almost laugh.

It's not the first time a fan of Manic at Midnight has

come into the bar asking if I know the newest member of Manic at Midnight, Hendrix Creed—*my brother.*

When Hendrix got the gig to temporarily replace Evans, their bass guitarist on tour, I knew he might gain some notoriety.

I just didn't realize it would happen so fast. The band's tour has barely started.

"A little," I reply as politely as I can. I may have agreed to these tour buses coming into the bar—purely for the financial opportunity they provide—but that does not mean I have to share personal information about the band members.

Especially the ones who happen to be my family members.

"Well, enjoy the rest of your night," I say, handing her the drink with the biggest fake smile I can muster. As much as I try not to judge what others are into, I just cannot get on board with this level of celebrity worship.

Love their movies, geek out over their music, but leave their personal lives alone. Zander hasn't been able to visit the bar in years. The attention is so intense, he can barely go to the pharmacy to buy cold medicine for his daughter without getting mobbed. Will that be my brother's life now that his name is plastered all over the internet? "Be sure to check out the pictures on the wall. I think there's a photo or two of him there."

"A photo of who?"

I turn to see my boyfriend sauntering up to me as if he has all the time in the world. He gives the redhead a wolfish grin before bending down to kiss the corner of my mouth. His hand slides around my waist as he brushes his lips over mine.

It's completely inappropriate for work, but I can't help but be momentarily distracted until I see the girl's cheeks flush. Her eyes quickly dart away just before he lifts his head and smiles. Was he looking at her while kissing me?

"Zander," the redhead answers. "From Manic at Midnight. I'm here with a tour group that visits all the MAM hot spots around LA."

"Well, there's no better place than Creeds." Jace gives her a flirty wink as he runs his hand through his unruly blond hair to push it away from his face. I really wish he were less hot. It would make being mad at him a lot easier. With his edgy style, ink, and piercings, he fits in perfectly with the rocker style the Creeds exude. The customers love it. Sometimes a little too much.

"I take it you're a big fan?"

The redhead bobs her head with enthusiasm. He strikes up a conversation with her about the band while I move around him, serving pints and mixing drinks. He doesn't seem to notice, leaning over the bar, like he's hanging on to her every word.

"Jace, I need some help here," I whisper into his ear about ten minutes later.

He hasn't moved an inch. Sweat is dripping down the back of my neck, and my feet are numb. It's barely eight, and I feel like I've already worked an entire shift.

"Yeah, I got you, babe." He gives me a lazy smile and grabs a bar towel, and slings it over his shoulder. "No worries."

I sag in relief as he begins to mix a drink until I see him reach for the Malibu rum and realize the drink he's making is for her.

Did she even ask for a refill?

I glance over and see that her drink is barely half empty.

"You know Zander used to work here, right?" he asks her, sliding the drink over the counter. He knows we're not in a financial position to be giving away free drinks, and yet, he doesn't even touch the register. Instead, he just leans in and watches as she nods eagerly in reply. "And I'm sure Presley told you about her brother?"

"Presley?" She says my name in confusion.

He jerks his head in my direction as I hand a pint of beer to the customer next to her. "My girlfriend, Presley Creed. She didn't tell you she's related to Hendrix?"

No, because I was trying to make her go away so I could work. Something you seem to be allergic to at the moment.

"Really?" Her voice jumps about five octaves, not caring in the least that I lied to her earlier.

"Yup." I politely smile, wiping the sweat off my brow, while she sits on the barstool across from me, looking fresh as a daisy, and sexy as hell to boot. "And I'd love to shoot the shit with you, I really would..." Total lie. I would rather clean the men's bathroom at closing time on a Saturday night. "But we've got beers to sling and drinks to mix, so if you'll excuse—"

"Since Pres is busy, why don't I walk you to the front of the bar?" Jace interrupts, giving her one of his megawatt smiles. "I'll take your picture in front of Zander's signed photo, and on the way, I can tell you some funny stories Pres has told me about him. He's practically her brother."

"Really?" she says in a daze, looking up at Jace like he's God himself.

Sorry, sweetheart. Pretty sure he's the devil.

He drops the towel he's been carrying around like a

prop for the last ten minutes on top of the bar and plants another kiss on my cheek before he whispers, "Gotta keep these Maniacs happy. I'll be right back."

I don't see him for the rest of the night.

The next morning, I wake up around eleven, bleary-eyed and sore. Forcing myself out of bed, I throw on a pair of sweats and an old Creeds T-shirt and shuffle into the kitchen in search of caffeine.

If I have one vice, it's coffee. I'm that person who doesn't believe coffee should be relegated to certain times of the day, and I definitely think decaf is a sin.

Even though I work odd hours, I usually don't allow myself to sleep in this late. But last night, when I got home, I was so tired I barely had the energy to strip off my clothes before my head hit the pillow. I've worked some tough shifts in my life, but that one was a doozie. It also didn't help that I was frustrated and angry with Jace and myself the whole time.

He had the good sense not to ask to sleep over. We barely exchanged five words after I locked up. When we finished closing out the register and cleaning, he walked me to my car, gave a quick kiss on my cheek, and scurried away.

Am I being too harsh?

He's not always late, and he did try to make it up to me by texting an apology this morning and offering to help with inventory.

I let out a heavy sigh as I make a large pot of coffee

and grab a leftover blueberry muffin I bought from a local bakery yesterday. My kitchen is small but modern, with updated appliances and cabinets. Hendrix calls it millennial white—white cabinets, white countertops, and a white-tiled backsplash to finish it off. Although it does lack a bit of charm, there is at least an island with a small breakfast nook.

Once my coffee is ready and the muffin is warmed, I head to the equally small living room and settle onto the sofa with a blanket.

Creeds is located in Malibu, close to where I grew up, but my apartment is about forty minutes inland. It's a bitch to drive at night, but there's no way I can afford to live in Malibu on a bartender's salary.

Not unless I live off my parents, and that's not fucking happening.

The Creed family is legendary, not just for our bar—or my brother's new rock star status—but also for the work my father does in the music industry.

Lance Creed, my dad, grew up with a deep love for music and traveled all across the country, chasing bands and doing all sorts of things I probably don't want to think about. But during those wild years of his youth, he also built relationships and made connections, which eventually led to the creation of the Creed Agency.

Today, my dad is the most sought-after music manager in the industry and represents some of the biggest names around.

A couple of years ago, he also added a recording studio in the mix, and shortly after, he officially handed the family bar over to me.

I've been trying to make him proud ever since.

I'm about halfway through my muffin and scrolling

through Creed's social media when my phone pings, alerting me to a new text.

I pull it up, but stop short when I see it's from an unknown number.

UNKNOWN NUMBER

Is this still Presley Creed's number?

Don't fall for it, Pres. It's probably a scam.

I know that as soon as I reply, someone will be blowing up my phone asking for money to get out of a foreign prison, my Social Security number to pay back taxes, or worse—sending me random dick pics because they think that's what women want.

Hey, maybe you'll luck out and get all three!

My finger hovers over it, ready to delete, but then, something stops me.

But what if it's not a scam?

They do know my full name...

Before I have a chance to change my mind, I type out a reply.

ME

Yes. Who the hell is this?

Chapter Two

HOLLIS

Hendrix Creed is in my nightclub.

It shouldn't come as a surprise to me. I've known about Manic at Midnight's visit for months. Ever since their publicist reached out to us about booking the VIP lounge during their tour stop in Nashville, Jonas Ellery—my business partner and best friend—and I have been prepping for their arrival to make sure it goes off without a hitch.

Of course, back then, I had no idea Hendrix would be part of the equation. That bomb was dropped about two weeks ago after he took over for the band's bass guitarist, and I've been dreading this day ever since.

"You gonna pop in and say hi?" Jonas asks as he steps into my office.

My eyes are glued to my monitor. I don't even bother looking up to acknowledge him. He walks behind my desk, but he already knows what I'm looking at so intently.

"Fuck, no," I answer, watching my former best friend

toss back a drink with Asher Knight, one of the most famous rock stars in the world.

A mixture of emotions swirls around inside my gut. Sadness, regret, pride. A touch of jealousy.

"So you're just going to sit back here and watch him all night like a stalker?"

"It's not stalking. I'm making sure my VIP guests are well cared for."

"That's what we have employees for, Hollis."

I lean back in my chair and run a hand through my unruly hair. God, I need a haircut. Letting out a frustrated sigh, I say, "I told you I didn't want to see him. He's touring with one of the biggest bands in the world. I highly doubt he gives a shit about the poor kid he hung out with in high school."

I continue to watch the monitor feed. Although the video isn't as detailed as if he were right in front of me, it's enough that I can see just how much Hendrix has changed in the last twelve years. Back in high school, he was always popular and good-looking, but now he looks like he belongs in that room.

I'm sure his dad is proud.

He laughs at something I'm assuming Asher said, but his blue eyes are set on a curvy brunette over by the blackout glass who's chatting with one of the other band members.

"You were more than just some kid he hung out with," Jonas reminds me, sitting on the edge of the desk. He is dressed to the nines tonight in a fitted Dolce & Gabbana suit. Jonas loves a good suit, and when he swaggered into my office in sapphire blue, bragging about how his wife was gonna devour him later, I just rolled my eyes and ignored him. He smooths out a nonexistent wrinkle on his lapel. "And who cares what he thinks? Don't you think you deserve some...I don't know, closure after all this time?"

I wince, sometimes regretting how much I've shared with Jonas over the past few years. But he's someone I can be myself around, and for me, that's rare.

I met Jonas right after I moved to Nashville. For most of my twenties, I hopped around from city to city, but when I started bartending for Jonas at one of his restaurants downtown, everything changed.

Within a year, I was managing several of his properties, and then when he decided to open Velvet, he offered me a partnership. We've been best friends since.

I've only ever had one other official best friend in my life, and he happens to be enjoying a single malt whiskey in my club at this very moment.

I shake my head, sadness seeping into my voice. "I'm not entirely sure I do."

The brunette Hendrix is fixated on begins to walk toward the stairs with the band member she was speaking to. Hendrix watches her closely and then moves to position himself in front of the blackout glass.

"I think your boy has a crush."

"He's not my boy," I snap, scrolling through the various cameras until I get the angle I need. It's not hard to find the brunette. The band member she's with—the drummer, I think—is huge. He must be six and a half feet tall and built like a fucking tank. They're in the middle of the dance floor, and his hands are all over her. "Not anymore. And can you please focus? I don't think we exactly prepared for the mayhem that will ensue once that guy is recognized on the dance floor."

Jonas leans down to get a better view. "Eh, seems like

it's fine. When I did my research on the band, it seemed like Darius—that's him." He points to the dude on the screen. "Doesn't have as big a following as the two leads, so he probably won't garner as much attention. Plus, we handpicked most of these people. They're used to seeing celebrities."

"Most being the operative word. Some of them insisted on bringing guests."

He blows out a breath. "Downside of having an exclusive club—it's filled with a bunch of rich, entitled assholes."

"Don't you mean a bunch of rich, entitled asshole's kids?"

He shrugs. "Oh, come on. I threw in a few tech bros and models to keep it interesting. Oh, shit—"

My eyes fly to the camera just as Hendrix comes onto the middle of the dance floor. Where the fuck did he come from?

"What is going on?"

"I have no clue, but I think it has something to do with that guy right there." He points to some random guy on the dance floor.

"Where the fuck did Darren go?"

"Darius," Jonas says.

"Huh?"

"The drummer. His name is Darius. Didn't you research the band?"

"No," I grumble. Hendrix looks pissed and appears to be yelling at the guy. The brunette is visibly upset. "I was too busy making sure we had extra security and top-shelf booze. Shit, do you think we should get Matteo?" Matteo is in charge of our security and would be either in the security room or making rounds.

Before Jonas can answer, the guy who appears to be wasted quickly scurries off. Hendrix's gaze drifts and, for a split second, I swear he looks directly at me. I freeze and watch him through the security feed, instantly feeling like I've been transported back in time. I can practically smell the salt of the ocean, hear his mom's musical laughter floating through the house, and see his sister's shy smile as we walk side by side down the beach.

I clear my throat, feeling a bit embarrassed when I realize he was looking at the bar where Darius had taken up residence. Some kind of emotion flickers across his face before he shifts his attention back to the brunette, and a moment later, they head toward the VIP suites near the back of the main floor.

"Looks like he took care of it all by himself," Jonas says. "And he even got the girl."

"Everything worked out then," I mutter, rising from my seat. "It always does."

Especially when your last name is Creed.

Chapter Three

HOLLIS

BEFORE...

I've been at this school for less than five minutes, and I already know I'm gonna hate it.

Everything is shiny and new, including the students, and the parking lot looks like a dealership for the rich and famous.

My mom is in heaven.

This is the kind of lifestyle she thinks she was born for. The kind of lifestyle she thinks she deserves.

She deserves—not us. Just her.

I'm just here because I have to be. She's not exactly sure who my father is, and her parents died years ago. So there's no one for her to pawn me off on, and she stopped pretending to love me a long time ago.

Her latest boyfriend, Todd Lockwood, is the richest man my mom has ever dated. He made a fortune selling some app that does something I don't give a shit about, and now he spends all his time golfing and trading stocks. He met my mom at a catering event she was working.

Now, here I am, living in fucking Malibu, going to a school that literally looks like something out of a nineties teen drama.

I look up from the paper schedule the registrar gave me, searching for a classroom number, and that's when I see her.

Standing a few feet away by the lockers, she's easily the prettiest girl I've ever seen. Even with her head turned slightly away, I can see the subtle slope of her tiny button nose and pink pouty lips. Her hair is long and golden blonde. She's tall. The black cutoff shorts she has on over a pair of ripped tights make her legs seem to go on for days.

Before I can even take a step in her direction, I hear someone shout in my direction, and my day instantly sours.

I've gone to enough new schools to know how to keep under the radar. Being the new kid has taught me that. But it doesn't matter. There's always that one guy.

And apparently, he's already found me.

I chance a look over in the girl's direction, and for a split second, our eyes meet. My stomach flips like in one of those cheesy rom-coms, and I swear it actually feels like fucking butterflies.

"Who the hell are you?" the generic bully asks, demanding my attention. His group of friends laughs, like he's just cracked the world's funniest joke.

"No one," I answer.

"Well, No One," he sneers. "You're in my way." He motions to the locker behind me. There isn't anyone on either side of us in the hall. He could obviously go around.

But this isn't about that, is it?

I've met dozens of guys like him, and they're all the same. Privileged, starved for attention, and maybe even a little deranged.

He'll probably be a politician someday.

When I step back without so much as a single word, his face goes slack, disappointment marring his face.

Not the reaction he was hoping for.

"You here on some sort of scholarship or something?"

My brow furrows. "It's a public school."

"Yeah. In Malibu," he emphasizes with a snort. "So did you just move here?"

"Sure," I deflect, adjusting my backpack.

He eyes me warily. "Why are you so shifty? Are you sure you go here?"

I scoff. "Why else would I be here, man? Do you think I snuck in to go to gym class or something?"

He shrugs. "We have one of the best athletic programs in the area."

"Whatever."

I try to step out of his way, but he blocks my path.

I am not a violent person. Not because I don't necessarily want to be, because there are times when I definitely want to be, like right the fuck now. I have plenty to be angry about, but I can't afford to be.

The last time I took a swing at a guy like him, my mom and I were out on our asses in less than two days.

While I hate most of my mom's boyfriends, I hate being homeless and hungry even more. Which is why I take a deep breath and calmly try to step around him. His friends, however, box me in, and suddenly I'm cornered.

No one else in the hallway pays any attention.

Or if they do, they pretend not to.

"I'm gonna ask you one more time," the guy says. He's up in my face now. Whatever his mom made him for breakfast still lingers on his breath, and I try not to gag. "What is your name?"

"Hollis!"

We all turn around. Yeah, I kind of want to know who's shouting my name too, especially when I don't know a single person in this school.

If these guys are quintessential jocks, then this newcomer is the bad boy. Dressed in ripped black jeans and a Megadeth T-shirt, he looks like he belongs on a stage with a guitar in his hand.

Or at least in someone's garage, dreaming of being on a stage.

He steps right up to me, with his bag slung over his left shoulder. A lazy smile hangs on his lips as he pushes his hand through his sandy blond hair. "You have first period bio, right?"

What the fuck?

"Uh, yeah."

"Cool. Let's go." Then he turns toward the ring-leader of the bully welcoming committee. "Hey, Alex."

"Hey, Hendrix."

"Might want to lay off the onions in the morning. Your breath is rank." Alex's eyes go wide a second before his expression hardens. If he was planning on offering a rebuttal, he doesn't get a chance, because Hendrix relaxes back into that easy-going smile again and pats him on the shoulder like they're good buds. Something tells me they're definitely not. "Thanks for looking out for my new friend, Hollis. I'm sure you were making him feel welcome."

That hand on his shoulder squeezes. Hard. "Yup," Alex winces.

"Oh, and Alex?"

"Yeah?"

"Stay the fuck away from my sister."

Hendrix motions for me to follow him, and I suddenly wonder if I'm just trading one bully for another, but I walk ahead anyway.

"I'm Hendrix," he says once we're out of earshot of Alex and his friends.

"I gathered that. What I don't understand is how you know who I am."

"Oh." He laughs. "I was in the front office when you came in this morning. Heard them say your name and go over your schedule. I'm nosy as fuck. But it worked out, right?"

"I can fight my own battles."

"Oh, no doubt," he agrees. "But I meant it more like now you have an excuse to be my friend."

"I don't really do friends."

That's usually a conversation ender. Not for Hendrix, though. He just seems to go with the flow and instead nods and says, "That's because you've never been mine."

Chapter Four

HOLLIS

On Friday morning, I wake up in a shit mood.

It's been years since I thought about the Creed family.

Okay, not years, but outside of my scheduled therapy sessions, I've managed to shove all those memories to the back of my mind.

But seeing Hendrix in the club last night was like opening a closet full of crap you don't want to deal with. You pack it so tightly that even the slightest turn of the handle could trigger an avalanche. Now, it seems I can't think about anything but the Creeds and the year I spent almost believing I could be part of their family.

After a shower and a cup of coffee, I finally break down and text my therapist. It's taken me a long time to realize that the shit I went through as a kid was still affecting me as an adult.

I think the tipping point was when I had a woman sleep over, and the next morning, as she was drinking a cup of coffee, she said something like, "Isn't moving the worst?" When I gave her a funny look, she pointed to the stack of boxes in the corner—the ones that had been there for more than two years. The ones I never ever unpack.

My therapist says I'm afraid to put down roots because I never got a chance to plant any as a child.

She's poetic like that.

My mom moved us around a lot, so much so that I lost track. It was always, "Oh, Steve's house is so nice, you're gonna love it," or, "There's a park near Mario's place that has ducks, and he says he'll take you for ice cream whenever you want."

But there were never any ducks or ice cream. And Steve, Mario, or whoever she'd conned into loving her in that moment was always the same—temporary.

Sabine, my therapist, texts me back almost immediately, and within a few hours, I'm in my home office, talking through my shit over Zoom.

I tell her about Hendrix coming to the club and how I hid in my office, watching him all night on the security camera instead of going down to say hello like I probably should have.

"And how are you feeling about that decision?" Sabine asks. Her gray hair is pulled back into a loose bun, and she's wearing a dark-purple sweater. She always wears a sweater. I'm beginning to think she's a knitter, but I've never asked. She never talks about her private life anyway.

I lean back in my chair and let out a nervous laugh. "I thought it would be fairly obvious given the fact that I requested a last-minute session—something I never do."

She doesn't offer a response and instead just waits for me to elaborate. I feel a little like a child being reprimanded, but it's probably justified. I'm not what you would call an easy patient.

"Okay, fine. I'm feeling…a lot of things." Too much. I feel too much, I want to say. But I leave it at that.

She's silent for a moment, then she says, "Have you considered you're feeling this way because you've been harboring some unresolved feelings regarding the Creeds?"

Uh, yeah. A lot of them, in fact. That's why I just keep stuffing them into that metaphorical closet.

I don't say that either. Instead, I reply with a simple, "Maybe."

I swear she can sense my bullshit from her office all the way across town. But she doesn't call me on it. Instead, she asks, "Do you think some of those unresolved feelings might have been addressed if you confronted Hendrix last night?"

I allow myself a moment to consider the question, and I come to the same conclusion as I have every other time I've thought about it over the last twelve hours. "I don't know."

She tilts her head, like she's pondering something. "What would you have said? If you had spoken to him?"

"We're assuming he remembers me in this scenario?"

A wry smile tugs at her lips. "Yes, Hollis. Let's assume that."

I try to picture walking into Velvet's swanky VIP lounge and approaching my former best friend, but instead of Hendrix standing there…it's his sister.

Presley.

I can almost smell her vanilla lotion, hear her goofy laugh, and see her lunging for me, tears streaking her cheeks as I walked out that final time.

I swallow hard and blink a few times.

"Ah, I don't know," I reply, my throat suddenly thick

with emotion. "I think I regret a lot of things—about how I left. About what was said. What wasn't."

Who I hurt in the process...

"Perhaps you should write a letter expressing those thoughts," she suggests.

"A letter?" The way I say letter makes it sound like she's just suggested I clean out a litter box or stick my hand down a dirty garbage disposal.

She laughs. "Okay, how about an email then, or you could even send a text? How you do it isn't as important as the actual exercise itself. Putting your thoughts and feelings into words can be incredibly helpful when you're unable to communicate face-to-face with someone."

"But then what do I do with the letter? Or email or whatever?"

"Erase it," she suggests. "Or print it out and rip it up. It doesn't really matter. The words are for you and your closure—not the person you're addressing it to."

"Okay, I guess I could give it a try," I say, and then, before I can stop myself, I ask, "What if I wanted to send it? This hypothetical text or email?"

She shrugs, completely unfazed by my random question. "Then send it. I can't tell you what to do with your life, Hollis. My job is only to guide and support. If you think sending the email is a good idea, then that's your decision. Just make sure you're prepared for whatever comes next, good or bad."

Her words resonate, and as we wrap things up a few minutes later, I can't help but reach for my phone. When I left home after high school graduation and changed my number, I deleted most of my old contacts.

All except for a few, and they all had the last name Creed.

I scroll to the Cs and stare at all their names all together in a group.

Like a happy little family.

I swallow the lump that has been forming in my throat for the past few minutes and hover over Hendrix's name.

But then at the last minute, I pull up a different name and number entirely. One that makes my heart race and my stomach clench.

Because out of all the Creeds, she might be the one I miss the most.

The one that meant the most.

Before I change my mind, I type a single sentence. Then I hit send.

No going back now.

Chapter Five

PRESLEY

ME

Yes. Who the hell is this?

My stomach is in my throat, and I feel instant regret for my impulsive decision. Because as soon as I send off my text, three tiny dots appear at the bottom of the screen.

Holy shit, the mystery texter is typing.

UNKNOWN NUMBER

I'll give you three clues. If you guess correctly, then we'll both know we're talking to the right person.

ME

This better not be some convoluted scam to steal my identity…because honestly, you should just give up now. I'm not that cool.

UNKNOWN NUMBER

Definitely not a scam.

ME

Oh, that's reassuring. Like a scammer would say otherwise!

UNKNOWN NUMBER

Glad to see your stubborn streak hasn't gone away.

What? My stubborn streak? Who the hell is this?

UNKNOWN NUMBER

First clue: We used to be neighbors.

I scoff and roll my eyes.

ME

You could literally be anyone. I've had tons of neighbors. Try harder.

UNKNOWN NUMBER

Okay, how about this one? Second clue: You taught me to surf.

My brows scrunch together. I don't think I've ever been that close with a neighbor. Unless…

UNKNOWN NUMBER

Third clue: We once spent seven minutes in heaven…

My heart starts to race.

Because, holy shit. I know who this is.

ME

Hollis?

His reply takes fucking forever. My hands start to shake. I even drop my damn phone.

UNKNOWN NUMBER

Hey, Pres.

Two words.

That's all it takes for twelve years to turn to dust.

I don't know how long I stare at my screen.

Hollis Beck is my mystery texter.

And he still calls me Pres.

I walk into the kitchen and come to an abrupt halt.

My brother is standing there.

But he is not alone.

With him is the boy from the hallway.

I only saw him for a moment by my locker that day, but the way he made my heart stop.

Dark reddish hair, dimples, and mesmerizing green eyes.

They're both laughing, but the second Hendrix sees me, they both stop and turn.

"Oh, hey! This is my friend, Hollis. He's new to town." He points a finger in my direction. "This is my little sister, Presley. She's a freshman."

"Hey, Hollis," I say awkwardly.

He smirks. "Hey, Pres."

I remember feeling both elated and despondent in that moment.

I'd been thinking about him ever since that day, and there he was, in my kitchen, like I'd conjured him with my thoughts alone.

But he was also my brother's friend.

And soon, he'd become so much more.

A few months after I met him in our kitchen, he ended up staying with us over a holiday weekend and just never left. His mom's boyfriend didn't like having a kid around, and she was more than happy to let him stay with us.

He ended up living with us for almost a year.

Hollis fit into our family seamlessly. My younger siblings loved him like a brother. My parents loved him like a son, and I—

Well, my feelings were slightly more complicated.

When his mom's boyfriend dumped her and subsequently kicked her out just weeks before his graduation, she showed up demanding we give him back.

He was just shy of eighteen and therefore still a minor, and according to my parents, there was nothing they could do. So he left.

That was the last I saw or heard from Hollis Beck.

Until now.

And he thinks he can just text me out of the blue like nothing happened?

Well, I've got news for him...

HOLLIS

It's been ten minutes since Pres figured out who I was.

Ten minutes of complete radio silence.

I can't decide if that's a bad thing or not.

She could just be busy. It is a weekday, after all. Normal people work on Thursdays, right? Since I have no fucking clue what she does for a living, she could be one of those people. She could be in a sales meeting or seeing a patient...

Yeah, that doesn't sound like her at all.

I get up and walk out of my office. I can't sit still any longer. I need to do something, so I head into the kitchen and—

My phone starts to ring.

I look down and, oh holy fuck. It's her.

Who answers a text with a phone call? *There are rules, Pres...*

My palms start to sweat as my phone buzzes, waiting for me to make up my mind.

"Answer the damn phone, asshole."

I swipe my thumb across the screen and lift it to my ear, but before I can open my mouth to greet her, she's already speaking.

And it's loud...and *animated.*

"I haven't heard from you in twelve years, Hollis. Twelve years! And that's how you decide to reach out? By acting like some creepy scammer? And then, after all of that, all you have to say is, 'Hey, Pres.'"

The way she mimics my voice by dropping her own is priceless. I can't help the tiny grin that tugs at the corner of my lips.

"I was going to follow up with a *how are you*, or

maybe a *whatcha been up to,* but it's kind of hard to get a word in with all the yelling and such."

"I am not yelling."

"Not now, no. But a minute ago, it was getting a little shrill. I think I heard one of the neighbor's dogs howl in response."

"You—" She huffs in frustration. "You do not get to be funny right now. I'm mad at you. Really mad, Hollis."

"I know, Pres." I swallow, instantly sobering. "I'm sorry."

"You've seriously had my number this whole time?"

I don't bother lying. "Yes."

"And you never thought to contact me until now?"

Fuck. The hurt in her voice is so palpable, it makes my chest ache. Sabine said to be prepared for anything, but I hadn't anticipated how hard it would be to hear the pain I'd caused by walking away. I'd been solely focused on myself and couldn't see past my own bleeding heart.

"Look," I run a hand through my hair as I pace in my living room. "I was a fucked-up kid back then. I pushed everyone away, and it's taken me years to get to the point where I can admit that. I'm sorry I hurt you, Pres, and if you don't want to ever talk to me, I'll understand."

"Why now?"

"What?"

"Why did you decide to text me now?"

"Oh, um—I'm not sure," I lie. "Guess I was just thinking of you."

"You were just thinking of me..." She says it slowly, like she's testing out each word herself to check for authenticity. "So after all this time, you happen to think of me on a random Thursday, and what? Decided to pull up my contact info that you've been ignoring for over a decade and say hi?"

"I—"

"Come on, Hollis," she says, her voice laced with annoyance. "I have four siblings. You know I'm trained in sussing out bullshit. Tell me the truth. Why did you text me this morning?"

"I saw Hendrix last night," I finally confess.

"You…what?" I can get the genuine confusion in her voice as she tries to make sense of what I just said.

"I run a club in Nashville, and he and the band stopped by," I explain.

"You manage a nightclub?"

I don't know why I don't bother correcting her about the fact that I own the nightclub. Maybe it feels like I'm bragging. Maybe I'm not ready to share that part of my life. Either way, I answer, "I've always been a good multitasker."

"I just can't imagine you choosing a profession where you willingly spend all your time with a bunch of spoiled rich people."

"It pays the bills," I reply. But in all honesty, it more than pays the bills. Velvet is the hottest club in Nashville. It's doing so well, we're considering opening clubs in other cities.

"So did Hendrix tell you to call to give me business advice or because he thinks I need an intervention?"

"What?" My brow furrows as I take a seat on the sofa and stretch out my long legs. "What kind of intervention? And I never actually talked to Hendrix. I thought about it, but he was in the VIP lounge with his bandmates, and I just—"

"He would have loved to see you," she says softly.

"Yeah, well...I wasn't so sure."

"So is that why you called me? Because you felt guilty or wanted a way to get in touch with him?"

"What? No," I press. "I still have his number, Pres, assuming he hasn't changed it. But I called you. I wanted to talk to you."

"Oh."

A silence settles between us, and it's not the comfortable kind we used to enjoy when we would walk on the beach together or sit side by side on her bed and listen to music.

No, this silence is awkward. It's the kind of silence that makes you feel naked and vulnerable.

"So why does Hendrix think you need an intervention?" I ask, literally reaching for any conversation topic I can grab.

"Oh." She laughs nervously. "I don't think it's just him. I'm pretty sure my whole family thinks I need an intervention when it comes to my boyfriend."

Boyfriend.

I don't know why the word makes me stop dead in my tracks. It's been twelve years. Of course, she has a boyfriend.

Why wouldn't she?

She's had a whole life since I left.

I swallow the lump in my throat. "They don't like him?"

"It's a long story."

"Well, I've got time."

I settle onto the couch, listen, and get to know Presley Creed all over again.

Chapter Six

PRESLEY

Hollis Beck.

I stare at his name in the chat history on my phone.

It's been a few days since he sent me those mystery messages and crashed back into my life.

We've been playing catch-up ever since.

Since that first phone call, it's been mostly texts. I left him a voice memo one night when I was too busy to type, and got a text back that said, "Nice to hear your voice. Especially when you're not yelling at me."

Jerk.

I want to be mad at him for all the times he could have called.

I want to hate him for leaving us...leaving me and never coming back.

Over the years, I would always look for him in crowds, at bars, and even searched for him on social media, but I never found him.

I eventually lost hope of ever finding him again.

To find out he had the ability to contact me this entire time? It hurts. But holding a grudge and staying angry at him would hurt a lot more. Because more than anything, I've missed him, and I like having him back in my life.

As selfish as it sounds, I kind of like having him to myself, too. I'm not ready to share him with the rest of the family—or anyone else, for that matter.

Since we started talking, I haven't told a single soul about Hollis Beck. Not my parents or my siblings.

Not even my boyfriend.

Sitting in the small office in the back of Creeds, I look at the latest text from him and can't help but smile.

HOLLIS

Do you still skip breakfast? You know that's an unhealthy habit for someone as advanced in years as yourself.

ME

Coffee doesn't count as breakfast? Also, advanced in years?!

HOLLIS

Well, you are almost thirty.

It should not impress me that he still knows my age, but it does. Is that how low my standards have fallen?

ME

Says the man who's 32.

HOLLIS

Exactly. I'm just offering sage advice from the other side. It's not pretty over here. Soon, you'll be bitching about all those rowdy kids on bikes and telling anyone who will listen about how when you were young...

ME

Were you gonna finish that sentence, Grandpa?

HOLLIS

Sorry, nodded off…

I snort out a laugh, then yelp in surprise when Jace suddenly darkens my office door. "What's so funny?"

"What?" My face flushes scarlet, like I've been caught doing something scandalous. It's a ridiculous reaction, but it doesn't stop me from answering, "Oh, nothing. Just a funny video I saw on Instagram. What are you doing here so early?"

I check my watch and nearly gasp. He's here a full half hour early. I don't think that's ever happened in… well, ever. He casually shrugs and saunters forward. I place my phone face down on the desk. Thankfully, it doesn't buzz again.

"I promised I'd come help with inventory." He smirks. "Plus, I'm just an awesome boyfriend."

"Yeah." I nod, remembering how much he used to help in the beginning. Maybe he is trying to make it up to me. "That'd be great."

"Great." He rocks back on his heels, looking far too eager for a stock run. "Let's go."

Ten minutes later, Jace seems to be more interested in the booze than actually stocking it. "What's this?" he asks, holding up a bottle.

"Oh, I ordered some new wine from this vineyard in Paso Robles."

"Expensive?" He eyes the label.

"A little, but our wine list is in need of a refresh. Plus,

I like supporting California businesses, and Paso has some amazing vineyards."

"I wouldn't know."

"You've never been to the Central Coast?"

He scoffs. "I've never been anywhere, Pres. Not all of us grow up in mansions on the beach."

His words feel like a slap across my face, and I'm momentarily stunned. He must notice because the hardened expression on his face suddenly disappears and is replaced with an easy-going smile. "I'm sorry, babe. Maybe you can take me there?" he offers. "And in the meantime, I'm gonna take a pic of this label so I can grab a bottle at the store. I like the idea of supporting local businesses too."

I try to brush it off, nodding as he snaps the photo and then types out something on his phone. For the next half hour, he's the model employee, helping me empty crates and restock the bar. But as we get closer to finishing, his mood shifts, and he decides a quickie in the stockroom is exactly what we need before the bar opens.

"Jace," I steady his hand as it slides down to grip my ass. I'm pinned between him and the stock shelves, and I can feel the cold metal digging into my back. "Mel will be here any minute."

"Then I guess we'd better be quick." He palms my breast as he drags my lips between his teeth. It stings.

My watch suddenly lights up, alerting me to a new text.

From Hollis.

It feels like pouring water on a fire, and I can't explain why. I try to refocus on Jace, but he's staring at my watch.

"Who's Hollis?"

"What?" My heart starts to hammer in my chest. Why

am I behaving like a cheating spouse? I haven't done anything wrong.

"He's just a friend."

"Just a friend?" He pushes away from me. I can hear the accusation clear in his tone.

"Yes. A friend. I've known him forever. He used to live with my family when I was in high school, and we recently reconnected."

"He's one of your parents' little pet projects, then? Like Myles? And Zander? Your parents sort of adopted him, too, right?"

My hackles rise. "Do not call my siblings pet projects, Jace."

"So is that all this Hollis guy is to you? A sibling?"

I wait just a second too long to reply.

"That's what I thought," he sneers, stalking toward the door like he can't get away from me fast enough. "I'm out of here. Enjoy serving a full house tonight without me."

Well, Jace was right about one thing. I definitely did not have a good night.

With him bailing on me and the packed house he promised, I was left short-staffed and overwhelmed. My bartender, Mel, helped out a ton, but it was just too much, and by the end of the night, I was breaking my own rule and comping drinks just to keep customers happy.

Now, it's three a.m., and I'm pretty sure I just woke up

all my neighbors when I dropped my keys at my front door, cursed, and then loudly burst into tears.

By the time I make it inside, I let go of everything—purse, shoes, and keys. It all goes onto the coffee table as I head to the sofa, bury myself in a pile of blankets, and try to forget the last eight hours.

It doesn't work.

I check my watch and see the minutes ticking by.

I'm dead on my feet, but I'm wide awake.

I'm so angry at Jace. I can't stop replaying those moments in the stockroom. How dare he get mad at me for texting an old friend when he flirts with every woman in the bar?

With a huff of frustration, I sit up and reach for my phone. I had hoped to just flop onto the couch and fall asleep from exhaustion, but clearly that's not happening.

Maybe a shower would help clear my head and calm me down. A little personal time with my battery-operated friend would definitely do the trick.

At that thought, I remember I have unread text messages from Hollis.

I should not be following up thoughts of an orgasm with Hollis Beck…

HOLLIS

Hope the band goes well tonight.

Make sure you eat. Old folks like us need protein.

I grin at that last remark and swoon a little at the first one. I barely remember telling him about the band I booked for the evening.

I can't believe he remembered.

But then, he seems to remember everything.

The other day, he texted me and asked if I still drank coffee like other people drank water. I laughed so loudly that the person in front of me in line at Starbucks turned around to see what was so funny.

I start to text him back, not expecting a reply. Like me, Hollis works crazy hours. He probably won't be up for hours.

ME

Does caffeine count as protein?

To my utter surprise, three dots start to appear almost instantly. I don't know why my heart begins to flutter.

When they disappear, I feel a pang of disappointment. But it's quickly erased when my phone starts to vibrate and I see his name flash across the screen.

"What the hell are you doing up?" I say, not bothering to say hello. I set my phone on speaker and place it on my lap.

"I could ask you the same thing."

It's still so weird and thrilling to hear his voice.

"I can't sleep," I admit.

"Rough day at the office?" His tone may be light, but I can sense the question isn't. He genuinely seems interested in my life, and it's nice to have someone to talk to about it.

I've never been great at making friends. Most people assume that because I work in a bar and enjoy going to concerts, I'm outgoing, but I'm actually quite shy.

When I'm around people I know and love, I can be loud and animated, but at work, it's easy to get overwhelmed surrounded by strangers all the time.

It's why I tend to hire people like Jace. People who are naturally charismatic and confident. People who can step in and handle the small talk when my social battery dies halfway through the night.

People who don't have to fake it.

"You could say that," I answer, letting my eyes close as I lean my head against the cushion.

"Something go wrong with the band? I looked them up, and they seem to have a good reputation. Nice following too."

He looked them up? "Um, no," I answer, feeling somewhat off kilter. "They were great. One of my favorites so far this year, actually."

"Yeah? That's awesome. I bet they filled the place up."

"Yup," I answer, feeling my mood souring. "We were packed."

"Short-staffed?"

"How'd you guess?"

"Call it my sixth sense from being in the business for so long," he says.

I hesitate for a moment before admitting to him. "Jace and I had an argument right before we opened, and he walked out on his shift."

"He what?"

"He walked out," I repeat. "He saw a text from you on my phone, went nuclear, and stormed out."

"Wait. Why would that set him off?"

I leave out the more intimate details of the encounter—like how he was feeling me up when he saw it. Or the slight hesitation I gave after he asked if we were more than just friends.

"He just got jealous," I explain. "Seeing another guy texting me."

"That's ridiculous, Pres. I'm nearly three thousand miles away."

"I know," I agree, even though I know there is more than one way to cheat—not that I think I have, but emotional cheating is still a very real thing.

"Did you have anyone else to cover the bar?"

"Yeah," I answer. "But there are supposed to be at least three of us on busy nights, and with it being so close to opening, I couldn't find a replacement for him. So it was just Mel and me all night. It was total chaos."

"You should fire him, Pres."

"I know, but—"

"And break up with him."

"What?"

"I'm sorry for being so blunt, but that guy is an asshole. You don't deserve to be treated that way—as a boss or a girlfriend."

My mouth falls open. "I'm not really sure it's any of your business, Hollis."

"I'm not sure it is either, but here we are."

I attempt to stop it, but the words come out of my mouth before I can catch them. "He's not an asshole. He just reacted poorly," I say, coming to Jace's defense like I always do whenever someone tries to question his place in my life.

"Poorly?" he scoffs. "Pres, he walked out on you. That's unacceptable."

"He was upset. Can you blame him? I'm not sure I would have acted much differently if I saw a text on his phone from some random girl."

There's a beat of silence. Just enough to make my pulse kick up a notch, and then Hollis says, "Random?"

Dammit. I'd been so focused on defending my boyfriend's shitty behavior that I'd inadvertently hurt

Hollis in the process. “No, sorry. But you know what I mean.”

“Yeah, I guess I do fall into the random category of your life.”

“No, Hollis—”

“Listen, it’s late. You should get some sleep.” I can tell by the tone in his voice that he doesn’t want to talk anymore tonight, so I don’t push it.

“Right, yeah. Of course. I’ll talk to you later?”

But he doesn’t answer. Instead, he just says, “Good night, Pres.”

“Good night, Hollis.”

As I hang up, I can’t help but wonder if I’ve just said goodbye to Hollis Beck for good this time.

Chapter Seven

HOLLIS

BEFORE...

I can't sleep.

I've been staring at the unfamiliar ceiling in this unfamiliar room for hours.

I should be used to this—the unknown. Thanks to my mom, temporary seems to be the only constant in my life. Even though the Creeds have assured me I'm welcome to stay with them for as long as I want, I know this time will be no different.

But it doesn't stop me from wanting it to be.

After my mom and her boyfriend went to Easter brunch at his parents' house and left me behind, it became clear I no longer fit into her world or his. Despite the legal ties that bind us together, she was more than willing to pawn me off to the Creeds when they offered to let me stay here instead.

I'm not even sure if she said thank you before she hightailed it out of here. It's been two months, and I haven't heard a word from her. I'm starting to wonder if I ever will.

I'm trying to decide if I care.

I continue to gaze up at the ceiling. It's a nice ceiling. One of the nicest I've slept under.

Not that I'm doing a lot of sleeping lately.

Tilly—that's Hendrix's mom—moved me in here days after the Easter debacle. I expected a simple guest room, but I should have known better.

Tilly Creed never does anything halfway.

Somehow, in just a few days, she managed to completely redecorate the room in shades of green and gray. It's moody and modern. I like it. I just can't seem to wrap my head around the fact that it's mine.

I roll over and check the alarm clock on the nightstand beside me. I double blink.

It's only twelve thirty? Fuck.

Sitting up, I run a hand down my face and look around the room. My jacket is draped over the desk chair, and my backpack sits in the corner. Tilly and Lance bought me some clothes and a computer since I moved in, but, like the room, I'm still finding it hard to call those things mine.

It's not like I did anything to deserve them.

With my focus still on the jacket, I stand up and make a quick decision. If I can't sleep, I might as well do something else. So I grab that jacket and head out into the hallway. I make it halfway when I hear the faint sound of singing coming from Presley's room.

I press my ear to the door and smile.

I had no idea she could sing.

I raise my hand to knock, but hesitate. Is it weird for me to do this? It's the middle of the night, and although

I'd never admit it to him, I've checked out Hendrix's little sister more than once or twice.

Even after I swore to myself I wouldn't.

Seeing her standing in Hendrix's kitchen, I experienced a fleeting moment of joy, which was quickly replaced by crushing sadness.

It was the girl from the hallway.

And she was Hendrix's sister.

Friendship is all we could ever be, especially now that I live down the hall. So I guess I might as well make the most of it.

With my decision made, I quietly knock on her door and wait. The singing comes to an abrupt halt, and I hear a shuffle of feet across the floor—then a curse as she trips.

I bite down on my bottom lip to stop the grin creeping up.

Suddenly, the door is pulled open, and I find a frazzled Presley on the other side. Her hair is in a messy knot on the top of her head, and she's wearing a tiny tank top and plaid pajama shorts.

I quickly glance up. "Hey," I say awkwardly. "Do you want to go for a walk on the beach?"

Her gaze darts toward her brother's room, and I know what she must be thinking. Did I knock on the wrong door? But nope, I'm exactly where I'm supposed to be.

I think.

God, I hope this wasn't a bad idea.

"Uh, sure," she finally answers. "Let me just grab a hoodie."

My eyes drift down her body, then quickly snap back to her face. "Good, yeah. Great idea."

She gives me a puzzled look. Probably way too much enthusiasm for a hoodie, huh? "What?"

"It's…cold," I say, feeling like an absolute moron.

"Yeah, I know." She smirks in amusement.

This is going great…

I shove my hands in my pockets as she goes into her room to retrieve a Creeds Bar hoodie. It does nothing to dampen my attraction to her.

Best friend's little sister, I remind myself.

"Can't sleep?" I ask in a hushed tone as she quietly closes the door behind her.

She shrugs. "I haven't even tried. I like to stay up late."

"All the time?"

We make our way downstairs, toward the sliding glass doors that lead out to the deck. "Most of the time. I like how quiet the house is. And I know they say we're supposed to get eight hours of sleep or whatever, but I swear my body needs less, because I cannot stay in bed that long to save my life."

I nod in agreement. "Same."

She flips the lock, slides the door open, and we are immediately hit with the salty smell of the ocean. The roar of the waves can be heard in the distance, never failing to surprise me.

Some people hope for decent neighbors on the other side of the fence or, at the very least, some trees to serve as a buffer.

But the Creeds have the whole damn Pacific right in their backyard.

We don't talk as we take the stairs down to the beach. The breeze from the ocean makes the night air chilly, and

I notice Pres wrap her arms tightly around herself as our feet hit the sand.

I shrug off my jacket and place it on her shoulder.

"Oh, you don't—" She shivers mid-sentence, causing her cheeks to pinken. "Okay."

"I'm pretty used to the cold," I say as I watch her slip her arms into it. I try and fight a smile as it nearly swallows her slim frame whole. "I spent a few winters in the Midwest, and you adapt pretty quickly."

Especially when your mom doesn't pay the heating bill...

"I'm not sure I could ever live someplace that cold," she replies. "Or someplace so far away from my family. Plus, I really like the ocean."

We've made our way close to the water now. The sand is wet here, and both of us have ditched our shoes, not caring in the least that our feet will freeze.

"I've never lived anywhere near the ocean. Until now."

"Do you like it?" she asks, bending down to pick up a seashell. It's broken. Imperfect. She hands it to me. I brush off the sand and stick it in my pocket, feeling like I've just been given a treasure.

"Yeah." I nod. "I think I do."

"Where did you live before this?"

"Uh..." I hesitate. I hate talking about this. It makes me feel exposed. "Arizona. My mom met this guy at a bar when we were driving out west one night, and we ended up staying for six months."

She looks over at me, her eyes squinted together like they're trying to read me. Finally, she says, "Isn't it like a million degrees there? I've heard the pavement literally melts?"

Relief floods me, and I grin. “Yeah, it’s really hot. Not sure about the melting pavement, though. Never witnessed it.”

“Yuck. I hate extreme heat. I’d take a cold day at the beach any day.”

I snort. “I mean, who wouldn’t?

“Right?” she sighs. “Look at that.” She points to the water, smiling, and it’s hard to turn away.

She’s stunning.

But I do, tearing my gaze away to see what she sees. The inky black water sparkles in the distance while foamy white waves crash one after another. The sound is hypnotic. Soothing.

“Yeah,” I agree. “It’s pretty epic.”

Her smile widens. “What about you? Do you like the cold, or do you prefer the heat?” She pauses for a second, probably realizing the double meaning of her question. She instantly blushes. God, she’s fucking cute.

“A few months ago, I would have said the heat,” I answer, giving her a meaningful look. “But the cold is starting to grow on me.”

“Yeah?”

“Yeah. But, Pres?”

We’ve completely stopped walking. We’re just two lone figures staring at each other on an empty beach in the middle of the night. “Hmm?”

“This is not cold. It’s mild at best.”

She laughs. “This isn’t, but go put your feet in the water. Or better yet, go spend a few hours in it and see if you change your mind.”

“You swim in that freezing ass water?” I raise a brow as I shove my hands in my pockets. I won’t lie. It does feel pretty chilly out here.

"God, no. But some swear a brisk swim in the Pacific keeps you healthy and young," she says with a shrug. "But I do occasionally surf."

"You can surf?" I'm learning all sorts of new things about Presley Creed tonight, and fuck, that should not be hot.

"You can't?"

"Remember the part where I said I've never lived near the ocean before?"

"Yeah, but I guess I just figured Hen would have offered to teach you by now."

"He did, but whenever he goes out, it's always with a group and—"

She nods. "I get it. I don't like crowds either."

A moment of understanding passes between us.

"I'll teach you."

"Pres, you don't have to—"

"I do," she insists. "You're not a real Californian until you wipe out on at least one wave."

My lips quirk. "Well, prepare to be amazed, because if there's one thing I'm bad at, it's organized sports."

Chapter Eight

HOLLIS

"I will never understand why you live here," Jonas says from my living room as I rummage through my fridge to find us some beers.

I really need to go grocery shopping. I'm usually good at cooking and fending for myself. I've been doing it most of my life, after all. But right now, with half a carton of milk and leftover Chinese food, the inside of my fridge is looking pretty damn pathetic.

I find the IPA he likes, grab two, and head back to the living room. He's lounging on my sofa in fitted khakis and a blue button-down. He looks far too regal for the bare white walls and sparse furnishings. I, however, fit right in with my jeans and plain white tee. "Don't knock my place. It's homey."

I hand over one of the beers, and he pops the top and takes a long drink. "If by homey, you mean small, sad, and devoid of life, then sure. It's very *homey*."

I take a seat across from him and roll my eyes at his theatrics. "You're just annoyed I didn't hire that fancy designer Keisha got to design your place."

"No," he argues. "I'm annoyed you didn't let me talk you into that spacious two-bedroom apartment in our building with the high ceilings and exposed beams. That place was stunning."

"And over a million dollars," I remind him.

He shrugs. "You can afford it."

If he notices me flinch at the mention of money, he doesn't comment. "I like this place," I say. "It's simple and uncomplicated."

"And temporary?"

"I got rid of the boxes in the corner finally," I point to the spot over by the small dining table. "See?" I fail to mention that I just stashed them in a storage unit a couple of blocks away, but he doesn't need to know that.

"Wow," he deadpans. "How long did that take you? Three years?"

"Did you come here to complain about my apartment choice, or did you have an actual reason for visiting?"

He grins, his dimples popping along his stubbled chin. "I came over to talk more about your thoughts on expanding. But first, I want to know how you're doing. I've barely seen you in the last few weeks."

"You've seen me," I try to argue, but even I know it's a lie. Ever since I texted Pres at the beginning of the month, I've become somewhat distant.

Because all my thoughts seem to revolve around her.

Talking with her feels natural, like no time has passed at all. It's easy, and I'm reminded of how close we once were in high school. I always considered Hendrix my best friend back then, but it was almost always Presley I would turn to when I needed someone to confide in.

That brief time in Malibu feels like ages ago, and so

uncomplicated that it's easy to fall back into a natural rhythm with her.

But we're not kids anymore, and life is far from uncomplicated.

We've both grown up. We live on opposite sides of the country. She has a boyfriend, and I'm...

I'm just some random guy.

"You know what I mean," Jonas presses, raising an eyebrow at me. "You've been hiding in your office and—"

My phone buzzes on the coffee table. I don't even remember leaving it there. Presley's name flashes across the screen, alerting me that I have a new text.

It's been two days since we've spoken.

Two days since that phone call when I told her she should break up with her boyfriend...

I reach for it, hoping to swipe it off the table before Jonas can see.

"What the fuck?" he exclaims. "Why is Presley Creed texting you?"

Too late.

After I started talking to Pres, I had no idea how to explain it to Jonas, so I did what I do best and avoided the conversation altogether. I told myself I would bring it up if our texts turned into something more. But after two days of radio silence between Pres and me, I was beginning to think that our resurrected friendship was finally dead, and there would be no reason to tell Jonas.

But now it seems I have some explaining to do.

"After Hendrix came to the club, my therapist suggested I write him a letter," I start to explain. "For closure or whatever."

He stares at me blankly. "And so you took that to

mean you should text his sister instead? I didn't even know you had any of their numbers."

I rub the back of my neck. "When I got a new number years ago, I saved all of them for some reason. When Sabine suggested the letter thing, I was going to write Hendrix a message, then delete it. But instead, I ended up texting Pres."

"On purpose?"

I nod. "On purpose."

"And how did that go?"

The corner of my mouth tilts into a smile. "She thought I was a scammer, and then she called and yelled at me."

He angles his head, tiny creases forming between his dark brows. "And this makes you...happy?"

"Her voice gets all high and squeaky when she's mad and—"

"Oh, fucking hell," he groans.

"What?"

"You like her."

"I—what?"

"You fucking like her."

I stare at him, my mouth on the floor as I process what he's just said. "I do not. I barely know her. We haven't seen each other since we were kids, and since then, we've shared a handful of texts. Besides, she's Hendrix's sister and—"

"And what?" he challenges with a smug grin.

"And she has a boyfriend." A really big asshole of a boyfriend. Even just thinking of him walking out on her that night at the bar makes me want to punch something.

If he worked for me, he would have been fired before his ass left the building. But he doesn't work for me, and therefore, it isn't any of my business—something Pres has made abundantly clear.

"So that's the real reason then?"

I scoff. "No. I'm just stating a fact. Presley and I have never been more than friends. I'd never do that to Hendrix."

"Do what to Hendrix?" he questions, looking exasperated. "'Cause I don't understand the whole bro code of 'I will not date my best friend's sister.' If I had a sister, I wouldn't give a shit if you wanted to date her. In fact, I'd be fucking thrilled for her—'cause you're a damn good egg. Not perfect by any means. You've got a few hairline cracks, but still one of the good ones."

"Thanks?"

"Welcome," he replies, then swipes my phone out of my hand. "Now, what did Presley Creed text us?"

"I don't believe she texted *us* anything."

He makes a show of typing in my password, making me seriously regret my decision not to change it after he gave me shit for choosing something as simple as 1234.

A moment later, I see his brow furrow.

"What?"

"You guys are boring." He hands me back my phone. "There's no sexting in here at all."

"We've been talking for less than a week."

"And?"

I roll my eyes and check her latest text.

PRES

Remember when Aimee Carroll asked you to the winter formal and I told you not to go?

I did remember.

The subject of the dance had come up on one of our chilly walks on the beach one night in December. Presley said she wasn't going. She hated school dances.

I did too.

But I made the mistake of mentioning I'd been asked. The look on her face told me everything I needed to know.

We were both treading into dangerous territory.

When she asked me not to go, I played it off, saying I wasn't sure, even though I had no intention of going. Then I tried to distance myself from Hendrix's little sister.

Tried being the operative word.

I finish reading the rest of the text.

> PRES
>
> It was none of my business, and I shouldn't have interfered. So, can we just call it even and forget about the other night?

"Are you going to text her back?"

"No. I think I'll call her. Our last conversation didn't end well, and this is definitely her way of apologizing—although I'm not sure I entirely deserve it." Jonas rises from the couch and makes like he's going to leave. "Wait. What about the expansion discussion? I didn't mean I was going to call her now."

"It can wait," he shrugs, as he heads to the door. He reaches for the handle and then turns. "Presley still live in Malibu?"

"LA, but yeah. Why?"

"Just curious," he says with a knowing look on his

face. "Oh, and a bit of advice, Hollis. Call her now. Despite what we've been told, it's best never to leave a woman waiting. Learned that one the hard way. Keisha never let me forget it."

Chapter Nine

PRESLEY

How do you know if you're in an unhealthy relationship?

Are you miserable all the time? Or are you just happy enough to ignore all the warning signs flashing in neon around you?

It's something I contemplate as Jace and I drive to my parents' house for Sunday dinner. It's a weekly tradition for the Creeds, but it's been months since he's made the trip out to Malibu with me, so I was surprised when he brought it up this week at the bar.

He has been working hard to earn my forgiveness for walking out on his shift—both as his boss and as my boyfriend—so perhaps this is part of that.

"How was the concert last night?" Jace asks. I turn my attention from the ocean view outside the window and focus on him.

"It was great," I say, unable to hold back the huge grin spreading across my face. Manic at Midnight's LA stop was last night, and everyone in the family was gifted VIP tickets to see my brother and the band. "Watching Hendrix on stage with Zander was surreal. My dad was practically beaming. He was so damn proud, and I think my mom cried at least three times."

A shadow seems to pass over Jace, but just as quickly as it appears, it's gone, and his megawatt smile is back in place. "That's great. Happy for him. I'm assuming he'll be at the house today?"

"Yeah." I nod as we approach the driveway. "And he's bringing his girlfriend."

"He has a girlfriend?"

He parks behind Cash's car, and I check my watch, grateful we're not late. I don't want to hear my eldest brother make a snide comment about that right now. "I don't think they've made it official yet, but yeah," I answer. "I've told you about her. Zara. The doctor?"

His blank face reveals no recollection as he unfastens his seat belt. "Right, the doctor. I remember."

Something makes me think he doesn't.

We both get out of the car, and he joins me on the other side as we walk up the walkway. His arm slips around my shoulder, and he gives me a lazy smile.

I try to copy him, offering one in return, just as the door flings open, and my niece races out. "Auntie Pres!"

"Tay Tay!" I meet her halfway and scoop her up in my arms. She's warm, wiggly, and smells like kids' shampoo and happiness. She bursts into giggles when I spin us around, her yellow sundress and pigtails flying behind her. Taylor has her mom's dark brown hair, but she got the blue eyes from her dad. "What are you doing out here? Are you escaping already?"

"No." She giggles. "I saw you from the window, silly!"

"Oh, man. Bored already? It's because your favorite aunt hasn't arrived yet, huh?" I set her down and offer a hand. "Let's go find something to do."

I turn to find Jace staring at the two of us with an unreadable expression. He's never really struck me as a kid lover, and that couldn't be more evident than right now. He's staring at my niece like she's an alien. "Coming?"

"You two go ahead," he says, giving Taylor a wary glance. "I'm gonna head to the kitchen and find something to drink."

"Okay." The acknowledgment barely leaves my lips, and he's already through the front door like his ass is on fire.

I shake my head. "Come on, Tay Tay. Let's go find some uncles to torment."

As it turns out, there is only one uncle in attendance tonight.

But Taylor and I do our best to tease my youngest brother, Myles, with a lively game of tag that makes me relive old memories of all of us running through the house while Hollis watches as my mom cooks turkey for Thanksgiving.

Hollis.

It's been a little over a week since that first text pulled him back into my life, and I haven't told anyone about him. It feels strange now to keep him secret, especially since I'm back at my parents' house, where the memories of him seem to be woven right into the foundation of the house.

He was once such a big part of our life, and then he was just...gone.

I don't know why I'm keeping it from them.

I guess I'm worried it's not real. That eventually our calls and texts will come to an end, and I'll be hurt and alone, wondering where he went all over again.

And I don't want my family to suffer that same fate.

Plus, there's the issue with Jace.

Since he stormed out of the stockroom, we haven't spoken about Hollis at all. It's like he completely forgot about it. He hasn't asked if I'm still talking to him, and I'm careful to keep my phone out of sight, because I sure as hell am not going to be the one to bring it up.

Does it feel wrong? A little.

But I'm also not doing anything nefarious. Hollis and I are just friends, whether or not Jace understands that.

"It's a bummer Zara got sick," Mercury starts to say as we all gather around the table later for dinner. She and I are very different when it comes to style. My little sister is all sleek lines and fine fabrics, and I'm...I look down at my frayed shorts and cropped tee. Thanks to my lack of time and funds, my style is whatever I can find in thrift stores.

"I know. Poor thing," my mom says from across the table. "Hendrix said it was pretty bad too. He sounded so concerned."

"Why are you smiling then?" Myles asks with a mouthful of salad. It's hard to believe sometimes that he's the same guy who can transform into a renegade duke or a charismatic professor on stage.

Of course, those were roles he played in college. Now, he's in the real world—also known as LA, and it's brutal for an actor.

"Because she thinks he's in love," Cash responds, not even bothering to lift his head as he points to the salad on his daughter's plate. I suppress a laugh as Taylor grimaces and shakes her head.

"Well, isn't he? You saw how he was last night when her ex showed up," I say, remembering that I hadn't filled Jace in on the backstage drama.

"All I remember is the way Asher told him to get the hell out," Mercury says, causing me to roll my eyes. My little sister has always had a little crush on the lead singer of Manic at Midnight.

"Kind of sorry I missed that," Myles says.

"You kind of missed everything," Cash reminds him. "Where were you?"

Myles shrugs. "Around."

I can tell Cash is about to press the issue, but the sound of a chair sliding next to me cuts him off, and Jace rises to his feet. "I'm getting another drink," he says darkly.

Looks are exchanged around the table, and I feel my cheeks begin to flush. "Is he all right?" my mom asks, a genuine look of concern on her face.

I attempt a smile and nod. "I'm sure he's just tired from having to cover the bar last night while I was at the concert." I scoot back from the table and place my napkin next to my nearly untouched plate. "I'll go check on him."

Walking into the kitchen, I see him pouring himself some vodka. Not a shot, though. No, he's taken a full glass from the cabinet and is filling it up as if he's pouring himself a glass of water.

I didn't even know he knew where my parents kept the hard stuff.

I watch as he downs it, places the glass on the counter, and begins the process all over again.

I slow blink. I've never seen him drink like this, and I'm kind of shell-shocked, wondering what could have caused it. Is my family that insufferable? Is that why he avoids family dinners?

"So your brother bails to take care of his sick girlfriend, and the rest of the band's a no-show as well?"

"What?"

He knocks back some more vodka and then turns toward me. His head hangs low, and his gaze is weary. "You're always going on about how your parents treats everyone like family. Zander, Asher...even that Hollis guy you were texting." My pulse quickens. "So where are they? If they're family, shouldn't they fucking be here?"

My brow furrows as I try to make sense of what he means. Zander usually shows up, but he's spending a quiet day at home with Elena and their daughter before they have to hit the road again. They don't get much alone time," I try to explain, but he cuts me off.

"And Asher? I thought he was a regular at the Creed family dinners now?" His voice is growing louder. I take a step forward, trying to quell some of his nerves.

Maybe he just feels intimidated, what with the band stopping in LA last night and everyone talking about the concert at dinner. "Asher's only been to dinner once, and you know you're considered family too," I press, reaching out to try to soothe him, but he pulls away.

It feels like a slap to the face.

"This whole night was a waste of my time," he mutters.

"What do you mean it was a waste of your time?"

He lifts his head and looks at me. His eyes are glassy,

and his expression grim. "Not all of us have daddies who can just snap their fingers and get us signed on a world tour. Some of us have to do whatever it takes to get noticed."

Noticed? That's when it hits me. He didn't come here tonight to spend time with my family or even as a favor to me. He came hoping the guys from Manic were here and he'd make some connections.

My family tried to warn me. *He asks too many questions about Dad's clients, Pres. He told Cash he used our last name to get into a club the other night. He texted Myles asking about acting gigs.* I refused to believe he'd use me like that.

I refused to believe any of it.

God, I'm such an idiot.

Before I have a chance to reply, he grabs the vodka bottle and heads for the sliding glass door that leads to the deck.

"Where are you going?"

"To the beach," he replies harshly. "Don't follow me."

I feel tears stinging the backs of my eyes, knowing my family probably heard every word of our heated conversation. "Wasn't planning on it." Then, before he walks out, I add, "Oh, and Jace, don't bother coming back. We're over."

He snorts, muttering under his breath. The door slams behind him, making me jump. I stand there staring at the empty glass on the counter. My lip starts to wobble, and I hate it.

I hate the way he makes me feel.

Weak, insecure, and untethered.

I glance toward the dining room, where I know my

family is waiting to offer words of encouragement and support.

But I just can't.

Not yet.

There is just one person I want to talk to, and I don't know why.

But I don't question it.

I just pull out my phone and call Hollis.

Chapter Ten

HOLLIS

BEFORE...

"Man, I thought you said you were gonna dump Sienna Turner last week?" I groan as we pull up to the curb and glance up. The house is ridiculous—modern and sleek, with floor-to-ceiling windows and lush landscaping.

I don't even know why I'm surprised anymore.

"I was," Hendrix says as we start to get out of the car. I walk around the front and meet him at the curb. "But then she suggested we go skinny dipping in her parents' pool, and I kind of forgot."

We head toward the front door. I try not to stare, but it's difficult. The sheer size of the place is intimidating, especially since the last place my mom and I lived was smaller than the driveway we just passed. "And now we're stuck going to her best friend's lame birthday party."

"Might not be lame." Hendrix shrugs.

An hour later, my best friend is eating his words as

we're both forced into a circle on the floor of Bethany's—that's the birthday girl—gigantic living room.

"Time for spin the bottle!" She claps her hands with glee.

"Ah, what the fuck?" Hendrix groans.

"Told you," I mutter, just as his eyes widen. I glance across the circle to see what has him so rattled and then laugh.

"Nope." His head shakes back and forth with force. "I will not play spin the bottle with my sister sitting across from me. That's way too hillbilly for me."

Bethany rolls her eyes as Sienna comes to sit next to Hendrix. Apparently, she has no qualms with the idea of her boyfriend kissing other girls. "If it lands on Presley, you will obviously spin again, Hendrix. Duh." She plops down beside me, and I get hit with the overwhelming scent of her fancy ass perfume. It reminds me of the flowery one my mom always wears. I try not to gag. "Now, if there aren't any other dumb questions, let's begin."

She then announces she gets the first turn because it's her birthday. She even points to the giant crown on her head as if we didn't all know.

She spins the bottle, and we all watch as it lands on some football jock across from her. They both grin, and she jumps up, smoothing the skirt of her dress as if she's about to walk down the aisle.

"Later, losers," the jock says.

"Wait. Where are you going?" Presley asks. My eyes jerk toward her. It's involuntary. Whenever I hear her voice, I can't help but look at her.

"To my bedroom. Set the timer," she says to Sienna. "Seven minutes."

My brow furrows. "You realize those are two different games, right?"

Her perfectly powdered nose scrunches. "What?"

"Spin the bottle and seven minutes in heaven? Two different games."

She rolls her eyes. "Whatever. It's my birthday. I get to do whatever I want."

"Yeah, cock block. Let her do whatever she wants," the jock hollers over her shoulder.

He's right. I don't even know why I'm arguing. It's seven minutes without those two. I should be celebrating. Instead, I awkwardly sit around and wait while Hendrix goes off to play his own version of the game with Sierra. Everyone else drifts off to grab snacks or beer.

"Hey, Hollis," Presley joins me. The scent of vanilla follows her. Unlike Bethany, it's not overpowering or pretentious. It's just...her.

"Hey, Pres. Didn't expect to see you here."

She shrugs. Our shoulders bump. She doesn't pull away. "Alex asked me to come."

"Alex Carpenter?" I fucking hate that guy, and I know Hendrix has warned him to stay away from his sister more than once.

She nods as both of our heads turn to see him talking to one of Bethany's friends across the room. He's clearly flirting with her, and although I have no idea what pretense he gave Presley tonight about bringing her, I do know ignoring her is beyond douchey.

"Want me to get Hendrix to take you home?" I ask, giving her a meaningful look.

She bites her lip, clearly torn, because we both know Hendrix is otherwise occupied. Before she can answer,

Bethany barrels down the stairs, still fixing her top, and shouts, "Gather up, everyone! It's time for round two!"

I raise a questioning eyebrow at her, but she just shakes her head. When Hendrix returns, I'm going to tell him he owes his sister coffee for sticking it out.

Especially when, a moment later, Bethany's eyes land on Presley, and she grins. "Since your brother bailed, you're up, Presley."

Presley is popular by association. She's Hendrix's little sister, and everyone knows well enough not to mess with her. However, when it comes down to it, much like me, Presley doesn't fit in with the popular crowd.

And it couldn't be more blatantly obvious than now.

She looks like she'd rather have the earth swallow her up than reach for that bottle. But she does it anyway. She uncrosses her long legs, gets on her hands and knees, and fucking crawls to the damn bottle.

God, kill me now.

Because try as I might, I am failing miserably at not checking out my best friend's little sister right now.

I've gotten better at looking away.

Over the last eight months, I've managed to put Presley firmly in the hell no category and not look at her in any sort of way that's sexual in nature.

But tonight, I appear to be slipping. And she is so fucking pretty...

She twists the bottle clockwise and then gives it a strong spin. It spins repeatedly, and with each turn, I can feel my heart race faster.

I do not want her kissing any of these guys.

The bottle begins to slow and comes to a stop, causing everyone in the circle to erupt. Because it doesn't land on someone. It lands between two someones.

Alex Carpenter and…me.

We all look to Bethany for guidance. After all, she's the one who decided to create this hybrid disaster. She looks around and realizes she's supposed to say something. Rolling her eyes, she shrugs like she couldn't give two shits. "Ladies' choice, I guess."

"Wait," Alex suddenly interjects. "Doesn't Hollis live with her? Isn't that, like, incestuous or something?"

Is he fucking for real? I turn to him. "We're not related."

"Yeah, but—"

"Hollis," Presley says, interrupting us and rising to her feet. "I choose Hollis."

"What the fuck, Presley?" Alex looks stunned, like he can't believe she'd ever pick the gutter rat over him. "You're my date."

She walks across the circle, holds out her hand, and I take it just in time for her to say, "Probably should have thought of that earlier. Come on, Hollis. Heaven awaits."

I take her hand, giving Alex a smug grin. "Later, losers."

Chapter Eleven

HOLLIS

It's been a couple of days since I got that apology text from Pres.

I took Jonas's advice and replied almost immediately and told her it was water under the bridge.

I was way out of line anyway.

Then neither of us talked about it again. We resumed our constant stream of texts and voice memos, slowly getting to know each other, but neither of us brought up Jace again.

Did it bother me? A little.

Okay, more than a little. I hate the idea of her dating someone who treats her like shit. But I hate the thought of never hearing her voice again even more.

I don't want to lose this friendship—this connection to my past—and I know that if I don't control this jealousy I'm feeling, it will push Pres away.

So that's exactly what I do.

All week, I push those feelings to the back of my mind.

I treat Presley like the friend she's always been and remind myself she is not mine to protect.

But then, my phone rings, and it all goes to shit.

"What's wrong?" I ask, hearing the pain in her voice almost instantly. I set down the plate I was about to shove in the dishwasher and dry off my hands.

"It's been a rough night," she says in a defeated tone.

"Aren't you at your parents tonight?"

"Yeah," she answers. "How do you know that?"

My brow scrunches. "You told me the other day, Pres. It's not that hard to remember."

My answer seems to give her pause because it takes a moment before she responds. "Jace came with me tonight, and I thought he wanted to spend time with my family, but..." She pauses, taking a deep ragged breath that I can hear through the speaker of my phone. "He was just hoping the band would be here so he could meet Asher and hang out with celebrities."

What the actual fuck...

I force myself to take a second and think before I answer because I have a feeling that if I fly off the handle again when it comes to her boyfriend, this will be the last time she confides in me.

Plus, I need that second to calm the storm brewing in my mind—the one that dreams of ripping this fucking guy apart.

"Where is he now?" I ask, leaving the kitchen to take a seat on the living room sofa. I was supposed to go out to dinner with Jonas tonight to finally have that talk about expanding the club, but I'm going to have to cancel.

This takes priority.

"Gone. He took a bottle of my parents' Grey Goose and headed for the beach."

My fist clenches at my side, but I manage to keep my opinions to myself.

Because it doesn't matter what I think right now.

I'm sure she knows exactly what everyone thinks about Jace. I'm sure deep down she even knows they're right. But bringing that up right now will only make her feel worse, and I won't be that guy.

I want to be the person who makes her smile.

"Okay, do me a favor," I say. "Can you go to the pantry?"

"The pantry?" There's a hint of amusement in her tone, and it's the first time since I answered her call that I sense anything in her voice besides sadness, so I run with it.

"Yup." I smile. "You heard me."

"Is there a secret passage in there I'm unaware of?"

"Maybe," I tease. "But you won't know if you don't get your ass in there."

That earns me a laugh, and the sound of it makes me feel like I've accomplished something truly remarkable. "This is a really weird request."

"Pres."

"I'm going, I'm going!" she assures me, her voice still a bit stuffy from the tears she shed.

I wish I could be there to wipe away every single one of them.

I hear her footsteps clack against the hardwood, and it feels like I'm right there with her. I can practically see the wide oak planks and the huge center island with the marble top. I still remember walking into that kitchen and thinking it looked like something out of a magazine. I expected to see a chef pop out of nowhere and offer us hors d'oeuvres, but instead it was just Tilly with pizza bites and Capri-Suns.

"You there yet?" I ask, running a hand through my unruly hair. In high school, I used to keep it on the shorter side because I was insecure about the color. It's on the darker end of the ginger spectrum, but it still made me stand out.

And since I was always the new kid, thanks to my mom, I hated any extra attention directed at me.

"Yup," she replies. "Does whatever we're doing only work with the door shut, or can I leave it open?"

"You can leave it open," I tell her. "Now, go to the back left corner."

The Creed family pantry is spacious, able to comfortably fit several grown adults or at least five teenagers.

Believe me, we tried.

"Okay, now what?"

"Sit down. Face the wall."

"Am I in time out?"

"Depends. Have you been bad?" My eyes widen. "Fuck, I mean—"

Laughter fills my ears, and I exhale in relief. "What am I doing in here, Beck?"

Hearing her call me by my last name makes me smile. There's something so familiar and easy about it, and I know then that I'll do whatever it takes to protect this friendship between us.

Not dropping flirty innuendos would be a solid start...

"You're treasure hunting," I inform her. "Now, what do you see in front of you?"

"Beans."

"Huh. Your mom used to keep the cookies there. Guess she's moved some things around."

"I think they're both on a health kick now—low sugar and sodium for my dad. We usually bring our own desserts now."

It's strange hearing her talk about her parents. Mostly because I still don't know how I feel about the eldest Creeds. As angry as I was when everything went down with my mom during those last few months of my senior year, I knew none of the blame fell on Presley or Hendrix.

I still distanced myself from them, but I never blamed them.

Tilly and Lance, though? I wasn't so sure.

They promised I was family. They loved me like a son, but the second my mom showed up at their door, they just stood there and let her take me away.

They didn't fight for me.

As an adult, I can rationalize why. I know their hands were tied, but the younger version of me didn't understand the legal issues they faced, and so I carried around that anger for a long time. It's a hard thing to let go of.

"Makes sense. Okay, so there's a story that goes with this, but first I need you to move those beans," I tell her, and then say with a chuckle, "And if that isn't a sentence I thought I'd ever say..."

She laughs, and I can hear the sound of cans being moved around and stacked. "Well, I didn't expect I'd be sitting in my parents' pantry tonight, so big surprises all around."

"Find it yet?" I ask, suddenly feeling anxious.

"Find what? Wait...what the hell?" I smile, because a small part of me wondered if Tilly may have erased it, but I'm glad to know it's still there. "Who wrote, 'Sometimes life sucks, but cookies never do,' on the wall in here?"

"Your mom."

"Are you serious?"

"Yup." I swallow, trying to maintain the levity in my voice as the memory replays in my mind. "She caught me in there not too long after I moved in, just sort of hiding. I'd had a shitty day, and everywhere I went in the house, there was someone. I wasn't used to being around that many people. And my room..." I let out a breath. "It didn't feel like mine yet."

"So you went into the pantry." She doesn't form it like a question. More like a statement—one she understands. We were always alike in that way.

"Yeah," I reply. "And when Tilly found me in there, she didn't miss a beat. She just walked over to that shelf, reached down, grabbed the Oreos, and handed me a stack. The next time I came in, I found that note."

I feel a lump in my throat.

That single motherly act was more than my own had ever done for me, and Tilly followed it up with a hundred more tiny gestures over the year I lived in that house.

She was the closest thing to a real mom that I ever had.

And then one day, she was just gone.

They all were.

"Thanks, Hollis," she says. "I really—"

"Hollis?" A voice I haven't heard in years echoes in my ear, and before I know it, I'm sitting up, heart pounding.

"Mom?" Pres says. She obviously isn't talking to me. Guess I should have had her shut that door after all.

"Did I hear you say Hollis?" I hear Tilly ask.

Pres pauses, and I realize she's waiting for me to say something. To tell her what to do, because although we haven't outright said anything, both of us have been keeping this thing between us on the down low.

"It's okay," I finally say. "You can tell her."

I may have complicated feelings about Tilly Creed, but I do not want to force Pres to lie to her mother on my behalf.

"Yes," she answers hesitantly. "We reconnected a week or so ago."

"You did?" Even I can hear the slight hurt in her voice. "Were you going to tell anyone?"

"Of course, Mom," Pres starts to say, and that light-hearted tone she had just moments ago is gone, and I hate that I've put her in this position.

So it's time to fix it.

I will not be that guy who makes her sad.

Not tonight. Not ever.

"Let me talk to her," I tell her, sitting up straighter like I'm preparing to face the principal at school.

"What?"

"It's about time I say hi, Pres. It's not like we have anything to hide, right?"

"Right," she agrees, although I can detect a hint of worry in her tone. Is that for me? "Mom, he wants to talk to you."

"Okay."

Then she hands the phone over, and I take another step further into the past.

Chapter Twelve

PRESLEY

BEFORE...

I awake to the sound of shouting.

It's not entirely unheard of in our house. I do have three brothers. But as I blink open my eyes and sit up, I quickly realize the noise I hear from downstairs isn't coming from my rowdy siblings.

It's coming from adults.

I quickly hop out of bed and put on a pair of pajama pants and a hoodie. Grabbing my phone, I check the time.

It's just after eight a.m. Who would show up this early—on a Saturday, no less—and cause such a scene?

Maybe one of my dad's clients?

No. My dad wouldn't put up with that, no matter who it was. He'd kick Mick Jagger himself to the curb if he showed up at his door and disturbed his family.

I pull open my bedroom door as the voices grow louder.

"Why don't we all just go into the dining room and talk this over?" I hear my mom say.

"There's nothing to talk over," someone replies, and it takes me a second to recognize that distinctive voice. I've only heard it a few times, but my pulse starts to race at the sound. "I'm leaving town, and Hollis is coming with me. End of discussion."

Hollis's mom is here?

And she wants to take him away?

My heart plummets just as I hear a door close behind me. I turn to see him standing there with a bag slung over his shoulder, eyes filled with defeat.

"But he's graduating in a month," my mom pleads. "Surely you wouldn't take him away from his friends and—"

"He can graduate somewhere else," she cuts her off. "Or not. It doesn't really matter either way. Not like he's going to college."

Hollis visibly flinches. Despite her harsh words, he had been accepted to several colleges, and my parents were more than willing to pay his tuition, but he had been hesitant.

Had he known this was going to happen?

Or just feared it might?

I take a step toward him just as Hendrix rushes out of his room. "What the fuck is going on?" He rubs his tired eyes, hair sticking up everywhere, but he's ready to do battle nonetheless.

"My mom is here." His voice is soft and monotone.

"What do you mean?"

"I have to go," he simply says.

Hendrix's eyes shift from Hollis to me and then back

again. I see the confusion and reluctance to accept what's happening. "Okay. When will you be back?"

"I don't think I'm coming back, Hen."

He just shakes his head. "No." Then he stalks toward the stairs. "Uh-uh. Not happening."

"Hen!" Both of us run after him.

We manage to catch up to him in the foyer, but it's too late. He's already in the middle of everything, surrounded by my parents, with an angry finger pointed at Hollis's mom. "You do not get to show up here after all this time and demand—"

"Hendrix." My mom's voice is calm and steady as she places a tender hand on his shoulder. "She can do whatever she wants. She's his mother."

Hen's head whips around to face her. His expression is riddled with betrayal. "You can't be serious? She is not his family." His voice cracks. "We are."

"I know," she soothes, pulling him into a hug as her gaze finds mine. "But he's still a minor, and she's his legal guardian."

"He'll be eighteen in a few weeks. Can't he just stay here until then?" I ask her, hoping she'll see reason.

But then I notice just how different she looks from the last time I saw her. Her light-blonde hair is pulled back in a messy ponytail, and there is makeup smudged and flaking under her eyes.

Her clothes are still designer, but they look like they need a wash. Honestly, the same could be said of her as well. What happened to her? And what exactly is she trying to drag her son into?

"No," she answers curtly, her eyes now pinned on Hollis. She gives him an appraising glance before turning away. "If I have to be miserable, so does he." Then she turns and heads for the door. "I'll be in the car. Don't keep me waiting."

We all watch her leave, and the sound of the door slamming behind her makes my heart lurch.

This can't be happening.

This isn't real.

Just yesterday, the guys were talking about going to Cabo for a graduation trip, and now Hollis won't even be here to get his diploma?

It feels like all the air has been sucked out of the room.

"Mom, Dad, you have to do something," I say, turning to both of them. They're staring at Hollis as if it physically pains them to see him so lost and bewildered.

"I'll call our lawyer, but—"

"It's okay," Hollis finally says. It's the first words I've heard him utter since we came downstairs. He gives us all a meaningful look, his face ashen as he tries to play off a casual shrug. "We always knew this was temporary anyway."

"Hollis—" my mom begins to say, but he simply offers a sad smile as he steps forward and hugs her. Her eyes well with tears.

"Thanks for everything."

My lips start to quiver, and my throat feels thick as I watch him pull back and step toward the door.

"Hollis," Hendrix calls out. "Don't go."

"Good luck at Stanford, man," he says, then heads for the door. I get one final look as he glances over his shoulder, and then he's gone.

Before I know what I'm doing, I'm running after him. I don't even make it halfway across the foyer before someone catches me around the waist. I cry out and struggle against their hold. "No," I plead. "No!"

"Let him go," my dad says, as the door softly clicks behind him. It echoes in my head, the sound so final. So resolute.

"Why aren't you fighting?" I yell. "Why aren't you doing anything?"

"I will," he promises. "I am. I'll call the lawyer right now, just like I said I would. We'll get him back, but we can't fight her. Not like this, okay?"

Tears fall down my cheeks as I give in to him, letting my father's arms engulf me as I weep, hoping he means what he says.

Because I do not want to lose Hollis Beck.

Not now. Not ever.

Chapter Thirteen

PRESLEY

"Hey, stranger." I smile as the sound of my brother's deep voice drowns out the noise from the bar that's bleeding through the walls.

"Hey, rock star. How's life on the road?"

"Exhausting." He lets out a haggard breath. "But good. Really good. I've tried calling you a few times. You never call me back."

"I text Zara."

"Oh, I see how it is." He chuckles. "Now that I have a woman in my life, you're just gonna ignore me now?"

Smiling, I say, "Of course not. You know you're my favorite sibling. That makes you irreplaceable. But Zara does an excellent job of keeping me updated on how you're doing. So I send her my appreciation in the form of emojis and IOUs."

"Do I want to know what you're promising my girlfriend?"

"Makeup tips and wine."

"Ah, so the standard IOUs then."

Snorting out a laugh, I reply, "Exactly."

I lean back and kick my feet up on my desk. The small office in the back of the bar hasn't changed much since my father's days. The ratty leather chair and the old wooden desk have been in here since I was a baby. The computer I've been staring at for the better part of an hour, however, is brand new.

Not that it seems to be helping me with my current conundrum.

"So how are you? You feeling all right?" I ask, tearing my eyes away from the screen. *Why do these stock reports not match our sales numbers?*

"Yeah," he says. "Mostly. Having Evan's back is nice. I'm able to take time away from the stage and rest. And I started movement therapy. The doctor is optimistic."

Tears prick my eyes, and I nod to no one in particular. When we all learned that my brother had a neurological condition affecting his ability to play bass, we were devastated. But Zara has been vigilant about finding him treatment, and they both remain hopeful.

So I will be too.

"That's good," I say. "I'm glad they were able to coordinate everything so quickly."

"Me too, and I feel incredibly lucky in that regard. Not everyone has the means or a doctor like Zara at their beck and call. She found an amazing specialist. We met with her between show dates, and I'm checking in with her virtually until we're back in LA," he replies warmly, and I shake my head. It's hard to believe this is the same guy who was trying to convince me he didn't have time for a committed relationship just a couple of months ago.

"And when is that exactly?"

"September," he says. "We're wrapping up in Florida this week, and then I'm taking Zara to Belize. Went all out and got one of those bungalows on the water. She's gonna freak. Anyway, we'll be there until we leave for the international leg of the tour. We both need the downtime."

"Do you actually hear yourself when you talk? 'Cause it sounds to me like you're complaining about going on an all-expense-paid trip to Europe."

"Not just Europe, Pres. We play in Australia and Brazil. We're very popular."

"God..." I fake a sigh. "The fame has already gone to your head, hasn't it?"

He laughs. "Totally. But seriously, I am excited to travel with Zara and the band, but we just need some time to decompress. Being on a tour, you're just constantly surrounded by people. It's a lot."

"I can understand that. I get that way after a week at the bar."

"Speaking of...how is the bar?"

I look down at the report, which still fills up the bulk of my computer screen. "Good." God, why do I keep saying that word? "I'm planning an even bigger Halloween event this year." I swallow a lump of nerves as the numbers on the report stare back at me.

Assuming I can afford it...

When I took over the bar, the profits were modest at best. Wanting to impress my father and prove he made the right choice in trusting me, I may have gone a little overboard. I booked more bands, stocked our shelves with premium liquor, and planned more events.

It's drained the coffers considerably, but the bar has never been more popular.

It's been worth it.

I think...

"Well, it was a huge success last year, so it would be stupid not to."

Stupid. Right... "You'll be back in town by then, won't you? You said September?"

"Did I? I think I meant November."

My eyes crinkle as a hint of a smile tugs at my lips. "Too late, Hen. Can't back out now. And just think of all the couples' costumes you can come as! Oh, what about Guinevere and Lancelot?"

"Hard pass."

"Bacon and eggs?"

"What the fuck? No."

"I bet if Zara asked you to dress up like an egg, you would totally do it."

"Uh, no. 'Cause I'm obviously the bacon. Duh."

I snort out a laugh. "I miss you, Hen."

"Miss you too, Pres. I didn't realize just how much I'd miss you guys being out on the road. Our time in LA was so brief, and with Zara getting sick, I didn't get to see you as much as I had hoped."

"Well, that couldn't be helped. You were needed elsewhere."

"Yeah, I was." That sugary-sweet tone is back in his voice, and I am almost one hundred percent sure Zara is close enough that he is either staring at her or has her in his arms.

An ache forms in my chest.

Things with Jace have deteriorated quickly. I thought he might quit after I broke up with him at my parents' house, but he didn't.

Instead, he's been on time for a month straight.

He completely ignores me, but acts like employee of the month in front of everyone else. It's fucking weird. I'd love to fire him, but I feel that doing so right after I dumped him would look bad.

"And you were apparently catching up with old friends?"

"What?" I try to pull myself out of my thoughts and focus on my brother.

"Hollis," he says, making my heart race at the sound of his name. I still haven't told him—or my brother—about my breakup, and I'm pretty sure the rise in my pulse when I hear his name has something to do with why. "Mom said he called out of the blue that night after the concert?"

That was the line my mom told the family when she strode into the living room, holding my phone and with Hollis on speaker. But not before she shot me a look over her shoulder that said, *We'll talk about this later.*

I'm not sure what she wanted to say because whatever talk she planned hasn't happened yet, and it has been weeks.

Maybe she felt a hint of betrayal finding out that Hollis and I had been talking for a week and I hadn't told her, but if so, she didn't show it that night when she waltzed into the living room with unshed tears in her eyes.

She and my dad talked to him for what seemed like hours.

Even Mercury and Myles joined in.

If Hollis felt overwhelmed by the sudden reunion, he never let it show in his voice. He joked about feeling old when Mercury told him about her job at the recording studio. He asked questions about Myles's acting gigs and where he'd traveled, and he indulged my parents by telling them all about his life in Nashville.

I pretended not to notice how he hadn't mentioned a woman in his life. He's never talked about anyone in our conversations, so I assume he is single, but I've been too afraid to ask.

Why? Well, I'm too afraid to ask myself that as well. Especially now that my relationship status has officially changed.

"Yes," I answer, choosing to stick with what Mom told him. If I told the truth, I would have to explain why I kept it secret, and that answer was more confusing than I was willing to admit. "He apparently still had my number saved in his phone, and with the band traveling to Nashville, I guess we were all on his mind."

"That's wild," he says, and I have to keep myself from laughing. If he only knew how wild it really was. But I wouldn't tell him about the nightclub Hollis works at. I know he feels embarrassed about avoiding Hendrix that night.

My legs start to ache from the awkward angle I'm at, so I lift them off the desk and slide them onto the floor. I accidentally hit my keyboard in the process and hit something that makes all the programs on my computer shuffle. Suddenly, I'm looking at the security feed instead of the stupid report I can't figure out.

I rarely watch the live feed. It feels a bit creepy to stalk my employees during their shifts. I tend to only check it when I have someone new on board and want to ensure they've got the hang of things, or if something goes wrong.

Tonight, Jace and Sadie are manning the bar. Sadie is relatively new, having been here for only two months, but she's a quick study. And since Jace has been here...

I double blink as I catch something out of the corner of my eye just before I click back to my sales report.

My brother is still talking about...actually, I'm not really sure. "Hen, can I call you back? Something just came up, and I'm needed up front." I say the first thing that comes to mind, never tearing my eyes away from the security monitor.

"Yup. Talk to you later."

"Love you."

"Love you too, Pres."

We don't bother with goodbyes, and as I end the call, I set the phone down and start to pull up the recorded feed from a few minutes ago so I can replay it, praying that what I saw was just my mind playing tricks on me.

Because if it wasn't...

I rewind about a minute or two before I accidentally pulled up the surveillance footage, hit play, and focused on Jace. He sets the drink down in front of the older blonde. They exchange a few words. He laughs, and she hands him a single bill before saying something else. I'm guessing she's telling him to keep the cash, because the next thing he does is glance over to Sadie, who's busy pouring a beer, and then he heads to the register and...

Oh, you've got to be fucking kidding me.

He hits the no sale button, opens the register, and then shifts his body. If he thinks he's hiding what he's doing, he's dead wrong, because I see it all.

I see him pretend to make change as he clutches the cash the woman gave him in his other hand. He grabs an extra twenty and then slyly shoves it all in his pocket before Sadie even glances his way. I rewind the tape to the beginning of the night and catch him doing it three more times.

I pull up his last week's worth of shifts and let out a curse, because now I know exactly why my report won't add up. My fucking ex is stealing from me, and I've been too stupid to notice.

I guess I have that reason to fire him now.

Fuck my life.

Chapter Fourteen

HOLLIS

I haven't heard from Pres in days.

Since we've been a constant part of each other's lives for the last two months, it's a decent cause for concern.

Especially since tomorrow is her birthday.

She and Jace were supposed to take a trip to Vegas, or at least that was the plan back in June when she still felt comfortable talking about him with me. Per our silent agreement, she hasn't mentioned him since that night in her parents' pantry, and I haven't asked.

So I have no idea what the status of their relationship is.

They could be getting married by an Elvis impersonator right now for all I know.

God, I fucking hope not.

Because what if she forgave him after that? What if she made excuses for his inexcusable behavior again? I'm not sure I'll be able to hold my tongue this time.

I want to support her. I want to be a good friend. But being supportive doesn't mean standing by while someone you love is being mistreated.

Because I do love Presley.

Maybe not in the way Jonas seems to believe I do, but I've always had strong feelings for the Creeds.

Especially her.

I pace the floor of my living room as the midday sun beams light across the dull couch and empty walls. Pulling my phone out of my jeans pocket, I stare at the unanswered texts from this morning.

They are still all unread.

She's never left any of my messages unread. Even at three in the morning, she'll message me back just to say, "Go to sleep, old man."

But for the last two days...silence.

An uneasy feeling starts to settle in my stomach. Sure, it might be nothing. She could be in Vegas right now, just too busy having fun to text me back, but something tells me that's not it.

Or maybe I'm just hoping.

I decide to call her either way.

She answers on the third ring. "Hey, it's my good friend, Hollis!" Her words sound slightly slurred together, and her voice has that dopey pitch that can only be achieved through copious amounts of alcohol consumption.

"Are you drunk?" I don't know why I bother asking. I already know the answer.

She whispers the answer like it's a secret. "Maybe."

If I weren't so worried, I might find Drunk Presley kind of cute. But I am. Worried, that is. Because it's only three in the afternoon here, which means it's noon on the West Coast, and she's already trashed.

"Where are you?" I press, ready to bolt out of my

apartment to...where? I'm in fucking Nashville. She's... not.

"Vegas, baby!"

I swallow my disappointment. I guess that birthday trip is still on. This information shouldn't bum me out as much as it does.

Friends do not get jealous, remember?

"Oh, okay. Well, I won't keep you. I just hadn't heard from you in a few days, so I wanted to check in and make sure you're okay."

"I'm great," she assures me in that slurred voice again. "Nothing a little vitamin D and a mai tai can't fix. Shit, how long have I been out here?" I hear the clanking of a glass, and she groans.

"Wait, where's Jace?"

She snorts. "That cheat? How the hell should I know? He's definitely not here."

Cheat? My brain is struggling to keep up. "He cheated on you?"

"Dirty rotten cheat," she murmurs into the phone. "He ruined everything, and now I'm in Vegas all alone."

She sounds devastated. "You're by yourself?"

"I have my mai tai." She hiccups before adding, "Well, I did. Now, I just have an empty glass."

I suspect she has more than one based on the sound of her voice.

I don't like the idea of her drinking alone, especially so early in the day. "Where are you?"

"I told you. Vegas," she says in an exasperated tone.

"No." I chuckle. "I mean, where in Vegas are you?"

"Ooooh..." She drags out the word and then giggles.

Jesus.

"I'm at the pool. It's so fucking hot."

Alarm bells start to go off in my head. It's the middle of summer, and Las Vegas is hot on a normal day. In July? It must be unbearable. "How long have you been out there, Pres?"

"I'm not sure. A while. I was going to get breakfast, but then I decided the pool sounded more fun."

Shit. "Is there a bartender around anywhere? Or a pool attendant?"

"Um." There's a pause, and I hope to God she's actually looking around the pool deck and not staring at her feet or something. "Oh! Found one! There is a bartender over there!"

Does she think I can see him?

"Great, that's perfect. Can you do me a favor and walk over to him?"

"Sure, why?"

"Call it an early birthday surprise."

"You remembered my birthday?" Her voice turns serious. It's the most sober I've heard her since she answered the phone.

"Of course I did."

"Jace never remembered anything I said," she says softly, and I don't know what surprises me more—the fact that she's comparing me to her ex or that I like that I come out on top.

"Well, he is an asshole and didn't deserve you." The words slip out of my mouth before I can stop them.

But I can't help it. I've been holding them in for over a month.

"You're right." She simply agrees before I hear her say, "I'm at the bar."

The quick change of subject jars me a little, but I remember why I sent her there and focus on that.

"Good. Now tell him your friend would like to talk to him."

"What?"

"Just trust me."

I can hear a hint of apprehension in her voice. "Okay."

She must press the phone to her chest or put it on the bar top because everything sounds a little muffled. But, from what I can hear, the bartender sounds slightly confused by her request, but is amenable.

That or he's simply flirting with her and willing to do whatever she asks in hopes of getting in her good graces.

Suddenly, there's a shuffle, and I hear a deep voice say, "Hello?"

"Hi, who am I speaking with?"

"Uh, Mike?" He answers as if he's not entirely sure. I hear Presley giggle, and I'm pretty sure I have my answer to my previous question—definitely flirting. Still is, if I had to guess.

"Hi, Mike," I say through gritted teeth. "My name is Hollis, and in front of you is my good friend, Presley."

"Your friend is hot, Hollis."

"Not really part of your job description, Mike," I growl.

"Just an observation."

"Yeah? Well, since you're so good at *observing*, how many drinks have you served her?"

"I don't know. I'm not anyone's keeper."

"Yeah? How long have you been bartending?"

"Not long."

No shit. It's why he was working the morning shift on the pool deck. Shitty bartender. Shitty shift. "And if she had passed out from alcohol poisoning or sun sickness?"

"I don't know, man? She looks fine to me." He feigns indifference again.

"Yeah, and you're going to make sure she stays that way. Otherwise, I'm going to have a nice long chat with your manager, and you'll be stuck working this sweaty pool deck shift forever."

He doesn't respond. "What do you want?"

"I want you to have someone from the spa come and escort her to her room. Have them treat her like fucking royalty, and don't fucking embarrass her. And then I want her to spend the whole day at that spa—"

"I can't charge that to her room without her approval. Do you know how much a full day at the spa costs?"

"I'll pay for it," I tell him. "And I don't give a shit about the cost."

"Are you rich or something?" He snorts.

"Nope," I lie. "Just a bartender who actually knows how to do his job. Now, hand the phone back over to Presley," I tell him as he mutters under his breath. "Oh, and one more thing. Stop fucking looking at her."

Pretty sure I hear him call me an asshole.

Not entirely sure I don't deserve it, though.

I got the text over thirty minutes ago and have been sitting here in my living room staring at it ever since.

She sent me a photo.

Presley sent me a selfie, and I can't stop looking at it because it's the first time I've seen her since high school. She looks fresh-faced and sobered up from her day at the spa. Her hair is wet, and she's wearing one of those fluffy white robes that every fancy hotel seems to have.

She's holding a glass of champagne with a huge grin plastered on her face.

She's the most breathtaking vision I've ever seen.

And now I'm thinking about doing something really, really stupid. I decide to call for reinforcements instead.

Jonas picks up the FaceTime call almost immediately. "Hey, what's up?"

I slow blink as I try to make sense of what I'm seeing. "Are you in the bathtub?"

He scoops up a handful of bubbles, smears them down the smooth skin of his chest, and smirks. "Yup."

I shake my head back and forth, trying to dislodge the mental image of my best friend naked in the bath. "You know you don't have to answer when I call, right?"

He shrugs, shifting so his shoulders dip slightly lower into the water, not showing any signs of being bothered by his lack of clothing. "Figured it might be important. You rarely call me. Plus, I am really comfortable in my own skin."

"I call you."

"No," he argues. "You're a die-hard texter. I can count on one hand the number of times you've called me outside of work shit. Wait, is this work shit? 'Cause if so —" A bare foot slides up his torso.

"Fucking hell, Jonas. Keisha's in there with you?"

"Of course she is. You think I'm sitting here, taking a bubble bath all by myself?"

"I don't know what you do when I'm not around."

"I fuck my wife in the tub—that's what. Now, hurry up and tell me why you called before the water gets cold."

"Fine. Jesus," I grumble, making both of them laugh.

I need new friends. "Presley's birthday is tomorrow, and she's in Vegas all by herself, and I'm this close"—I hold up my thumb and index finger, almost touching—"to buying a plane ticket and joining her. Talk me out of it."

"Why?"

"Why what? Why is she all alone or—"

"Well, sure, I guess. But—"

I cut him off mid-sentence. "Her boyfriend cheated on her, and she dumped him. Vegas was supposed to be the trip they took together."

"Go!" both he and Keisha shout together.

I throw my free hand up in exasperation. "You're supposed to talk me out of it!"

"I never agreed to that," Jonas says. "Baby, did you ever hear me agree to that?"

"Nope," I hear Keisha reply.

"See?" He shrugs. "And why wouldn't you want to go? Like you said, she's all alone. On her birthday."

I wince, hating the idea of her spending the whole day by herself. "I know, but she's also fresh off a breakup, and I'm—"

"You're what?"

"I'm not sure I'm the friend she needs right now."

"And why is that, Hollis?" God, he's a smug asshole sometimes.

I let out a frustrated sigh. "You're really gonna make me say it, aren't you?"

He grins. "Yup."

"I don't think what I feel for her is just friendship anymore, okay? Happy?"

It doesn't mean I am in love with her, I try to convince myself. It just means that my feelings for her are a bit more complicated than I realized.

"So happy." His grin turns wickedly mischievous. "I'd be happier if you'd just admit you've been obsessed with that girl since high school, but this will do. Now, do you want to leave tonight or tomorrow morning?"

"What?"

"Oh, while you were working your way through all that, Keisha was busy looking up flights. So I'll ask again. Do you want to leave tonight or tomorrow morning?"

I bite my bottom lip, trying to find a reason not to go. But I just keep picturing her alone and miserable on that pool deck. "Tonight," I finally say. "I want to be there when she wakes up."

"Who knew our boy was a romantic?"

"It's not like that, Jonas."

"But you want it to be," he reminds me.

"It doesn't matter what I want. She just broke up with her boyfriend, and right now she needs a friend."

"But it's Vegas!"

"What is that supposed to mean?"

He shrugs. "Crazy things always happen when you're in Vegas."

Chapter Fifteen

PRESLEY

Thanks to a holistic guru at the spa and the detox massage she gave me, I wake up feeling pretty damn good despite the copious amounts of alcohol I drank the day before.

Or should I be thanking Hollis? Because even though the spa said it was "their treat," I have my doubts. At the pool, I remember handing over the phone to the bartender and seeing the color drain from his face.

Whatever Hollis said to him apparently had him shaking in his boots because as soon as he was done, that guy got on the phone and suddenly I was being treated like a celebrity with VIP status.

I don't even want to know what Hollis threatened him with...or why.

But I enjoyed the day regardless.

Someone from the spa came up and escorted me back to my room, where they brought me lunch and a strong pot of coffee. After I ate a bit and had some caffeine in my stomach, the alcohol started to wear off, and I was taken away for a full day of spa treatments.

It was divine.

I was so relaxed by the end that I did something a bit reckless. I could blame it on the glass of champagne, but after the morning I had, I barely took two sips.

No, I was pretty damn clear-headed when I flipped the camera around, snapped a picture of myself, and sent it to Hollis with a single word attached. *Thanks.*

Was I hoping he would acknowledge the picture? Tell me how beautiful I'd become? Maybe. But all I got in return was, "Glad you're feeling better."

And I was—feeling better, that is. Until about five minutes ago, when I woke up and realized I'm officially thirty, single, and completely alone.

Best birthday ever.

I throw off the covers and sit up in bed. The room is still covered in darkness because of the curtains I pulled shut last night, so I force myself out of bed to open them.

The strip is already fairly busy with young families and locals trying to get to their shifts on time. I've been here for two days already, and I have yet to actually explore any of Vegas.

At least anything beyond the casino and pool in my hotel.

To say I've been sulking is an understatement.

It's not the breakup bothering me. I've been over that for weeks. It's the betrayal and my total lack of judgment that made me blind from the very beginning. Now the bar—our family's bar—will suffer, all because I fell for the wrong guy.

Moisture coats my cheek, and I lift my hand, only to realize I'm crying. "Ugh, not again," I say to myself. I've lost count of the tears I've shed since I broke up with—and fired—Jace.

I should have called the cops the second I saw that video feed.

Instead, I just pulled him into my office, showed him the video of him slipping that cash into his pocket, and told him to get the hell out. I should have known something was up when he didn't even bother arguing and just grabbed his stuff and bailed.

I thought that would be the last time I'd ever have to deal with Jace Vaughn.

Two weeks later, he proved me wrong.

Now I'm here, drowning my sorrows, trying to figure out how I'm going to pull the bar out of this mess—without my family finding out. Because the last thing I need is my parents finding out how close the bar is to closing because I didn't listen when they all warned me what an absolute jerk my boyfriend was.

Moving forward, there'll be absolutely no confusion about who the family fuckup is. *Thanks, Jace.*

"Happy fucking birthday to me," I mutter, wiping away the rest of my tears as I head to the shower.

Thirty minutes later, my hair is washed and blown dry, and I stand in front of my suitcase and reach for a floral sundress, hoping it will improve my mood. It's not my typical attire, but Vegas isn't my typical scene either.

Here's to hoping both will improve my mood.

The thin fabric feels light and airy as it slips over my skin, and the bodice offers just enough support so I can ditch my bra for the day. Always a win in my opinion.

I check myself out in the mirror and give myself a nod of approval.

I somehow managed to avoid a sunburn yesterday, but I am rocking a gorgeous new tan, which helps make my long legs look endless.

Not bad, Pres.

Just as I'm about to order room service, my phone starts to vibrate on the nightstand next to the bed. When I pick it up, I see Hollis's name flash across the screen. It's barely nine in the morning here.

"Someone's up early," I say in greeting, unable to hide the grin that spreads across my face.

"I wanted to be the first to wish you a happy birthday."

"Well, you are. Or at least you will be."

He chuckles. "Happy thirtieth birthday, Pres."

Chills race up my spine at the sound of my name on his lips. "Thank you."

"Hey, I have a surprise for you."

"Another one? 'Cause I know you paid for that spa day, Hollis Beck."

"I plead the Fifth," he says with another laugh. "Besides, you deserved it."

"And I deserve this one too?"

"I don't know. You may want to send it back once you find out what it is," he says playfully, though I can sense a hint of nervousness behind his words.

What did he get me that's got him so anxious?

"Anyway, it's, uh...rather large. So you'll need to go down to the lobby to pick it up."

"It's here? In my hotel?"

"Well, yeah. How else was I supposed to make sure it arrived on time?"

Once again, I am dumbstruck by his thoughtfulness. The only men I know who do such sweet things like this are fictional. "But you didn't know I was here until yesterday."

"I'm not following, Pres. They do deliver in Vegas, yes?"

"Yes," I reply, my cheeks flushing. "It's just...it must have cost you a fortune."

Plus, the cost of the spa day he still refuses to admit to paying for...

"Someone once told me it's not the cost of the gift that matters, just the thought behind it."

I smile. "I did say that, didn't I?"

"Yeah, you did. It was Christmas morning, and I believe I was staring at a stack of presents that were all addressed to me. I felt so overwhelmed and guilty that I was sure the homemade cinnamon rolls your mom made were about to reappear."

"Gross." I laugh.

"Go get your surprise, Pres."

"Okay. Do you want to stay on the phone with me?"

"Nah," he says. "I'm sure I'll be talking to you real soon."

Before I can say anything in reply, he hangs up, and I'm left staring at my home screen, wondering what he meant by that.

"Maybe he wants me to call him after I pick it up?" I mumble to myself as I grab a pair of sandals and my purse. I threw on a bit of blush and mascara after I did my hair. In this heat, that's all I can handle. Everything else just melts off.

I double-check my purse for my keycard before heading out and manage to slide into the elevator just before it closes. An elderly couple from Texas greets me and asks where I'm from, and then, when I say LA, they do that thing everyone does—ask if I've ever seen any famous people.

I shake my head and lie. Their disappointment is instantaneous.

Do I feel bad lying? Sure, but it's a lie that protects my brother, so it's justifiable, right? Besides, I doubt they even know who Manic at Midnight is.

Thankfully, the elevator makes its way down to the lobby quickly, and our conversation is cut short. I give them a polite nod and step out toward the concierge.

But instead, I come to a complete stop.

Standing in the middle of the lobby is Hollis Beck.

I feel a strange sense of déjà vu because, like that first moment I saw him standing in the school hallway or my parents' kitchen, I feel completely blindsided.

He is still the hottest man I've ever seen.

His dark-red hair is longer and curlier than I remember. I would definitely remember those curls. They frame his ruggedly handsome face and piercing green eyes. He looks like something out of a Highlander novel. All he needs is a kilt, a Scottish accent, and a sword because that body is ridiculous.

He definitely wasn't so...*fit* in high school.

"You're here," I manage to say, somewhat in a daze as I close the gap between us.

"Surprise?" His voice is deeper than it sounds on the phone. Sexier.

"How?" Apparently, seeing him has greatly reduced my vocabulary.

"I took a red eye," he explains sheepishly with a shrug. It's adorable, and suddenly I find myself throwing my arms around his shoulders. He grunts in surprise.

"It's so good to see you."

His arms wrap around my waist. They're large and familiar, and I can feel their heat through the thin fabric of my dress. I forgot how tall he is, and because of our height difference, I'm practically using his pec as a pillow.

"It's good to see you too," he says softly. "Really good."

I pull back, suddenly realizing I've been clinging to him like we're reunited lovers, rather than just old friends.

Just friends, I remind myself.

"Um...do you need to check in or something?" I ask awkwardly. "How long are you staying?"

"I already checked in, but I haven't gone up to my room yet." He points to the small bag by his feet that I hadn't even bothered to notice. How could I with him standing there? "And as for how long I'm staying...it depends."

"On?"

"How long *you* are staying."

"Oh, I'm headed back tomorrow morning," I say, suddenly wishing I could stay longer. But I'm already pushing it being away this long since the bar is now down an employee.

Thanks for that, Jace.

"So we have twenty-four hours, then?"

"Yes," I answer with a grimace. Is he going to regret coming all this way for a single day?

He grabs my hand, and I'm suddenly being dragged toward the elevator. I let out an amused laugh. "Where are we going?"

"To drop off my bag," he announces as if it's the most obvious answer in the world. "We've got twenty-four hours, Pres. Don't want to waste it!"

Chapter Sixteen

HOLLIS

"So you never explained to me how you became a manager of a nightclub," Pres says next to me as we wait for the waitress to come with our drink refills.

We've had the best day. We ate breakfast at the Paris Hotel, took cheesy photos in front of the Fountains of Bellagio, and even did the zipline on Fremont Street.

Spending time with her like this again? It feels just as natural and easy as our phone conversations. We've talked about everything, from reminiscing about high school to the many years that followed. She told me about her early days at Creeds and the roommate struggles she faced in her early twenties.

One subject that doesn't come up is Jace.

I try not to dwell on what that means.

After a quick trip back to the hotel to change our clothes, we're starting the night off at a trendy bar down the street from our hotel.

"I was a bartender," I confess, trying to keep my eyes from wandering south. Having her in front of me in that sequined gold dress with the plunging neckline is proving to be a huge distraction.

Her jaw drops. "You? A bartender?"

"Is that so hard to believe?" I smile. "You're a bartender!"

"Yeah, but I'm a hell of a lot nicer than you are."

I scoff, pretending to be offended. "I'm nice."

She leans forward, and I try not to groan when the familiar scent of vanilla hits my nostrils. Fucking hell. "You're nice to the people you like. You're just standoffish with everyone else. It's why we would always end up hanging out at parties while Hendrix talked to literally everyone."

It's one of the reasons why we became so close in the first place. Pres had a calmness to her that I gravitated toward. The teenage boy in me craved the normalcy that Hendrix's friendship gave, but I think I formed a deeper connection to Pres in those quiet hours on the beach.

"I'm nice to you," I counter.

Her eyes sparkle with amusement. "That's because you like me."

"Yeah." I smirk, watching her lips curve upward. "I do."

Even in the low light of the bar, I can see her blushing. I like being the reason for all that color on her cheeks. The waitress chooses that moment to bring us our refills—a whiskey sour for me and a martini for her.

We offer our thanks before she walks away, and as Pres reaches for her glass at the same time I do, our fingers brush. It's not the first time we've touched today—sometimes by accident, other times on purpose. But right now, this small bit of contact—under the dim lights, with the whiskey warming my blood—feels electric.

Neither of us is quick to pull away.

I can't get over how gorgeous she is, from those mesmerizing blue eyes to the high cheekbones and scattering of freckles. She's everything I remember.

And more.

Like me, she's changed since high school. Back then, she thought she was too tall and gangly. I thought she was perfect.

I still do.

Adult Presley's body is a work of art—tight and curvy in all the right places. Her hair is longer, lighter, with wisps of honey and sand woven in. There are also other things I notice too, like the tiny tattoo behind her ear that I can't stop looking at. She has her last name on the inside of her forearm, like the rest of her family, in swirly, delicate script, but it's the other one that has me so intrigued.

It's stars—a cluster of tiny stars—and I can't help but wonder what it means.

I watch as Pres takes a sip of her drink. Her throat bobs as the cool liquid slides down. Finally, she says, "So I guess what I should have asked was how did the introvert stumble into bartending?"

I smile. I've never really labeled myself an introvert, but I suppose it fits. I don't like crowds, and I always hated parties in high school. Even at the club, I tend to stay in my office while Jonas handles the front, greeting guests and VIPs.

"I was broke. It was decent money," I explain with a shrug. "And I was good at it. I was punctual, never missed a shift, and my standoffish behavior..." I say with air quotes, causing her to laugh. "Meant that I never crossed a line with customers."

A shadow crosses her face. "Not always easy qualities to find in an employee," she says absently, before blinking and asking, "So you've bartended all over then?"

I nod, wondering just exactly what happened between her and Jace to cause such a reaction, but I don't want to sour the mood by bringing him up.

"I had a hard time settling down in one place until Nashville. I've lived in Phoenix, Seattle, Baltimore...even spent a few months in Dallas. I am not a fan of Texas."

"No?" Her eyes crinkle as she laughs. "I wouldn't think it's much different from Nashville."

"It is," I say firmly, which only causes her to laugh harder.

"What made you decide to put down roots in Nashville?"

I take a sip of my whiskey before I answer her. "I'm not sure I would call them roots exactly. I like Nashville, but it's not exactly where I envisioned I'd end up."

I'm not sure I actually ever envisioned ending up anywhere long-term, at least not since—

"So why do you stay?"

"Jonas."

"Your best friend?"

I nod. I've talked about him before, but failed to mention he's my business partner too. I don't know why I've kept up with the illusion that I'm the manager at Velvet, rather than co-owner. I should be proud that I've worked my way up from bartender to business owner, but sometimes when I look at all those zeros in my bank account, I feel like a sell-out.

I used to hate guys like me when I was a kid.

"He's the closest thing I've had to family since..." I swallow, and her expression softens.

"It's okay," she says, placing her hand gently on top of mine. It's small and delicate. "I get it, and I'm glad you found that. I always hoped you would."

I run my thumb over her wrist, feeling her pulse dance beneath my touch. I told myself I'd stick to the role of a friend on this trip. But so far, I am failing miserably.

Picking up the rest of my drink, I down it in one gulp. She laughs and does the same. "Okay, so what do you want to do for the rest of the evening?"

"Well, it is my birthday, and we are in Vegas..."

I grin. "Uh-huh."

She leans forward, a challenging glint in her eyes. "What exactly can I talk you into?"

"You don't have to talk me into anything, Pres. It's your birthday. I'm down for anything."

"So if I told you I wanted to get matching tattoos?"

I shrug, acting completely unfazed. I've never gotten a tattoo. I can barely commit to a six-month lease. Why the fuck would I be okay with permanent ink? But the idea of doing it with Pres has me rethinking the idea. "I'd ask that you not pick the neck or forehead, but otherwise, I'm game."

"You didn't even ask what it would be!"

Another shrug. "Not my birthday. Not my decision. Although you might want to keep that in mind, 'cause for my birthday, I want a Goonies tattoo."

"Oh my god, you still love *The Goonies*? Hollis, it's been twelve years. Pick a new favorite!"

I shake my head, eyes crinkling with laughter. "Nope. Can't. It's a classic."

She chews on her bottom lip. "Okay, well, luckily for you—and me apparently—I don't want a tattoo. But I do want something."

Why does my whole body seem to come alive when she utters those last few words?

She's not going to ask for you, asshat.

"Then ask me, Pres."

Her eyes glance down at my mouth for a heartbeat or two. I swear my own heart stops. Then she looks at me and says, "I want to go dancing."

"That's it?" I laugh. "That's your big ask? That's tame compared to a tattoo. Why did you think I wouldn't want to go?"

An amused expression crosses her beautiful face. "I don't know. I wasn't sure if being in a nightclub would feel too much like work to you."

I smirk. "We're at a bar, Pres. Do you feel like you're at work?"

Her lips curve into a smile. "No."

"All right, then let's go dance. But only on one condition." I grin, finally feeling like the perks of my job might actually come in handy for once.

"Okay?"

"I get to choose the club."

"Deal."

Thirty minutes later, after a quick call to Jonas, we are walking past the long line of people waiting to get into one of Vegas's hottest clubs.

"Take notes," Jonas said to me over the phone when I told him where we were headed. He wanted me to work tonight?

Yeah, no.

Tonight is all about Presley.

The bouncer takes my name, checks his list, and gives us the go-ahead. I take Presley's hand, and we walk through the nondescript black door to his right.

Like any good club should be, it's like stepping into another world.

The music is loud, but the DJ has the bass just right so you can feel it vibrating deep inside your chest rather than your eardrums. The lights are a mix of deep purples, blues, and pinks, and the fog machines add a bit of mystery.

It's different than Velvet, but no less luxurious, and the large crowd reflects that. It is absolutely packed in here. Vegas doesn't seem to understand the meaning of a weekday, so I imagine this place is like this every night.

We push through the crowd until we reach the bar. I turn to Pres and lean in. My lips brush her ear. The alcohol from earlier is messing with my inhibitions, so I'm not entirely sure it was unintentional. She shivers. "Another martini? Or something else?"

Her lips quirk. "Surprise me, Mr. Bartender."

"You may regret that," I say, before motioning to the actual bartender. I make sure she can't hear me when I order, even angling my body so she can't read my lips.

When he goes to fetch my request, and I turn back, her arms are folded across her chest, and she's pouting. I laugh and then see her eyes widen as the bartender returns with a bottle of tequila.

"Shots?"

"Yup."

"Are you crazy? It's my thirtieth, not my twenty-first!"

I chuckle. "Yeah, and what did you say at the bar earlier?"

"That it's my birthday, and we're in Vegas?"

"Exactly!" I emphasize. "If we only have a few hours left together in this crazy town, we're gonna make the most of it—starting with shots."

She watches as the bartender pours two shots and then slides them over. I wait as she stares them down, clearly thinking it through. Decision made, she reaches down, grabs both shots, and shoots them back, one right after the other.

"Your turn."

I guess I'm getting drunk tonight.

"You are not a bad dancer," Pres whisper-shouts into my ear as we once again wait by the bar for the bartender.

"Did you expect me to be a bad dancer?"

She shrugs. Her face is flushed from all the dancing and tequila. She pulled her long blonde hair into a ponytail a while ago, and all I can think about is all the wicked things I could do with that wrapped around my wrist. "It's just that most guys I've dated aren't great at dancing."

I try not to imagine Jace's hands all over her like mine just were. A surge of jealousy rises up, nevertheless. "We aren't dating, though."

"No..." She pauses, looking at me intently. "We're not."

The bartender approaches, and I hold up two fingers.

He nods. But this time, when he comes back around with our drinks, I ask for two lime wedges and salt. I'm probably going to regret this later, but the tequila is giving me all kinds of stupid ideas tonight.

Pres watches as the bartender sets down a small glass with several limes and a saltshaker. Her eyes slowly meet mine. "Who goes first?" I challenge.

She bites her bottom lip, and I nearly groan. "You can," she answers, her cheeks flaming red.

"Okay." I grin. "Where do you want it?"

"What?"

Chuckling, I clarify, "The salt, Pres. Where do you want the salt?"

"Oh, um..." She looks down at her dress and her arms before slowly pointing to her neck.

Excitement races through me. Exactly where I was hoping she'd pick. I pick up the lime and hand it to her. Despite her earlier fluster, she's a bartender, so I know she knows what to do with it.

With one hand, I grab the salt. With the other, I grip her waist and pull her closer. I can feel the heat of her body and the warmth of her breath. She looks up at me, and I give in to my earlier desire and wrap my hand around her ponytail, using it to tilt her head to the side.

She lets out a tiny gasp.

The sound of it practically undoes me, and I imagine what other noises she'd make if I had the chance to coax them out of her.

I lean down and slowly drag my tongue over the soft skin of her neck. God, she smells good. Vanilla always reminds me of her. For the last twelve years, I've barely been able to walk into a bakery without getting semi-aroused.

She grabs hold of my shirt, gripping it hard between her fingers, but lets go the second I go to sprinkle the salt. She shivers when I lick the same spot, lingering just a second longer than necessary.

Pulling back, I go to grab the shot off the bar. But Presley swipes it away before I get the chance.

"Any good bartender knows that's not how you do a body shot," she tsks with a hell of a lot more confidence than she had a moment ago. "No hands allowed, Hollis."

She grins like the Cheshire Cat as she takes that shot of tequila and wedges it between her fucking tits.

"Jesus fuck," I mutter, staring brazenly at her low-cut dress and the ample cleavage I'd been trying to pretend didn't exist all night.

Someone wolf whistles, and that knocks me out of my boob haze. I angle my large body, blocking most of hers. I know it's stupid. We're in public, doing drunken body shots, for god's sake.

But it doesn't mean I want some asshat staring at her.

Besides me, that is.

I lean forward, my hand firmly around her waist as I close my mouth around the shot glass. God, what I wouldn't give to toss the glass aside and lick every inch of her.

But instead, I tilt my head back and down the liquor. When I place the shot glass on the bar, she's ready for me with a lime wedge between her teeth.

I have a split second to decide how far I want to take this.

Because in that moment everything in me is screaming to toss that lime wedge aside and kiss the hell out of her.

"Fuck it."

Chapter Seventeen

PRESLEY

A very naked-looking Hollis is in my bed.

No, wait. This isn't my bed.

His bed, maybe? I haven't quite figured out where I am right now or how I got here. I've only been awake for two minutes, and nothing makes sense.

Not a damn thing.

Especially the words that just came out of his mouth...

"What do you mean, you think we got married?"

That's crazy. *He's crazy.*

I look down at the ring on my finger.

"I mean exactly that, Pres. I think we got drunk off our asses last night and got married."

I press my palm to my forehead. My head is throbbing. It feels like there is alcohol literally leaking out of my pores, and everything is so fucking hazy, but there's no way I drank so much that I lost an entire day.

"Okay, let's think," I say as calmly as I can. "You said the last thing you remember was sightseeing? What about after that?"

"I don't know." He shakes his head. "I think we went to a bar?" He grips his head and grimaces in pain. I guess I'm not the only one with a headache.

Maybe we both need a little sustenance.

Scooting to the edge of the bed, I stop short. "Shit."

"What's wrong?"

I glance down at the blankets covering me and feel a faint blush warming my cheeks. "I was going to order some food and coffee since we both look like we could use it. Plus, there's Advil in my purse, but I, um..." I look down, hoping he'll catch what I'm trying to convey.

"But what?"

"I don't have any clothes on, Hollis!" I say in a fluster.

"You're naked?" His voice jumps a whole damn octave, I swear. And why does he sound so shocked? He doesn't look any less naked than I do.

"No," I say. "But considering how skimpy my undergarments are, I might as well be."

I hear him groan. "Did not need to know that."

"Figured you already knew, given our current situation."

"My memory isn't exactly serving me any favors today, Pres," he grumbles.

I feel the bed shift beside me, and I turn without even thinking. When I see Hollis getting up, I almost look away, but then I notice his black boxer briefs.

Oh, so he's not naked either...

Confusion overwhelms me. "Did we—" I stop mid-sentence because he turns around to face me and...*sweet baby Jesus.*

That's a whole lot of man candy right there. I don't know where to look first. His chest and abs are a fucking work of art. Toned and tanned with the finest dusting of hair trailing down to...

"We didn't," he says firmly, abruptly ending my blatant ogling.

"How do you know?"

"'Cause there are a lot of things I could forget—like my own wedding, apparently—but that's not one of them." The way he says it and the intensity with which he looks at me send shivers down my spine.

I open my mouth to respond, but he moves before I can say a word, heading toward the phone on the small desk by the window. "I'm just gonna order a little of everything. Okay?"

"Just no eggs," I plead. That's something my wonky hangover stomach can't handle right now.

He grimaces. "Agreed."

While he talks to room service, I glance down at the simple gold band on my left hand, trying to make sense of how it got there. I don't even notice when his call finishes or the bed dips, and Hollis sits down beside me.

"Hey," he says softly.

I look up and see that he's now wearing a pair of low-slung pajama pants.

"Is this your room?" I ask, trying to remember if I've been in here before. I think we came up here to drop off his bag when he surprised me yesterday, but I don't remember it being so grand.

"It's ours, apparently."

My eyes widen. "What?"

His eyes track mine as he softly says, "A wedding present to ourselves, according to the front desk."

I feel my stomach clench at his words. "So we are married."

"The marriage license by the phone would make it look that way, yes."

I lift my hands in an exasperated motion. "How does this even happen? What idiot would marry us? Like, I know we're in Vegas and—"

"Pres?" His voice is strained, with a note of panic.

"Yeah?" I immediately look to see what's wrong.

His gaze is firmly pinned on the floor, avoiding all eye contact. "I'm gonna need you to put clothes on if you want me to stay focused."

I look down and gasp. My wild hand gesture made me drop the firm grip I had on the sheet, and now, aside from my thin lace bra, I'm naked from the waist up. "Shit!" I curse, gathering up the sheet to wrap around my torso. "Sorry!"

I stand, which causes him to stand with me since I'm dragging the sheet along. He turns, keeping his back to me, which, considering our current situation, makes me snort out a laugh.

"Something funny?"

"Kind of," I answer. "The way you're averting your gaze. Doesn't seem very husbandly of you."

He briefly glances over his shoulder, and the heat in his gaze makes me blush. "Would you prefer I watch?"

I swallow, and suddenly everything feels so real in that moment.

The hotel room.

The ring.

Him.

"I'll just go grab some clothes," I awkwardly blurt out before looking around. "Wait, do I have any in here?"

He nods. "Looks like the hotel staff transferred everything from our separate rooms to here last night."

My brow furrows. "So we were too drunk to remember getting married, but cognizant enough to combine our rooms?"

He shrugs as he looks out the window in an attempt to keep his focus off me, I'm sure. "When I inquired, they said we came in announcing our nuptials to anyone who would listen and then asked for the biggest suite they had."

"How very Ross and Rachel of us," I mutter, looking around at the tall windows and the large bed. I can't even imagine how much a night in a room like this costs. "How are we going to pay for this?"

He finally looks up at me. "I'll take care of it."

"I can't let you do that," I argue.

"How does the saying go?" A wicked smile spreads across his face. "What's yours is mine, and what's mine is yours?"

My brow furrows in frustration. He cannot seriously be suggesting...

"Go get dressed, and then we can eat and try to make sense of the last twelve hours."

But that's the problem.

Nothing makes sense.

Nothing at all.

HOLLIS

Married.

We got fucking married?

Standing in the shower, I let the water pour over me as I try to remember exactly how the hell we went from something as innocent as ziplining to vowing to love and cherish each other for the rest of eternity.

And why do I feel like this might all be my fault?

I finish up, turn off the water, and dry myself off. Just as I'm pulling my shirt over my head, I hear Pres talking to someone from room service on the other side of the door.

"Thank you," she says politely.

"Of course," they answer. "Will there be anything else, Mrs. Beck?"

"N-no." Pres stumbles over the sound of my last name. My heart does too.

Fucking hell.

Standing in front of the mirror, I hold out my hand and glance down at the ring that now resides there. It should feel heavy, burdensome. Wrong.

But it doesn't. It feels like it's exactly where it's supposed to be. It feels right.

And isn't that a kicker?

In my thirty-two years, I don't think I've ever really considered the idea of getting married. After spending my childhood with a woman obsessed with the idea, it didn't appeal to me all that much.

But now?

When I open the bathroom door and find Pres gazing down at the nearly identical gold band on her finger, though, I know I have a problem.

Because I don't think my new wife sees that ring the same way I do.

How could she?

She just got cheated on by her boyfriend and then wakes up to find herself married to her childhood friend? Jonas said that Vegas had a way of stirring up trouble, but even I couldn't have imagined this.

She turns toward the sound of the door opening and gives a hesitant smile. "She called me Mrs. Beck."

I flinch. "I heard."

"My parents are going to be thrilled," she says at the same time I announce, "We can get an annulment."

Her eyes go wide as I suck in a breath. We stare at each other for a moment. Then another.

Finally, she speaks. "You want to get an annulment?"

My heart starts to hammer in my chest. "I just thought with everything going on between you and Jace —" I blurt out, before landing on, "You don't?"

"You know about Jace?" She seems surprised.

"You told me when you were drinking mai tais by the pool. You called him a dirty, rotten cheater. Do you not remember?"

She covers her face with her hands. "No. Obviously. God, this is so embarrassing. I'm never drinking again," she groans, plopping onto the bed. She's wearing a pair of tight yoga pants and a sweatshirt. I wish I could say it made me want her less, but it doesn't.

She's gorgeous in everything.

I really need to get a grip on this attraction I have for her, especially now that we're fucking married.

"I second that—the drinking thing, I mean. My head is killing me," I say, moving toward the breakfast tray. I go straight for the coffee, pour two cups, and hand her one. "I know you're particular about how you like it."

"I am," she agrees, but seems taken aback by the observation. It doesn't stop her from reaching for the cream and three packets of sugar. Then she looks over the food offerings and grabs a plain bagel and returns to her spot on the bed.

I stick to black coffee, but take a seat at the desk across from her.

"Tell me what you want to do, Pres."

Those baby blues meet mine. "Go back in time and make better choices?"

Ouch.

She must see me flinch at her choice of words because she instantly starts to backpedal. "I'm sorry, Hollis. I didn't mean you. I don't know what led us here, but getting drunk and married to you isn't half as dumb as dating Jace Vaughn. My family has been telling me what a skeevy piece of shit he is for months, and all I ever did was stick up for him and now..."

Her words falter, and now I feel like a piece of shit. I should be supportive and understanding like any good friend, but instead, all I feel is jealousy. She might be married to me, but her heart still belongs to the man who cheated on her.

I swallow down all those emotions and try to focus. "I doubt they'll hold that against you. Your family loves you and has always supported you."

She snorts and rolls her eyes. "You've been gone a long time, Beck. A lot has changed."

My brow furrows as I take a sip of my coffee. "What do you mean?"

"I mean, I'm surrounded by a bunch of overachieving

siblings. Cash is set to take over the entire Creed empire from Dad. Hendrix is a literal fucking rock star now. Mercury is like this evil genius when it comes to music production, and then there's Myles, who I swear is just one role away from being the next Chris Hemsworth."

I tilt my head. "Chris Hemsworth? Really? From the pic you showed me, I was thinking he looked more like that guy from that Viking movie."

"The blond guy?" I nod, and she seems to ponder it before saying, "He would make a pretty excellent Viking."

I give her an amused grin. "I know all about your siblings, Pres. Between what you've told me and the hour-long phone call with your mom during that family dinner, I'm all caught up on the many achievements of the various Creed children. What I don't know is what that has to do with you."

She tosses a hand in the air, clearly frustrated. The other clutches her precious cup of coffee. "Can't you see? I'm the family fuckup. I dropped out of community college. I don't have any special talents. I'm not good at anything. I'm an embarrassment." She lets out a ragged breath. "And once they find out about what happened with Jace, it will only confirm that."

"First of all, not true. Have you ever heard yourself sing? Fucking angels, Pres."

She snorts out a laugh. God, I forgot how good it feels to make her laugh. I used to crack the stupidest jokes during our late-night walks just so I could hear it. "I knew you used to stand outside my door and listen to me. Stalker."

"Couldn't help myself," I say, before turning serious. "You really think your family will judge you for his infidelity?"

"His...what? You think he cheated on me?"

My brow scrunches. "That's what you told me. I assumed that's why you broke up."

Then I feel the blood drain from my face. "You did break up, didn't you?"

Please tell me I didn't wake up to find out I'm married to the one woman I've been sort of crushing on for years, only to discover she still has a boyfriend.

"Yes," she says, making me exhale a breath I didn't know I was holding. "We broke up a month ago."

I gape. "A month?"

She nods. "The night I called you from my parents' house."

"Then why did you say he cheated on you that day by the pool?" I ask, hoping it doesn't come off accusatory. I'm just trying to make sense of that phone call.

She stares at the floor for a minute, then I hear her mumble the words *dirty, rotten cheater* under her breath before her face collapses into her palms. "I am such an idiot," she laments. "I was calling him a cheat. Not a cheater. Because what he did was something so much worse."

I tense. "What did he do, Pres?" When she looks up at me, her face is a mixture of guilt and embarrassment. She shakes her head, like the truth will cost her. "Tell me."

"He stole from the bar."

Anger courses through me, but I manage to keep it in check. "How much?"

Her eyes gleam with unshed tears. "A lot," she confesses. "I caught him on the security camera lifting cash from the register. I went back several weeks and caught him doing it dozens of times."

"But that shouldn't be enough to—"

"There's more," she continues. "After I fired him, I figured that was the end of it. I knew he'd stolen a lot, but it wasn't enough to ruin us. But then he broke into the bar and stole all of our inventory."

"He what?"

"It's my fault." Her bottom lip starts to quiver. "I should have changed the security pin, but I had no idea he even knew it. Since the alarm wasn't tripped, he was able to waltz right in. I didn't find out until the next day when I walked in and discovered the entire stockroom empty."

"How do you know it was him?" I ask, just to play devil's advocate, because of course it was him.

"We only have a security camera in the hallway, with none in the stockroom. But the few glimpses I caught of his shadowy figure moving through the hallway were enough. It was him."

"You should go to the cops," I press. "File a report with your insurance.They'll cover it."

"No." She shakes her head. "Thanks to me, the bar was barely skating by, and after this, I'm worried it could ruin us. I can't let my family find out how badly I..."

She can't even finish her sentence, and I can't stand to see the look of fear in her eyes at the possibility of failing her family. So I say the first thing that comes to mind. "What if we stay married?"

PRESLEY

"I'm sorry." I blink, my tears forgotten as I try to process what he just said. "I think I just hallucinated. Did you say we should *stay married?* Didn't you suggest we get an annulment like ten minutes ago?"

He checks his watch and gives me a lazy smile. "It was about five minutes ago, but yes, I did."

"Why?"

"Why, what?"

"Why do you suddenly want to stay married?"

He leans forward, the muscles of his biceps straining against the thin fabric of his T-shirt. I get the briefest flash of a memory—my hand fisting a black button-down as he leans forward in a crowded bar. I can feel every rock-hard inch of him pressed against me. My breath comes out in shallow rasps, as he grips my waist, leans over and...

"Pres?"

"Huh?" I say in a rush.

"You asked me why I suddenly wanted to stay married. I never said I didn't."

"You didn't?"

"No," he replies, taking a slow sip of coffee. "Could be beneficial for both of us."

"How so? 'Cause I hate to break it to you, but my health insurance is shit."

He barks out a laugh. "I don't need health insurance, but we can switch you to mine. It's awesome. I do need a place to stay, though."

"You what?"

"In LA," he explains. My head is spinning trying to keep up with him. "The nightclub I...manage is expanding, and LA is one of the cities they chose. I would need to be here to scout locations, approve the designs, and basically oversee every single detail."

I eye him suspiciously. "Why didn't you tell me about this sooner? Seems like you would have mentioned a temporary move to LA before now."

"I wasn't sure I wanted to take it," he says evenly. "Now, I don't seem to have a reason not to."

So being married to me is a convenience?

"This project sounds way beyond the scope of a manager."

He shrugs. "They trust me."

"If they trust you so much, why do you need to stay married to me?"

Another shrug. Why is he being so calm about all of this? We're talking about a marriage, not a business merger. "I don't, but having a more permanent attachment to the area can't hurt when I'm working with contractors and such."

"Especially when you're married to a Creed?"

That seems to shake his calm and casual demeanor. "What? No. I'd never use your family or last name like that. I just meant that it's easier to work with people when you're not an outsider."

"Oh." I nod, with understanding. "And what do I get out of this deal?"

"Like you said, your family will be thrilled," he explains. "They love me. It will distract them from everything that went down with Jace, and you'll have the added bonus of me."

"You?" My stomach does a little flip.

"I manage one of the hottest nightclubs in Nashville. I

have the knowledge and experience to help you get Creeds back on its feet."

"I don't need your—"

"I promise not to overstep," he assures me, as if he already knows what I'm about to say. "And you can oversee everything. I know your trust in others is probably at an all-time low. I'll do whatever you feel comfortable with."

I swallow down the lump in my throat. Am I really going to agree to this? "Okay," I find myself saying. "But you're forgetting one thing." I raise an eyebrow.

"And that is?"

"A marriage is supposed to last forever. Are we just going to fake this thing until we're old and gray, Hollis? Have a pretend family and go on fake anniversary trips? Buy a make-believe time-share in the Caymans?"

He shakes his head, amusement shining in his eyes. "Never buy a time-share, Pres. Hasn't anyone ever told you that?"

I roll my eyes. "You know what I mean, Beck."

"I do, and you're right. We should have an exit strategy."

Exit strategy. It was the sanest idea to come out of this whole ridiculous plan, and yet, I hated it the most. Because it means we will once again be going our separate ways, and I will have to say goodbye to Hollis Beck.

And this time, I fear it might be forever.

"Okay." I steady my breath and steel my spine as if I'm preparing for war. "Let's talk details."

Chapter Eighteen

HOLLIS

It is nine in the morning.

I just flew in from Las Vegas on a redeye. I am running on zero hours of sleep, five cups of coffee, and I'm currently knocking on Jonas's front door, hoping he doesn't kill me for the early morning visit.

He pulls the door open, dressed in nothing but a pair of black sweats, and gives me a once-over. "Man, you look like shit. What the hell happened to you?"

"I got married."

His brows shoot up so high, they nearly touch the door frame. "I'm sorry, can you repeat that? 'Cause what I think you said was—"

"I got married. Do you have coffee?"

"Of course I have coffee." He ushers me in, and we both head to the kitchen. Keisha is at the stove, humming and making pancakes in a long, fuzzy pink robe. My mouth waters. I don't remember the last time I ate. I headed to the airport with Pres around noon for her afternoon flight back to California.

Our goodbye was awkward as fuck. Do you kiss your fake wife at the airport? Shake hands? We settled on a brief hug, and even that went terribly.

After that, I just sat around for hours on standby until I could get back to Nashville.

I hadn't wanted to leave in the first place.

But I needed to come back and make arrangements.

Which is why I am here at Jonas's house at nine in the morning on a Saturday.

"The expansion idea..." I jump right in, eager to sell him my plans—the ones I came up with on the fly when I blurted out the crazy idea that we stay married. I'm practically bouncing on the balls of my feet with the need to get this all out. "Are you still on board with that?"

"You mean the one we've barely had the chance to discuss because you've been too preoccupied with Presley Creed for the last two months?"

"Yeah, that one," I answer, not even bothering to deny it. I know I've been distracted. But to be fair, he was equally distracted during the first six months after he met Keisha, so I'd say I'm ahead of schedule.

"Yeah, why?"

"'Cause I want to open a club in LA," I announce. "And I'd like to be on site to oversee everything."

Keisha pivots to gawk at me while Jonas simply gives me an assessing gaze. "So let me get this straight." He folds his arms across his bare chest. "You get married in Vegas..." Keisha gasps, covering her mouth as her husband continues, "And now you want to run off to LA and open a club just so you can live with your wife, who I'm assuming is also Presley Creed?"

"Yes."

We look at each other for a moment, then a huge

smile spreads across Jonas's face. "I told you crazy things always happen in Vegas."

He steps forward to pull me into a hug. "Congrats, man."

"Don't congratulate me yet," I warn. "We don't even remember getting married, and right now she's using our drunken marriage as an excuse to distract her family from her thief of an ex-boyfriend."

"Wait, what?" Keisha exclaims over her shoulder. "I'm gonna need you to back up and explain."

So I do. Or at least what I remember. I tell them about the rush I felt when I saw her again, about our day of sightseeing, and how easy it was to fall back into our natural rhythm.

How I never wanted the day to end.

Then I recount the moment I woke up yesterday—the confusion and the realization that I wasn't alone in that unfamiliar hotel room.

The ring on my finger.

I explain the deal we worked out.

Three months. That's how long we decided on. Three months of living together, pretending to be in love and married, and then I'd make an excuse for why I can't stay in LA anymore.

It's too crowded.

I'm needed in Nashville.

We're better off as friends...

I'll be back in Nashville before Thanksgiving.

"Three months?" Jonas scoffs. "You know that's not enough time, right?"

"Of course I do," I snap back.

It's barely enough time to get designs planned out. Definitely not enough time to get it opened, but I know I can't stay any longer than that.

If I do, we'll be heading into the holiday season, and I can't imagine going through another Christmas with the Creeds, knowing it's not real.

"It's the best I could do," is all I end up saying to Jonas.

I know I'm setting myself up for disaster because walking away from her was hard the first time around. Doing it again—no matter what time of year it is—will simply destroy me.

"You know you could just give her the money she needs to save her bar, right? You don't have to stay married to her," Jonas says. Keisha slowly turns around and stares at her husband. He looks back at her and then at me before raising both hands. "What?"

"I promised her I wouldn't overstep. That's definitely overstepping. And besides..." I nervously grip the back of my neck. "She doesn't know about the club."

His brow furrows. "What do you mean she doesn't know? Surely you mentioned your job once or twice over the last two months."

"I did. I just may have led her to believe I work for you—not with you."

"Oh, for fuck's sake, Hollis." He throws his hands up. "Why?"

"When I first told her about Velvet, she assumed, and I just didn't correct her."

He lets out a frustrated sigh. "You need to stop feeling guilty over your success."

"I don't feel guilty."

"Okay, then, whatever it is—shame, unease, insecurity. It doesn't matter. It's unnecessary, and it's a lie you don't need to be bringing into your marriage."

"You're right," I agree. "About all of it. And I'll tell her eventually, but right now, I want to be there to help her, and I worry if she knows I can bail her out at any point, she won't trust me to help."

"And what if she doesn't trust you when she finds out you've been lying?"

My throat bobs. "Then I'll cross that bridge when I get to it."

"And she agreed to all of this? What did you tell her you were getting out of this deal?"

"I told her I needed someplace to stay?"

"Jesus fuck," Jonas mutters as Keisha turns off the burner and starts to plate a few pancakes for me. I graciously accept, so hungry I don't even bother with syrup. "Tell me she didn't fall for that?"

"I may have said some other stuff," I say between bites. "I honestly don't remember. I just knew I needed to stay."

"Why?" they both ask.

"Because she needed help," I answer, remembering the way she compared herself to her siblings. It broke my heart that she didn't see herself the way I did, and I intended to show her every day for as long as I was able. "And I wanted to be the one who offered it."

"And if that's all it is? Help from a friend?"

"Then I'll find a way to be okay with it," I say, my voice strained. "And I'll see you in three months."

Three days later, my apartment is packed up, keys turned in, and what I couldn't fit in two large duffel bags is stored away.

"You sure you don't want to keep your apartment?" Jonas asks for the third time. I have a mid-morning flight, and we're meeting one last time at Velvet to go over everything before I leave.

"No," I answer, leaning back in my chair. I didn't bother cleaning out my office. There's nothing here, no personal items at least. I'm sure Sabine would have something to say about that, but it makes packing simpler.

Shit. Sabine.

I probably need to update my therapist on my major life changes.

Are therapists still allowed to provide telehealth over state lines?

I push that issue aside and focus on the present. "I have no attachment to the place, so I don't really see the point in wasting three months of rent holding onto it. Besides, I thought you'd be thrilled. Now you'll have an excuse to talk me into something extravagant when I get back."

He gives me a sideways glance. "I love you, Hollis, so don't take this the wrong way, but I'm really hoping you don't come back."

I swallow, my throat thick with emotion as I try to stay grounded in reality. He and Keisha caught me at a vulnerable moment that day in his kitchen. I can't go back to LA with the idea that this could be anything more than the deal Pres and I agreed on. Doing otherwise will only hurt me. "That's not what Pres and I agreed on. And besides, everything is temporary, right?"

"No, Hollis." He gives me a sad smile. "The people who matter? They stay. Real love isn't fleeting."

I know he's right. He's been doing a damn good job convincing me he's a permanent part of my life for years, but I'm afraid there will always be a part of me that doubts it all.

Who's ready to run at the first sign of trouble.

He lets the subject go, knowing when not to push, and clicks on a file on his laptop labeled "LA." I choke back a curse at the sheer number of files it contains: real estate listings, revenue and crime reports, demographics, maps. It's all there.

"What the hell, Jonas? I thought I was supposed to be the research and numbers guy?"

He shrugs, pulling up some of the real estate listings. "Who do you think was the research and numbers guy before you came along? Anyway, this is where I think you should start."

He points to a rundown-looking building. "Is that a hotel?" I ask.

"Yeah." He nods, his eyes gleaming with excitement. This is why Jonas is so successful. He sees potential where others don't, and it's why he was able to grow a single restaurant into a multi-million-dollar business. "Used to be kind of a big deal back in the day, but bigger, more extravagant hotels popped up in the nineties, and it was sort of forgotten. Several owners have tried to revive it since, but nothing's stuck."

"And what makes you think we can succeed where others have failed?"

He grins. "We're not in the hotel business."

* * *

About ten hours, two flights, and one layover later, I'm in Los Angeles for the first time in over a decade. I've traveled a lot since I went out on my own. I've lived all over the country. In all that time, I've never returned to California.

Not once.

As the Uber heads toward the coast, I realize I wasn't just avoiding the Golden State. I was avoiding them.

I was avoiding the Creeds.

The Malibu city limits sign comes into view, and a million memories seem to hit me all at once. That first day of school. Long walks on the beach. Lance teaching me to drive in his Mercedes as if it were no big deal. My first college acceptance letter.

My heart starts to race as we get closer to Creeds.

Since it's late and Pres already took several days off, I agreed to meet her at the bar so I could grab a spare key before heading to her apartment.

I haven't been to Creeds in years, and even when I lived with them, I rarely visited their family bar. We would all sometimes go during the day to help clean or restock, but I've never been there at night.

Tilly and Lance weren't strict about much, but they were about that. No minors at the bar—especially their own kids.

The driver lets me off in front. I grab my bags and thank him. The salty smell of the ocean hits me immediately, and it's like a balm to my soul. If I could bottle up all the good memories from my life, most of them would be on the beach—with her.

I take a minute to look up at the old bar. It's had some updates. Fresh paint and a new sign, but otherwise, it looks just as I remember it. I head for the entrance. The door creaks as I walk through, but the music playing inside dampens it.

With the heavy bags slung over my shoulder, I look completely out of place, but no one seems to notice because everyone is focused on the band up front.

Everyone except me.

My eyes are pinned on the woman behind the bar—*my wife.*

Jesus, the thought alone sends a jolt through me, and suddenly I'm pushing through the crowd to get to her.

That's when I notice how frazzled she appears. Her blonde hair is pulled back into a messy bun. Sweat dots her forehead, and she's faking a smile while talking to someone and filling a glass from the tap at the same time.

I look to the other side of the bar, where there is a petite blonde pouring a line of shots while several people try to get her attention.

Pres once told me she requires a minimum of three bartenders when a band is playing, but I only see two. Firing Jace has left her short-staffed.

I don't even think. I just move. Heading toward the back, I drop my bags behind the bar and pass the very confused-looking blonde. "Hey," I greet her.

"Hi?" she stares, a little longer than necessary.

I make my way toward Pres, who's trying to grab a bottle from the top shelf. Her eyes widen when our fingers touch, and I easily lift the bottle and hand it over to her. "Hi! You're here! I didn't realize what time it was. Sorry, it's been—"

"Busy?"

"Yeah." She nods, turning back toward the bar with her bottle of rum. "If you give me a sec, I can grab your key so you can get out of here."

"Just give me the office key."

She stiffens. "Office key? Why?"

"I just need to drop off my bags."

"But I thought you were headed to the apartment?" she asks, mixing a mojito with the kind of ease that comes from years of practice. It's impressive and kind of hot.

"And leave you to have all the fun? Nah. Besides, the band is great."

She slides the drink over to the woman, who hands her a card and asks to start a tab. "You don't have to, Hollis. It's okay, really. I'm sure you're tired and—"

"Pres. Let me help," I tell her. "We're a team now."

Her gaze meets mine, and I wait until she finally relents. "Okay. But I'll go drop off your bags. I don't like people in my office. How about you take the next order? Brush up on those bartending skills of yours."

"You got it, boss."

"I'm not your boss!" she yells over her shoulder.

"No? Then what should I call you when we're at work?" I ask innocently, not knowing where this flirty banter is coming from. Five minutes ago, I felt like I was about to drop from exhaustion, and then one look at her...

"Call me Presley. That is my name."

"Nah. I think I'll call you wife."

"You're ridiculous." She rolls her eyes, taking the towel from her shoulders and placing it on mine.

"Doesn't change the fact that you're still my wife." I shrug.

She rises on her toes and leans in close, so close I can feel her tits brush my chest. *Fucking hell.*

It reminds me of something. A memory I can't quite recall. Did she touch me like this the night we got married?

Her lips brush my ear. "For three months," she whispers. "Now get to work, *husband*."

Chapter Nineteen

PRESLEY

I've been mentally preparing myself for the arrival of my hus—*of Hollis,* for days.

I cleaned my apartment from top to bottom. I made room in my closet and cleaned out the drawers in my dresser. I even gave him precious counter space in the bathroom.

I don't know how any of this is going to work. I haven't lived with anyone in years. I tried having a roommate back in my early twenties and quickly learned it wasn't for me. It was like having an intruder in my personal space all the time. I never felt like I could relax.

And I've definitely never lived with a man.

Will he feel like an intruder too? Will this drive us apart?

Before my shift starts at the bar, I try to come up with a list of rules or boundaries, if you will. We came up with some basics back in Vegas, but those were more parameters than actual rules. Having a general housekeeping rule for your fake marriage is always a good idea, right?

But the whole time I try to come up with something, I

draw a blank. All I can think about is him, coming in that door. Being here. *Here.* In my bar.

I don't know how many times I've lain in bed over the years, wondering where he was and if he was all right. I'd picture him walking through that door and coming back to us.

To me.

And when he finally does, just a few hours later, nothing could have prepared me for the way he looks behind the bar at Creeds.

Why does he have to look so...at home? So natural and at ease. He settles in quickly, learning the register in minutes. He's polite to the customers, but not creepy. He and I move around each other like we've been doing it for years.

I try to convince myself it is because he's a former bartender, and it would be exactly the same with anyone with this much experience. But even I know that's a lie, and that's what makes this whole situation so dangerous. That's why we need rules.

Otherwise, one of us is bound to get hurt.

"Did you like the band?" Hollis asks, making me jump.

I drop my keys just as we walk up to the door of my apartment.

He bends down to pick them up, and I try not to notice the way his thighs flex in his jeans. I am very interested in what his workout routine is, because it has to be...*intense.*

He rises and hands them over, just as I realize he asked me a question. "Oh, um...yes. I've booked them several times, and they always bring a crowd. Even on a Tuesday, which is a rarity. Usually we're pretty slow."

I unlock the door, and he waits for me to go first.

Why am I suddenly so nervous?

Flipping the lights on, I turn just as he steps inside. I see him take a tentative look around, and my stomach flips. Does he hate it? Is he regretting this?

Am I?

"It's nice," he finally says.

"It's not much," I try to argue. Nearly everything in here is secondhand. After living in my parents' house, he must think this is a dump in comparison.

He drops his bags by the sofa and takes a step forward. His eyes meet mine. "I've lived in a lot of places that weren't much. This is perfect, Pres. I'm grateful for the hospitality."

My cheeks warm at the compliment and his intense gaze. "Not sure offering up my sofa is great hospitality, but you're welcome nonetheless."

His expression dims ever so slightly. "I've slept on a lot worse." I suddenly wish I could take it back, but he doesn't give me the opportunity. "Where do you want my things? I doubt you want it all dumped on your floor?"

"Oh, you can just leave them there for now. I made some room for you, but it's late and..." I glance around, feeling awkward.

This is all feeling very real.

He's going to be sleeping in my living room, just down the hall.

His stuff will be next to mine in the shower. Does he sleep in? What if he sees my underwear in the laundry? Will I see his?

A week ago, these were all questions I would have felt comfortable bringing up with him. We would have laughed about it, but I doubt there was a subject between us that was off limits—except maybe romantic relationships. I don't think I want to know about his dating history. Like ever.

But since we woke up in that hotel room, things have been weird between us. I feel like I'm talking to a stranger at the checkout line in the supermarket, rather than a lifelong friend I just happened to marry on a wild night in Vegas.

"Are you hungry?"

I expect him to say he's too tired. It's after three in the morning, and he's still on Eastern time, which makes it even later for him, but he just nods and replies, "Starving, actually."

"Okay." I smile to myself. Maybe we just need food to help smooth things over. I begin walking to the kitchen, but he stops me.

"Why don't you take a seat, and I'll make us something?" He points to the single barstool tucked under the kitchen island that I use instead of a dining table.

Shit, I should probably have two of those now.

I stand there staring as he walks over and starts to wash his large hands in my tiny sink. In fact, my whole kitchen looks ridiculously small with him in it. "But you've had a long day, and you don't even know where anything is."

"We've both had long days, and I can manage. Plus, I still don't sleep much. Kind of handy in my chosen profession." He shrugs as he starts to roll up his sleeves. I always thought I preferred tattooed men, but his muscular forearms, with their smooth, tanned skin, are beginning to prove me wrong.

Why am I suddenly picturing him with a Goonies tattoo then?

"Besides, I like to cook."

I shove that thought aside and fold my arms across my chest, trying to look offended. "I like to cook." He gives me an amused smirk, already rummaging through cabinets until he finds a sauté pan. "Okay, fine. I don't mind cooking. I just prefer when someone else does it."

"Well, consider me your personal chef for the next three months," he says lightly, though his voice is strained. "Grilled cheese, okay?"

I nod. "It's either that or eggs. I'm pretty low on food. I probably should have gone grocery shopping."

"We can go tomorrow," he suggests. "Then I'll know what you like."

"Seems like you already do."

His gaze finally lifts to meet mine. "Always have. Doesn't mean I don't need a refresher, though."

"Right." I swallow, watching as he reaches into the fridge to grab the butter and cheese. "And maybe while we're spending some time together, we can work on what exactly we're going to tell my family on Sunday."

He arches a brow and smirks. "And how are we going to convince them we're in love when things are so very awkward between us?"

I let out a relieved breath. "Yes. It's bad, right?"

He chuckles, and the sound of it instantly soothes the anxiety storming inside of me. "Yeah, we've been a little off since Naked Friday."

"Naked Friday? Is that what you're calling that morning in Vegas?" I snort out a laugh. "Also, we weren't naked!"

He shrugs. "Sounds better than half-naked Friday. And a guy can dream, right?"

I throw a towel at him, and he tries to duck but

catches it at the last second and throws it back in my direction. I laugh when it lands on the counter next to me. He was never great at sports.

Decent runner, though.

“Thanks for the help tonight,” I say as he assembles the sandwiches and places them on the pan. “I really appreciate it.”

“I was happy to do it,” he answers. “I meant what I said, Pres. We’re a team now. I can help with the bar’s financials, but I can just as easily cover behind the bar.”

“You were pretty good at it.”

“*Pretty* good?” He raises an eyebrow.

“You know how good you are.” I roll my eyes. “Do you really need me to stroke your ego?”

“Of course I do, but I’m always up for a little... stroking.” He waggles his eyebrows in an overly suggestive manner, and I choke out a laugh. He grins.

I watch as he butters the bread and assembles the sandwiches. The flirty banter has me thinking about earlier.

“Do you think we need rules?”

He looks up from the pan, a note of curiosity in his expression. “I thought we already had those.”

“Setting an exit plan and deciding what we’ll tell people is more like building the foundation than actually creating rules.”

“Okay,” he agrees with a slow nod. “So what were you thinking?”

I steady myself and gather the courage I need to say, “I think we should keep things platonic.”

His eyes meet mine, and for a split second, there is a searing intensity in those green eyes that makes my stomach flip. Then, a moment later, he straightens, and it's gone. "I'm sleeping on the couch, Pres. I figured that was implied."

"Right." I laugh nervously. "Of course."

"But we will have to make an exception when we're around others—like your family or friends. They'll expect a certain level of...intimacy."

I gulp. "Sure."

"And we might want to practice—"

"Practice?" My voice jumps an entire octave.

"You didn't let me finish." He chuckles, making me blush. "We might want to try holding hands in public or whatever so we don't appear awkward around each other."

"Oh." I relax. "Yeah, that makes sense. But that's all it is? Practice?" His eyes meet mine again. "Because I don't want there to be any confusion. You're my friend, Hollis. I can't risk that."

His hand finds mine and gives it a gentle squeeze. "Just practice, Pres." I nod, unsure what to feel. Grateful, maybe? For his understanding. But all I feel is a sharp wave of sadness.

This isn't how it's supposed to be.

"What else you got?"

"Oh, um..." I pause, biting my lip. This one I'm even less sure about, but I need to say it. "I don't think we should date, even if we're not—"

"Done."

He flips the sandwiches, each a rich golden brown. The kitchen smells like melted cheese and butter. My stomach growls.

My brow lifts. "Just like that?"

He sets the spatula down, giving me his full attention. "Pres, you are my wife. Even if that is in name only, it means something to me. I would never even think of looking at another woman while your ring is on my finger."

Emotions clog my throat, and I'm at a loss for words. "Okay," I manage to say.

A hint of a smile tugs at his lips as he plates our food. Sliding one of the plates my way, he asks. "Anything else? Want to talk about monthly expenses? Chores?"

I shake my head, needing a break from this conversation for now. "We can figure that out as we go, but I do want to make one thing totally clear."

He goes still, his eyes turning serious. "Yeah, sure."

"The toilet seat always stays down, Beck. Always."

He barks out a laugh, and I join in just moments later. "Got it, boss."

"I am not your boss!"

A slow grin spreads across his face. "Okay, wife."

Chapter Twenty

HOLLIS

JONAS

How's it going?

ME

Meeting with the broker tomorrow to tour some properties.

And yes, before you ask, the hotel is at the top of the list.

JONAS

Excellent. Send me pics.

ME

Will do.

JONAS

How is everything else going?

ME

It's...going.

JONAS

Really? That's it. That's all you're gonna give me.

ME

It's been an adjustment. We're still trying to figure things out.

That is the understatement of the year. After that first night, I thought we'd found our rhythm again. Or we were at least getting there. We joked, and the conversation flowed.

It felt good. Normal.

Even when the conversation could have gotten awkward.

I understand her hesitance and her need for rules. I need them too. She may be trying to protect our friendship, but I'm trying to protect my heart.

The morning after my arrival in LA, we both slept in. When she stumbled into the kitchen in skimpy sleep shorts and a hoodie, I tried to act like I didn't notice and made us breakfast. She made coffee. We moved around the kitchen like we'd done it a hundred times. I unpacked my stuff, and in the afternoon, we headed to the grocery store and Target since I'd only brought the bare essentials on the plane.

We even stopped for an early dinner at a place Pres loves near her place, and I met the owner. She didn't even hesitate to introduce me as her husband.

I took it as a good sign.

But then, evening arrived, and I offered to help out at the bar. She waved me off, saying she had it covered and was just going in to do some paperwork.

When she returned a few hours later, her mood was different. Darker. She went straight to bed, and ever since, she's been quiet. Guarded.

JONAS

That's understandable. There's always an adjustment period. Keisha and I had ours, remember? You just need to give it time.

ME

You adjusting to having all of Keisha's stuff around is not the same thing.

JONAS

I had to give up half my closet.

ME

I feel for you, I do. But, I've got to go.

JONAS

Say hi to the Mrs. for me!

It's now been five days since I got here, and thanks to our mismatched schedules, I've barely seen Presley. When she's bartending at night, I'm sleeping. When I'm working, she's back at the bar doing inventory or catching up on more mysterious paperwork.

I know from our weeks of texting that she doesn't usually clock this many hours unless she's understaffed. But the loss of one employee wouldn't account for the number of hours she's putting in during the day.

Unless she's just using it as an excuse to avoid me.

As I step out of the shower, I try to think of a reason why. Is it something I said? Maybe she's having second thoughts. I wouldn't blame her. What we're doing isn't exactly normal.

I dry off my hair and reach for my shirt, but quickly realize it's not there.

Shit, I forgot my clothes.

I keep everything in Presley's room to maintain the

pretense that I sleep there in case anyone visits, but I always pull out fresh clothes the night before so I can shower when I wake up.

I did all that, but left them lying on the chair in the living room.

I glance at the door and then at my phone. It's still early, and I'm usually the first one up. I don't like the thought of her having to tiptoe around her own living room.

Plus, I like having the coffee ready for her when she wakes up, which probably won't be for another thirty minutes.

I should be safe.

I turn the handle, step into the hallway, and run straight into my wife.

She gasps in surprise as I try to jump back, but my smart watch with the chunky metal band that Jonas insisted was stylish gets caught in her hair, and we're instantly stuck together.

Stylish, Jonas? Try deadly.

"Shit, Pres. Are you okay?"

"Mm-hmm, yep." Her voice sounds strained, and I look down to see that her face is practically plastered to my chest. I can feel her hot breath against my skin. She's in one of those tight tank tops she likes to wear to bed and flannel sleep shorts that have no right looking that sexy.

No bra, of course.

Focus.

"Just give me a second and I can—" Before I can finish my sentence, she reaches up and unclasps my watch from my wrist and takes a giant step back.

"I'll untangle it and get it back to you in a minute." She turns toward her room.

"Yeah." I nod. "Um, thanks."

Then she flees back to the safety of her room.

PRESLEY

It's times like these that I wish I had more friends. Because right now, I could use some good advice.

You had a friend, Pres, and then you went and married him.

And that is essentially my problem.

I don't know how to be just friends with Hollis anymore. Sure, I've always had an attraction to him. I mean, who wouldn't? He's gorgeous. Seriously fucking gorgeous.

But, first and foremost, he's always been my friend.

Until Vegas, that is. Until we got married.

Something happened that night that changed—obviously—how I see him, and now that simmering attraction between us feels almost electric. It doesn't help one bit when he comes barreling out of the shower in nothing but a towel.

God.

That's a memory that's going to live rent-free in my mind for eternity. I could feel every hard inch of him pressed against me. Every. Inch. That towel was thin.

I briefly consider calling Zara for help, but that would

mean my brother finding out about my recent nuptials, and I'm not sure I'm ready for that.

I'm not even sure I'm ready to tell my parents.

But it's a little too late for that now, as we're heading down the PCH toward Malibu for Sunday dinner.

"You look nice," Hollis says, breaking the ten-minute-long silent streak we've got going.

"Thank you," I answer, brushing an imaginary piece of lint off my black jeans. I paired it with an off-the-shoulder sweater. It's nicer than I usually wear for Sunday dinner, but I am hoping it might distract from the obvious awkwardness Hollis and I have between us.

Thanks, partially due to me. Okay, mostly due to me.

After our little "rule talk," I felt better about the situation. I put myself first and took steps to protect my heart and maybe even our friendship as well.

I woke up the next morning feeling optimistic.

Maybe this crazy idea we came up with could actually work, and I could be platonically married to my superhot friend for three months while he helps me save my family business.

Then I went to work and resumed my deep dive into the bar's finances. That's when I realized just how fucked we were.

I'm so lost in my thoughts that I don't even realize the car has stopped. I look up to find Hollis staring at me.

"We're here."

"Oh." I see the familiar walkway to my parents' house just beyond his shoulders. "Sorry. Guess I spaced out for a bit."

He opens his mouth to say something, but decides against it. We both get out, and I walk over to the other side of the car where he's leaning against the driver's door, waiting.

He's dressed in dark khakis that are doing all sorts of amazing things for his ass. The fitted black Henley with the rolled-up sleeves is a nice touch too. His curly hair is a little wild, probably in need of a trim, but I love it like this. I have to fight the urge to reach up and run my hands through it, reminding myself that's usually not something friends do.

"Wait a second," he says, reaching for my hand.

"What's up?" I ask, trying to come off as casual.

"I just wanted to make sure you're okay before we go in there. That we're okay."

I attempt a smile. "Yeah, why?"

"Pres, come on. You've been avoiding me for days."

"I have not," I argue, trying to tug my hand away, but he just pulls me closer. "I've just been busy."

"Okay, then let me help."

I glare at him. "No."

"No? Why?"

"I'm just not ready for help," I answer defensively, trying to focus on anything but him. My mom's roses look particularly nice this year...

"Pres." He gazes into my eyes in a way only he can. In a way that seems to reach into my soul and tug at my heartstrings, begging me to answer back.

"Fine," I relent with a sigh. "I have been avoiding you."

"I know that," he says smugly. "Why?"

"Because I realized the money problem at the bar isn't completely Jace's fault, okay?" I throw my hands up in frustration. "I knew we weren't doing well, but I thought I could handle it. I pushed extra money into bands and events, expecting it all to pay off. But I risked way too much, and now with all the money and stock Jace stole..."

His jaw tightens, and I wait for it. I wait for the insults or the insinuations that I'm in over my head. But they never come. "What can I do to help?" he simply says.

I stand there stunned. "What?"

"I said I would help, and I meant it. What do you need me to do?"

It's such a simple response, but so powerful. He doesn't offer any unwanted opinions, doesn't drown me in false sympathy, or try to bulldoze me and take over everything like most men do. He just offers a hand.

"Right now, if you could help me convince my parents we're head over heels for each other, that'd be great."

A sly smirk peeks out of the corner of his mouth. "All right, but I may need to bend that rule of yours."

"Why?"

"Because if we're going to convince anyone, we need to loosen up around each other, Pres. And we need to do it fast."

"Okay."

His expression shifts, and he licks his lips. Is he nervous? "And since you've been avoiding me all week, we haven't exactly had a chance to work our way up to anything. So I might have to resort to something drastic."

My stomach flutters with anticipation. "Like what?"

"Like this," he says, right before he grabs me around the waist, pulls me close, and kisses me.

I let out a tiny gasp of surprise as his mouth closes over mine, and then I'm completely lost to it. The feeling of his lips against mine. The swirling desire grows deep in my belly. The sexy groan he lets out as he slides a hand down to cup my ass.

So this is what it feels like to kiss Hollis Beck? It's electric and consuming and slightly...familiar?

In one quick motion, he lifts me up and turns so I'm pressed against the side of the car. My fingers sink into his hair, finally touching those soft red curls of his.

Just as my brain is starting to short-circuit and my libido is primed and ready to take over, I hear the sound of someone gasp.

I open my eyes, and standing there behind us is my mom.

Her gaze falls on Hollis, and her eyes widen. "Hi, Mom," I say awkwardly. "Um...surprise!"

Chapter Twenty-One

HOLLIS

I turn to see Presley's mom staring at me as if she's just seen a ghost.

Her eyes blink back tears. Apart from a few more laugh lines and gray hairs, she hasn't aged a day since the last time I saw her. She still has that laid-back West Coast vibe, complete with loose linen pants and a long cardigan to fend off the late-day chill from the ocean. "Hollis?" She steps forward like she's about to hug me. My fingers dig into Pres's waist, pleading for an intervention.

It's not that I don't want to hug her mom.

It's just that I don't want to hug her *right now.*

Not after I just experienced the most earth-shattering kiss of my life, and I'm suffering the physical consequences of it.

I shift behind her, a futile attempt to adjust myself.

No, definitely no hugs right now.

"Mom, why don't we go inside and find the others? Then we can get all the reunions done all at once?"

She eyes us suspiciously. "And you'll explain what I just walked in on?"

"Yes." Pres laughs. "We'll explain everything. Promise."

She takes my hand, and we follow Tilly up the walkway, but I slow my pace so we fall behind a little. "You're a lifesaver," I whisper in her ear.

She snorts. "Pretty sure that's not the introduction you were envisioning."

"The making out or the boner?" I joke. "Because walking in on us making out looks pretty convincing." Is it still considered walking in when we're outside? I'm not sure.

She snickers under her breath. "The boner, you idiot."

"Oh yeah, that would have been awkward," I answer, but then add, "Sorry. I may have let things get a little out of hand."

"It wasn't just you," she whispers. "And like you said, it was convincing."

I swallow, remembering the feel of her body pressed against mine. "Very."

"What are you two whispering about back there?" Tilly says over her shoulder, a contented smile now replacing her tears.

"Nothing!" we both answer.

"Some things never change," I hear her say as we all step through the familiar front door.

The foyer is spacious and open. It gives off a California coastal vibe without coming off corny. The walls are light to match the white oak floors and the contemporary art. It feels like I'm stepping back in time. "No, they don't," I murmur as memories assault me of the last time I stood in this very spot.

If I have to be miserable, so does he.

After she dragged me out of here, we ended up in

some no-name town in some no-name state, where my mother could lick her wounds after being dumped. Again. I never learned the reason he kicked her out, and honestly, I didn't care. I started making plans to leave as soon as I could.

And I never looked back.

As if she senses my discomfort, Pres takes my hand and pulls me toward the family room. "Come on," she says softly. "Let's go find everyone else."

Nerves start to settle in the pit of my stomach. I've been so focused on Pres and the growing distance between us that I hadn't given much thought to how I'd react to seeing her family today.

And now I've run out of time to prepare.

We round the corner past the impressive staircase to the living room that overlooks the Pacific. I don't know how many hours I sat here watching the water wink out in the distance.

But today, I barely notice it because sitting on the sofa is Lance Creed.

"Hi, Daddy," Pres greets him, still clutching my hand. "I brought a guest. Hope you don't—"

"Hollis!" Lance pops up from the sofa to greet us. His dark hair has turned a bit more salt and pepper than I remember, but he's still rocking the vintage band tees and worn jeans. He's always kind of reminded me of an older version of Dave Grohl. He's even got a pair of stylish black-framed glasses now.

Lance doesn't even bother with a handshake and just steps right up and pulls me into a tight hug. I tense as years of unresolved feelings toward this man surge to the forefront of my mind. But when I catch a glimpse of my wife, I push it all aside.

I am not here for that. I am only here for her.

"Good to see you, Lance," I say when he finally lets me go.

"This is such a wonderful surprise," he replies. "I wish the rest of the kids were all here to see you."

"We're the only ones?" Pres asks. Now that he mentions it, the living room is unusually quiet for the Creed family.

"Yeah, I'm afraid it's just us this week," Tilly says, coming up to join her husband. "Myles is rehearsing for an audition he has tomorrow. Mercury is sick, and obviously, Hendrix and Zara are still on tour."

"Cash?"

"Oh!" Tilly laughs at her unintentional omission. "Taylor has a birthday party. Parents are required to stay the entire time."

Now it's Pres's turn to laugh. "Oh, I bet he was thrilled about that."

"Immensely. You know how much he loves social gatherings."

"And people," she adds.

"Wait? Are we talking about the same Cash?" I ask, because the Cash I remember was a total book nerd, but he was also immensely popular. He rarely came home from college because he was always busy with some club he was in or he had plans with friends.

Tilly shrugs, a shadow falling over her. "People change."

Lance takes her hand as his expression shifts. "So what brings you to Malibu, Hollis?"

"Yes." Tilly smiles, eyeing us both with a knowing grin. "I'd love to know that as well."

Oh, here we go...

"Uh...actually, Dad, that's actually something we'd like to discuss. You see, the thing is..." She falters, trying to find the right way to tell them.

So I just come out and say it.

"We got married!" I announce, grabbing Presley's hand in mine as both her parents' mouths drop open. Two sets of eyes land on the matching gold bands they now realize they somehow missed.

"You're married?"

"It was a spontaneous thing," Pres says, the words rushing out. "But we're happy about it."

"More than happy," I add. "And we hope you'll be happy for us."

They both just stare at us. I can't tell if being at a loss for words is a good thing—like they're just processing and trying to catch up—or if they're trying to find the nicest way possible to tell us we're completely crazy.

Because, as much as they love me, or used to anyway, this does come off as a little nuts. Especially when a few weeks ago, Pres was here for a family dinner with a completely different man.

A man they all hated, but still.

"Why don't we go sit?" I suggest, realizing we're still all standing in the middle of the living room, awkwardly facing each other.

"Good idea," Pres agrees. She takes my hand again as we all head toward the oversized sectional. It's different from the one I remember, and now that I look around, I notice several new things in the room. A new abstract painting over the mantel. A fancy TV. A toy box.

Tilly's gaze stays fixed on our joined hands as we all settle in. Even though I know Presley is holding it to sell our story, I can't help but feel a little more at ease with her fingers curled around mine.

Her presence has always had that effect on me.

"So maybe we should start at the beginning?" I suggest.

Tilly and Lance nod. "That would be helpful."

"I'm sure by now Mom has told you that Hollis and I have been talking for a couple of months. It started before that night he called during family dinner."

Lance's bushy gray brows furrow as Tilly's cheeks go red. "Uh…no, I actually hadn't mentioned that to your father yet. He's been busy with work, and I wasn't sure it mattered since we all got to chat with him in the end."

"Oh." Pres looks around awkwardly. "Well, that night Hollis called—that wasn't spontaneous. I called him. We'd already reconnected. Mom was just covering for me."

"Why did you keep it a secret?" Lance asks.

"Because it was new," Pres explains. "And confusing. When Hollis first contacted me, I was so glad to have him back in my life, but then my feelings for him started to change, and I didn't know how to handle that."

She says it so effortlessly, I almost believe her.

"Wait," Lance holds up a hand. "Your mother made it sound like you reconnected with him through social media. But he contacted you? How?"

Oh, fuck.

"He texted me."

Lance's gaze settles on me. "How did you get her number?" he asks, but it's not really a question. He already knows the answer.

I let out a heavy sigh. This is a conversation that's been a long time coming—one I wasn't exactly planning on having five minutes after walking through the door. But I guess we might as well get it out of the way. "I always had it," I confess. "I never lost any of your numbers."

"So all the texts I sent..."

I shake my head, knowing this is gonna hurt. It's taken a lot of therapy to get me to this point. To finally understand all the things I did to sabotage my own happiness in a futile attempt to protect myself. "I never got them, Lance. I blocked all of you the moment I walked out of this house."

"Why?" He looks as wrecked as I felt that day.

"Because leaving you was something I could control. Walking away hurt a lot less than staying and someday finding out you didn't want me," I admit, as Pres squeezes my hand. I rub my thumb over the smooth skin of her knuckle. "I grew up believing I didn't deserve anything good. That year I spent with you guys almost changed my mind. But when my mom showed up here demanding I come with her, it all just fell apart. Every ounce of self-worth I'd built crumpled at her feet, and I was nothing but a scared little kid again."

"I'm so sorry, Hollis," Tilly sniffles, her eyes glistening with tears.

"We tried everything," Lance says, his voice hoarse. "I hired a lawyer, but by the time we could work anything out, your mother was long gone, and I couldn't get a hold of you."

I manage a sad smile. "It's okay. I left as soon as I finished school, and I've had a good life." I glance toward Pres, whose own eyes are a bit misty. "I'm exactly where I'm supposed to be."

She smiles, and when we turn back to her parents, they both grin. "Yes," Tilly agrees. "We can see that."

Since it's just the four of us, Tilly decides to forgo cooking anything for dinner and just order Thai for everyone. I'm a little bummed none of Pres's siblings could make it, but also a bit relieved.

Telling Tilly and Lance has been stressful. Breaking the news of our marriage to the entire Creed family would have been exhausting.

While we wait for the food to arrive, Pres and I give them the edited version of our Vegas wedding story—one that does not involve copious amounts of alcohol or waking up with the world's worst hangover and no recollection of the night before.

Well, almost no recollection. I haven't told Pres this, but every once in a while, I'll get a tiny flashback—a glimpse—and then it's gone.

I'm hoping this means that eventually I'll be able to piece it together and have at least a roadmap for how we ended up at a wedding chapel in the middle of the night.

I'm not sure it will solve anything, but at least we'll know.

"And, um...am I allowed to ask what happened with Jace? Last I heard, he was still working at the bar?" Tilly's mood has been light, happy even, since we broke the news. Now she's hanging on our every word as we gather plates and napkins. Lance is tracking the Uber Eats driver like a hawk. I've never seen him act more his age than when he jumped up to announce, "He's just down the street!" and then raced toward the front door.

Pres scoffs, handing me the bottled water I asked for. "I fired him. He was never on time and seriously unprofessional."

Her mom simply nods. They obviously already know she broke up with him, but Pres clearly expected a comment or two about how they always knew he was bad for business or a horrible person.

But neither of them says a word.

Maybe our plan of distraction is working after all.

We all head into the dining room, and I try not to gape when my eyes land on the massive new table they've put in here. It's got to be maple or some sort of birch. It's easily twice the length of a normal table and must seat over a dozen people.

"It's ridiculous, I know." Tilly motions with her hand. "But the family's grown a bit since you've been gone, and you know us. We always have room for a few more."

"A few? Pretty sure you could fit half of Malibu in here," I joke.

"At least a football team or two," Presley chimes in. "And hey, if you need a side gig, you could always rent it out for parties or formal events."

"You could host a state dinner," I offer.

"Maybe extend an invitation to the king?" Pres snickers.

"What about a wedding reception?" Lance interrupts her as he enters the room with two large bags in his arms. He sets the food on the table and looks up at us.

"A wedding reception?" Pres parrots back to him. "For who?"

"You two, of course."

Presley's eyes widen. "Why? We're already married."

"Doesn't mean you can't celebrate," Lance tells her. "That's what a wedding reception is for, after all."

"Oh, I love that idea!" Tilly places a dramatic hand on her chest like she's got a serious case of the feels.

"We wouldn't want to cause a fuss." I try to derail this idea before it gets away from us. "And wedding receptions are expensive. We can't ask that of you."

Lance dismisses my concerns with a wave of his hand. "It's no trouble, and it will be ages before we'll have the opportunity to do something like this for one of our daughters, since Mercury is still so young. Please—it's the least we can do.

"I..." *Shit.* My mind goes blank as I try to come up with another excuse.

"Listen," Tilly says as Lance starts to pull the food out of the bags and set it on the table in front of us. "I don't mind that your wedding was spontaneous. In fact, I find it incredibly romantic, and anyone can see you two are meant for each other." They can? "But I can't deny the fact that I'm devastated we weren't all there to celebrate with you."

"I know you hate crowds, kiddo," Lance says to Pres, who looks just as shocked as I am. This is not something we planned for. Questions about how we fell in love so quickly, sure. How we're adjusting to married life, of course. But this? Totally left field. "So we could keep it small. Just close family and friends."

"But we'd have to wait until everyone gets back from tour," Tilly chimes in.

"True." Lance nods as he and Tilly eye each other. "Very true."

"And when is that?" I ask, feeling nervous. Our deadline is supposed to be the beginning of November. It would be bad form to have a wedding reception right before I'm supposed to leave my wife and skip town.

"September," Tilly answers. "But we're going to need some time to plan. Right, Pres?"

My wife is currently sporting a deer-in-the-headlights look, but manages to glance over at her mom and say, "Um…right?"

"And you'll be too busy planning the Halloween party at the bar in October," Lance chimes in. "And then there's Thanksgiving…"

"Oooh, what if we did early December?" Tilly exclaims, her excitement growing with every second. "It's close to the holidays, but I think we could make it work."

Lance's head bobs up and down in agreement. "I do love Malibu in the winter. Don't you?"

"Yeah, sure," I say absently.

Tilly claps her hands together excitedly. "Great, then it's all settled. Let's eat!"

Pres and I just look at each other. What the fuck just happened?

It looks like I might be staying a bit longer…

Chapter Twenty-Two

PRESLEY

After my parents ambushed us with a surprise wedding reception, Hollis and I slowly start to settle into a nice routine.

He works during the day, doing whatever managers do to get a new nightclub up and running, while I run errands and take care of things around the apartment. In the late afternoon, we both head to the bar. I'll either work a shift with him behind the bar or, if we have enough coverage, I'll go back to my office and try to find ways to keep the doors open.

On days when we both have off, I act as a tour guide and take him to the beach or a museum. We even spend an entire day at Disneyland, where we buy matching mouse ears and ride Space Mountain three times in a row.

We talk endlessly about the past—his and mine, together and apart. I learn so much about him and the life he's lived. I think it's been a lonely one.

And the more I listen, the more I start to wonder if mine might have been too.

We do not discuss the kiss in my parents' driveway.

And I definitely do not think about it when I'm alone in the shower. Or in bed late at night. Or that one time I locked the door to my office...

Occasionally, my mom calls and asks us questions like, *Do we want the reception inside, or on the beach under a tent,* or *do we want a cake or a dessert bar?*

I have no idea how to answer, because all I can think about is the fact that Hollis was supposed to move back to Nashville in November, and now my parents are throwing a lavish celebration of our love a month later.

He told me he would stay, but how is it going to look when he leaves a few weeks later?

Or a month?

God, this will break their damn hearts.

In all my self-loathing over the bar and Jace's break-in, I never stopped to think how this fake marriage might affect anyone else. When Hollis suggested we stay married, all I could see was how it would benefit me and solve my problems.

Now, I'm worried about how much collateral damage we might cause because of my selfishness. This revelation is why I decided to ask them to hold off on telling my siblings.

Maybe if they have less time to become attached to him, it will hurt less when he's gone.

My mom was initially resistant to the idea, so I may have laid it on a bit thick, telling her at dinner that night that we just wanted a little time for ourselves before everyone else found out. I watched as her expression softened, and she gave us a sappy smile. She agreed we'd tell the rest of the family when Hendrix and Zander return from Europe next month.

That was two weeks ago, which means I have two more weeks of dodging my siblings before the news of my marriage gets out.

I'm honestly surprised my mom has managed to keep a secret this long, especially one so big. She's been dying for one of us to get married for years. Pretty sure she almost got her wish when Cash was dating Taylor's mom, but that all went to shit—to put it mildly.

Speaking of...

Sitting in my office, I look up from the report I've been staring at and do a double take as I catch a glimpse of my brother entering the bar on the security camera I now keep open on an extra monitor on my desk.

"Fuck."

We've barely been open an hour. There are maybe five customers milling about while Hollis and Mel prep behind the bar for the crowd we're sure to have later on.

I'm about to get up and go out there when I notice how Cash marches right up to Hollis without a hint of surprise on his face.

"You were doing so well, Mom," I mutter under my breath, wishing this camera had audio, but California has strict laws, and I already feel like a creeper with how much I watch my employees since Jace was fired.

I sneak out of my office and walk down the hall.

Cash and Hollis are close enough to the end of the bar that I can just make out what they're saying without actually leaving the hallway.

And yes, I know eavesdropping isn't cool, but is it that bad if it comes from a good place? What if a fight breaks out in the middle of the bar? What if my brother is his usual jackass self and hurts Hollis's feelings?

A lot could go wrong.

"So you're not going to tell me?" Cash's authoritative voice comes through loud and clear.

"Tell you what, man?" Hollis asks, sounding calm and unruffled by my brother's grizzly demeanor.

"The real reason you and my sister got married. 'Cause I'm not falling for this insta-love bullshit my parents told me."

I knew my mom would cave.

"And why's that?"

"Because it's ridiculous. Only an idiot would think they could fall in love that quickly, and although my sister can be a bit impetuous—"

"Hey, now." Hollis's voice grows cold. "That's my wife, Cash. Don't start badmouthing her in front of me. I know we're brothers now, but don't think that'll stop me from putting you in your place."

"Unbelievable," Cash grumbles. "So that's the party line? That you, what? Suddenly remembered she existed after twelve years, and after a few texts and phone calls, you fell madly in love with her?"

I squeeze my eyelids shut. I hate how much his words affect me. I love all my siblings. I really do. But with Cash, it's always been a struggle. Our personalities are completely different, and for years now, I've felt like all he does is judge me and everything I do. It makes me feel small.

And I hate feeling small.

"First of all," Hollis says. "I never forgot her. Not for a second." My breath catches as Hollis's words affect me in a completely different way. I try to remind myself he's just playing a part. Selling the story. "Just because I didn't contact her—or any of you—doesn't mean I didn't want to. We all have our shit, Cash. I was dealing with mine. Maybe you should go deal with yours?"

"What the fuck does that mean?"

"Last time I saw you, you weren't such a self-righteous dick," he says bluntly. *Oh, damn.* I smother a laugh. "I don't know what happened between then and now, and it's frankly none of my business, but maybe you should figure it out. In the meantime, try not to take it out on my wife, yeah?"

God, why is that so hot?

Friends, Pres. You are just friends.

A beat of silence follows, and then Cash says, "Yeah. Okay."

"Cool. You want a beer?" Hollis asks, his icy demeanor changing in an instant. I can't help but grin.

"Yeah, man. I'd love one."

"Coming right up. You still like that bougie microbrew from Washington?" He must nod because the next thing I hear before I turn to leave is, "Hey, so tell me all about this niece of mine. Does she like movies?"

I smile the whole way back to my office.

"That was wild," Hollis exclaims just before he stifles a yawn. We just got home. It's around three in the morning, and we're both dead on our feet. "I know you've told me about the tour bus thing before, but experiencing it was something else."

I laugh, toeing off my shoes one at a time by the front door. "I tried to warn you."

"Listening to people gush about your brother all night long has got to be weird."

"It's beyond weird, which is why I never tell them who I am," I explain, hobbling on my sore feet to the sofa. "Because they all end up treating me like I'm some sort of celebrity adjacent, and I hate it. Plus, I can't do my damn job."

"How do they know?" he asks. "Because everyone on that tour seemed to recognize you straight away."

He joins me on the couch, his head falling back on the cushion. He looks as tired as I do, but I worry it might actually be worse. He's been putting in a lot of hours during the day, touring properties and meeting with contractors. Then he comes home and leaves again to work another full day with me.

It can't be sustainable.

"Jace is an attention whore," I grumble. "And he loved to brag that he was dating the sister of Hendrix Creed?"

"That's fucked up, Pres. Being with you should be the reward. Not anything else. Just you." I feel momentarily stunned. Is he talking for himself or just in general? Before I can answer, he continues. "Feel free to hide in the office next time they come."

"What? No way," I argue. "We were too busy. I can put up with a few fan girls asking about my brother's chiseled abs."

"That's horrifying. Truly."

I laugh. "It could be worse. I could be Asher's sister. That poor man never gets any peace."

"I saw him that night at Velvet. Even on the security camera, he never looked completely relaxed. Like, he always seemed to be looking over his shoulder, even when he was joking with his bandmates. Is it really that bad?"

"Yeah. When he came over to our house for dinner a couple of months ago, he had to use a decoy driver and switch cars halfway here, just so that he could throw off the paparazzi that park outside his house twenty-four seven."

"That's insane."

I nod, noticing how he's not showing an ounce of jealousy as I talk about Asher. I couldn't even mention his name in Jace's presence without him storming off in a tantrum. "It's definitely not glamorous."

I adjust my sitting position, trying to take all the pressure off the balls of my feet, but I can't seem to get comfortable. Hollis must notice because he motions toward me. "Give me your feet."

"What?"

"Swing your feet onto my lap, Pres. They are obviously killing you, and I guarantee a foot rub falls safely within the guidelines of our friendship."

Are you sure about that?

I eye him warily but do as he says, and the second his fingers press into the arch of my foot, I let out a small moan.

"Well, shit, give me a fighting chance here, Pres."

I burst out laughing. "Sorry, it just feels really good."

"Exactly what I was aiming for," he tells me with a smirk. "Just try to keep the sex noises to a minimum, 'kay?"

My lip twitches. "Will do."

He resumes his massage, and I try my damndest not to whimper or moan or do anything else remotely sexual while he releases the tension from my tired feet.

He is really good at this.

Is it a natural talent, or is there a string of women before me who have benefited from his skilled fingers?

A surge of jealousy flares to life deep in my belly.

Nope. Not gonna think about that.

In fact, I'm not going to think about anything except reciting the alphabet backward. That and plain oatmeal.

Dirty socks.

Anything but the feel of this man's hand on my—

"Cash visited the bar today," he says, interrupting my thought spiral.

"I know. I saw him on the security camera," I say casually, deciding to go with the partial truth. I'll leave out the part where I stood in the hallway like a stalker. "I'm assuming he knows."

"He knows," he confirms. "He doesn't believe us, but he knows."

I snort, his words helping to distract me as he continues to work his thumb into the arch of my foot. "That's not surprising. He's the most pessimistic person I know. How'd he find out?"

"He overheard your dad at the office talking with your mom," he explains. "It worries me that he doesn't believe us, Pres. What if the others don't either?"

I shrug. "My parents did."

He tilts his head. "Your mom believes us because she wants it to be true. And your dad is probably so relieved it's not Jace you married in Vegas that he's willing to believe anything. I don't think your siblings will be nearly as easy to convince."

He has a point. But also... "So what? Who cares what Cash thinks? I'm pretty sure he doesn't even believe in love anymore, so I'm not sure what we could do to convince him."

"But we need to try, Pres."

"Why?" I fold my arms across my chest, feeling defensive. I always get this way when it comes to Cash. I shouldn't have to prove myself to him, even if it's over a fake husband.

"Because if he doubts us, he may start looking for a reason."

Fuck. He's right. Cash is one of those people who is never satisfied until he has an answer, and if he doesn't get one, he'll just keep digging and digging. "The bar's finances," I say under my breath. All the family's businesses are linked. "He could access them without much difficulty."

And then this whole thing would be for nothing.

"So what do you propose?"

His hand slides up to my ankle, all the way to my calf muscle, and gives it a gentle squeeze. I think it's supposed to be a comforting gesture, but my brain doesn't see it as one. I swallow and try to look as unfazed as he does. Meanwhile, I feel like I'm melting into a puddle on the floor.

Is it hot in here?

"What if instead of telling them all together, we told them individually? And we start with the one who is most likely going to join our team."

"Our team?" I don't even bother hiding the amusement in my tone.

"Yeah, you know, like when you watch one of those sappy movies with a love triangle, and everyone is either Team Broody Man or Team Emo Guy?"

I let out a laugh. "You would so be the Emo Guy."

"What? I can pull off broody. Just give me a little time to practice your brother's scary scowl, and I'll have it down."

"Okay, Mr. Tall, Ginger, and Brood-*ish*," I joke. "But you're getting your terminology wrong. What I think you're looking for is someone who is most likely to 'ship' us or root for us."

"Okay, yeah. We need that," he agrees, his hands now just splayed across my calves. His wedding ring glints under the light, and I try not to stare, mostly because I don't want him to notice and pull away. "We tell that sibling first and then work our way up, basically creating a support team as we go."

"That's—"

"Genius? Brilliant?"

"A lot of work," I finally say. "We're going to have to be very convincing, not just once, but several times."

"Yes."

"Which means a lot of physical contact. A lot of hand-holding and touching."

His eyes bore into mine. "Yes."

Suddenly, his hand feels scorching hot on my calf. It moves the slightest inch north, and I suck in a breath, my body coming alive in a way it hasn't since that day he pressed me against the car in my parents' driveway.

I watch his throat bob. We stare at each other until suddenly he jumps up like his ass is on fire. "I should get ready for bed."

I blink, feeling like some spell has just broken. "Yeah. Yeah, me too," I say, looking up, but he's already gone, disappearing down the hall.

Oh god, I think I'm falling for my fake husband.

Chapter Twenty-Three

HOLLIS

After much debate, it's been decided that Myles will be our first victim. Ally? Whatever.

I suggested we go with Mercury, but I was shot down. Since they are Presley's siblings and I haven't exactly been around for the last decade, I decided to trust her judgment over mine.

Plus, she says Myles is a closet romantic at heart, so there's that.

With Myles's crazy schedule, it takes a week to arrange, but Pres goes with the story that I'm in town visiting and would love to catch up.

We decide dropping the marriage bomb is better in person when we've had a chance to properly display our love and affection for each other.

That's the plan, at least.

Ever since I ran out of the living room last week like I was being chased by a wild boar, I haven't touched Presley. At all. Not even a friendly pat on the shoulder. I just...can't.

Because if I learned anything from that night on the

couch, it's that I can't be trusted around her. Touching her leads to wanting her, and then I'm contemplating all kinds of bad choices that have nothing to do with friendship.

Which is probably how we ended up in this mess in the first place.

Of course, none of this helps my current situation because tonight, to play the part of doting husband, I will definitely have to touch her.

And it's going to be torture.

At this point, maybe I deserve it.

"I can't believe my brother chose a nightclub of all places," Presley exclaims as our rideshare pulls up to the curb. I thank the driver, and we hop out. I'm actually familiar with this club. It's one of the places I recently toured after meeting with the owner. Not every club owner was as receptive to my meeting request, knowing we would soon be competition. However, Sonia Laurant was one of the exceptions, and she was more than happy to offer her advice and expertise on the LA club scene.

She also offered to take me out to dinner. Whether or not she saw my wedding ring, I'm not sure, but I politely declined.

"He's twenty-five, single, and trying to make it in Hollywood," I say with a shrug. "He probably lives here."

She laughs, then her eyes widen. "Oh my god. Did we go to a nightclub in Vegas?"

I was wondering if she would remember that. I have the credit card receipts to prove we did, but the memories of it are gradually starting to come back as well. "We did."

She grimaces, her cheeks flushing red. "Was that my idea?"

"Maybe a little bit of both," I lie. It was one hundred percent hers.

"I think you're lying." She laughs.

"I'll never tell." I grab her hand, pulling her toward the front of the line, trying hard to ignore the way the black satin of her dress clings to her curves. "Come on. Time to enjoy the perks of being married to a VIP."

"Do you get to skip all the lines? Is that like your superpower as a club manager?"

"Fuck no." I laugh. "I'm not that important. I just happen to know the owner of this one, and she said she'd put our name on the list."

"She?"

I steal a sideways glance, grinning. "Calm yourself. She knows I'm a married man."

"I'm not..." she says in a fluster before relenting. "Okay."

"Myles knows to meet us inside?"

She nods. "He texted to say he's waiting for us at the bar. He told me to tell you thanks for the 'royal treatment'"

I chuckle. "See, he's already on our side."

"Why does it sound like we're going to war?"

Because we're risking everything, I want to say. "He's rooting for us? Does that sound better?"

"Much."

We walk up to the bouncer and receive the usual dirty looks from a few people waiting in line. I give him our name, and he nods quickly, ushering us inside.

Although I've been inside La Notte, it looks completely different now. It's like stepping into a fancy Italian villa under the night sky. Thousands of twinkling lights mimic stars, while stately marble columns and plush velvet seating create a sense of luxury without feeling like you're in a theme park.

"Okay, this is pretty cool," Pres admits, leaning in so I can hear her. She practically has to shout in my ear, and because of the crowd we're fighting to get to the bar, her body is pressed right up against mine. "Is this what your nightclub is like?"

"No," I answer, trying to keep my gaze steadily on her face and not the plunging V-neck of her dress. When she walked out of her room in this short satin number, I nearly died. I swear she's trying to torture me, one dress at a time. "We're very exclusive."

"You mean snobby."

I laugh. "Yeah. It's incredibly hard to get through our doors and even harder to get one of our VIP rooms."

"There are multiple?"

"We have a large VIP area that overlooks the main dance floor, but we also have about eight smaller rooms. They're fully staffed and completely private. Hendrix didn't tell you about it?"

She makes a face. "I know you didn't grow up with siblings, Beck, but what the hell do you think we talk about?"

I chuckle, wrapping a protective hand around her waist as I steer us the rest of the way toward the bar. "Fair enough. We should take a trip to Nashville sometime, then. I can give you a private tour."

I don't mean it to sound sexual, but that's the way it comes off. Luckily, she doesn't have any time to react because, out of the corner of my eye, I catch Myles, or at least I think that's him sitting by the bar, laughing it up with a tall Black guy in a fitted suit Jonas would die for.

Aside from a few pics, I haven't seen the guy since he was eleven.

He looks up, does a double take, and then his face lights up. He waves. He says something to the guy next to him before walking away.

Jesus, it is him.

He looks so damn grown-up.

Will he even remember me? He seemed to when we talked on the phone that one time, but he could have just been trying to be polite.

We push through the rest of the crowd, and before we even reach the bar, Myles is already off his stool, pulling me into a big bear hug. "Hollis!"

"Jesus, Myles." Pres laughs. "Don't break him."

"God, he just might." I laugh, pulling back to get a good look at him.

His features have always been similar enough to the rest of the Creeds that no one really questioned his parentage, but if you look closely, you can see the slight differences. His hair is lighter than the others, a pale blond, and his eyes are a striking arctic blue.

That and—"You're huge. Are you trying out for WWE or something?" While he's just as tall as Hendrix, he's more filled out. God, he really does look like the guy from that Viking movie.

I really wish I could remember his damn name...

"Jealous?" He grins.

"Kind of, yeah," I admit. "I thought I was pretty fit until just a moment ago."

He puffs up, looking smug. "I've been bulking up 'cause I'm trying to prepare for this role I heard might be coming around."

"Oh?" Presley perks up at this news. She's always

talking about how talented Myles is. I know she's hoping he gets his shot soon. "What's it for?"

"Don't really want to talk about it quite yet. Afraid I'll jinx it, you know?"

She sighs, shaking her head. "You theater types and your superstitions."

"You won't be thinking that when I win an Oscar."

She reaches up to pinch his biceps. "Get any bigger, and you'll break the damn stage walking up there."

He fakes a wince, acting like he's in pain, but then laughs. "Nah. If Jason Momoa can manage, then so can —" His words come to a screeching halt as his eyes land on her left hand.

Oh, fuck. I hadn't expected those icy blue eagle eyes of his to lock onto the tiny gold band so quickly. I thought we'd have some time to order drinks and ease into it.

Presley's gaze darts to her wedding ring and then to me. I glance back over at Myles, who has a puzzled look about him.

"What am I missing here?" he asks, now noticing the matching ring on my finger.

"I'm not actually visiting," I say, deciding to just come out with it like I did with his parents. Rip that band-aid right off. "I moved here a couple of weeks ago. We got married!"

He quietly looks at me, then at his sister. A moment passes. Then another. Finally, I see his mouth curve into a big grin as he opens his arms wide. "Dude, are you serious?"

We both nod.

"Give me a hug, guys! This is awesome."

Well, that was easy.

One down. Three to go.

Myles is so happy you'd think he was the one who just got married. He's telling everyone at the bar our joyous news, including the bartender, and every stranger that passes by. He even waves over the guy he was talking to earlier to introduce us.

"This is the sister I was telling you about," he beams, speaking into the man's ear. "And this is her husband, Hollis. They just got married! This is Omar. We've worked together on a few projects."

Something tells me, by the way they stand just a little too close, that they are more than just work buddies.

"Congratulations," Omar says, offering me a handshake. "So I guess you're not in town to visit then?"

"No." I chuckle, giving my wife a sideways glance. "Definitely not visiting."

"Aww." Myles sighs. "See the way he looks at her? I always knew you had a thing for each other."

"You were twelve." Pres scoffs. "How would you even have known?"

"I may have been twelve, but I wasn't blind, Pres. And neither was anyone else. We all knew about you two sneaking off to the beach at night and all your"—he holds up his hands to do air quotes—"study sessions in your room."

She points a finger at him, with a hint of amusement in her expression. "Okay, those really were study sessions, I'll have you know."

He laughs. "Sure, sis. Sure."

I don't bother correcting him. If he wants to believe we were fooling around in high school, then let him. It only solidifies our case.

And God knows, it sure as hell crossed my mind a time or two.

"Come on." Myles motions with his hand. "Let's do a round of shots to celebrate!"

I can practically hear Pres groan, but she agrees, and I drape an arm over her shoulder as we join her brother and Omar at the bar. Myles signals to the bartender, and when she approaches, he leans in to tell her his order. She nods, and a few minutes later, she's pouring a line of tequila shots for us.

I stare at them, and a strange sense of déjà vu begins to wash over me. I turn toward Presley, and then the memory slams into me.

It's so vivid I can almost taste the salt on her neck, smell the citrus from the lime, and feel her eager body pressed against mine as I lean forward and—

Oh, fuck.

"To Pres and Hollis!" Myles shouts, pulling me back to reality. I lock eyes with Pres, who's staring at me with a mixture of concern and confusion.

We both take a shot of tequila and down it at the same time. The liquid burns all the way down, but I barely notice it as I grab Presley's hand and say, "We're gonna go dance."

"Maybe we'll join you!" Myles shouts back.

"Take your time," I tell him. And good luck finding us.

I pull us onto the dance floor, but when we reach the middle, I just keep moving us through the crowd.

"Where are we going?" Pres hollers into my ear as we make our way to the other side.

"Somewhere we can talk," I simply tell her.

When I was here last week, there was a discreet hallway somewhere nearby that led to Sonia's office and a few supply closets. If it were my club, I would have a security guard stationed at its entrance to keep people like me from wandering in, but thankfully, Sonia isn't me.

We slip relatively unnoticed down the hallway. There are a few people lingering around the entrance, but it's dark, and they're...distracted. It's fairly empty as you venture further, and the locked doors probably serve as a deterrent for anyone looking for a place to hook up.

Luckily for me, I happen to know the code.

I'll apologize to Sonia later.

We stop at the second door, and as I begin to enter the code, I hear Pres gasp behind me. "How the hell—"

"I saw her punch it in." I shrug. "I can't help that she didn't bother to hide it or that I happened to remember it."

"You remember everything."

Not when I'm drunk, apparently...

Just as the light turns green and the lock clicks open, I turn. "Usually just the things that matter, but I guess this came in handy."

I push the door open, and we step inside. I quickly close it to avoid any unwanted attention, and we're immediately plunged into darkness. I feel around for a light but can't find one, so I do the next best thing. I pull out my phone and turn on my flashlight. Pres is standing in front of me, the satin of her dress shimmering in the dim light.

"What exactly are we doing in here, Hollis? What was so important that you had to pull me into a"—she looks around—"broom closet to talk?"

"Because I think it's my fault we ended up married."

"What? Why?"

I set my phone down on the metal shelf next to me and absentmindedly run my hand through my hair. It's getting way too long. The curls are gonna turn into fucking ringlets if I don't get a haircut soon.

Pres watches me, waiting for a response. "You were right earlier. We did go to a nightclub, and it was your idea. But everything that happened after that was entirely mine." Or at least, I think it was.

"What do you mean?" she asks tentatively, taking a step back. That's never a good sign.

"It was the shots that brought it all back," I explain. "I remember standing next to a bar just like that in Vegas, challenging you to do tequila shots for your birthday."

"Okay. I don't see how that leads to us getting married, though."

"We ordered shots at the club. A lot of shots," I emphasize. "And then we danced for a while. When we returned to the bar, I challenged you to a body shot, Pres. And when it got to the part when I was supposed to suck on the lime..."

Her eyes go wide. A hand jerks to her mouth like she's remembering the exact moment when—

"You kissed me."

"I kissed you," I confirm. "I grabbed the lime you had wedged between your lips, tossed it to the floor, and kissed you instead. I'm so sorry, Pres. I shouldn't have. You were drunk and nursing a broken heart, and I—"

"You were drunk too."

"Still." I shake my head. "It doesn't excuse my behavior."

"And I wasn't nursing a broken heart."

"You—what?"

Her steady gaze meets mine. "I was pissed and embarrassed for not realizing what Jace was doing behind my back, but I was not heartsick over it. Jace and I had been broken up for a month by then."

My pulse quickens. "Then why didn't you tell me?"

"I don't know," she admits. "I wanted to tell you that night in the pantry, but I was afraid."

"Afraid of what?" I take a tentative step forward.

Her breath hitches, and it takes every ounce of willpower I possess not to reach out and touch her.

"I didn't want things to change between us."

"Change is inevitable, Pres. I probably know that better than most. My whole childhood was a lesson in adapting to change. But I've learned since then that it's not all bad. Change can be a good thing."

"It can?" She swallows in anticipation as I watch her tongue dart out and lick her bottom lip.

Fucking hell. I want to bite that lip with my teeth.

I want to press her up against this wall, run my hands all over the smooth satin that barely covers her body, and keep her here until she's crying out my name.

But I will not break her rule.

I won't be another guy who breaks her trust.

It doesn't mean I can't take advantage of the evening, though.

"Come on, let me show you," I say, holding out my hand.

She takes it, and I quickly lead us out of the stuffy stockroom and back toward the dance floor. I do a quick scan for Myles and find him near the center dancing with Omar. They're practically glued together.

Yeah, definitely not just work friends.

I hear Pres groan, and I turn to see her grimacing. "I do not want to watch my baby brother make out on the dance floor, Beck."

"Then focus on me," I tell her, grabbing her hips and pulling her close. "Gotta sell it, remember?"

The sudden gasp of surprise that escapes from her lips is an instant turn on, and she doesn't need any more convincing to keep her attention.

I forgot how well we move together.

Like everything, dancing with Pres is easy. Every movement is fluid and effortless, like we've been doing it for years.

God, and now I'm thinking about sex.

Her arms twist around my neck, pulling us closer. The satin fabric of her dress makes me want to run my hands all over it. All over her. It's like a dirty slip and slide.

She leans in, her lips brushing my ear, and she says seven words that make my heart stutter. "You can kiss me if you want."

My first reaction is, *hell yes.*

But then I replay the words in my head.

If you want...

"Do you want me to?" I pull back to gauge her reaction.

She bites her bottom lip like she does when she's trying to hold back some strong emotion. The problem is, I don't know which one it happens to be—anticipation? Nervousness? Anxiousness?

All three?

"If it helps," she says, her gaze briefly darting over my shoulder in the direction of her brother and his dance partner.

My heart sinks, and I reach up and tip her chin back to face me. "That's not what I asked," I emphasize. "Do you want to kiss me, Pres?"

I can see the indecision in her eyes, and I already have my answer. I lean in, making sure she can hear me. I swear she shivers as I curl my hand around her waist. "I'm happy to play the part of a loving couple for your family, Pres, but I can't kiss you." She starts to pull back, but I hold her, needing to finish. "Not like this."

She jerks back to look at me, so I have to raise my voice for her to hear the next part. "The next time we kiss, it won't be for show, Pres. And there will be nothing platonic about it."

As confident as my words may sound, all I can think in that moment is...please, let there be a next time.

Chapter Twenty-Four

PRESLEY

CASH

Is there a reason I don't have access to the bar's financials?

I've been staring at this text from Cash for twenty minutes, trying to figure out how to respond.

Yeah, because we're royally fucked, and I'm trying to figure out how to get us un-fucked, so I removed the bar's financial records from the server before you could find them.

Also, could you stop being such a snoop and maybe obsess over something else? Thanks.

Somehow, I don't think that will go over with my super anal, super grumpy older brother.

ME

Uh, I don't know. Maybe something is wrong with the interwebs?

Interwebs—a term used by people who don't know shit about technology. It's also good for diverting snobby older brothers who think they know everything about everything.

He's probably rolling his eyes right now, mumbling under his breath about how awful his life is that he has to deal with crap like this.

CASH

I can send out someone from IT to look at your computer and modem.

Fuck. I didn't think about that.

ME

No need. I'll have Hollis take a look.

CASH

Still blissfully happy, then?

I roll my eyes. Asshole.

ME

Yep. You should try it.

CASH

No fucking thank you.

I set my phone on the coffee table and look up just in time to see Hollis walking down the hall. My stomach does this annoying little flip at the mere sight of him.

It's an epidemic, this attraction I have for him, because it's getting worse day after day.

Yesterday, he bent over in the kitchen to get a dish towel off the floor, and I swear I had to hold back a moan. His ass in athletic shorts should be illegal.

And ever since the club, when he simultaneously

turned down my request for a kiss and then promised a real one at some future date, I've been a mess.

What does that mean?

Does he like me?

Does he want more?

And aren't those stupid questions to ponder over in regard to your own freaking husband?

I try not to think about it. That's healthy, right?

I watch as he walks down the hallway in gray sweats and a hoodie. He's been holed up in my room all day. I let him borrow the space to work because it's private and quiet. He rarely uses it since this project mostly involves meeting people in person, whether they are contractors or pretty club owners.

Okay, so I looked her up. Whatever.

But today, he's home, and since it's Monday and the bar is closed, we have a whole night to ourselves.

He's requested a movie marathon—eighties themed, of course. I still remember a similar night back in high school, where we were all arguing over which one to watch first—*Back to the Future* or *Ferris Bueller's Day Off*—and my dad turned to Hollis and asked which one he liked better, and he sheepishly answered he hadn't seen either.

The truth was, he hadn't seen any of them.

We sort of made it our mission to make sure he got caught up on all the cult classics after that. You truly haven't lived until you've sobbed into a bucket of popcorn during the swamp of sadness scene in *The NeverEnding Story*.

"All done?" I ask as he joins me on the couch.

"Yeah, I think so," he replies, leaning his head back on the cushion. His messy curls frame his face, and I resist the urge to reach out and touch them. "I sent everything over to Jonas to look over. He'll let me know what he wants to do next."

His boss appears to have a very hands-off approach. So far, this is the most I've heard him talk about the man who also happens to be his best friend.

"Is he going to come check on the progress at some point?" I ask.

He gives me a sideways glance and smirks. "Don't trust in my abilities, Pres?"

"What?" I exclaim. "No, I just mean—" He chuckles, clearly pleased with himself. I push him playfully on the shoulder. "You're mean."

"He trusts me," he answers. "And we talk every day."

"You do?" That was news to me.

"We do," he confirms.

"Do you..." I hesitate. "Talk about me?"

His lips twitch. "Sometimes."

"Only sometimes?" I joke, hating the way my heart is pounding. I shouldn't care what his best friend thinks about me.

But I do. God, I really do.

Now he breaks out into a full grin. "If it were up to Jonas, we'd do nothing but talk about you. He finds your presence in my life very interesting."

"Because I'm your pretend wife?"

"Because you're a woman."

My brow furrows as I try to make sense of what he's saying, and then it dawns on me. "Do you not usually date women? Are you—"

"No." He laughs, the corners of his eyes crinkling with amusement. "I'm not gay. Or bi. I just don't usually date."

"At all?" The words come out louder than intended, but seriously, he's gorgeous. How can he not date?

"Not in the traditional sense." Which translates to... he's strictly a hookup guy. Oh great. My husband is a fuckboy.

I raise my hand, plastering on a smile, before he has a chance to respond. "I have three brothers. No need to explain."

"Clearly I do." He shakes his head. "'Cause I can see how you might have interpreted that, and while yes, when I do spend time with a woman, it's usually brief—"

I groan. "Hollis, this is—"

"Uncomfortable? Yeah, it is. But I need you to understand, okay? Will you let me try to explain?"

I nod.

"Good, okay." He lets out a breath. "I'm not good at letting people in. I never have been. It's why I move around so much, why I suck at making friends. I don't know. Maybe growing up the way I did broke something in me."

"You're not broken, Hollis," I say.

He stares up at the ceiling, clearly unconvinced. "I used to believe her, you know, when I was little? She'd tell me we were moving and things would be better, and I'd believe her. I'd think, finally, I'm going to have a real home like everyone else. But then a few months later, I'd be alone in a dingy hotel room, eating stale Cheerios, wondering what I did wrong this time."

Fucking hell.

He's never opened up this much about his past. Even when he was living with us, I'd just get snippets, and then he'd close himself off with a broad smile and quick-witted joke.

"You didn't do anything wrong," I tell him.

"I know that now. I do, but it still doesn't make it any easier to trust people. To let my guard down."

"Sounds lonely," I say, feeling a heavy weight of emotion settle on my chest.

"It can be."

"So you…" God, please don't make me say it.

"Sometimes," he thankfully answers for me. "When the loneliness gets unbearable."

I nod, the pain in his voice making me focus less on my jealousy and more on him. "My family never really understood why I stayed with Jace so long. It was because the thought of being alone was more unbearable than staying with him."

He turns to face me, his eyes full of sadness. "Pres."

I shake my head, trying to keep the tears at bay. "It took me a while to realize that. I have an amazing family. Why would I ever feel lonely, right?"

"Like you've said, they all have their own lives. It's easy to feel isolated."

I nod. "When I took over the bar, I thought it would bring us all closer together. Instead, it just felt like I was more on my own than ever. Maybe that's why I latched on to Jace. It's definitely why I defended him so fiercely, because even though Jace was a shitty boyfriend, he was still better than not having one at all. Than not having anyone at all."

"What made you change your mind?"

I manage a smile. "An old friend reminded me I was worth more."

"You are."

Our eyes meet, and it's so intense that my heart begins to race, forcing me to look away.

"You, um…you've never found anyone you've trusted? That you've thought might be worth pursuing?"

"Not romantically," he says. "Just Jonas. And I only let him in because he's incredibly insistent."

"You let me in," I say, before adding, "You sought me out."

"Yeah." He smiles softly. "I did. And that's why Jonas is so taken with you."

"And what about you?" I ask. "Are you…taken with me?"

He looks at me with those light green eyes. "Presley Creed, I've always been completely and utterly…taken by you."

"Are you sure that it's okay if I come with you?" I ask for the fifth time since we left the apartment.

"Yeah, Pres, it's fine," he assures me, looking hot as fuck sitting in the driver's seat of my black Jeep as we head down the 101. This old thing has seen better days, but when he's behind the wheel? Automatic upgrade.

"You won't get in trouble?"

His lip twitches. "No. I can promise you I won't get in any trouble."

"'Cause I can sit in the car while you—"

He takes my hand in his and squeezes. "I want you there," he says. "It will be nice to show you what I've been working on when I sneak off during the day with your car for hours."

"Okay." I try not to let it show, but that tiny bit of

contact has me reeling. Since the nightclub, we haven't needed to pretend or show any public PDA, so he's been the perfect gentleman.

He follows every single rule I put in place.

He's kept his word, going to great lengths to maintain work boundaries. Everyone at the bar knows we're married, but it never gets in the way. When we work together, he's professional, both with the staff and the customers.

He is nothing like Jace, and yet I have him permanently stationed behind the bar when I know he could be doing so much more. Hell, I won't even let him go into the stockroom unaccompanied.

But then again, I haven't let anyone go into the stockroom alone in weeks. It's like ever since Jace fucked me over, I've completely lost faith in humanity.

I don't even know how to trust my husband.

He came here to help me save the bar. I'm assuming he thought that meant helping me go through the finances and find a way to keep us from closing. But instead, I have him slinging drinks and taking out the trash.

"We're here," he announces.

I look up, and a small gasp escapes me. When he said he needed to stop by the club, I was expecting something similar to the place we went to a couple of weeks ago with Myles.

This is... "Wow," I exclaim. "This is gorgeous."

It looks like something out of an old Hollywood film. Mature palm trees frame the Spanish architecture of what looks to be a boutique-style hotel. The stucco arches and carved doors are straight out of my damn dreams.

"You may retract that statement when you see the

inside." He chuckles. "It's definitely been neglected over the years."

"Well, it has the curb appeal. Don't they say that's the most important part to win over a potential customer? Or is that something I'm remembering from *House Hunters*?"

"I think it works either way." He shrugs. "Jonas found this place and swore it had that special something that would make our club stand out. Since he seems to have a knack for this, I didn't argue."

"Your club?" I tease.

He tenses, but quickly recovers. "You know what I mean."

We both stare up at the building for another moment before I turn to him. "So are you going to take me inside or what?"

"Right, yeah." He laughs. "Let's go. Don't want to be late meeting up with your sister."

"Assuming she can actually tear herself away from work," I quip. "This is the third time she's rescheduled."

"Why lunch?" he asks. "Why not dinner, or I don't know...bowling?"

I snicker, trying to imagine my prim and proper sister bowling. She'd probably show up wearing a sweater set and pearls. "Mercury is like the female version of Cash, but without the permanent stick up her ass," I explain. "She's super smart and detail-oriented and a complete workaholic. But unlike some people who are married to their jobs, she actually enjoys it."

"You said she's some sort of musical genius?"

We head toward what I assume will be the main entrance. The intricately carved double doors are both propped open, and inside I can see a construction crew hard at work.

He was not wrong. The inside is a hot mess.

But it's also absolutely stunning.

Old carpet is being pulled from a grand staircase. A man to our left is carefully repairing the plaster on a massive column, while another works on salvaging the old tile floor.

"We call her a genius," I say absently, distracted by everything going on around me. "But it's not like she's been tested or anything. She's just insanely talented. Dad is lucky to have her. All of them, really."

He stops dead in his tracks and turns. "You know, he's lucky to have you too? They all are."

I avoid his intense stare, choosing to focus on the rich brown terracotta floors. "Sure."

"Are you, though? Because sometimes the way you talk about your siblings makes me think that you don't, and I can't help but wonder why. Did someone make you feel that way?"

"What? No." I jerk up. "You know my family. They're awesome."

"Then where does this come from? Because when I see you at the bar, you are confident and competent. Everyone who works there respects the hell out of you and feels lucky to work there."

"Then why did I mess it all up?" I blurt out a little louder than I mean to. The words bounce off the walls of the massive space, and a few of the workers look up and finally notice us.

Oh god. Please, let the ground swallow me whole.

One of the workers, a tall guy about our age, waves, sets down his paintbrush, and pulls his phone out of his back pocket. He quickly types a message and then puts it away again.

"He's probably letting the general contractor know we're here. And you didn't fuck it up, Pres," he says, going right back to our previous conversation.

"I don't recall my dad ever being worried the bar might close."

"How would you have known?" he asks, raising an eyebrow. "Do you think he would have shared something like that with you as a kid? With any of you?"

I open my mouth to respond that, of course, he would have. My parents shared everything with us, but then I think about it—really think about it—and I shake my head. "No," I find myself saying. "He wouldn't want us to worry. He never wanted us to worry. About anything."

"And I love that about your father. I really do. He's fiercely protective, but I think by shielding you from his struggles, he inadvertently gave you the illusion that he had none."

I think about it and nod. "I know you're right, and I know my parents aren't perfect, but it's hard to remind myself of that when everything feels so bleak. I'm still so worried he's going to regret giving me this responsibility. I've had it for less than two years, and we're so fucking close to losing it all."

"Then it wasn't in that good of shape to start with, Pres. I know you think you did all this, but I guarantee you didn't. I wouldn't be surprised if the bar has been hanging on by a thread for years."

"It wasn't doing well when I took over," I admit. "But I assumed that was because of the economy. Dad's never mentioned the bar struggling, so I focused on bringing in more cash. I wanted to make him proud."

"But what if it wasn't just a short-term thing? What if the bar was struggling for a long time?"

"Don't you think my dad would have done something? That he would have been scrambling to—" And then it dawns on me. The numerous times over the years when the bar would barely reach capacity on the weekend. The half-empty stockroom... "Oh, fucking hell. He didn't care. This bar has never been about the money for him. It has always been his passion project, a gift he gave himself after his first client went platinum. And as long as the door remains open, he's happy." I let out a shaky breath, realizing just how much is on the line. "Oh god, Hollis. We've got to keep that bar open."

"We will," he says fiercely, pulling me into a tight hug. "Don't worry."

I melt into his arms. He smells like the woodsy soap he uses in the shower. My head rests against his chest, and he runs a hand through my hair.

Nothing about this is sexual. It's comforting and sweet, so why do I want him to stop being gentle and kiss me?

The next time we kiss, it won't be for show, Pres.

My throat goes dry, and I take a small step back.

Distance. I need distance.

"I think I'm ready to ask you for something," I say, my voice slightly hoarse.

His eyebrow quirks. "Okay."

"Will you look at the bar's finances and help me figure out a way to save the bar?"

A tiny smirk tugs at the corner of his mouth. "Yeah, Pres. I'd be honored."

Chapter Twenty-Five

HOLLIS

Just as Brian, the general contractor, is finishing up with our tour around the club, Pres gets a text from her sister. She lets out a heavy sigh as she reads it.

"What is it?" I ask as I wave goodbye to everyone. "Did she cancel again?"

"Not exactly. She says she can't get away, but has a short break in forty-five minutes if I want to meet her there."

Mercury didn't exactly know this lunch date included me. She just thinks Pres is doing the big sister thing and trying to catch up since they haven't seen each other in a while.

"At the recording studio?"

She nods. "Honestly, this may be our best bet if we want to see her in the next month." I snort, and she looks up with a tilted brow. "You think I'm joking, but I'm not. Outside of Sunday dinner, which she only makes time for because she knows Mom and Dad love it, she's a hard woman to pin down."

"Well, since you're still adamant about telling her

before Hendrix, I say we swing by. We can even grab some takeout and feed her before she has to get back to work." I throw my arm around her shoulder, taking full advantage of the loophole that allows PDA in public.

God, her hair smells good.

"I doubt she's even thought about food today. That's actually a great idea."

"See, I'm not just a pretty face."

She laughs as we get to the Jeep and stop. She turns to look up at me and smiles. "No, you definitely aren't."

A wicked grin spreads across my face. "Did you just call me pretty?"

She scrunches her face and gives me an assessing gaze. "You're all right, I guess."

I take a step closer to the car to cage her in. "All right? I think you might be lying."

Her eyes flash with anticipation. "Why would I lie?"

I take another step until our bodies are flush.

"Because I don't think your heart would be beating this fast if you thought I was just 'all right.'"

"What do you want me to say?" she asks, looking up at me. My hand stays on her chest, the frantic rhythm of her heart thumping beneath it. "That I'm attracted to you? I think you already know that I am."

"Doesn't mean I don't want to hear it."

"Why?"

"Wouldn't you want to know if I found you attractive?"

I can see the question in her expression even though she doesn't voice it. *If?* Instead, she asks, "Do you?"

"The first time I saw you, Pres, I thought you were the most beautiful girl I'd ever seen. You were standing by your locker, and I remember thinking this school might not be so bad after all. But then Hendrix stepped in between an altercation between Alex Carpenter and me and decided we were going to be best friends."

She snorts. "That sounds exactly like him."

"He was very persistent about it." I smile, remembering how hard I tried to dodge him those first few days. I didn't really do friends back then. Honestly, I still don't, but like Hendrix, Jonas had been insistent. In school, forming attachments was messy, and it only got harder when my mom decided it was time to pack up and leave. But Hendrix wouldn't take no for an answer.

"I remember that, you know?" she says, looking up at me. "That moment by my locker."

"You do?" She'd never mentioned it. I just figured our brief eye contact was nothing more than a passing glance for her, and I'd been just another student in the hall.

"When you've gone to school with the same kids forever, it's kind of hard not to notice a new face. Especially when they look like yours."

I grin. "There you go, calling me pretty again."

Her cheeks heat. "I don't think pretty is the word that came to mind."

"No?"

"Definitely thought you were the hottest guy I'd ever seen." Her mouth quirks into the cutest little smile.

"Yeah?"

"Yeah, but you were also my brother's best friend."

"True," I agree. "But I'm not anymore. Hendrix has a new best friend. He has Zander and the band."

I search her face, feeling like I'm standing on the edge of a cliff. I know I could fall for this woman—hell, I think I might be already there.

Maybe I always have been.

But what if it ends badly?

What if it doesn't work out?

I cannot lose her again.

"Yeah, but you're still *my* best friend," she says.

I smile, an understanding settling between us. "And that is one thing that will never change."

When we pull up to the address Pres punched into the GPS, I look around and then glance over at her, asking, "Is this it?"

She nods. "Yup, why?"

I scan the area again. It's in an industrial park. The buildings are all very plain, with flat roofs and aluminum siding. There is no signage over the doors to identify one business from another, except for a small sign that reads *CS*.

"It's so underwhelming," I say, recalling my first tour of the Creed Agency when I was in high school. Everything in that building was impressive, from its high-rise location to the swanky furnishings and wall-to-wall windows overlooking downtown.

"That's the point. It's supposed to be underwhelming. Can't exactly advertise the place," she explains as I put the Jeep in Park. Since I moved in, I've realized that Presley hates driving and is always happy to hand the task over to me, which I'm more than willing to do.

I kind of want to buy her a new car, though.

This one has seen better days.

"Because of all the high-profile clients?"

She nods. God, she looks good today. I don't know how she manages to make a simple pair of jeans and a T-shirt look so sexy, but she does. *Stop staring, asshole.* "It doesn't completely deter unwanted guests, but it helps. Plus, we have a wicked security system."

I help her with the takeout we grabbed on the way here, and we head toward the entrance. Other than a camera perched in the corner and a keypad on the door, there is nothing that stands out. But, like she said, I guess that's the point.

Pres takes out her phone and types something in. A second later, she punches in a code. "Okay, we're good."

I grab the door and follow her in, and instantly we're transported. It's like walking through the wardrobe into Narnia. Only instead of snow and lions, there's vinyl and guitars.

The lighting is moody, and the floors are made of warm wood with wool rugs running up the center to dampen the sound. The dark walls of the hallway are lined with records—all gold and platinum. Since we're in a hurry, I don't stop to check out the artists, but the sheer volume is impressive.

We head down the hall, past some offices and bathrooms, and then Pres leads us to the sound booth.

Sitting in front of the biggest soundboard in existence is a grown-up version of the girl who used to stomp into my bedroom, critique my music choices, and then come back twenty minutes later with a playlist she insisted was better.

Damn if she wasn't always right.

While Pres favors her mother's fairer features, Mercury takes after Lance. Her long chestnut hair is tied back in a practical ponytail at the nape of her neck, and she wears tailored black pants and a cream-colored sweater.

With large headphones held to her ear, she's so immersed in what she's doing that she doesn't even seem to hear us come in.

"See what I mean?" Pres says, leaning against the door. She gestures to her sister. "Total nerd."

"Come here and listen to this." Merc waves Presley over, not even flinching at the abrupt sound of her voice.

Pres gives me a *what-the-fuck* look, and I just shrug. "Bat hearing?" I mouth, and she snickers.

I set the food down and watch my wife walk over to join Mercury at the soundboard. She takes the seat next to her. Merc hands her a twin set of headphones, and Pres mimics her, holding them up to one ear so she can still hear with the other.

Her brow scrunches together as they listen to the track together. She closes her eyes ever so slightly.

She looks so in her element.

Pres talks about Mercury's talent for music, but she has it too. All the Creed kids do. It's in their blood, and right now, it's showing.

The selection must come to an end as both women set down their headphones, and Merc looks at her sister. "Well?"

I lean against the wall, quietly observing the exchange. "It needs something," Pres says.

"I know, but I can't decide what exactly it's missing, and I'm running out of time."

"Wasn't this supposed to be your break?" Pres teases. It earns her a glare. She lifts her hands in defense. "Okay, okay. I get it. You're stressed. Let me listen to it again, and I'll help you out, okay? But in the meantime, will you do me a favor?"

"What?"

She gestures over her shoulder at me. "Will you turn around and meet your new brother-in-law?"

"No," Pres says firmly, shaking her head.

"Yes! It was your idea," Merc reminds her.

They're face-to-face, arms crossed, glaring at each other. Presley is half a foot taller, but Merc is twice as determined. They both turn to me, and I instantly raise both my hands. "Oh, no. Do not make me decide. I am not voting against my wife."

An accusing brow rises on Presley's face. "But you want to, don't you?"

Oh my god, I can't win.

Right after Mercury congratulated us with hugs, we regaled her with our edited Vegas wedding story, fed her semi-cold tacos, and then she got back to work.

Or she and Presley did, that is.

I can't tell if she's accepted the idea of our quickie marriage so easily because she genuinely believes us or because she's just so focused on what she's doing.

Either way, about five minutes ago, after much deliberation, Pres suggested adding another vocal element to the song—someone to play off the male lead in the chorus.

Mercury thought it was the perfect solution. Pres

thought so too until her sister said she thought Pres would be the perfect person to do it.

That's when all hell broke loose.

"Do I think you'd be great at it, Pres? Yes. You have a phenomenal voice." I give her sister a hard stare. "But no one is going to force you. Right?"

Mercury folds her arms across her chest. "What if I ask nicely?"

Pres scoffs. "Nicely? You didn't even ask! So far, you've just dictated."

"You did sort of do that," I agree.

Merc huffs, looking up at the clock mounted on the wall. "Okay, yeah. You're right. I got a little intense there, didn't I?"

"A little?"

She slowly blinks.

Definitely not up for humor right now. "Okay, fine." Pres throws up her hands. "But how exactly do we do this?" Pres asks. "'Cause the only singing I've done is in the shower."

"Thank you, Pres," she gushes, rushing to hug her. "You're a lifesaver. And I'll make sure you get credit, okay?"

"What?" Presley's eyes go wide, realizing she doesn't just mean name credit. She means money. "No, that's crazy. I don't need to—"

"Take the credit, Pres," I urge, pulling her into my arms. It feels effortless being able to touch her without rules or boundaries. "You can put the royalties into savings or invest them in the bar. Or buy a new car."

She snorts. "What's wrong with my car?"

"What isn't wrong with your car?"

"Okay, newlyweds," Mercury interrupts, motioning in

our direction. “Love this for you. Truly. But I don’t have time for whatever this is. Go be gross on your own time.”

I let her go, grinning as she slips away to help her sister.

It doesn’t take long to set things up, and in no time, Pres is sitting on a stool directly in front of a large microphone on the other side of the glass.

She looks incredibly nervous.

“Tell me what to do,” she says. I can hear her voice shake through the headphones.

Merc presses a button and speaks into a mic. “Okay, Pres, listen to me. You’re probably not going to like this, but I need you to just go with your gut on this.”

“What?” she practically screeches. “What do you mean, go with my gut? Aren’t you the one who says music is all about precision?”

“I am.” She nods. “Which is why I knew this song was missing something. It was missing you.”

“I am not precise, Merc. I am chaos at best.”

Merc smiles. “I know, Pres. I’m not asking you to be anything but yourself. It’s that wildness in you that will make this song perfect. So just close your eyes and feel it. Let the music take you, and I guarantee it’s all going to be fine.”

I can still see her nervousness, but she tries to shake it off as she sits a bit straighter and takes a calming breath. “Okay.” She nods. “I’m ready.”

Mercury starts the track from the beginning, so Pres can get a feel for it without jumping straight into the chorus. I’ve heard it a few times now, so I know it’s a rock ballad with an emotional chorus about a love that endures.

The male voice is powerful, with a deep, raspy tone

that sounds almost perfect. But when it reaches the chorus and I hear my wife echo the haunting lyrics, I know Merc has a masterpiece on her hands.

"Fucking hell," I mutter, watching the way she transforms before my eyes. She sings with her eyes closed, completely swept up by the music as she sways back and forth.

It's the sexiest thing I've ever seen.

She finishes the chorus, and her eyes open and land straight on me. For a moment, I feel like the world melts away.

"You really are in love with her, aren't you?" Merc says.

Without tearing my gaze away from my wife, I nod. "I really fucking am."

And I have no idea what to do about it.

Because the days are slipping away from me. Soon, it will be November, and my time here will be over.

Chapter Twenty-Six

PRESLEY

HENDRIX

Are you guys avoiding me?

MYLES

What? No.

MERC

Of course not.

CASH

Yes.

MYLES

Cash, wtf.

CASH

He asked.

ME

Just ignore him, Hen. We are not avoiding you.

We are one hundred percent avoiding him.

And it's all my fault.

Out of my four siblings, Hendrix is the last to know about Hollis.

Manic at Midnight recently got back from tour, and since then, I've been dodging his calls and texts.

Hen and Zara even showed up at the bar the other night, and I begged Lamar to lie and say I had the night off. Meanwhile, Hollis and I hid in the stockroom while Hendrix and Zara enjoyed drinks, and I tried not to think about all the wicked things I could be doing in there with my husband.

Bright side? I got over my trust issues with the stockroom. With Hollis, at least.

It's not that I don't want to see Hendrix. I do. I really do. I've missed that big, dumb idiot.

But I'm scared.

Of all my siblings, Hendrix was the closest to Hollis.

I mean, they were best friends.

What if he feels betrayed somehow? Or mad because Hollis didn't tell him first? It shouldn't matter what he thinks. This marriage isn't even real, and Hollis will be going back to Tennessee next month anyway.

But lately, this thing between us feels a lot less fake, and a whole lot like something...more.

So yeah, I want my brother's approval.

HENDRIX

Are you sure? You guys don't resent me cause I'm super famous now?

MYLES

Oh, fuck right off.

MERC

You're just a bass player. You're not that cool.

CASH

You are all idiots. I'm leaving.

ME

...And yet you're still here.

MYLES

That's cause Grinchy Cash loves us.

HENDRIX

Omg, you really are the Grinch! 😆

MERC

He reminds me more of that grumpy guy from Ted Lasso.

ME

The hot, grumpy soccer player? No way. Do not compare our brother to that man. You'll ruin the entire show. Forever.

MYLES

He does kind of look like him, now that you mention it...

ME

Stop this right now.

CASH

I am still here...

ME

Yes, and?

HENDRIX

Hey, I thought of a new name for the group chat while I was gone.

MYLES

Does it suck?

ME

It's gonna suck.

CASH

Veto.

HENDRIX

You haven't even heard it yet! You can't veto!

CASH

I'm just saving us a little time.

MYLES

And suffering.

A giggle escapes my lips as I set my phone down on my desk. I'm supposed to be working, but those four are really distracting.

I didn't realize how much I've missed my siblings over the last few weeks. Months?

With Hendrix traveling all over the globe with the band and Myles trying to get his acting career going, it's getting harder and harder to find time to see all of them.

I shouldn't have avoided telling them the truth about Hollis.

They deserve a chance to reconnect with him. He deserves that too—a family. And even if he doesn't stay, they can still keep in touch.

Even if I don't.

Because I fear that may be a real possibility if I take this leap. If I give in to these feelings.

So do I fight my attraction to him to preserve our friendship?

Or do I take that leap and hope that love is the ultimate reward?

Everything is nearly ready for the Halloween party. As I originally planned, it will be bigger and better than last year, but thankfully, it won't also blow the budget. Hollis and I have been working on it for weeks, and together, we've come up with ways to cut costs while still bringing the wow factor that will attract customers.

I honestly don't know what I would have done without him. He's patient and attentive. He supports my ideas and vision for the future. And for the first time in a while, I think the bar might actually make it through the long haul.

Perhaps we could too.

It's late, and we're the last two left in the bar. We've closed out the register, and Hollis is putting up the chairs so he can sweep the floor. In a few minutes, we'll be done and heading home.

I don't think I want to sleep alone tonight.

I think I'm ready to step off that ledge. To take that leap. To make this marriage...*real.*

Every day we're together, we grow closer. Our bond strengthens. Our friendship deepens. And this yearning I have for my husband never wavers.

If that's not love, I don't know what is.

I don't want to live my life with regret.

Before he sees me standing there, watching him, I turn and head to the back, eager to finish up now that my mind is made up. I grab the trash and push the door open, not bothering to look as I prepare to chuck the bag into the dumpster.

That turns out to be a dire mistake.

Someone pushes me, and the door slams shut behind me, locking me out instantly. A sudden wave of dread washes over me as I turn to see Jace looming over me with malice in his eyes.

"What are you doing here?" I ask, and at the same time, he knocks the bag out of my hand. Trash goes everywhere.

He doesn't even flinch and instead reaches up to brush a stray hair from my face. "Paying my girl a visit, of course."

I bat his hand away. "I am not your girl, Jace. We broke up months ago."

"Yeah, but we had such a good thing going."

I try to step back, but the corner of the dumpster digs into my hip, pinning me in place. Jace uses this to his advantage, getting into my personal space. He smells like pot and cheap cologne.

I can't remember a single reason why I liked this man.

He looks the same as when I last saw him, but there's a desperation in his expression that scares me. I once wouldn't have thought him capable of violence, but that was before he broke in and emptied my stockroom.

"You mean, good for you? Tell me, when exactly did you decide to start stealing from me? Was it before or after I gave you the job? Just trying to decide how calculating you are."

"Can't blame a guy for taking advantage of an opportunity." He shrugs.

"I trusted you," I seethe.

He ignores me as a cold smile appears on his face. "When I met you at that concert, I thought you were a little shy. Kind of boring. But then I looked you up and realized who your family was, and I thought I'd go for it. Plus, you were hot, so it wasn't like it was a hardship, you know?" He winks, and my stomach turns. I try to side-step, but he blocks me. "With your family's connections, I thought I'd have no trouble getting into the hottest clubs and exclusive parties. But then I actually met your family. And you know what, Pres? They're just as boring as you."

"They're not boring," I argue. "They're just normal."

He laughs. "I got news for you. Normal people don't grow up where you did, princess."

"So are you mad at us for having money, or not having enough to benefit you?" *Shut up, Pres. Stop antagonizing him.*

"I'm mad because, thanks to you, I'm in serious debt. And you're gonna get me out of it."

I blanch. "What do you mean?"

"I needed that cash to pay someone off," he says through gritted teeth.

"Who?" I press.

"It doesn't matter!" he explodes, his face just inches from mine. I try to figure out how I used to look at this man with love and affection.

But then I realize...

It was never love.

It was barely affection.

If anything, it was a need to feel wanted, which he fulfilled—all while he drained me dry. "It's none of your business," he spits. "But you're going to help me. It's the least you can do."

"The least I can do?" I scoff. "I would have thought all

the liquor you stole from me would have been more than enough. I mean, it was enough to nearly destroy me, so..."

He shifts his eyes slightly, and I already have my answer.

I shake my head in disbelief. "You spent it, didn't you?"

"I don't have to explain myself to you, Pres."

"You stole my fucking money, Jace!"

"It's not like you don't have more. I know you like to pretend to be a regular girl with your beat-up Jeep and hand-me-down couch, but it's all an act. You're a Creed. I know you have money."

God, he really didn't know my family at all.

"Look, I don't know what you got yourself into, Jace, and honestly, I don't really care. It's not my problem. But I'm not letting you have another free pass in my stock-room. I should have called the police the first time."

I should have changed the fucking security code the second I fired his ass.

He grins. "But you didn't. 'Cause you're afraid of disappointing Mommy and Daddy, aren't you?"

"Fuck you, Jace."

His hand grips my waist, and when I try to push it away, he only tightens his hold. "Since you brought it up, I do have something I wanted to show you. Just a little something I've kept to remind myself of our happier days." He pulls out his phone with his other hand. "I'll text you a copy, but remember, I have the original."

He taps a few buttons on his phone and then turns the screen toward me.

It's hard to see at first because of the camera angle

and dim lighting, but I'd recognize those pleated velvet curtains and four-poster bed anywhere.

It's my bedroom.

And in the center of my bed, there's a perfect shot of me, straddling Jace as his hands grip my waist just like he is now.

I feel physically ill.

"Turn it off," I beg, pushing the phone away.

"What? No. It's just getting to the good part, babe. I really do miss those sounds you make."

I push him. Hard. "I said, turn it off!"

The bar door bursts open just as Jace stumbles backward. The phone clatters to the ground, face up. Tears stream down my cheeks as Hollis steps out, his eyes darting between me, Jace, and the phone.

"Who the fuck are you?" Jace demands.

"I'm her husband. Who the hell are you?" Hollis growls, though I'm sure he already has a pretty good idea. He steps up beside me and gently places a hand on mine. I lean into it, needing the connection. Needing him.

"Husband? And here I thought you were boring." He smirks just as a moan echoes from his phone and pierces the silence. My whole body tenses. Jace chuckles. "Well, not *that* boring."

Hollis lunges, but I grab his arm, and he instantly stills. "Don't, Hollis. He's not worth it."

Jace's cold smile turns deadly. "*Hollis?* This is Hollis? The guy you said was just a friend? Wow, you rich bitches really all are the same, aren't you?"

I physically have to hold Hollis back as Jace continues to talk.

Jace just shakes his head, a mixture of amusement and pure rage in his expression. "Since I'm a nice guy, consider the two days I'm giving you to pay up a wedding gift. But if you go to the cops, Pres, this video will go straight to the press. I doubt your brother's band will appreciate another scandal."

Zander joined the band a couple of years ago after their former lead guitarist (and childhood best friend) got a minor pregnant and tried to cover it up. Hendrix once told me that Asher felt responsible for not noticing Mitch's erratic behavior. The band has never been the same.

I'm not sure they can survive another scandal.

I'm not sure I can either.

Still clinging to Hollis, I watch as Jace slowly reaches down, picks up his phone, and then walks away. When he's finally out of sight, Hollis turns to me, and I take one step and crumble into his arms.

Chapter Twenty-Seven

HOLLIS

Presley has barely spoken since we left the bar.

It's like she's in shock, and I don't know what to do or how to help her.

Mainly because I have no idea what happened outside that bar—except that my wife was alone, and I wasn't there when she needed me.

I should have checked on her sooner. I should have noticed she was gone, but I had been so focused on finishing everything so we could leave that I missed the sound of the back door closing.

When I finally went to look for her, I already knew something was wrong. The dumpster is literally right outside. You don't even need to step all the way out to toss out the trash.

And Pres was definitely a toss-and-go kind of girl.

We walk silently to her apartment. It's late, quiet. Everyone else has already turned in for the night. I fish out my keys so she doesn't have to. She stands there with her arms crossed over her chest, as if she's holding all the pieces of herself together.

I worry she just might be.

Turning the lock, I let her go in first. The apartment is dark. I go to turn on a light, but she stops me. I turn.

"I'm so sorry," she says softly, barely able to meet my gaze. It's the first words she's uttered since the bar, and it's an apology?

I take a step closer and lift her chin. Even in the darkness, I can see the tears coating her lashes. "What in the world would you have to be sorry for, Pres?"

"The video. I didn't know that he...I never agreed to —" She can't finish her sentence, but it doesn't matter. I reach out and pull her into my arms.

"I'm so sorry, Pres. I'm sorry your trust was violated like that." I pull back, wanting her eyes on mine when I say this next part. "But I need you to know I wouldn't think any less of you if that video had been consensual. I would still be here supporting you every step of the way. Nothing would change my opinion of you."

Or the way I feel about you...

Her bottom lip begins to wobble as she digests my words. Then a single tear trickles down her cheek. "What am I going to do? How—"

"Right now, we're not going to worry about it."

"But—"

I smooth a hand over her hair. "We'll worry about it tomorrow, Pres. It's late, and you need to sleep."

She tenses. "Will you come with me?"

"Yeah." I nod. "Of course."

We leave everything in the living room, and I follow her down the hall. When we reach her bedroom, she hesitates, lingering at the entryway before stepping inside. Her gaze drifts to the drawn curtains and then to her unmade bed.

"I can't," she murmurs, shaking her head. "The bedding, Hollis. I can't..."

I didn't get a good glimpse of the video, thank God. Otherwise, I'm not sure even Presley's pleading would have held me back from taking a swing at that guy, especially if I'd known he filmed her without consent.

But I saw enough to know it was her bedroom.

And now, nothing in here must feel safe to her.

"I'll take care of it, Pres." I move quickly, ripping the comforter off the bed. I dump it into the hall closet, then head to the living room, where I grab the sheets I use to cover the couch each night. They're in a storage ottoman, along with a pillow and some blankets. I grab those too.

I come back to find her standing in the exact same spot. I don't even bother checking if she wants the sheets changed. At this point, I'd replace everything in the damn apartment if it gave her a sliver of peace.

With the borrowed sheets and blanket in place, I walk back over to her. "I'll look for another blanket in a minute. Can I take off your shoes?"

She nods, and I slowly drop to my knees, leaning back on my heels. I look up to see her watching me with those round blue eyes.

She's so fucking quiet.

It's killing me.

I reach out and wrap my hand around the back of her ankle, guiding it onto my thigh. If this were a normal day, she would probably comment about not wanting to get her dirty work shoes on my pants, but she doesn't say a word. She just watches as I undo the laces and carefully slide them off. I pull off her sock too before moving to the other shoe.

When I finish, I stuff her socks into her boots and set them aside. All shit we can deal with later.

I rise to my feet, and right away, I can tell she's holding back tears. Her face is blotchy, and her lip is trembling. I hesitate for a split second, worried that my touch might be unwanted in this space, but then she closes the gap between us and presses her face into my chest.

I wrap my arms around her. "What do you need, Pres? What can I do?"

"I feel..." She struggles to find the words. Her body shudders. Finally, she says, "I need a shower, I think."

Dread washes over me as I piece together her words. I pull back. "Did he touch you?" I ask. "Before I came out?"

"No." She shakes her head, but then says, "A little. He got in my face. Pinned me to the dumpster and grabbed my waist." I grit my teeth. The fucker is going to regret that. "I swear I can still smell the trash. His cologne. I need it all gone."

Keep it together, Beck.

"Come on." I hold out my hand and lead her to the bathroom, focusing all my energy on this single task, because if I don't, I'm going to lose it.

I cannot think about his hands on her.

Or the irrational jealousy I felt when I realized what was playing on his phone. Or the immense guilt I'm carrying because even after learning that the video wasn't consensual, even after seeing my wife fall apart in my arms at the very sight of her own bedroom, I can't shake it.

I want that video gone.

I turn on the light, and we both walk in. It's small,

with just a single sink and a shower-tub combo. Pres once told me that everything in her apartment looks smaller when I'm in it. I took it as a compliment.

I turn on the faucet and adjust the water temperature. Based on how steamy it is in here after she showers, I make sure it's plenty warm. When I turn around, Pres is standing there in her bra and underwear. She's got her jeans and T-shirt balled up in her hand, with a lost look on her face. If this were any other situation, my eyes would be everywhere, getting my fill of her nearly naked body.

But this is definitely not normal circumstances. "Can you?" she asks, holding out her hand.

"Yeah," I answer, keeping my eyes locked on her face. "Absolutely." I grab the clothes and head out into the hallway. I stop momentarily, unsure whether to just chuck the clothes or wash them. I decide to leave them on top of the washer for now.

She might feel differently in the morning, and I'd hate to toss her favorite pair of jeans or something.

By the time I return to the bathroom, her undergarments are on the floor, and I see her shadow behind the shower curtain. I make a little noise to let her know I'm here and take a seat on the edge of the counter.

I try not to watch her too closely, not wanting to seem like a creep. But when a sob echoes through the small space, my eyes snap back in her direction.

"Pres?" I call out, but she doesn't answer. I can see the faint outline of her body under the showerhead. Water pours down, but she barely moves.

Another sob pierces the silence.

Fuck.

Instantly, I'm kicking off my shoes and hopping off

the counter. I don't even bother with anything else. I just pull back the curtain and step into the shower fully clothed. The second she sees me standing there, with water soaking my shirt and jeans, she crumbles.

"I've got you, Pres," I say softly, holding her as I gently stroke her wet hair. "I'm not going anywhere."

She pulls back, eyes searching. "Promise?"

Somehow, I know we're not talking about just right now. My throat works, and I nod. "Promise."

Chapter Twenty-Eight

PRESLEY

It's dark in my room when I wake, but I can tell from the bright beams of light peeking through the curtains that it's well past morning.

My eyes linger. I used to love those curtains.

They were a total splurge and one of the first things I bought that made my bedroom feel grown-up. Now they just remind me of the grainy porno I unwillingly starred in.

The one that's going to go viral if I don't somehow come up with a huge amount of cash in the next day and a half.

My pulse quickens, and my stomach clenches with memories of those moments with Jace. I've never felt so scared. So angry. So violated.

God, I don't want to think about that right now.

I shift in bed and turn to face a sleeping Hollis.

The last time we were in a bed together, it was our wedding night. I woke up disoriented, confused, and okay, yes, maybe a little turned on.

This time, there is no confusion when I look at him.

No indecision. No regret.

He is exactly where he's supposed to be.

This man was an absolute saint last night. While others might have tried to take advantage of my vulnerability, he never did. He stripped my bed, washed my hair, and held me until I fell asleep.

When I needed it, he put me first.

I reach out and brush one of those auburn curls back. A scattering of freckles dusts his tanned cheeks. There's a faint scar on his chin that he got in a fight long before I met him.

He's lying on his stomach with his arms tucked under the pillow. The white T-shirt he changed into after we got out of the shower is a sharp contrast to the dark green sheets he put on my bed.

A few minutes pass, and eventually his eyes flutter open. This time, there's no awkwardness when he sees me. This time, he just smiles. It's a little sleepy and kinda boyish, but it's all for me.

"Hi," he says.

"Hi."

He props his head on his hand. "Do you know that you snore?"

My mouth drops open. "I do not!"

He chuckles. "No, you don't. But you do steal the covers." He glances down, and sure enough, the extra blankets he added last night have all shifted to my side, leaving him with a single sheet.

"Sorry?"

"It's fine." He flashes a grin. "I'm a hot sleeper."

I try not to giggle at that remark, because *yeah, you are.*

"How are you?" he asks, his voice turning serious.

I blow out a breath. "I'm better, I think. Not one hundred percent, but getting there. I think I'm mostly just pissed now." Last night, all I felt was despair. Complete and utter despair, and Hollis had kept me from drowning in it. "Thank you for everything."

He shakes his head. "You don't have to thank me, Pres."

"I do. You protected me. Stood up for me. You took care of me."

His throat works, indecision warring in his gaze. "You're my...best friend."

I inch closer to him. He tracks me, barely breathing. "I'm also your wife." Our bodies are so close I can feel the heat radiating from his skin.

"Pres." He says my name like a prayer. Or maybe a plea.

"I don't want to pretend anymore, Hollis," I say, the words rushing out of me. "I don't want a husband who sleeps on the couch. I don't want rules or exit strategies. I just want something real—with you."

He reaches out, cupping the back of my head. His green eyes blaze as he pulls me closer. "It was never pretend for me, Pres."

When his mouth covers mine, I feel it all the way down to my toes. His lips are soft yet commanding. My fingers dig into his hair as his tongue slides into my mouth.

His hand brushes the hem of my shirt, and my breath hitches in anticipation. But then, he hesitates and pulls back. He presses his forehead to mine and slowly exhales, as if he's trying to calm a raging storm. "That should have been our first kiss. Not some sloppy bar kiss we barely remember."

"It doesn't matter how we started, Hollis. Only where we go from here."

"And where do you see us going?" His eyes turn heated.

"Well, for the next couple of hours, I was kind of hoping we'd stay right here in this bed?"

His brow furrows slightly. "Are you sure? Last night was a lot and—"

I meet his gaze. "I'm sure."

His lip twitches as he tries to fight a smile. "And are you okay with—" He motions with his finger, pointing to the room. "'Cause if not, we can move to the couch or kitchen counter. I can be really creative when the situation calls for it."

I playfully slap him on the arm. "I'll be happy to explore this creativity of yours later on, but no. I think I'm actually okay. I want to make good memories in this room."

"I can definitely help with that." He slowly lifts the hem of my T-shirt. It creeps up to reveal just the undersides of my breasts. He leans down and kisses my belly, then my rib cage. I exhale sharply. "I've thought about having you like this for so long, Pres." He pushes my shirt a little higher. His hand grazes the side of my tit, and I nearly fly off the bed.

"How long?" I run my fingers under his shirt along his stomach. His breath hitches. I love knowing I have that effect on him.

"Too long."

"How long?" I press.

"Since the moment I saw you in that hallway—and nearly every moment since," he confesses. "I've always tried to do the right thing. You were Hendrix's sister, and your family gave me a home. But you were never just a friend, Pres. Not then. Definitely not now."

His eyes are blazing, and he looks like he's ready to devour me. Still, I ask, "What am I now, Hollis?"

"You are my wife."

"Prove it."

It's like those two words are the permission he needs to unleash the firestorm he's been holding back. His mouth slams down on mine, and there is nothing slow or languid about this kiss.

It's frantic. Needy.

With my shirt still askew, he runs a hand up my torso until he's cupping my bare breast. His thumb rubs my pebbled nipple, and I swear, I feel it between my thighs.

I lift up, ready to rip this shirt off my body, Hulk-style, if he doesn't do it for me. But he's already one step ahead of me, and within seconds, it's on the floor, along with his.

I take a second to admire him.

He does the same.

"You are so damn beautiful, Pres."

My cheeks heat at his words. Jace used a lot of words to describe me—hot, sexy—which are all fine, but when he said them, they always just felt like empty words.

When Hollis calls me beautiful, I know he genuinely means it. There's honesty in his words, and because of that, I truly feel beautiful.

He kisses me again, and we tumble back to the bed. The feeling of my nipples rubbing against his naked chest is like another level of foreplay I didn't know existed, and I find myself wrapping my legs around him in desperate need of friction.

"Fuck," Hollis groans when his very obvious erection

presses against my core. "I'm gonna come in my fucking pants if you keep grinding your hips against me like that, Pres."

Still squirming, I practically whimper.

He definitely notices. "Does it ache?" I nod. "Does my wife need to be taken care of?"

Hell yeah, I do.

I should have known Hollis would be like this in the bedroom. The caretaker. A giver through and through.

"Yes."

He hooks his fingers into the waistband of my shorts. "Tell me what you like, Pres. Tell me what you need."

"You," I say automatically. "I just need your hands on me."

He grins. "I'm gonna put more than my hands on you. By the time we're through, you're going to be well acquainted with my hands, my fingers...my tongue."

Kind, compassionate, and a dirty talker in bed? Did I hit the holy trifecta of husbands?

I lift my hips, and he slides my shorts down, taking my panties along with them. He drops them on the floor, and then his eyes sweep over my naked body with heated intensity.

He leans down and plants a kiss just below my ear, working his way down. He makes a path to my collarbone and then the valley between my breasts. His thumb rubs slow circles over my rosy nipple. My back bows.

I've never been much into nipple play, but this man makes me a believer.

He kisses my stomach, then my hip bone, inching closer to my center. My body is practically vibrating in anticipation.

He thought I was aching before. My pussy is fucking throbbing now.

He slides down so he's in line with my lower body. He places his hands on both sides of my hips. "Spread those legs for me, Pres. Show me what's mine."

Dirty talker and possessive?

I have a feeling I'm really going to enjoy this new side of my husband.

My legs fall to his sides, and he wraps a hand around each, holding me in place. "You're dripping for me, aren't you?"

"Yes," I moan.

"Have you ever made yourself come thinking of me?" He kisses my inner thigh and drags the tip of his nose along my feverish skin. It's close to where I want him.

"Yes."

He likes this admission. I mean, what guy wouldn't? Especially your husband. "How many times?"

"Too many to count."

"In high school?"

"How do you think I taught myself to get off, Hollis? I had a picture of you hidden under my mattress that I'd stare at while I dry humped my pillow."

"Jesus, that's hot. I'm gonna have to have you reenact that." He pauses. "Later."

Then his mouth is on my pussy and—

"Oh, holy fucking shit balls!" I cry out. My back arches, but the way his arms are wrapped around my thighs, I'm basically pinned to the mattress.

All I can do is lie there and take everything he's giving me.

It's a hardship, honestly, especially when I lift up on

my elbows and get to not only feel what he's doing but see it.

His muscled frame is bent over, arms flexed, face buried. His freckled shoulders move as he licks and sucks with enthusiasm. The sight of him ratchets my pleasure up to an insane level because he's not just pleasuring me for my enjoyment. He's getting off on it.

His tongue flicks my clit in just the right spot, and my hand shoots out, grabbing his head and holding him there.

"Right there. Don't stop," I beg.

It usually takes me forever to come like this, but that single tongue flick and I'm already starting to feel that delicious fluttering deep in my belly.

He does exactly what I ask, staying exactly where I told him, and when I start grinding my hips against his face, he lets out the sexiest groan.

"Oh fuck, Hollis." My orgasm starts to build. "I'm gonna come."

His arms tighten around my thighs, and then they start to shake as the orgasm hits me. I cry out his name, my legs clamping around his head as wave after wave of pleasure crash over me.

When I come back to earth, Hollis is staring up at me with glossy lips and a contented smile. "That was the hottest fucking thing I've ever done."

"Ever?" I level him with a mischievous grin. "That was pretty tame."

He shakes his head, still grinning ear to ear. "Don't mess with me right now. My inner caveman is feeling very possessive."

I run my thumb along his bottom lip, still wet from

me. His eyes flare with heat. "I noticed. Where did my sweet best friend go?"

He climbs off the bed, and I watch as his thumbs slip under the waistband of his athletic shorts. "I'll always be your best friend, Pres. But right now, I'm your husband, and I really need to fuck you."

His shorts fall to the floor.

Oh damn. I mean, I knew he was well-endowed based on the towel incident a few weeks ago, and he wasn't even hard then, but I had no idea—

"Pres, you're staring."

"Yeah." My lips quirk. "There's a lot to stare at."

"Was that a dick joke?" He gets back on the bed and slowly crawls up my body.

"Maybe."

That boyish grin returns as he leans in to kiss me, but he suddenly stops himself. Eyes wide, he says, "Shit. I don't have any condoms. Seemed kind of presumptuous before. But now—"

"I don't either. I threw all mine out when—"

"Nope." He shakes his head. "We are not bringing his name into our marital bed."

I snort. "Marital bed?"

His eyes crinkle at the corners. "We're married. This is our bed. What the fuck else do we call it?"

"I just like that it's ours."

His expression instantly softens. "Yeah, me too."

"I'm on birth control," I offer as an alternative. "And I've been tested."

I don't elaborate. He doesn't need or want the details, but I got tested regularly when I was dating Jace. I didn't trust him.

Probably should have been a red flag, huh?

"So have I." He doesn't elaborate either, but follows it up with. "Are you sure?"

"I don't exactly plan on being with anyone else. Do you?"

He leans down, his gaze meeting mine. "No. This is it for me, Pres. *You* are it for me."

He kisses me again. It's soft at first. Slow. But eventually our need for each other takes over, and neither of us can wait any longer.

I feel like I've been waiting for this moment my whole life.

"Lift your hips," he instructs, shoving a pillow under my ass to raise me up. I watch as he strokes himself, beads of pre-cum leaking from the tip. Someday, I'm going to give him the blow job of his life, but right now, I just want him to bury himself in me.

When he lines himself up, his eyes track every detail like he's trying to memorize it.

But then those green eyes find mine as he pushes inside.

"Fuck," we both groan.

"Are you okay?" he asks.

"Yes. It's just a lot."

A cocky smirk tugs at his lips. "You say the sweetest fucking things, wife." Then he captures my lips in another scorching kiss. He pushes in deeper.

It feels exquisite. But I need—

"More," I beg. "I need all of you, Hollis."

He gives me a fierce kiss on my forehead before he pushes his hips forward and slides all the way home. We both groan. "You have all of me, Pres. You always have."

He gives our bodies time to adjust, peppering me with

kisses. I run my hands up and down his muscular thighs. I reach around to grab his round, perfect ass.

Every touch feels intentional. Every kiss has meaning, like we're getting to know each other all over again in an entirely new way.

Our eyes lock, and he starts to move. Slow, shallow thrusts at first, like he's teasing me. He slides my hands above my head and then pins them with one of his. His fingers lace with mine, and I feel the cool metal of his wedding ring rub against mine.

That's way fucking hotter than it should be.

He picks up the pace and does this crazy little hip thing that has my eyes rolling in the back of my head. After that and the earth-shattering oral he gave me, I'm starting to wonder if my husband is some sort of sexpert.

Oh no. Seriously wrong train of thought to have right now.

"Whatever you're thinking, the answer is no," he says, slowing his movements.

"How do you know what I'm thinking?"

"Because it's written all over your face." His hand ghosts up my ribcage to cradle my face. "It's never been like this with anyone else. It's just you. Just us."

I kiss him hard. He groans, grabbing my waist and in one fluid motion, switching our positions. I pull him toward me so we're face-to-face. My legs straddle his. His hands circle my waist as I start to move, slowly at first until I'm riding his dick so hard my tits are bouncing, and the bed is shaking.

"Yes," I cry out. We're both panting and moaning so much, I'm surprised none of the neighbors haven't pounded on the walls.

"I need you to come, Pres. I'm not going to last much longer with you riding my dick like that."

"Touch me."

He doesn't need any further instructions. He just slips a hand between us and starts working my clit. The extra stimulation is exactly what I need. I come so hard, I see stars. While I'm still riding out the aftershocks of my orgasm, Hollis flips us, and I find myself on my back, being fucked just like he promised.

He pushes my knees up to my chest and pounds into me. I think I scream "Oh god!" at least a dozen times. It's that fucking good. I don't know how, but it prolongs my orgasm.

That familiar feeling deep in my belly starts to flutter.

"Oh my god," I cry out. "I think I'm gonna come again."

He just grins.

This time, he comes with me. I watch in fascination as his whole body tenses, and he lets out a low guttural groan. When he calls out my name at the end, it's the sexiest fucking thing I've ever heard.

Chapter Twenty-Nine

HOLLIS

"More," she demands, and I swear that one word goes straight to my dick.

Unfortunately, that is not what my wife is referring to.

"Are you sure?" I swing around to face her. She's got her plate held out, with several neatly stacked pancakes covered in maple syrup. But she doesn't seem to care about any of that. All she wants is—

"Give me the bacon, Beck."

I grin, holding up both hands. "Okay, okay. I'm just looking out for you. You're thirty now. You've gotta watch out for cholesterol and shit."

"You're thirty-two. Are you sure you should even be having any at all?" She flutters her lashes, and I can't help the chuckle that escapes my lips.

God, she's fucking cute.

After we thoroughly consummated our marriage this morning, we had an encore performance in the shower and then on the couch.

Just for good measure.

Got to make sure it sticks.

Now, it's late afternoon, and the two of us are fucking starving. So I offered to make us a very late breakfast.

I don't think I've stopped smiling all damn day.

"Are you trying to steal my bacon?"

She shrugs, her oversized sweatshirt slipping off her shoulder. "Just trying to save you the cholesterol. Plus, I worked up quite the appetite."

I smirk. "Yeah, you did."

She squeals with excitement when I add several more slices of bacon to her plate. This woman would eat breakfast for every meal if given the chance.

I top off her coffee, hand her the creamer, and then work on fixing my own plate. By the time I take the seat next to her at the kitchen island, she's grown silent.

"What's up, Pres?" I ask, sensing her quick change in mood.

She turns to me, her expression somber. "What am I going to do about the video, Hollis?"

I knew our post-coital bliss would eventually fade, and reality would rush back. It had to. Jace's deadline was approaching, and we needed to come up with a plan.

I set down my fork and take her hand. "I think you mean, what are *we* going to do."

She opens her mouth to argue. "It's not—"

"You're my wife, Pres," I press. "Not just in the bedroom or when it's convenient. I know we don't exactly remember our vows, but I will still do everything in my power to uphold them. I will honor and cherish you. And right now, I will protect you."

"Jesus, Hollis, you're gonna make me cry all over my bacon."

I huff out a laugh, planting a soft kiss on her forehead. "There's more in the oven."

"God, you really are perfect."

I give her a hesitant smile. "You may not think so when I tell you this next part. I think we should go to the police."

Her eyes widen. "But he said not to."

"I know." I offer her my hand. She takes it willingly. "I know. But here's the thing with people like Jace. He's gonna keep coming back, Pres. He'll use that video to squeeze every last dime he can out of you, 'cause he knows you're terrified of it damaging Hendrix and Zander's careers.

"But won't he just do that anyway if I go to the police?"

"Not if he's behind bars. What he did was a serious crime. He filmed you without your consent, blackmailed you, and threatened to distribute it. That's at least three felony charges, not including what he did to your bar."

She looks genuinely conflicted, and I get it. "I know it's a risk, so I will support you no matter what you decide. If you want to pay him off, that's what we'll do."

"But I don't have the money, Hollis. Even if I wanted to, I can't pay what he's asking. I'd have to go to my parents, and then I'd have to tell them about everything —the stealing, the break-in..."

This is the part of the conversation I'm dreading. "I can."

Her eyes widen. "What?"

"I can pay it."

"That's...a lot of cash. How?"

Breakfast forgotten, I nervously lick my lips. "When we first started talking, and you asked me about my job, you made an assumption, and for some reason I never chose to correct you."

"What assumption did I make?" she asks softly.

"That I'm the manager of Velvet."

"You're not?"

I shake my head. "I'm the owner."

"The owner? But I thought that was Jonas."

"We co-own it." Jonas and I co-own several other restaurants and properties in Nashville, but we handed off day-to-day operations a while ago. Judging by the shocked look on my wife's face, I think I'll save that explanation for later. "He's the face of the company. I run everything behind the scenes."

"Why didn't you tell me?"

"At first? Because money makes me uncomfortable. Jonas says I'm a guilty millionaire, and maybe that's true. Growing up the way I did, having a mom who constantly chased wealth..." I shrug my shoulders. "I never want to become one of those people who think money fixes everything."

Her throat works. "And then later on?"

I let out a humorless laugh. "Because I didn't want you to think I was one of those people who use money to fix everything."

"What do you mean?"

"The bar was struggling, and I wanted to help you, but I knew you'd never take it if you thought it might be monetary."

She just stares at me. "So you've been sweeping my floors for two months with no pay, when you could have bought the whole damn bar without breaking a sweat?"

I shrug. "Basically."

Her mouth hangs open, stunned. "I don't know whether to kiss you or kill you right now."

"I vote for kiss. Our marriage isn't fake anymore. I

have the scratch marks down my back to prove it. I'd hate for you to go to jail for murdering your very real husband." I fake a grimace.

She throws her head back and laughs. I live for that fucking laugh.

"So you don't hate me?"

She snorts. "Because my oopsie husband happens to be a millionaire? Nah, I'm good."

"I don't love the term 'oopsie husband.' Can we workshop that?"

She laughs. "Sure, Daddy Warbucks. But I'm not letting you pay off Jace."

"Pres—"

She holds up her hand. "No. You're right. If we pay him off, he'll just keep coming back."

"So what do you want to do?"

She lets out a slow exhale. "I want to go to the police. I want that fucker to pay."

By the time we return from the police department, Presley is emotionally drained but feeling confident in her decision. The detective assigned to the case, Stephanie Cortez, was extremely patient and knowledgeable, praising Presley's bravery.

She told us it would hopefully prevent him from victimizing other women in the future. I think that meant a lot to Pres.

After we handed over the evidence, including Jace's text and the bar's surveillance footage, Detective Cortez asked Pres to describe exactly what happened last night since the security footage didn't have sound.

Hearing her recount some of the things he said to her was...*challenging*. Having Presley back in my life has stirred up a lot of unfamiliar emotions in me. I don't think it's a bad thing, but sometimes I feel overwhelmed by them, like my need to protect her from her asshole ex.

I haven't been able to find a new therapist since I moved to LA. Honestly, I haven't made much effort to look. I've been so swept up in work and my new life that I put therapy on the back burner.

I think it might be time for that to change.

Because if there is one thing I refuse to fail at, it's her.

Pres is quiet when we step into the apartment. She has been since we left the station. I set my keys down on the counter. When I turn, she's standing in the living room, nervously chewing on her bottom lip.

"What's wrong?" I ask.

"Do you think I'm stupid for not seeing it sooner?"

"What?" My brow furrows.

"Jace was robbing me blind for months, and I didn't even notice. How is that possible?"

I thought she had moved past this. I thought with the Halloween event approaching and things beginning to look up, she'd given herself a little grace.

But I should have known better because when things go wrong, she always feels responsible. She considers herself the family fuckup, so of course, everything is her fault.

"Did I ever tell you why my mom's relationships never worked out?"

"'Cause she was selfish?"

"Yeah, actually," I answer with a humorless laugh.

"Wait, really?"

I shrug, motioning for her to sit. We both settle on the couch. She tucks her feet under and nuzzles into my side. "My mom was really good at charming people. Teachers, cops, men," I explain. "On top of that, she was young and good-looking. Finding a guy was never an issue. If she had really wanted to, she could have found someone. Fallen in love. But she always wanted more."

"I remember this one guy, Aaron. He was nice. Had a good job. I think the poor bastard actually loved my mom. Unfortunately for Aaron, I'm not sure she was wired that way. When he found his mother's wedding ring stuffed in her sock drawer, I think a part of him broke that day. Pretty sure he would have given it to her eventually if she'd just waited."

"God, Hollis. That's horrible."

"Selfish people do selfish things, Pres. It's not anyone's fault but their own," I say, trying to shake off the memory. It was the only time in my childhood, other than that year with the Creeds, when I felt safe. Aaron wasn't perfect, but he tried.

It was more than my own mother ever did.

"You're right," she says. "I've blamed myself for his actions for far too long. I'm done letting Jace fuck with my head. I'm…"

I wince. Presley isn't the only one trying to recover from what she saw on that video. "Can we not use the words 'Jace' and 'fuck' in the same sentence?"

"Oh!" She looks up at me and snorts. "You know I was faking it, right?"

My lips quirk. "I've become well acquainted with the sounds you make when you come, Pres. Yeah, I know."

Her eyes twinkle with mischief, and I watch as she

swings her leg over my hip to straddle me. My hands immediately settle on her waist. "Are you? 'Cause I could demonstrate if you need a refresher?"

I groan. "I'm gonna hate myself for saying this, but can I take a rain check?"

She gasps dramatically. "Are you sick of me already?"

"God, no. I just want to take you out on a date."

"A date?"

I laugh. "You say the words like it's a foreign concept to you."

Her arms wrap around my neck. "I understand the concept. I just wonder if it's maybe a little backward. Aren't you supposed to do the dates first, then get married?"

"Nah," I reply, kissing her slow and sweet. "I think the way we did it worked out just fine."

She rolls her hips as our kiss turns heated. Her tongue slips into my mouth, and I groan. It's been mere hours since I had her, and I feel fucking desperate to be inside her again. I've never felt like this before.

It's addictive.

"About that rain check?" I say, my breath ragged. "Can I cash it in now?"

She's already got her sweatshirt halfway off. "Fuck yes. We can go on our date when we're done."

Sounds good to me.

She tosses the sweatshirt onto the floor. I give her a once-over. She's completely naked from the waist up. "Were you braless this entire time?"

She shrugs. "They're uncomfortable. I rarely wear one when I'm not at work."

I eye her perfectly round tits. Tits I spent all fucking

morning sucking and licking. "I'm so glad I didn't know that before today."

"There are a lot of things I'm glad I didn't know about you until today," she says, reaching for the hem of my T-shirt. "It would have made this friendship thing a hell of a lot more difficult."

I help her out by lifting my arms. She yanks the shirt over my head and tosses it to the floor. Her eyes sweep over my upper body appreciatively. I've always worked out to keep in shape, but seeing the way she looks at me makes those hours on the treadmill worth it for an entirely different reason. "Yeah? Like what?"

"Like how you like to dirty talk in bed."

"I do not." *Do I?*

"Uh...yeah, you do, sweet husband. And it's hot as hell."

"I just say what I'm thinking."

She rolls her hips, and I let out a hiss when her body rubs against mine. "And what are you thinking?"

"Right now?" I ask.

She nods.

"Right now, I'm thinking that I've already had you in this position today. And although it was really fucking good, what I'd really want to do is rip these leggings off and fuck your tight little cunt hard and fast against that wall over there." I pause, sliding my hands underneath her ass. "Was that dirty enough for you?"

She bobs her head up and down with enthusiasm.

"Good."

I rise from the couch, with her wrapped around my torso. I walk us over to the living room wall and press her back against it. She unhooks her legs from my waist and puts her feet on the floor, watching me. Hooking my thumbs into the waistband of those skin-tight leggings, I slide them off her hips until they're a heap on the floor.

I know it's only been a few hours, but I don't think I'll ever get used to the sight of my wife naked. I've been dreaming of what she might look like under all those clothes for years, but my fantasies were nothing compared to the real thing.

She's still got tan lines from the summer, reminding me of her birthday and the night of our wedding. Her silky blonde hair is so long that it nearly reaches her small waist. I reach out and brush it over her shoulder, exposing those rosy nipples I'm obsessed with.

I reach for my belt buckle.

She licks her fucking lips as she watches me undress. As soon as my pants hit the floor, she pounces. She grabs my shoulders, and suddenly I'm the one against the wall.

"Change of plans," she announces.

"What?"

"It's just that we've fucked three times today, and all day, I've been dying to do this one thing."

She drops to her knees.

"Oh shit."

She looks up at me, and I about lose my fucking mind.

"When you went down on me, you asked me what I liked."

"And you told me all you wanted were my hands on you."

Mischief twinkles in her eyes. "Is that what you want, Hollis? Just my hands on you? Or do you want my mouth too?"

"The only reason I ever want you on your knees is when you're using that pretty mouth to suck my dick." I give her a wolfish grin. "But feel free to use your hands. I like those too."

She mutters something about holy trifecta, but all thoughts are lost the second she rises up and runs her tongue along the sensitive tip of my cock, lapping up the beads of pre-cum leaking out.

I let out a low groan, my head lulling back against the wall with a loud thunk. But I jerk back when I feel her wet mouth close over my shaft and suck.

"Jesus," I drawl, watching as she works to take all of me. It's a struggle, but she manages. She runs the tip of her tongue along the thick vein underneath as her hand reaches up to cup my balls. "Pres," I moan, running my hands through her silky hair.

She pulls back. "Fuck my face."

Now who's the dirty talker?

She takes me back into her mouth, only this time, her jaw is loose. She wraps her hands around my thighs as I grip her head.

I thrust into her. She moans.

"Touch yourself, Pres. Get yourself off."

She doesn't hesitate. She spreads her legs and works two fingers into her pussy. I swear my dick gets harder just watching her.

My hips surge forward, fucking her face just like she asked. Her mouth is so warm. So wet. So fucking mine.

Her moans turn frantic. My spine starts to tingle. "Pres, I'm gonna come."

Her eyelids start to flutter, and I know she's right there with me. I let go, shooting my release into the back of my wife's throat as she writhes below me.

She swallows and then wipes the corner of her mouth, smirking. "Now, about that date."

Chapter Thirty

PRESLEY

ME

Who's coming tonight?

MYLES

Can't. Working. Out of town.

ME

Do you only speak in fragmented sentences now?

MYLES

Time is money, baby!

ME

Ew. Never say that again.

MERC

Agreed.

MERC

Also, I can't come either.

ME

Why?

MERC

Oh, I just don't want to.

CASH

I can't come either. Taking Taylor trick-or-treating.

CASH

Also, I don't want to.

I roll my eyes. I don't know why I expected any of them to show up. Myles is rarely home, and when he is, it's for an audition or to meet someone about an audition. I'm incredibly proud of his hustle, but just hearing about how hard he's working makes me tired.

Mercury is another story. When she's not working, she's at home. While I don't consider myself a true introvert, my little sister definitely is. She may love rock music, but she is not the quintessential rock-chic. She would rather spend her evenings at home watching concerts than actually attending them.

Cash...well, Cash is a grump who doesn't remember what fun even is anymore.

ME

You know, I don't feel very supported right now.

ZARA

We're coming!

ME

Omg! ZARA! When did you join the sibling group chat?

ZARA

I'm not actually sure. Hen must have added me cause you guys just started blowing up my phone while I was waiting for him to finish movement therapy.

MYLES

That sneaky little shit. He just wants to get another vote on his side when it comes to choosing a name for the group chat.

ZARA

Well, I've got news for him. I've heard some of his name ideas (Creed It and Weep?!?!), and they're shit. He doesn't get my pity vote.

MERC

That's horrendous. Also. you're my new favorite sister.

MYLES

Same.

ME

Honestly, that's so fair. You are the only one coming to my Halloween party, after all.

MERC

RUDE.

ZARA

I'm just excited to see what Hen picked out for a costume.

ME

You don't know?

ZARA

It's a surprise!

MYLES

And he kept it? That's impressive.

ME

Speaking of... Tell Hen I have my own surprise tonight.

CASH

Oh, it's a surprise all right.

ME

Shut up, Cash.

I set my phone on the bed and turn toward the hallway.

Where is he?

Hollis said he needed to run an errand, but that was a while ago. When I asked if it had to be done today of all days, he nodded and said, "Yes, it can't wait."

Now, we need to be at the bar in two hours, and I'm starting to get nervous.

What could be so important that—

The front door opens. I exhale in relief, trying not to seem panicked or frazzled, even though I definitely am. I turn my attention to the costume pieces I've laid out on the bed, just as he enters behind me.

"Hi," he says.

I turn to see him leaning against the doorframe with his arms crossed, looking at me as if he doesn't have a care in the world.

"Hi. Did you finish your errand?"

A small smirk forms at the corner of his lips. "Mm-hmm."

"Okay..." I begin to let it go, but then I remember I'm married to a millionaire. "Is it a car?"

He tosses his head back and laughs. "No, Pres. It's not a car. Although now that you mention it..."

I glare at him, and he grins. "Kidding. Mostly."

"Your costume is in the closet," I tell him over my shoulder, grabbing the lacy thigh highs I bought for tonight. Part of our impromptu date the other night was going to the costume shop together. I'd been putting it off, so focused on making sure every little detail went as planned, but he convinced me it was okay to have fun too.

We had the best time. I'm convinced Hollis will do just about anything to make me laugh. That man dressed up like the tooth fairy and Pooh Bear, but my favorite was when he squeezed his six-foot, two-inch frame into a cheerleader costume with the super-short skirt and pom-poms. He was such a good sport about it, posing for silly photos that I totally sent to my entire family—minus Hendrix.

Hollis was a bit more focused when choosing costumes for me to try on. He definitely stuck with a theme. Sexy nurse. Sexy maid. Sexy princess.

We may have taken a few of those home. For later.

For the Halloween party, though, we settled on two classics—a witch and a vampire. Not exactly a couple's costume, but close enough.

I'm just finishing up getting everything on when I hear Hollis's footsteps echo behind me. "That is not what your costume looked like in the store, Pres."

I turn around and see him staring at the leather bustier I added. "The dress was a little plain," I explain. "Plus, it wasn't fair that only one of us got to wear leather."

I give him an appreciative glance. He makes one hot

vampire. Black shirt and pants that hug his muscular frame, but it's the leather vest and long black velvet trench coat that really give him that otherworldly vibe.

The coal eyeliner and pointy teeth I'm going to help him put on later will also help.

"Pretty sure this is pleather." He flashes a grin.

"I think the term is faux leather, and so is mine."

"Well, whatever it is, it's sexy as fuck. If I drop anything tonight, just blame it on your tits."

I snort out a laugh. "This new, unedited version of you is wild. You've just had all those dirty thoughts running through your head all this time?"

A cocky grin spreads across his lips as his gaze trails down my body. "And you didn't?"

"Oh, I definitely did. But until recently, I just thought it was very one-sided."

He closes the distance between us. "I fought them, but I've always had feelings for you. I just don't think I realized it until I heard your shrill voice yelling at me over the phone for ghosting you for twelve years."

"My voice is not shrill."

He smiles. "No, it's actually pretty fucking perfect."

I look up at him. I'm so gone for those soft green eyes and freckled cheeks. I can't believe I ever thought I'd be able to let him go. Now, I just want to stand on that bar top tonight and scream, "He's mine! That hot vampire right there—he's all mine."

Shit. That reminds me...

"Hen and Zara are coming tonight."

He nods. "You thought they might. Didn't you sort of tell Hendrix he had to?"

"Yeah, but that was ages ago. Before—"

He smirks. "Before you married his former best friend and then purposely avoided telling him?"

"Yeah. That."

He places his hands on either side of my face, taking care not to mess up the makeup I spent forever applying. "It's going to be okay."

"You sure?"

He nods. "Like the others, I'm sure he'll be thrilled. But if not, we'll handle it. Just like we have with everything else that's come our way. I told you from the start, we are a team, and nothing will ever change that."

A team. I've never been on one before.

I avoided sports in high school. I never joined the choir. Even at the bar, I was always the boss's daughter until I eventually took over.

Even in my own family, I've felt sort of set apart. Different.

But I like the idea of being part of something with Hollis.

A team. A partnership.

A marriage.

The bar is quiet when we arrive. A few employees volunteered to come in earlier and decorate, but they left hours ago.

It's just Hollis and me.

I go to flip on the lights behind the bar, but his hand stops me. "Wait," Hollis says.

"What? Why?"

"Just stay here for a second, okay?"

It's dark, and we're both covered in black from our spooky costumes, so I have a bit of difficulty tracking him as he moves through the space. But, a moment later, the entire bar is engulfed in tiny twinkling lights.

Red, green, and purple lights hang from the ceiling, the bar, and almost anywhere they can be displayed safely. There are spiderwebs and holy shit. Is that a fog machine in the corner?

My eyes are everywhere, taking it all in. "Oh my god! This must have taken hours!"

"Mel and Lamar were happy to do it."

"Remind me to thank them, 'cause this is so over the top. I mean, people are going to—"

"Pres."

I turn back to the sound of his voice and gasp. My vampire husband is down on one knee, holding a ring. I clutch my chest like a woman from the 1800s suffering from the vapors. "What is that?"

He smirks. "What does it look like?"

"It looks like an engagement ring."

"It is."

"I—wait. Is this what you went to do today?"

"Yes."

"You do remember we're already married, right?"

His lips twitch. "Can a guy propose?"

I try to fight a smile, looking at his costume and the spooky lights. "Don't you mean boo-pose?"

He shakes his head back, shoulders shaking. "You're really gonna make this difficult, aren't you?"

I nod. "Uh-huh."

"Get your ass over here, Pres."

I close the gap between us, allowing me to get a better

glimpse of the ring he's holding. "Oh my god." My attempt at shitty puns is instantly forgotten as my eyes begin to water. It's ornate and classy. The gold filigree band wraps around a large oval diamond. It's exactly what I would have picked. "Is that—"

"Antique? Yeah." His eye soften. "It's why it took me a while. Had to find just the right one."

I blow out a long breath. I don't understand why I'm getting so emotional. It's not like I really have anything to say yes to. I'm already married to the man.

It's not like he can ask me to marry him again...

"I want to marry you again," he says, making a total mockery of my thoughts.

"You what?" I laugh. "Why?"

He takes my hand, his expression turning serious. "Because I want us to have something to remember. I want to be able to close my eyes and see you walking down the aisle, know the vows we promised, remember the feel of your lips on mine when we kissed. Shit, Pres. I don't even know if we said or did all those things."

"It would have been nice if they had at least taken a picture."

"Based on my very empty wallet, I'm pretty sure all my cash went to bribing them to marry our drunk asses. There was no money left over for official wedding pics."

"So are you asking me to marry you again or telling me?"

"I'm not stupid enough to believe I could ever tell you to do anything." He chuckles. "This is me asking. But just so you know, if you say no, your ass is still married. You're stuck with me one way or another."

"Stuck with you, huh?"

"Like fucking glue."

Hell yeah, you are.

"Well, I guess we'd better call my parents then." His brow furrows. "A wedding reception would be the perfect time to have a wedding, don't you think?"

His eyes light up. "Is that a yes?"

"Hollis, I'll marry you as many times as you want."

"I just might hold you to that."

I hold out my left hand and wiggle my ring finger. "Keep buying me pretty rings, and I'll let you."

He slips the ring on, and it fits snugly against my wedding ring. We both stare at it before he grips my chin and turns my face upward.

"I love you, Pres. I know it might seem soon, or maybe not, since I just got down on one knee and asked you to marry me—again. But I think I've loved you longer than I even understood what the word truly meant."

My eyes start to water again.

"You were a friend and confidant when I needed one. You gave me a family when I had none. And now you've come back into my life and shown me the kind of love I never thought was possible. Thank you for loving me—every broken piece."

I swallow, my throat thick with emotion. "You are not broken, Hollis. We're all just painfully human, full of scars and imperfections. And I love all of you—the strong and silent side you show everyone else, and the sweet and caring side you save for me. I don't remember how we ended up in that chapel or why, but I thank God we did, because it brought us here. It brought me you."

He kisses me hard, pouring all his emotions into that single kiss. Love, devotion, passion. Then he pulls back, heat blazing in his eyes. “How long until everyone else shows up?”

I look at the clock over the bar. “Thirty minutes.”

“Good. Turn around. Hands on the bar top.”

My core clenches at his command. He looks downright feral in his badass costume and dark makeup. I’ve never really been into vampire romance, but I might be after tonight.

I do as he asks, placing my hands on the cool wood. I turn my head to see him eyeing me up and down. “Spread your legs. Keep your hands right there. I want to see that ring on your pretty finger while I fuck you, Pres.”

Oh, damn.

He makes fast work of his belt and unzips his pants. He’s so impatient that he just slides his pants down enough to pull his dick out. I watch as he strokes himself. His lashes flutter as he reaches out and slides a hand under my skirt.

“A thong and thigh highs. You wanted me to fuck you tonight, didn’t you?”

I bite my lip. “Well, I have been a *very* good girl.”

I feel his hot breath on my shoulder as he gives it a playful nip. Really glad we ditched those fake vampire teeth at the last minute. They would have definitely gotten in the way tonight. “Life with you is never going to be dull, is it?

“Never.”

His hand slides between my legs to cup my pussy. My thong is already drenched. He gives it a tug, letting the fabric slide between folds. It brushes my clit, and I gasp. Then I feel his hot breath next to my ear. “We’re pressed for time, so I’m going to take you hard and fast. But later tonight, we're going to celebrate the proper way." He gives a short pause. "For hours."

He pushes my wet thong to the side and grabs my hips. "Bend forward, Pres." I feel his hand smooth over the globe of my ass cheek as I bend my back to give him the perfect angle. "That's it." I feel the head of his cock work its way into my entrance, and then he slams into me.

I cry out, the pleasure so intense I don't even care how loud I'm being. Hollis doesn't let up once he starts. He promised hard and fast, and that's exactly what he gives me.

His belt buckle is digging into my ass. My makeup is probably trashed, but I don't care. I really don't fucking care.

"Fuck, Pres."

"Don't stop," I beg. "I'm so close."

He reaches a hand up, sliding it over the ring he just gave me. "Never," he says against my ear.

His sweet declaration and the possessive way he grips my hand—it's all too much, and I come seconds later, screaming his name. He follows right behind me, groaning as he empties himself into me.

When our breathing levels out, he kisses my temples and pulls out. A knowing smile spreads across his face as he starts to stuff himself into his pants and buckle his belt. "Don't you dare think about cleaning yourself up. I want you leaking my cum all fucking night."

I just shake my head. "There's that dirty talk again."

"Only for you, wife."

Chapter Thirty-One

HOLLIS

I watch Presley from across the bar, laughing as she hands a drink to a guy in a pirate costume. He takes it and then leans over to hand her a twenty. As she takes it, he says something that makes her brow rise. She shakes her head and then flashes her left hand, that new diamond ring sparkling under the lights.

I knew it was the right one the moment the salesclerk pulled it out. Seeing it on her finger, though? Fucking perfection.

I finish mixing my rum and Coke, smiling as I see the disappointment on the guy's face. He says something else, and Pres turns, points at me, and waves.

I wave back, and his face turns pale.

By the time I serve my customer, ring her up, and make my way over to my wife, the guy is already long gone.

"What was that all about?" I ask.

"Oh, he hit me with the good old, 'Are you a witch? 'Cause you just put a spell on me.'"

"You have to hand it to him. It's a classic."

Pres and I get hit on at the bar almost every night. It's an unfortunate part of the job. If I got jealous and broody over every guy who hit on her, we wouldn't be able to work together. Plus, I know she can handle herself, and if she's ever in a situation where she can't, I'm right here.

"Yeah, so I flashed my sparkles and told him I was married, and then he had the audacity to say, 'It's Halloween. Want to pretend you're not for a night?'"

"Bold."

"That's when I motioned to my very hot husband and said, 'No thanks.'"

I grab a pint glass and walk over to the bar tap. "So you're saying he was intimidated by my hotness?"

She shrugs. "You do look very hot. And intimidating."

I cock an eyebrow. "Well, I am a vampire."

"You guys are cute," a woman at the bar says. She's dressed as a mermaid with an iridescent shell bra and a bright red wig. Maybe Ariel? I don't know. I didn't exactly watch many Disney movies growing up. "How long have you been married?"

"Just a few months," Presley answers with a shy smile. She eyes her engagement ring, and I practically beam with pride.

When I woke up this morning, I had no intention of proposing today. But after breakfast, while rearranging some of my things in the apartment, I found our marriage license.

It made me think of the day we told her parents we got married. They were so happy, yet a part of them was devastated that they missed the wedding.

They weren't the only ones. We missed it too.

I want more than blurry tequila memories for my bride. I want photos on the wall that we can show our kids someday. I want to write vows I can recite to her year after year on our anniversary. And I want her to know that I would choose her again and again.

"Hey, Hollis!" Mel hollers over her shoulder as she pours a line of shots. "Can you grab some more triple sec from the back? I'm out over here."

I give Pres a gentle squeeze. "I'll be right back."

I head to the stockroom and enter the code on the new lock Pres installed. While we trust all of our current employees a hell of a lot more than Jace, Pres and I are the only ones allowed in here.

It reduces risk and Presley's stress level, which is always a win in my book.

It takes me less than a minute to grab a bottle of triple sec and head back to the bar. But as I turn the corner of the hallway, I stop dead in my tracks. Sitting toward the end of the bar with a familiar-looking brunette is my former best friend, Hendrix Creed.

He's wearing teal blue scrubs that seem almost too small for his large frame. His head is tilted back in laughter as Pres works behind the bar, pouring him a pint while she talks.

He looks so different.

I knew he would. I've seen his face everywhere—at Velvet that night, in pictures at Presley's apartment, and even in the damn grocery store aisle. But seeing him in person is a whole other experience.

As a kid, I thought he was destined for the stage. He just had a quality that made people sit up and notice him.

Now, there's no questioning it.

Hendrix Creed is a honest-to-god rock star. And he's about to find out I married his sister.

I stand there, sort of frozen.

What the fuck do I do?

We hadn't exactly planned this part out. Pres was nervous about telling him, so she was kind of hoping the element of surprise would do most of the work for us.

But now I'm standing back here, and they're...there.

Pres turns to grab a bottle of wine and catches my gaze. Her eyes grow wide, giving me that look that says, *Get your ass over here*, then turns back to her brother without even missing a beat.

I take a step back toward the bar, but stop myself.

Hendrix is now my brother-in-law. I shouldn't greet him for the first time in twelve years like a stranger behind the bar. I should greet him like a friend.

So I step into the crowd instead.

Creeds is packed tonight, which is good for us, but bad when you're trying to get from one end to the other. It takes a little while. I have to sidestep a Barbie, give directions to the bathroom to a gruesome-looking chef, and endure a chorus of wolf whistles from a group of women in the corner who probably need to be cut off.

Finally, I make it to the other side. I step up to Zara and Hendrix just as I hear him say to her, "What the fuck is that?"

Presley nervously licks her lips. "Oh! That's the surprise I wanted to tell you about. I got married!"

Zara and Hendrix look at each other. Hendrix turns back to his sister. "To who? If you say Jace, I swear to God..."

My wife looks up, eyes pleading. Time to intervene.

"Hey, Hendrix."

He whips around in his seat and looks me up and down as if he doesn't quite believe what he's seeing—or who.

"You remember Hollis, right?" Pres says, behind him.

His eyes narrow on my left hand before turning back to his sister. "What do you mean, *do I remember Hollis?* Are you asking if I remember my best friend? Of course, I do. What I don't remember is being invited to your goddamn wedding. What the fuck, Pres?"

"Hen..." Zara places a hand on his thigh.

"I wanted to tell you in person." Pres's eyes start to water.

"I've been home for a month!" He fumes.

"That's enough." I step forward, my voice calm. "You got something to say, Hen? You say it to me. But you will not raise your voice to my wife."

Hen looks momentarily stunned, but says, "Fine. Let's go talk."

Zara and Pres exchange worried glances, concern etched on both their faces.

"You okay if I step away for a bit?" I ask her. She quickly nods. "I'll be in the stockroom if you need anything."

"Okay."

Hendrix hops off his stool as I step up to the bar, leaning over so only Pres can hear me. "It's gonna be okay, remember?"

She nods again. "Don't beat up my brother. He looks scary, but he's really just a softie."

I choke out a laugh. "I'll be sure to tell him you said that."

"Don't you dare."

"I love you."

Her expression softens. "I love you too."

I turn to see Hendrix watching us. When his gaze

meets mine, he turns and slips into the crowd without saying a word.

That's fine. He can find the stockroom himself. It's not like he doesn't know where it is.

Once again, it takes a while to reach the other side of the bar. Luckily, there's no catcalling this time, but I still need to point out the bathroom again. I also see more than my fair share of weird costumes.

I don't know how Hendrix manages to avoid being recognized.

Or how he beats me.

"It's the costume," he says with a shrug when I give him a quizzical look, stopping in front of the stockroom door. He's leaning against it as if he's been standing there for ages. His sandy-brown hair is buzzed short on the sides and longer on top. The scrubs do little to conceal all his ink, including the signature Creed tattoo on his inner forearm. "No one expects to see me in scrubs. I'm honestly thinking about buying them in bulk and just wearing them to the grocery store. Maybe on our next date."

"Sure. 'Cause plenty of doctors go to the movies straight from the OR."

"I would. These things are hella comfortable."

I step up to the stockroom door and punch in the keypad. He watches in silence. "This is new."

I slowly swallow. "A lot of things around here are new."

"I can see that."

I guess joke time is over. "Come on." I push the door open. "It's quiet in here. We can talk."

He follows me inside and looks around. Pres has done a decent job replenishing the supply since Jace emptied her out, but it still looks sparse compared to what it used to be.

But I doubt Hendrix ever came in here enough to notice.

Besides, he's got other things on his mind.

"So how long have you two been lying to me?"

"Hendrix, it's not—"

He holds up a hand. "Hollis, I just found out my sister got married. Now, don't get me wrong. I'm really glad it's you and not that other guy. But I'm just trying to figure out why she didn't tell me. So maybe you start from the beginning, yeah?"

At one point in my life, I would have placed my loyalty to Hendrix above everything else. After all, he saved me.

From those assholes in that school hallway. From my mom.

He gave me a family, and for that, I would have done anything for him.

But the moment I woke up with that wedding ring on my finger, my priorities shifted.

My world shifted.

And now, Presley is my world.

I won't jeopardize that.

"I don't know what to tell you." I shrug, shoving my hands in my pockets, and sticking with the story we tell everyone. That's all he'll get from me. I won't betray my wife's trust. "We started talking after I called her that night she was at your parents', and we just fell for each other."

Leaning against one of the shelves, he asks, "And Jace?" He doesn't know about Jace? Man, he really is out of the loop.

"Dumped him a while ago."

"Thank fuck. That guy is..." He shakes his head.

"In jail," I finish, figuring I can at least share that bit of information for his peace of mind.

"Seriously?"

"Yup, and he'll stay there for a long time, if I have anything to say about it. Fucking deserves it after what he did."

His face blanches. "Did he—"

"No." I shake my head. "No. But I can't say any more. Your sister doesn't want anyone to know."

Those blue eyes of his watch me like he's still trying to piece me together. "Okay." He nods. He pushes off the shelf and walks a few steps. "Okay. That's fine. As long as you're sure he's gone."

"He's gone." I hired Pres the best lawyer money could buy. Money makes me uncomfortable, but when it comes to her safety, I'm grateful to have it.

"Good. That's good. But I'm still stuck on a few details when it comes to you and Pres." *Of course you are.*

He begins slowly walking the length of the room. Why do I suddenly feel like I'm being interrogated? "You and my sister start talking on the phone, right? You're in Nashville. She's here. And in a matter of weeks, you decide to uproot your life, relocate, and get married? Am I getting that right? 'Cause none of that seems like shit Presley would do."

"We got married in Vegas."

He pivots on his heels to face me. "Come again?"

"We went to Vegas for Presley's birthday, and getting married was sort of a spur-of-the-moment sort of thing."

He glares at me. "Was alcohol involved in this decision?"

I shrug. "Maybe a little."

He lets out a frustrated groan. "I really don't want to have to kick your ass."

"Well, I'm not allowed to kick yours. According to your sister, you're just a big softie."

"Like hell I am." He snorts. "Pretty sure I saved your ass a time or two."

"Yeah." I nod. "You did. You were more than just a best friend to me back then, Hendrix. You were family. You still are. I know you might doubt my feelings for Pres, but I fucking love that woman. She's it for me. Hell, I love her so much, I just asked her to marry me again."

His mouth quirks. "I'm not sure you can do that."

"People renew their vows all the time."

"Yeah, when they're like fifty." He snorts.

"Well, your parents are already throwing us that wedding reception—" My words cut short as his eyes widen.

Oh, fuck.

"What wedding reception?"

"Shit," I breathe out.

"What wedding reception, Hollis?"

"You know? I think I've left Pres out there by herself long enough." I motion to the door with my thumb. "I think I'm just gonna..."

He moves far too quickly for a dude his size and blocks my exit. "What. Fucking. Wedding. Reception?"

I blow out a breath. "When we told your parents we got married—"

He raises a hand. "Hold up. Exactly how many people in my family know you're married?"

I really wish my wife were here. "All of them?" Not sure why I phrase it like a question.

"All of them?"

I nod. "Pretty much."

"Myles?"

"Yup. He was thrilled. Bought us a round of shots."

His brow furrows. "Mercury?"

I nod. "She was preoccupied at the time, but happy for us."

He groans. "Cash?"

"He was pretty grumpy over the news. But, from what I hear, he's pretty grumpy all the time."

"He is," he agrees, momentarily distracted. "Myles called him the Grinch in the group chat last month."

"Does that mean his heart's gonna grow three sizes?"

He snorts. "Doubtful."

"Zander?"

"Uh..." I pause for a moment as his eyes fill with hope. "No, actually. Pres was worried he'd just go and blab the news to you before she could, so she hasn't told him."

"Yes!" He fist pumps.

I'm going to overlook the fact that he seems more excited about not being the last to know about our marriage than about our actual marriage.

Silence settles between us again, and I shift, looking around the small room as he steps away from the door.

"So you really just up and moved your whole life to be with my sister?"

I glance over at him. "It wasn't much of a life, but yeah. And happily. Wouldn't you do the same for Zara?"

"Happily," he echoes my words.

"I heard you two moved in together?"

A goofy smile spreads across his face. "Yeah. Never thought I'd be the domestic type, but here we are." He shrugs. “We spent last weekend picking out area rugs and plants for our living room. Like, who gives a shit if the rug goes with the curtains? Apparently, I do.”

I snort. “Happy for you, man.”

“Yeah, you too.” He pauses, and his mouth quirks. “I guess.”

I chuckle. “Such enthusiasm.”

His expression turns serious. “I couldn’t pick a better guy for my sister if I tried, Hollis. I know you’ll cherish her better than any man alive.” He pauses. “And I fucking knew you had a crush on her in high school.”

I open my mouth to protest, but end up just bursting out laughing. “To be fair, I really tried not to.”

“Well, I’m glad you figured it out. Although I’m pissed I’m always the last to know.” He shakes his head, muttering, “Those fuckers think I can’t keep a secret, but I can. When Zander signed with Manic, I didn’t tell anyone!”

“You really think you can keep a secret?”

His head whips around. “Yeah.”

I grin. This idea has been brewing in my head for months, but I didn’t think I’d ever get the chance to pull it off. Now that I know this is the real deal... “I have something I might need you to help me with, but you can’t tell Presley.”

“Just Presley? Cause I can totally keep a secret.”

I raise a brow. “Okay, it will just stay between us, then. No one else.”

I really don’t care, as long as it doesn’t get back to my wife. But, Hen looks so eager...

I step in closer. “Okay, here’s the deal...”

Chapter Thirty-Two

HOLLIS

I fucking hate ties.

Actually, I just hate dress clothes in general.

When I'm at the club, I'm always in a suit. Since moving to LA, though, it's just t-shirts, jeans, and what Pres calls my slutty sweats.

But not today.

I fiddle with the bow tie around my neck for the hundredth time, letting out a frustrated sigh. My phone starts to vibrate on the dresser beside me.

I pick it up and see Jonas's name flashing across the screen. I swipe to answer, and his face appears on the video call.

He's lounging on his leather sofa. The sun has already set on the East Coast, and even though it's not even Thanksgiving, their apartment is covered in Christmas lights. "Oh damn, you look snazzy."

My expression turns doubtful. "You can only see me from, like, the chest up."

He motions with a finger. "You're standing in front of a mirror, genius. I can see your reflection."

I raise a brow. "So basically, you're checking out my ass?"

He snorts. "No, I'm checking out your tux. Is that Armani?"

I set my phone back on the dresser, propping it against a picture so Jonas doesn't have to stare at the ceiling. I need to get this tie figured out. Pres is in the bathroom finishing up her makeup, and I want to be done by the time she comes out.

"Fuck if I know," I answer, trying to remember the directions the salesclerk gave me. "Hendrix sent me to this place he goes to. They picked it out."

"I could have helped you. Hell, I could have just shipped you something from my closet. No—the other way." He motions with his finger, pointing at my tie. "It goes under, then over."

I do what he says, but shoot him a sideways glance. "And risk ending up in something in a jewel tone or velvet at my first public outing with the Creeds? No thanks."

"You could totally pull off emerald green."

"Maybe," I say. "But I decided to stick with black. I don't know what Pres is wearing. She wanted to surprise me."

"Kind of like how I was surprised today when I got a wedding invitation in the mail…from my best friend."

I abandon my bow tie and grab the phone from the dresser. "Shit. I didn't know those went out already." Halloween was less than two weeks ago, and nearly every second we haven't been working or at the bar, Pres and I have been making up for lost time.

I've taken her out on at least half a dozen dates—museums, movie theaters, restaurants. We drove to

Malibu and walked on the beach. We went bowling with Hendrix and Zara in Hollywood. And we've fucked. A lot.

In that time, I meant to tell Jonas. I wasn't intentionally keeping anything from him. The club is at a point in the development process where I'm not needed every day, and I may have taken advantage of that. I let the real world go for a moment and just enjoyed being happy for once.

I didn't realize Tilly would end up accidentally telling him for me, but I guess she wants to make sure people have enough time to plan, since it's right in the middle of the holiday season.

Jonas's phone is snatched away from him, and Keisha's face appears. "What my husband is trying to say is, spill. Now."

I lick my lips, my eyes darting to the bathroom door where my wife is getting ready. A slow, goofy smile creeps across my face. "Oh shit," Jonas says. "You're not coming back, are you?"

I shake my head. "No. I'm exactly where I'm supposed to be."

"Hell fucking yeah, you are!" Jonas shouts out at the same time his wife yells, "That's our boy!"

They side hug like they're congratulating each other for a job well done.

I roll my eyes.

"This mean you're finally gonna unpack all those boxes you've been carrying around?" he asks. "I'll pay to have all that shit from your storage unit shipped myself."

I shake my head. "No, not quite yet."

They give each other a quizzical look, and I don't offer any more on the subject, so Jonas moves on. "So I'm your best man, right?"

I tug at the tight neck of my shirt collar. So fucking tight. "About that—"

"What do you mean *about that*? You were my best man. Now return the favor."

Keisha smacks his chest. "It's not a gift exchange, baby."

"We're not having a bridal party," I explain. "She has too many siblings, and the numbers don't work out. Too many groomsmen, not enough bridesmaids. Plus, we just want to keep it simple. Her niece is going to be the flower girl, and that's it."

A shocked expression paints his face. "So...no best man?"

I give him a knowing grin. Was he really that worried I'd choose someone else? "Nope."

"All right. I guess I can live with that."

Keisha pats him on the shoulder, holding back a laugh. "You sure, baby? 'Cause you seemed pretty jealous there for a second."

I chuckle as I resume the struggle with my tie. I set my phone back on the dresser. "Was not," he mutters. "Just concerned he was going to put me in some boring ass tux like that." He gestures toward me, then both his and Keisha's eyes go wide.

"Oh shit," Keisha curses. "Nothing is boring about that."

I turn to see what's caught their attention. Standing in the middle of the room is my wife in a stunning red satin gown. Her hair is in loose curls and pinned to one side. She's wearing a pair of sexy red heels, and I swear that slit goes all the way up.

"Jonas, I gotta go," I say without even bothering to look back. My eyes are glued to the woman in front of me.

"Yeah, you do." He chuckles, but quickly adds before hanging up, "Happy for you, man."

"I need help with the zipper," she says.

"In a minute. Let me just look at you."

She watches as I stalk toward her. Her gaze drags down my body. "You look really good in that tux."

"Not as good as you look in this dress."

"I chose it because of the color. I remember how you kept checking me out in my red summer dress when we were walking down the strip in Vegas."

I grin as my eyes wander over every inch of her. "Oh, that had nothing to do with the color. I just couldn't stop staring at your legs. But I do believe red is quickly becoming my new favorite color."

She instantly blushes. "Do you think we'll ever remember that night?"

I walk behind her, placing a tender kiss on her shoulder before my hand reaches her zipper. "I hope so. But if not, I'm just happy it brought me here."

I slowly zip her up, smoothing my hand over the curve of her spine. She's so fucking beautiful.

"Me too," she answers, turning in my arms to place a soft kiss on my lips. "But it would still be nice to know who came up with the idea."

She stares at me innocently, batting her eyelashes. My mouth gapes open. "You think it was me!"

"Well, it wasn't me." She laughs. "I would have been way too scared to mess up our friendship."

"But I wouldn't? I pined after you for months like one of those sad heroes from those romance novels you have lying all over the apartment."

Her eyes crinkle with amusement. "It's called yearning, Hollis. Get it right."

"Pretty sure it's just called jacking off every morning with your name on my lips."

Her mouth falls open, and we both laugh. "You're probably right, though," I admit. "I am the one who kissed you that night. I wouldn't be surprised if I'm the one who thought up the idea of getting married. Doesn't alcohol bring out your deepest desires?"

Her eyes soften. "So you're saying that when we were blackout drunk, your deepest desire wasn't to get me naked, but to propose marriage?"

"Hell yeah," I answer. "Why have one night when you can have them all?"

When Pres asked if I was nervous about tonight, I told her no. I was used to the glitz and glamour of wealthy people. I owned an ultra-exclusive nightclub that celebrities frequented.

This was basically the same thing, right?

It was not.

As soon as we stepped out of the limo, I knew I was in over my head. There were cameras flashing, people shouting, and I couldn't see a damn thing.

"Don't look at the camera. Save your eyes for the red carpet," Pres says, as I button my jacket and wrap an arm around her.

"Now you tell me."

The whole family is here for Lance. He's been in the

industry for decades, and tonight he's being honored with a lifetime achievement award in artist management. It's basically the equivalent of a Grammy in his field, which is why there is so much press. Nearly every artist Lance represents is here, as well as a bunch of other celebs and people in the industry.

The family met for dinner at a restaurant owned by one of Lance's old friends. He closed the whole place to accommodate us, allowing everyone to enjoy the meal without worrying about cameras or Manic fans.

That part of the evening is over, though.

Hendrix and Zara are ahead of us and getting most of the attention. His arm is protectively around her waist as the paparazzi try to get their attention. They throw out questions about his health and updates about the band. He gives a polite wave, ignoring their questions and requests to stop for photos.

Pres and I do the same until—

"Presley! Do you have a response to the rumors that your ex threatened to release a sex tape of you?"

My head snaps in the direction of the speaker. He's a younger guy, probably mid-twenties. He has a press pass around his neck, and all I can make out is the huge smile stretched across his face. "What the fuck did you just say?" I take a step in front of Pres, shielding her from the cameras flashing.

His grin widens, and he takes a step forward. Messy beard. Black beanie. Calculating eyes. "Simply wondering if the rumors are true."

But that's the thing. There are no rumors. On top of hiring a top-notch lawyer, I also recruited the expertise of a cyber tech genius recommended by Detective Cortez. He's been monitoring social media, gossip sites, and everything in between to make sure Presley's name never makes it to the headlines. And so far, there's been nothing. Not even a whisper.

So how the fuck does this guy know?

Hendrix steps up to my side. "My brother-in-law is quite protective. Especially when there are baseless claims made against his wife."

"So the rumors aren't true?" the pap presses.

"I'm not even going to dignify that with an answer," Hendrix answers in a cool and calm voice. I'm so angry, I'm not even sure I can speak right now. He casually pats my shoulder. "Now, if you'll excuse us, we're here to celebrate our father, not entertain rumors."

He turns, giving them his back, and then leans, whispering, "Just focus on Pres. Try to act normal, and we'll figure out what the fuck he's talking about when we get inside, okay?"

It's like he flipped a switch in my brain.

Pres.

I nod, and he steps back in line with Zara as if nothing ever happened. I turn back to my wife, who's standing tall in her gorgeous red gown. Her eyes meet mine, and I know by the way her throat works that she's trying to hold it together.

I need to distract her.

"Did you know that when we were at that birthday party in high school, I spent the entire seven minutes in Bethany's room trying to think of a reason to kiss you that wouldn't piss off Hendrix?"

A laugh escapes her lips, and I can tell she's fighting tears. "What were some of the reasons you came up with?"

I keep up my distraction technique as we continue

toward the red carpet. Lance and Tilly have already posed for photos, as well as Cash and Myles.

"Well, keep in mind that I was seventeen and an idiot back then, but a few of the better ones were offering to teach you CPR."

"Oh my god." She laughs.

"Oh, it gets better," I warn her. "There was also one from way out in left field that I heard you could pass on healing energy through kissing, and I was feeling a little under the weather."

"That doesn't even make sense."

"I told you I was an idiot." I shrug. "But the best one was that I was going to tell you I was a bad kisser, and I needed lessons. But we needed to keep it a secret—obviously."

"Now that one I might have actually fallen for."

I look down at her and grin. "That I was a bad kisser or that I would come to you for lessons?"

"You never dated, so—"

I bend down and kiss her, causing her to laugh. It's music to my fucking ears. Two minutes ago, she was near tears, and now she's laughing. If I can keep making her laugh like this for the rest of our lives, I'll forever be a happy man. "Because I was *yearning* for you."

"Never gonna hear that word and not think of you in the shower again."

"I'm actually okay with that."

Mercury is about to be photographed next, and she looks super nervous. Her dark brown hair is down for a change, and she's decked out in a shimmering gold gown. Her bright blue eyes flick around, unsure of what to do with her hands and where to look.

"She hates these kinds of things," Pres whispers.

"We've all had some media training, but Mercury just kind of freezes whenever she's in the spotlight."

"Shouldn't someone have gone with her?"

Her face contorts. "It's usually me. The guys probably didn't think about it."

Merc looks so miserable. I'm seriously thinking about going up there and rescuing her. But then there's a commotion, and all the cameras start swinging to the left as Asher Knight walks onto the red carpet.

"Asher! Asher, over here!"

He ignores all of them and instead walks up to a stunned Mercury. He whispers something in her ear, and she laughs and nods. Then, they turn together, and the cameras begin flashing.

"Did I miss something?" I ask, watching the two of them.

"What?" Pres looks at me, then at them. "Oh, no. Asher is just a family friend. He's just being nice."

I watch how Merc glances up at Asher. Mostly gratitude, for sure. But there's something else there too. Longing, maybe? I would know, I guess. "You sure?"

"Yeah. I mean, Merc had a crush on him when she was younger, but she's over it now. Besides, can you imagine her with a rock star like Asher? She'd never handle that kind of attention."

Hendrix and Zara go next, and the camera goes crazy as the two make eyes at each other. "Your brother looks happy."

She smiles. "I'm so glad he found Zara. Not just because she helped diagnose him so early, but because they're so good together."

I nod, understanding what she means. "They bring out the best in each other."

She looks into my eyes. "Exactly."

When it's our moment to step into the spotlight, I do exactly what Hendrix told me to do. I focus on my wife.

I mimic Hendrix and stand slightly angled toward Pres with my hand on her hip. She beams up at me and then faces the cameras.

And then it's over.

We head inside, where we're ushered into a VIP room reserved for family and guests. Champagne and fancy hors d'oeuvres are being passed around. Lance is shaking hands with someone as Tilly beams with pride for her husband.

We barely step two feet inside when Hendrix grabs my arm and tries to pull me aside. But I raise a hand, halting him.

I turn to Pres. "Are you okay if I talk to Hen about this?"

She nods. "He already knows, thanks to that guy outside."

I take her hand. "Doesn't mean I have to discuss it with him, or anyone else, if you don't want me to."

She brushes her thumb over mine. "No, it's okay. I think it's time we stop hiding everything."

My brow lifts. "Everything?"

She laughs. "Maybe we just start with this."

She heads over to the bar with Zara while Hen and I find a quiet spot in the corner. His expression looks almost murderous by the time he finally speaks. A softie, Pres? Really? "Is that what that asshole did to her? A sex tape?" he hisses. "I thought you said it was taken care of."

I scrub a hand down my face. "It was. It is," I stress. "I don't know how this guy knows. There are no rumors—"

"He seemed to think there were."

"There aren't. Believe me. I hired a digital intel guy who's been monitoring the internet since the day we filed the report. It's been quiet."

"And Jace is still in jail?"

"Yup. No one posted his bail after his arraignment, so he's rotting in there until his trial. Our lawyer thinks she can get him at least three to five, even if he asks for a plea deal."

"Good." He pauses, then asks, "Does Pres know you've got a guy cyber stalking her?"

I scoff. "Of course she does. I don't keep things from my wife." He arches a brow. "Well, not those kinds of things."

"Speaking of secrets, I talked to Zander."

I decide not to remind him that he promised to keep this a secret and let him go on. As long as Pres doesn't find out what we're planning. "And?"

"He gave me a recommendation."

"Are you going to give it to me?"

"Depends," he answers.

I tilt my head. "On?"

"I'm curious, and don't take this the wrong way, but how exactly can you afford something like this? I know Pres said you do something in entertainment? Are you a famous juggler? Stuntman?

"Juggler?" I snort out a laugh. "That's all you could come up with? Why couldn't I be a comedian or a social media influencer?"

He gives me a lackluster stare, and I laugh. "Social media influencer, Hollis? Seriously?"

I laugh. "Yeah, okay. Bit of a stretch. Wrong kind of entertainment too. I run a nightclub."

"You? Really?"

I chuckle. "Why is that so hard to believe?"

"I literally had to drag you to parties in high school. I thought you were allergic to fun, Hollis."

"I wasn't allergic to fun," I argue, remembering my nights on the beach with Presley. "I was just allergic to that kind of fun."

A server comes by and offers us champagne. He takes a glass. I decline. "So you make that kind of cash running a single nightclub?"

"No. My partner and I own several other businesses as well." I hesitate, feeling nervous. He notices and meets my gaze. "I own Velvet, Hen."

It takes him a moment to connect the dots, and then his eyes widen. "The swanky club the band went to in Nashville?"

I nod.

"So you knew we were there?"

Another nod.

"And you didn't think to drop in and say hello to your former best friend?" His expression is pained. "I died a little that day you left, Hollis. We all did. Pres walked around like a ghost for weeks. My dad tried everything to find you."

I look away, too overwhelmed to speak. But then I feel the warmth of a familiar hand slip into mine. "Let it go, Hen," Pres tells him, coming to my side. "He wasn't ready to confront you that night at Velvet, and you guilt-shaming him for it isn't going to help."

"I wasn't—" Hen tries to argue.

"You were," Pres stands firm. "You may not have done it intentionally, but the result was the same. All that matters is that Hollis is here now, where he belongs—with us. And when he's ready, I'm sure he'll be happy to sit down and talk with you about everything."

Both Hen and I stand there sort of stunned.

"You're right," Hen agrees, then shakes his head, eyes crinkling with amusement. "You two really are crazy about each other, aren't you?"

"Yup," Pres answers. "Now go check on your girlfriend. I left her with Darius, and I'm pretty sure he's hitting on her."

His eyes jerk up. "Oh, for fuck's sake. He promised me he'd stop that!"

He stalks off to go after his bandmate, and I turn to her. "That was—"

"I'm sorry if I overstepped. I was just coming over to see if you wanted a drink and—"

I silence her with a kiss. She lets out a little gasp of surprise. I pull back before I get too carried away. "You stuck up for me."

"Well, yeah." She laughs. "We're a team, remember?"

I smile. "Hell yeah, I do."

But we're not just a team.

She and I—we're a family.

Chapter Thirty-Three

PRESLEY

I should be reviewing the menu my mom just sent over to approve for the wedding. Instead, I'm staring at my husband's face right in the center of a celebrity gossip page.

CREED FAMILY DRAMA! NEWEST MEMBER CLASHES WITH PAPARAZZI AT FATHER-IN-LAW'S AWARD GALA!

On the bright side, he looks incredibly hot. That black tux he wore fit him like a dream, and the fierce look in his eyes? Well, let's just say the comment section is less about the headline and more about my husband's broad shoulders and chiseled jaw.

Seeing lewd comments about Hollis would usually make me livid, but in this case, it works in our favor.

This paparazzo who confronted me at the gala wanted to sell a story. When we got home, we contacted our digital intel guy. After some digging, he discovered a link between the pap and Jace. They used to be roommates.

"Still looking at that, huh?" Hollis walks up behind

the couch and catches me with my computer resting on my lap.

"Just checking out the comments again," I tell him, before tossing a grin over my shoulder. "And you, of course."

He rolls his eyes. "It's not that good of a picture."

I scroll down and down. "Hundreds of thousands of commenters would disagree with you."

"Hundreds of..." He shakes his head. "People need better things to do."

"Well, those people are doing what some in the industry pay a fortune for. They're killing a story before it even begins—all because they're distracted by my superhot husband."

"Well, it's not like the story had any merit to begin with. Jace might have reached out to his former roommate about selling the video, but the guy turned him down."

"Yeah." I laugh. "Because Jace is an idiot. You don't go to paps to sell that kind of stuff. They sell it to you."

"Too bad the pap decided to use the info to cause a scene."

I reach up and yank on his shirt, pulling him down to my level. He grunts out a laugh as he bends over the back of the couch and kisses my lips. "Too bad he underestimated the power of a hot man on the internet."

He kisses me again, and this time he takes his time, cupping my chin while my hand grips his biceps. When we finally pull apart, I ask, "How was therapy?"

"Good," he replies. He started seeing a new therapist a couple of weeks ago. I'm proud of him for talking to someone about his past and the trauma associated with it. Not a lot of men do. "I like my new therapist. He's different than Sabine. Asks more questions. He's funny."

"So you think he'll work out?"

He nods. "Yeah. I mean, it's always awkward to rehash my childhood to a complete stranger. But I feel comfortable with Troy, so I think it will be all right."

"I'm glad."

"Hey, do you want to go out to lunch with me?"

"Don't you have work stuff today?" He has been seriously slacking on his duties to the club over the last month. I am beginning to believe the honeymoon phase of a relationship is a real thing because we literally want to spend every second together.

When we almost got caught fucking in the stockroom the other day—again—I started to wonder if there was something wrong with us. Like, this can't be healthy, right? I've never been this obsessed over another person in my life.

So I did the unthinkable. I asked Hendrix for relationship advice. His response, "When it's the one? Totally normal. Fucking weird, right?"

"I do have a bit of work," Hollis answers my question. "But I was kind of hoping you might help me with it?"

I turn to face him because he looks hella nervous all of a sudden. "Oh?"

"Well, seeing as you're my wife..." A shy smile forms on his lips. "I thought it might be nice to get your input on some of the finishes that will go into the club."

I gape at him. "Shouldn't you ask Jonas?"

"I did. He agreed I should handle it, and I want your input."

"But I don't know the first thing about running a club. How will I know what looks good?"

"The designer has already set aside a few pre-approved choices."

"So you're saying I really can't mess it up?"

He laughs. "No."

I stand up and join him on the other side of the couch. "Lunch with my husband and an afternoon of spending someone else's money? Count me in."

I lead him to the kitchen counter, where he can grab the keys. I don't even offer to drive anymore. He knows he's in charge of that now. I kneel down and start putting on my shoes.

"Someone else's money?"

"Huh?" I blink up at him.

"You said you enjoy spending someone else's money." His tone is light. Amused, even.

I rise, shoelaces secured. "Well, yeah. The club is—"

"Ours," he says firmly.

"What? No, it's yours. You and Jonas—"

"The morning we woke up in Vegas, I said something to you. Do you remember?"

"You said a lot of crazy things that morning, Hollis." I grin. "Also, I was kind of distracted the first ten minutes or so because your abs were out."

He chuckles, wrapping his arms around my waist. "I said what's mine is yours. I meant it then, and I mean it now. Everything I have is yours."

"Even your company?" I ask, knowing I have nothing to give him in return. I don't own Creeds. It seems kind of like a shit deal for him.

"Yes." His mouth tips up. "Kind of the definition of everything."

"Okay." I sigh dramatically. "But it's not going to be

nearly as fun when I know it's our money. Don't be surprised if you find me in the clearance aisle."

He snorts. "I'm sure the designer will love that."

"Hey." I shrug, patting my thrift store couch. "Nothing wrong with a good deal, right?"

"No, now that you mention it..." He smirks with some hidden meaning. "Can we make one more stop today?"

Thanksgiving was last week, but you wouldn't know it while driving around downtown Los Angeles. The sun is shining, the palm trees are swaying, and everyone is in shorts.

It's as if someone forgot to tell Southern California that Old Man Winter is coming to town.

Hollis and I walk hand in hand down the street. We just finished lunch outside at a little bistro and are now on our way to the design showroom he needs to visit.

I'm actually kind of excited about this. I've always wanted a house of my own to fill with funky furniture and pretty things. When Mercury was in college and dorm life would get overwhelming, she'd come over, and we'd watch HGTV and bitch about the shitty decisions couples would make.

Now at least I can pretend for a little while.

We're nearly to the showroom when a woman stops us. "Are you Presley and Hollis Creed?"

Hollis's face goes pale. We've never discussed last

names. Now I'm wondering if we should. "Um..." I hesitate, realizing my short-sleeve shirt has already given me away. My Creed tattoo is staring her right in the face. "Yes."

"Oh my god, I knew it! I saw you on *Celeb News*, and I just have to say I love how you stood up for Presley! So romantic. It's no wonder 'Hero Hollis' is trending."

"Hero Hollis?" I try to keep a straight face.

"You didn't know?"

"Personally, I think it should be 'Hollis the Hero,' but I was an English major! Anyway, you're a big hit with BookTok."

"Book what?" Hollis's brow shoots up.

I choke out a laugh, patting him on the shoulder. "I'll explain to him later. Thanks for letting him know."

Her cheeks go red, and then she blurts out. "Do you mind if I get a pic? My book club will die when they see!"

I look over at my incredibly embarrassed husband. He shrugs. "Sure."

This place is huge.

It's like Disneyland for home design. Everything you could possibly want—from Spanish tile to bamboo floors and designer light fixtures—it's all here.

"I like this one," I say, pointing to the black quartz sample on the left.

"Then why do your eyes keep going over there?" Hollis asks with a smirk on his lips.

"You can't bring me to a place like this and not expect me to shop for myself," I inform him as I longingly stare at a stunning veined marble that would probably make my eyes water if I saw the price. "That counter would be gorgeous with oak cabinets and brushed gold hardware."

"Planning your dream kitchen?" he muses.

"Just getting distracted," I tell him, refocusing on the task in front of us. "Now, what's next?"

We've mainly been choosing finishes for the club's restrooms. Since they want to preserve as many historical features of the hotel as possible, the rest of the remodel has focused heavily on restoring what already exists, rather than replacing it.

The restrooms, however, have been a complete gut job. Not only because they needed to meet code, but also to be expanded to accommodate the number of people using the club on a nightly basis.

After reviewing the designers' choices, I appreciate how carefully she stayed true to the hotel's original design and the overall vision Jonas and Hollis have for the club.

I can't wait to see it all come together. It's such a big project, and Hollis and Jonas have worked so hard. There's been some pushback from the city on zoning, and permits have been tricky, but Vine will officially be opening early next spring.

Jonas is already talking about opening a third in Chicago. Hollis told him he'll have to hire a project manager for that one because he's not going anywhere.

Fucking right, you're not.

Hollis taps out a message on his phone and looks up. "Actually, I think we're all done."

"Does that mean you're going to tell me where we're going after this?" He's been keeping this extra stop he added a secret all day. It's driving me crazy.

He smiles. "Nope."

We thank the staff and head out. "That was surprisingly easy," I tell him, as we make our way to the Jeep. "I'm pretty sure your designer just wanted to give you the illusion of a choice because most of those samples were nearly identical."

He chuckles, taking my hand in his. "I think you might be right. But I did enjoy spending the day with you."

"I'd enjoy it more if you told me where we were going." I huff.

"So impatient."

We walk the short distance to the car, hop in, and soon we are on the freeway heading west. "Are we going to see my parents?"

"Nope."

"If we just end up at the bar, I'm really gonna be disappointed."

His deep laughter fills the air, and I sit back to watch the LA jungle give way to mountains, sand, and sea. We pass the bar and my parents' house and just keep driving.

"So we're just going all the way to San Diego, then?"

He just keeps driving.

Jerk.

My mind has gone on all kinds of wild tangents by the time he pulls off Highway 1. Are we visiting a former classmate? No, he doesn't care about anyone from high school. Maybe we're meeting an investor? No. He wouldn't take me along for something like that, would he? And if he would, I sure hope he gives me a heads-up so I can wear something other than jeans and a cropped tee.

The driveway we pull into is circular. Private. The

once well-manicured landscaping is now overgrown with weeds and bottlebrush. The house itself is in decent shape. The slate tile roof and white stucco exterior have seen better days, but it's obvious someone put a lot of thought into its design.

"Whose house is this?"

He palms the back of his neck. "Let's just go inside, okay?"

Why does he look nervous all of a sudden?

"All right."

I unbuckle my seat belt and step out of the car. The smell of saltwater feels like a warm hug, and I can't help but smile. Some people love the mountains or the desert, but my soul will always belong to the ocean.

He joins me by the hood of the car, taking my hand. "You're being weird," I tell him.

"I know."

Well, at least he's aware of it. We walk up the walkway. There are more overgrown plants and dead flowers in the planters. "Do the people who own this house know we're here?"

A smile plays on his lips. "They know."

Vague much? "All right."

We walk up to the door. Just as I'm about to ring the doorbell, Hollis turns to me. He has that same nervous energy about him. He opens his mouth to say something, but he's interrupted by the sound of clacking heels on pavement. "Sorry I'm late! Traffic was a bitch."

I turn to see a tall brunette rushing toward us. She's wearing wide-leg jeans, an oversized tee, and carrying a large manila folder.

"That's all right," Hollis says. "We just got here."

"Oh, good," she says, a bit winded. She offers her hand to Hollis, then introduces herself to me as Lara.

I still have no idea what Lara is doing here.

"Thanks for doing all this last minute. I know it was…stressful."

She waves her hand. "Nonsense. I'm used to this from my high-profile clients."

High-profile what? I stare at the two of them, waiting for someone to explain. Of course, no one does.

"Right. Well, let me just grab the code for the lockbox…"

The what?

I look down, and sure enough, there's one of those weird key-code box things secured around the door handle. How the hell did I miss that?

"Is this house for sale?" I ask.

"Not exactly," Hollis answers.

"I'm so confused."

Lara, the traitor, remains quiet as she enters a code into the lockbox. A second later, out pops a key. She sticks it into the lock and pushes the door open.

"I'll just give you two some time alone." She smiles. "I'll be out here if you need anything."

Hollis offers his thanks while I stare into the empty house with wide eyes.

"What are we doing here, Hollis?" I ask, almost too afraid to step inside. I can see the floor-to-ceiling windows from here that overlook the Pacific.

I don't want to fall in love with this place.

They already said it wasn't for sale. And besides, a beach house in Malibu? Please. This is not Barbieland. They don't just give these out for free.

"Why don't you come in and take a look?"

I hesitate, but step inside nonetheless. God, those windows are even more stunning up close. And of course, today had to be beautiful. Not a cloud in the sky. Bright blue water as far as the eye can see. "Do you need me to pick out tile for someone?"

"Yes, actually." A smile touches his lips, then he turns to me. "Us."

"What?" My hands start to shake. He can't mean... "You said it wasn't for sale."

"Technically, it isn't. I put a down payment on it this morning."

I glance around. Surely, he's joking. I try to communicate that to him, but all I manage to get out is, "You... but...what?"

He chuckles. The man actually laughs while my brain is short-circuiting because he just told me he put a down payment on my fucking dream house.

"Come on," he says as he offers a hand. "Let's head out on the deck. The ocean air always helps you think better."

He unlocks the sliding glass door, and we step outside. The sounds of birds and waves crashing against the shore fill my ears. There are people walking barefoot in the sand, while others brave the cold water for a mid-afternoon swim.

I take a deep breath, feeling my mind settle. I turn back to him, armed with questions. "Tell me how we can afford a house in Malibu—'cause I know you're rich, but Malibu is billionaire territory. I once looked up my parents' house on Zillow—mind you, they bought it in the nineties, so it's gone way up in value—but seriously, I almost had a heart attack. You have to be Asher Knight rich to afford beach houses in LA nowadays."

"Not everywhere," he argues. "But in Malibu, usually yes."

"Usually?"

"I wanted to surprise you," he confesses, heat creeping up his neck. "I had this grand idea to surprise you Christmas morning with a card, and inside would be the keys to our new house."

"That's romantic."

"It is," he agrees with a shrug. "But also incredibly stressful. Hen helped me find a realtor—that's Lara. She gave me this huge list of places to check out, but then I started to worry. What if I pick the wrong one? What if I find out after the fact that you hate Long Beach or Playa del Rey, and I never stopped to ask?"

"I don't, but I can see how that might be stressful."

We both lean on the railing, looking out at the beach. "I started second-guessing myself almost immediately. Until this morning when you made that comment about loving a good deal."

"It was a joke." I laugh. "Although I do love a bargain."

"Well, here's your bargain." He gestures back to the house.

"How much of a bargain?"

He snorts. "It's still Malibu, Pres. But it's priced to sell. The interior is outdated." As soon as he says it, I realize I didn't even look at anything inside except the floor-to-ceiling windows. Clearly, I have my priorities. "And it's small—much smaller than the surrounding mega mansions."

"It is?" I gape, looking back. "It looks huge."

"That's because you're used to living in a shoebox."

"Fair."

He turns and pulls me by the waist. I go willingly, looking up into those jade-green eyes. "I've been talking a lot with my therapist about permanence. It's something I've struggled with my entire life. I never felt like I had a real home growing up, and when I had the opportunity to put down roots as an adult, I was too scared. I couldn't even unpack all the boxes when I moved from place to place because I was worried it'd hurt too much when I inevitably had to pack them back up again."

"Hollis..." God, my heart hurts for him.

"I want to unpack all those boxes with you, Pres. I want to share a closet and a bank account. I want that permanence, and I want it with you."

Tears sting my eyes. "Are you going to propose again?"

"Only one grand gesture today. Promise." The corner of his eyes crinkle. "The down payment is just a hold, Pres. I can pull it if this isn't the place, and we can keep looking until we find the perfect one."

I look back toward the ocean. There are steps from the deck that lead to the beach. I picture moonlit walks in the evening, breakfast on the deck, and a hundred other memories just waiting to be made. "No need," I say. "It's perfect."

"Are you sure? You haven't even looked at the bedrooms or the kitchen."

"I've seen the most important part." I shrug, gesturing toward the Pacific. "The rest is all just details."

Chapter Thirty-Four

HOLLIS

"How are things going with the house?" Troy and I are meeting a bit later this week because of a scheduling issue on my end. Talking to him as the sun starts to set feels different somehow, and I let out a yawn, as if my body is aware of it.

"Good," I reply. "We had the inspection on Monday, and we will officially close in a few days. But we're waiting to move in until after the holidays. With the wedding next week, it's just too chaotic. Plus, we have some projects that will be easier to tackle if we're not living there quite yet."

"Sounds like you're making progress on finding permanence."

"Yeah." I smile. "I am."

He taps a few notes into his tablet. Then he looks up and says, "Speaking of the wedding? Everything going smoothly? I know from experience that it can be a stressful time, both for the couple and the family."

"Is it weird if we're not? Stressed, that is?"

"Do you think it's weird?"

I love it when a therapist throws your question back at you. "No, I guess not. It just sort of feels like a big party, you know? We're already married. I already got the girl. Nothing to stress over." I smile wistfully. "And her family has been a huge help. I'm pretty sure her mom has single-handedly planned the entire event and loved every minute."

He pauses, that contemplative look on his face. Then he says, "Why do you refer to the Creeds as Presley's family?"

"I..." I stumble over my words. "That's just what they are. They're her siblings. Her parents."

"But didn't you tell me that when you lived with them, it felt like the closest thing you had to a family?"

"Well, yeah." I wasn't kidding when I told Pres he asked more questions than Sabine. She would just sit back and patiently wait until I reached the point she was waiting for me to get to.

Troy doesn't wait. He just plows forward.

"And aren't you married into that family now?"

"Yes."

"So wouldn't it be fair to say that you are, in fact, part of the Creed family now?"

A knot forms in my stomach, remembering that day on the street when that woman referred to Presley and me as the Creeds.

There is no doubt in my mind that Pres is my family. She is, and always will be, my person. But as for the rest of them...

"Is there a reason you still struggle to reconnect with the rest of the family?"

I open my mouth to reply, but I'm interrupted by shouting in the living room.

"Time to come hang out with the boys, Hollis!" Is that Hendrix?

"Shh! He's in therapy, you big dumb oaf!" I hear my wife scold him.

"What the fuck?"

"Maybe we should continue this next week?" Troy chuckles. "Sounds like you've got some unexpected company?"

"Apparently."

We say our goodbyes, and I close my laptop, place it on the dresser, and head out into the hallway.

"There he is!" Hendrix's deep voice fills the small living room. I look around and find Myles in the kitchen raiding our fridge. "The groom to be!"

I eye my wife, and she just shrugs, mouthing, "I have no idea. They just showed up."

"Hey guys, what's going on?" I try as a greeting, because I don't know what else to say, other than, *What the fuck are you doing here?*

"We've come to steal you away for the evening!"

"What?"

"It's your surprise bachelor party," Myles informs me with a mouth full of lunch meat.

I raise an eyebrow. "I don't want a bachelor party. I have no desire to go to a strip club or drunkenly celebrate my last days of freedom or whatever other idiotic things guys do at those things. I'm good."

"See, we knew you'd say that." Hendrix grins. "Which is why we're just taking you to the bar."

"But the bar is closed for a private—" Pres starts to say before her mouth gapes open. "Wait. You booked the bar under a false name? Why?"

"'Cause I couldn't book it under my own." His eyes

gleam with mischief. "First, it was a surprise. Second, I'm famous now, Pres."

She rolls her eyes, muttering, "You're something, all right."

He laughs. "Anyway, it's just going to be Myles, Dad, and me. Zander. Oh, and Asher might come by if he can swing it. I hope that's all right?" I raise a brow. He's asking if it's okay that a super-famous rock star might casually stop by my bachelor party. "He's become somewhat of a recluse because of all the media attention. I think he's lonely."

Well, that's just fucking depressing.

"Yeah, no—that's fine."

"And what exactly am I supposed to do while you all are stealing my husband?"

A knock sounds at the door. We all turn. "Pres! Open up!" I hear someone shout on the other side. "We have food and wine! And penis-shaped balloons!"

"Oh." She beams, skipping over to kiss me on the cheek. "Have fun!" Then she turns to her brothers and says in a stern voice, "No tequila."

"I don't remember the last time I was in the bar when it was closed. Kind of weird seeing it so empty," Myles says after taking a sip of his lager. We moved a few of the tables around to make a larger one in the center, and we all helped ourselves to drinks. No one is officially behind the bar tonight.

"I don't remember the last time you were even at the bar, period," his dad quips.

We all chuckle.

"Ha ha, old man." He tries to look unamused, but those ice-blue eyes betray him. "But I don't remember the last time you were here. Or any of you, for that matter. I think we've all kind of been slacking on our duties to the family bar lately."

"And maybe taking our sister for granted in the process," Hen pipes up.

Everyone shifts, looking uncomfortable. But no one bothers trying to deny it.

"It's true," I speak up. "Lance, when you handed the bar over to her, it's like everyone disappeared. She suddenly had all the responsibility and none of the support."

I might be crossing a line, especially when all of them were nice enough to take me out tonight, but I don't care.

I will always stick up for my wife.

"I appreciate you saying that, Hollis," Lance says, leaning back in his seat. He scratches a hand down his wiry beard. "I didn't mean to make her feel like she didn't have our support. I..." He shakes his head. "I thought I was giving her space to make it her own."

"I don't have a good excuse. I've just been too wrapped up in my own shit," Myles admits. "But I'll try to make more of an effort and stop by more often."

"Unfortunately for me, casually stopping by the bar is impossible now," Zander says as he nurses a beer. "It's a damn shame because I miss this place. But it doesn't mean I can't check in. Pres is my sister. Period. And I've been seriously slacking on my big brother duties."

How does he do that? How is it so easy for him to

claim the Creeds as his own? He even has the fucking family tattoo on his arm. Meanwhile, I can't even hear someone call me by my wife's last name without freaking out.

"She should be proud of everything she's accomplished in the last year." We all turn. Cash looks around and rolls his eyes. "What? I can say nice things."

Everyone erupts in laughter. He just keeps glaring at everyone like we're all fools. When the noise finally subsides, he turns to me and leans in. "I know things haven't been easy for her the last few months." He gives a meaningful look. "I'm glad to see they're looking up."

He then turns back to his whiskey and doesn't say another word.

Holy shit, he knows. Maybe not about the fake marriage to cover up Jace's break-in, but he must know enough, and he's not saying anything.

I suddenly have a new appreciation for my grumpy brother-in-law.

The back door opens, and we all turn. In walks Asher, wearing a flannel, baseball cap, and tennis shoes.

"Damn, Ash," Zander calls out. "You look almost normal with that disguise."

"Almost." He chuckles, walking behind the bar to pour himself a beer. He's surprisingly adept at it. Considering Pres told me his family is Scottish royalty or something, I didn't figure it was a life skill he would have acquired. "Not sure how long it will last, but it was nice to take a drive down the coast without someone on my tail for once."

"Well, dressed like that, you kinda look like the dude I stood behind at the pharmacy, so I think you might get away with it for a while," Myles chimes in.

I don't think anyone, including Ash, believes Myles for a second, but I'm sure he appreciates the sentiment. Even in a simple flannel and faded jeans, there's something about Asher that makes people turn their heads and notice him.

With his beer poured, a dark stout, he takes a seat. He looks around the table before that intense gaze settles on me. "Congrats, mate. Or should I say congrats again?"

"Either works." I chuckle.

"So what'd I miss?"

"Actually," Hen says. "I was just about to go around the table and ask everyone to bestow their words of wisdom on our young groom."

"Words of wisdom?" Cash grunts. "Zander and Dad are the only two who are actually married."

He shrugs. "Doesn't mean they're the only two who have been in love. Come on, it'll be fun. Dad? Why don't you start? Age before beauty and all that."

Lance rolls his eyes, but looks amused. "Advice, huh? Well, there's the classic never go to bed angry. But I'm guessing you want something a bit more personal."

"Not too personal, please? None of us wants to leave here permanently scarred," Myles pleads.

"All right." He chuckles. "I'll try to be mindful of that."

"Appreciate it."

"Best piece of advice I can offer is to always put your marriage first," he begins. "It sounds simple, right? Isn't that what you're supposed to do? But priorities change. Someday, you might want kids, or one of your careers is gonna take off. Life is crazy and stressful, but if you keep making time for each other—nurturing the love that brought you together—it will carry you through the tough times."

"Thanks, Lance," I say, my throat suddenly thick.

"How are we supposed to follow that?" Zander croaks, his voice hoarse with emotion.

"I don't know, but you're next, dude," Hen tells him.

"What the fuck?" He groans. "Okay, um...I'm gonna go the non-sappy route—no offense, Lance—and offer some practical advice."

"All right." I give him a nod to go ahead.

"If your wife tells you her doctor said it was safe to go bare while she's switching from one birth control pill to the other, unless you want a surprise in nine months, do yourself a goddamn favor and use a condom."

I tip my head back and bark out a laugh.

"You're just never gonna let that one go, are you?" Hen chuckles.

"Elena has since confessed she may have misheard her," Zander says with a smirk, but then just shrugs. "Whatever. Marisa is fucking cute, and I'm damn lucky. Hen?"

"Travel," he simply says. "Before Zara went on tour with the band, she'd barely left California. Getting to see the world through her eyes was like falling in love with her all over again. So yeah, travel. Explore. Make memories on every continent if you can. You'll be happy you did."

We all stare at him, sort of stunned.

"What?" He stares back, confused. "I'm romantic as shit. Don't look at me like that."

I shake my head, grinning, and take a sip of my beer.

"Cash, what about you?" Zander asks. "Got any advice for the groom to be?"

Cash looks up from his beer, his expression grim. "Yeah," he replies. "Always get a paternity test."

An uncomfortable silence lingers between us until Myles pipes up and says, "Well, I've never been in love, so we can just skip right over me. Ash? What about you?"

Asher has been pretty damn quiet the whole time. I don't know if he's uncomfortable or if this is just how he is. Broody, loner rock star seems to fit his vibe. "Never had the privilege," he replies. "Doubt I ever will."

"You know, I thought for a minute you and Pres might date—when you came to family dinner back in May."

"What the fuck, Hen?" Z slaps the back of his head before he sends an apologetic look my way.

"Ouch, what? Obviously, they didn't. Pres didn't even bat an eyelash at him. I think she's the only woman alive immune to charm."

Asher flashes a grin. "I wouldn't go after your sisters, Hen. There's a code." Everyone turns to look at me. Asher's brow furrows in confusion. Apparently, he doesn't know all the sordid history between the Creeds and me. "What did I say?"

"Yeah, Hollis. What did he say?" Hen smirks.

I roll my eyes. "It's a stupid code. Also, we weren't even acquaintances, much less best friends, when Pres and I got married, so technically I didn't break any code."

"Am I missing something?" I hear Asher whisper.

"Hollis and Hen used to be best friends in high school," Myles whispers back.

"You want to claim a technicality." Hendrix raises a brow.

"No, I want to claim bullshit."

Hen looks dramatically over the group. “I still think he deserves punishment. What say you, boys?”

“Like a spanking?” Myles looks oddly intrigued.

“How are you and I related?” Cash mutters.

“What kind of punishment?” Asher questions.

“I’m thinking shots. Specifically, tequila shots.”

My brows shoot up. “Pres said no tequila. I do stupid shit when I drink tequila.”

“Exactly.” He grins. “Time for a little brother bonding.”

I groan. *Forgive me, Pres.*

Chapter Thirty-Five

PRESLEY

I never thought I'd see my mom posing with a cartoon penis balloon, but here we are.

"A little to the left, Tilly!" Elena shouts over the top of her iPhone. I giggle into my wine. I might be a little tipsy.

"Are you okay with all this?" Zara asks, motioning to the chaos that has descended upon my living room. She's sitting next to me on the sofa with a paper plate filled with cheese, fruit, and crackers nestled in her lap. Our tiny apartment feels positively cramped with Zara, her younger sister, Violet, Elena, Mercury, my mom, and me. But we're making it work. We pulled in chairs from the breakfast nook for Elena and my mom. Merc is sprawled out on a pile of pillows on the floor.

When the guys whisked Hollis away for an evening at the bar, the girls barreled into our apartment, loaded with appetizers, booze, and a ton of party favors.

"Yeah." I smile. "I didn't want a bachelorette party, but this…this is great."

"Good." She pops a grape into her mouth. "We all

wanted to do something for you, but didn't think a traditional bridal shower was your scene. So we sort of threw this together. Kind of a grown-up sleepover—without the sleepover." She laughs when she sees the horror spread across my face. "Don't worry, we're not all crashing here."

"Thank God," I breathe out. "'Cause I have no idea how I'd fit all of you."

She pops another grape. "Are you excited about the new house?"

I grin from ear to ear. "So excited. We're fitting in a few days before the holidays for a honeymoon. We're driving up the coast. Hollis has never been to Big Sur or even San Francisco. So I'm going to show him some of my favorite places. But when we get back, we'll meet the designer and finally get started."

"I'm really happy for you," she says. "I realize we haven't known each other that long, but Hendrix talks about you so much, I feel like I do. I know his reaction to your marriage wasn't the greatest at first."

"He was just being a big brother."

She smiles. "He was, but he was maybe a tad overdramatic."

"Hendrix? Never."

We both laugh, and I take a sip of my wine. Elena and my mom have finished their photo shoot and are now settling back in the living room. My mom sits, but Elena remains standing, holding a small box. "Pres, I'd personally like to thank you for getting married—"

"Twice!" Merc hollers, making everyone laugh.

"Twice," Elena echoes. "It not only gave us all a reason to celebrate you, but it also means I get a whole night—kid-free—with my husband!"

Hoots and hollers ensue.

"But in the meantime, we have some serious girl time to make up for—'cause Zara and I have been out of town for way too long."

"Me too," Violet agrees, squeezing in next to her sister. "I feel like I've barely been home in months." She's a successful model. She does runway shows all over the world, but you can also see her face in perfume ads and high-end clothing lines. She's widely popular and obviously gorgeous.

"Well, I'd say you haven't missed much, but..." Merc gestures to the rings on my hand, making everyone laugh.

"What's with the box, Elena?"

She looks down and suddenly perks up. "Oh! It's this game I found called *The Newlywed Game.* It's technically for the bride and groom. You ask questions, and both of you answer, and it's supposed to be cute and funny. But I just thought it'd be a good way to ask you questions without seeming super nosy."

"Probably should have kept that part to yourself." I laugh.

"Eh." She shrugs. "Let's play!"

I'm not exactly sure how the game really works, but Elena, who also seems a little tipsy, just slings off the top of the box and plops down in her chair, tucking one long leg underneath her. "Okay, I'll go first. I'm just going to pick a random card, ask the question, and pass the box. Sound good?"

Everyone agrees.

Why do I suddenly feel so nervous?

Oh, right. Because our marriage started out as a sham, and everyone thinks it was real.

This is going to be fun.

She pulls out a card from the middle and holds it in front of her. Frowning, she mumbles. "Why did I get the boring card?" She blows out a frustrated breath. "Which one of you cooks more?"

"Hollis. Next."

That is easy.

The box goes to my mom. She digs her fingers into it. Please God, don't be a sex question. "What is your spouse's pet name for you?"

"Oh." I cock my head to the side. "We don't really do pet names. Well..." I blush. "He likes to call me *wife*."

"Like, just...wife?" someone asks.

I nod.

"That's hot," Vi says.

"Agreed," Elena echoes.

I snuggle back into the sofa with my wineglass. This is fun. I can totally do—

"Where's the craziest place you've had sex?" Mercury asks, her wide eyes peeping over the top of the card. She flips it over and points. "That's literally what the card says."

My faint blush turns fire-engine red. "Oh god. Mom, can you cover your ears?"

"Nope." She laughs, taking a gulp of her wine.

I cover my face with my palms. "The bar," I mumble.

"The what?" Elena giggles. "I'm not sure we heard you."

"The bar!" I groan, making them all cackle with laughter.

"Pretty sure that bar's seen all our bare asses at some point." My mom just shrugs.

“Mom!” Merc and I shout while Elena and Zara double over with laughter.

“Not mine.” Vi pouts. “I feel left out.”

“Bucket list,” Zara suggests to her. “The bathroom is a little cramped, but it works.”

“Single stall too!” my mom chimes in.

“Oh my god.” I shake my head. “I have not had enough wine for this.”

“Well, at least we know Mom and Dad’s meddling worked,” Merc says, but then immediately sucks in a breath. “Shit, I did not mean to say that. This is why I shouldn’t drink.”

I whip my head to my mom, who looks way too pleased with herself. “What meddling?”

“Yeah, what meddling?” Elena and Zara say at the same time.

Her grin widens. “You know we have a security system at the house. With cameras and audio.”

My brow furrows. “Yes, but what does that—” I gasp, my palm slapping across my face. Our kiss. The talk *before* the kiss… “The driveway!”

“I got the notification that someone drove up, and when no one came to the door right away, I pulled up the camera. That’s when I saw Hollis. I probably shouldn’t have spied on you, but I had no idea why he was here or what we were about to walk into.”

“That’s for sure,” Merc mutters.

Zara looks around the room. “Can someone explain what the hell you’re talking about?”

I grimace, ignoring Zara. I’m completely focused on my traitorous mother right now. “So you’ve known the whole time that we were—”

“Faking it? Yes. But after a few minutes with you that

day, we knew there was something else going on. Maybe you thought you were faking, but there was no denying the way you two looked at each other. You obviously had feelings for each other, whether you knew it or not."

I can totally picture it now—my parents secretly texting each other back and forth, as they conspire and plot a way to bring us together without tipping us off.

God, they're sneaky.

And surprisingly good actors.

"So you just played along?"

"Not only did they play along…" Merc snorts. "But they decided to give you a little push by throwing that wedding reception."

"Mom!" Then I turn to my sister. "Wait, how do you know?"

"I had to tell her," my mom explains. "When has Merc ever just accepted something at face value without asking a hundred questions first?"

My mouth drops open. I had found that part a bit strange. "I just figured you were distracted."

Merc shrugs. "I was, but not that distracted. Thanks for the help, by the way."

I give her a sharp glare. I haven't told anyone about the song recording. I'm sure my dad knows, and probably my mom too. But I really don't want to make it into a big deal.

It's not that I'm not proud. Merc sent me a copy of the finished track, and I love how it turned out. When, or if, it ever makes it to the radio stations, it will be the thrill of a lifetime to hear my voice everywhere.

It's just that I don't want anyone to get any ideas.

My family is all about music, and don't get me wrong, I love it too. But just not in the same way. Recording that track was fun for a single afternoon, but I know it's not something I want to pursue as a career.

It may sound silly to some, but I enjoy my life at the bar. I love the history and the family connection. Searching for new bands and giving them a place to showcase their talent is rewarding. In the grand scheme of things, it may not seem like a lot, but for me, it's home.

Just like Hollis.

"So the whole wedding reception was just a ploy to keep us together?"

"Of course it was! I didn't know what you were doing or why, so I suggested the idea of a reception, knowing you'd have to keep up the ruse until then." She shrugs. "Anyway, it obviously worked, and I won't apologize for it. That boy loves you to the moon and back, and I'm so happy to know you've found each other."

I open my mouth to argue that her meddling didn't really have anything to do with Hollis and me falling in love. But did it? If my mom hadn't planned that wedding reception, would I have made such a big deal about telling each of my siblings in person? Or would I have just let their busy schedules work to my advantage until our inevitable "break up" in an attempt to protect them?

Shit.

My mom's smile simply widens.

"Well, now that we all know your marriage started out as a sham," Elena says, breaking the silence. "I say we toss the cards and ask the really nosy questions!"

Oh, boy.

"Fucking ouch. Stupid dresser..."

I awake to the sound of someone stumbling through our room.

No, not just someone.

My very drunk husband.

"What the...damn these pants."

I stifle a giggle, but not well enough because suddenly the bed shifts and Hollis is hovering over me with a stupid grin on his face.

He smells like a tequila factory.

I'm gonna kill my brothers.

"Hi." Red curls fall in front of his mischievous green eyes. His grin widens.

"Hi." I laugh. "Have fun?"

"Your brothers made me do shots."

"They made you, huh?"

He shifts so he's lying on his side next to me. I look down, and his damn pants are still halfway down his legs. Shaking my head, I sit up and crawl to the end of the bed. The drunk idiot still has his shoes on, which isn't exactly conducive to removing pants.

"There's a code," he explains as I start to untie his boots. "I had to."

"A code?"

"Yeah, you know, the bro code. You're not supposed to hook up with your best friend's sister. Definitely not supposed to drunkenly marry her in Vegas because her feet hurt and the jewelry store was open."

I freeze. "Wait, what did you say?"

"There's a code, Pres. Bro…code," he says it slower, his head sloshing from side to side.

I drop his other shoe on the ground and abandon his pants. He can deal with those later. I need to know what he just said. I scoot back up to the top of the bed and lie down next to him. His jade-green eyes are half closed, and he's looking at me with a sleepy smile. "You're pretty."

"I know," I say dismissively. "About Vegas. You said my feet hurt?"

"Uh-huh." His voice is groggy. I swear, if he falls asleep right now, I will pour a bucket of water on his head to wake him the fuck back up. "You were wearing those gold fuck-me heels with the tiny straps that wrap around your ankle. All I could think about was how they'd look wrapped around my neck."

His eyes flare with heat as he looks me over, like he suddenly just realized I'm lying beside him in bed.

Stay focused, Pres.

"Then what?" I ask, clearing my throat. "Did I take them off? Ask for a piggyback ride?"

"You tried to tough it out, but I suggested we go find a shoe store so you didn't get blisters." He hiccups. "Don't you remember?"

No, I want to tell him. *And until my brother plied you with tequila, neither did you.*

"It was the middle of the night, though," I question.

He shrugs. "It's Vegas. They have stores open twenty-four hours a day. But not a shoe store, apparently. It closed at midnight. The jewelry store next door, however…"

I cover my mouth with my palm as the memory suddenly resurfaces.

"Look at all those tennis shoes, Hollis," I whine. "They're just sitting there on the other side of the glass—mocking me."

I plop my ass on the bench in front of the store and sag against the back of the seat. My feet hurt, and my whole body feels like Jell-O.

I haven't been this drunk in a very long time.

"I really can't believe the shoe store is closed, but the jewelry store is open? Why?"

"It's Vegas," he says, as if that's an explanation. I raise a brow. "Pres, it's the wedding capital of the world. Where are all the lovebirds gonna get their rings?"

My eyes grow comically wide. "That's the reason it's open?"

He shrugs. "Why else?"

"Insomniacs with a shopping addiction?"

"Illegal gambling den?"

I frown. "But it's Vegas? Wouldn't it just be legal?"

"Fuck if I know. I hate gambling."

A giggle bursts free. "You are in the wrong city, dude."

He sits down right next to me. He turns to face me, placing an arm across the back of the bench. "I think I'm right where I'm supposed to be."

The way he's looking at me is the same intense stare he gave right before he kissed me back in the bar.

Neither of us has discussed it, but I swear I can still

taste him. I still feel the way his body molded against mine. The way we kissed felt desperate, like I'd been waiting my whole damn life for him to finally toss caution to the wind and make his move.

But then he pulled back, a warring expression in his gaze.

He paid our tab, and we left shortly afterward and took a walk.

And now I can't stop thinking about that kiss. About how right it felt. About how it left me wanting...so much more.

"Not sure if you remember," I say, glancing up at the jewelry store. "But you once promised to marry me if I ended up old and alone."

His eyes follow mine. Among the gold bangles and earrings, the designer watches, and the glittery necklaces, there's a small sign in the window that says, "Wedding Bands 50% off."

"I remember. You were watching some sappy movie and rambling about how if Kate Winslett couldn't find love, then what hope was there for the rest of us. Pretty sure I meant it as a joke to make you laugh, but go on..."

I stand and hold out my hand, my heart hammering like a jackhammer. I give him a wicked grin. "Remember how you said I'm practically geriatric now?" His eyes go wide, and then I say, "Wanna do something really crazy tonight?"

"Oh my god," I whisper, my hand still covering most of my face. "It was totally my idea."

"Of course it was." Hollis shrugs and then gives me that half-lidded grin again. "You looove me."

I brush a loose curl from his face. "Yeah." I smile. "I do." And that is all that really matters. But then I lean down close to his ear. "But if you wake up tomorrow and forget you told me all of this, we're just gonna keep acting like it was your fault, 'kay?"

He snuggles into my shoulder, a tiny chuckle escaping his lips. "Never fucking happening."

Dammit.

Chapter Thirty-Six

PRESLEY

Growing up, I was never one of those girls who dreamed about her wedding. I didn't dress up my Barbies in glittery gowns or write my name next to my latest crush in a diary that I hid under my bed.

I didn't even have a diary—or Barbies, actually.

It's not that I didn't want to get married. I just couldn't picture being a bride. There was just so much tulle and glitter...and white. I couldn't imagine myself being the center of such a spectacle.

Getting married in Vegas would have actually been a perfect solution...if I'd been sober. If I'm being honest, I was a little nervous at first about the idea of having a second wedding. But with my mother in charge, I should have known I had nothing to worry about.

She's kept the wedding small and intimate, just like we wanted. Everything from the flowers to the cake is simple and understated, and there isn't a speck of tulle or glitter in sight.

Hollis and I decided to do the traditional thing and spend last night apart. It felt kind of silly, since this is really more of a vow renewal than an actual wedding, but he wanted to.

He wants to do all the wedding things.

It's kind of adorable, actually.

Sitting at the desk in my old bedroom, I put the finishing touches on my makeup. I had a stylist come in and help with my hair, but I like doing my own makeup.

Plus, it gives me something to do. My sister was here earlier and hung out with me while the stylist did my hair. She even brought me lunch and a glass of wine from the kitchen.

But eventually, she had to go help with the setup in the tent, and I was left wondering if this is why brides have bridesmaids? To keep them occupied leading up to the ceremony?

Because the hours just seem to drag.

The door creaks open, and I turn to see my mom enter. She's changed since the last time I saw her. She's now wearing a gorgeous blue floral wrap dress and espadrilles. She stops the moment she sees me, placing a palm over her head. "Oh, Presley," she says, her eyes already wet with tears. "You look so beautiful."

I stand and do a turn. "Do you like my hair?"

I had the stylist create beachy waves, pinning pieces back with baby roses. She nods, dabbing at her eyes. "It's perfect. And you were right about the dress. It's stunning."

My mom was a bit surprised, shall we say, when I told her I bought my wedding dress online. I think she had hoped for that mother-daughter moment where I'd find *the dress* and we'd both cry happy tears. I didn't exactly mean to take that away from her, but the second I saw this beachy beauty online, I knew my search was over.

The mermaid style enhances my slim frame, creating the illusion of an hourglass shape, and the plunging neckline is both sexy and sophisticated. The delicate modern ivory lace screams beach wedding, and the small train gives me just enough bride vibes without making me feel like a pageant princess.

"Is it almost time?" I ask, walking over to the window in my room that overlooks the beach. I peek through the blinds where the tent has been set up for the reception. Beyond, toward the water, a cluster of chairs has been arranged, and guests have begun to gather and take their seats. The ceremony itself is small, reserved for close family and friends. The reception, however, will be slightly larger, with some extended family and my parents' friends attending.

"Almost," my mom replies. "But I was sent to give you this." She hands me a small box and a card.

I look down and immediately recognize Hollis's slanted handwriting. He told me no gifts. I look up at her with an incredulous expression. "He literally said no gifts!"

"Don't shoot the messenger," she says, patting my arm. "But if you want to open it before we head down, you'd better do it now."

"Yeah," I answer as I take a seat on the corner of my bed, being mindful of my train. "Okay."

I slide my index finger under the sealed flap and tear open the envelope. Inside, there's no card—just a plain piece of paper folded in half.

Pres,

I know I said no gifts, but that's only

because I don't need any. You already gave me the greatest gift by marrying me.

Plus, I am the king of grand gestures. How could I not get you something? Don't worry—it's not a car.

I laugh out loud, trying hard not to mess up my makeup.

I remember you once saying that you love moonstones. Did you know they symbolize new beginnings, protection, and love?

I smile to myself. Yes, I did know that. They also represent femininity and good fortune. It's why I like them so much. Well, that and they're pretty.

I don't know if I believe in stones having special powers, but I like the idea that when you wear these, you know I gave you something that symbolizes not only our wedding day—a new beginning—but also the love and protection I give with it.

See you soon,
Hollis

I exhale deeply and set the note on the bed. I haven't even walked down the aisle yet, and he's already trying to ruin my mascara with his sweet words.

I lift the lid of the box and gasp. I knew there would be moonstones, and from the wording, I gathered they were earrings, but I was unprepared for how stunning they would be.

"That man," I whisper under my breath. The moonstones, set in white gold, are teardrop-shaped. Their milky white color catches the light and shimmers with hues of blue, purple, and green. They're simple and elegant, just like my dress. I turn to my mom. "Can you help me put them on?"

"Absolutely." She takes the box and pulls them out one at a time. While she helps hold back my hair, I place them in my ears. When I'm done, I take a minute to look at myself in the mirror.

My mom stands behind me, tearing up once again. This woman is always crying. She gives me a gentle squeeze and asks, "Ready to get married?"

"Yeah." I smile.

"This time, maybe try to remember it?"

I choke out a laugh. "I'll do my best, Mom."

HOLLIS

I can't breathe.

That is how I feel the moment our eyes meet. The moment I see her in that dress.

Like the oxygen has been ripped from my very lungs.

She looks so fucking pretty. There are flowers in her hair and sand between her toes.

I want to race down that aisle, meet her halfway, and scoop her up in my arms, but I force myself to stay put. I've been waiting all day. I can survive thirty more seconds.

It feels like a damn eternity, though.

Did it feel like this the first time? Like my heart's about to beat out of my damn chest from the all-encompassing awe that this woman has chosen me.

The tequila haze I was in after the bachelor party gave me some of the memories back from that night, but the actual wedding? Still fuzzy.

Maybe someday we'll remember it.

But at least I know I'll never forget this.

She reaches the end of the aisle and kisses her father on the cheek. God, Lance. I've been so focused on Pres that I barely even noticed he was there. He's looking sharp in a slim black suit and a crisp white button-down —no tie. He whispers something in Presley's ear, and she nods before stepping forward.

She looks up at me, and I take her hand.

Fucking butterflies, I swear.

"Most people try to get married once. And only once," Hendrix begins, pausing for effect. "But apparently, my sister and Hollis like to do things the rock and roll way—go big, go to Vegas, and then...not remember any of it."

The small crowd chuckles. Yeah, everyone knows we accidentally got married now. Apparently, none of the women at Presley's bachelorette party can keep a secret from their significant others.

I doubt any of them are ever gonna let us live it down either.

"But in all seriousness, we are all here today to celebrate a love that's been twelve years in the making. And I think we can all safely say, we're so glad you found your way back to each other."

A few whoops and cheers fill the air. The moonstones hanging from Presley's ears catch the light, and I smile. They look just as beautiful as I knew they would be.

"Now, this is usually the part of the ceremony where the officiant might talk about love being patient and kind, but we know from their first wedding that neither of these two is patient." He smirks. "So we'll just skip ahead and focus on what really matters—the vows. Pres, you want to go first?

"Shit, yes. Do you think I want to follow him?" she says, making everyone else and me laugh. Then she squeezes my hands and looks up at me with those sapphire blue eyes. "Everyone knows that I love the beach. They probably think it's because I grew up here, which is partly true. As a kid, I liked coming down here to build sandcastles and dip my toes in the sand. It was, after all, the coolest backyard a little girl could have. But I didn't really fall in love with the beach until the summer before my sophomore year, when a boy knocked on my bedroom door and asked if I wanted to go for a walk."

My eyes start to sting. I'm going to fucking cry in front of everyone, aren't I?

Her eyes lock with mine. "I thought I fell in love with you in the weeks and months since we were married, but I realized I've been falling for you for years. Since those quiet moments when we walked on this very beach."

I let out a deep breath. She does the same.

"Hollis, I don't know where life will lead us. I don't know what obstacles are ahead. But I do know I'll be by your side, walking under the moonlight, and finding our way back home, again and again."

"Well..." Hendrix clears his throat, his voice a bit hoarse. "Not sure what you were worried about, sis." Then he turns to me. "Good luck following that."

"I—" My voice cracks as I blink back tears. "Fuck." Shaking my head, I scrub a hand down my face as a few quiet chuckles echo over the sound of the breaking waves. "I did not think I was going to be this emotional."

"I did," Pres and Hendrix say at the same time.

"I had a whole speech prepared. I was going to talk about the first time I saw you at school and those walks on the beach. I was going to tell you how happy you make me, and how I'm going to spend the rest of my life trying to do the same for you." A tear trickles down her cheek. I'm pretty sure a few fall down mine too. "But now all I can think of is getting to the part where I get to pull you into my arms and kiss you senseless." Someone wolf whistles in the crowd. "You are my home, Pres. The only one I've ever had, and I will love you until my last dying breath."

Her eyes glisten as she mouths the words, "I love you, too."

"Well, I guess that's my cue to move on to the rings portion of the ceremony, huh?" He looks at us expectantly. We look back, waiting. Just when I begin to second-guess our choice of officiant, his brows go up, and pats his suit jacket. "Oh, sorry! Forgot." He reaches in and pulls out two familiar gold bands, handing one to each of us.

My left hand has felt empty ever since I gave Hen my ring this morning. As if she knows what I'm thinking, Pres smiles and holds out my wedding ring. I give her my hand. "I promise to love you, to cherish you, and to always be by your side wherever life may take us." She slides the cool band back onto my finger—right where it's supposed to be.

I hold out her ring, and she offers her hand. With a smirk, I say, "I promise you forever, and this time, I'll remember every second of it."

The crowd laughs as I take her hand again. We don't turn to Hendrix. We don't break eye contact. We just wait until he chuckles and says, "Well, I guess I can now say by the internet powers vested in me by the golden state of California, I can now pronounce you husband and wife... again!"

She grabs the lapel of my tan suit and pulls me toward her. Nothing about our kiss is chaste or brief. I wrap my arms around her waist and lift her off the ground as people clap and cheer.

I've never been happier.

Chapter Thirty-Seven

HOLLIS

"Oh my god, Hollis," Pres moans, her voice slightly muffled. "Don't stop."

She's got her wedding dress gathered around her waist. My pants and boxers are pooled around my ankles, and we're going at it like horny teenagers in the closet of her old bedroom.

Or two newlyweds who just snuck off for a quicky before their wedding reception.

I slide my dick out, watching the way her body squeezes me. Then I give her a single thrust. She whimpers, reaching back to dig her fingernails into my thighs. That's her way of saying I need to stop with all the teasing and just fuck her already.

"You want it hard and fast? Is that what you're asking for?"

"Yes," she pants.

I grip her hips. "You gonna be quiet? Anyone could hear."

She looks back, grinds her ass against me, and grins. "No."

Jesus.

"Gather your skirt with one hand and hold on to that rod with the other," I instruct, pointing to the empty closet rod near her head.

This is a nice house. It should be secure.

She does as she's told, wrapping the delicate lace of her skirt around her arm. Her hand reaches up to grip the bar. Mine circle her waist, resting on her hips. Then I give her what she wants.

The first thrust makes her cry out. The second makes her moan. Now she's just a mess of garbled words and gasping breaths.

"You're gonna get us in so much fucking trouble," I whisper into her ear.

"I don't care. I love getting into trouble with you."

God, I love this woman. I slide my hand up her torso, underneath the bodice of her dress.

No fucking bra.

I squeeze her tit, running my thumb over her sensitive nipple. Her skin is so soft, I just want to touch her everywhere. Reaching over the layers of fabric, I find her soaking-wet thong. It's already askew. I part her labia and start to rub tight, slow circles over her clit.

Her knees almost buckle.

"Yes," she moans. "God, yes. Right there."

I tighten my hold around her chest, give her clit all the attention it deserves, and fuck her until we're both crying out so loud, the whole West Coast is probably blushing.

Still panting, a laugh escapes my lips. My forehead falls to her shoulders, and soon they're shaking with high-pitched giggles.

"Oh my god," she gasps, then snorts. "My mascara is gonna run."

"Do you think they sent out a search party yet?" I carefully pull out, making sure to keep her dress out of the way. I may enjoy knowing she's got the evidence of our lovemaking still on her skin, but I think she'd kill me if it left a giant cum stain on the train of her dress.

"Nah." She straightens and fans out her skirt. I start to pull up my boxers and pants, but stop to take a second to just look at her.

"You really are beautiful," I tell her. "I thought so from the first moment I saw you in high school, but then I got to know you, and realized your beauty is just part of you. It radiates out of every pore."

She turns, smoothing out her dress one last time. She bends down and picks up my jacket, which fell on the ground at some point, and slings it over her shoulder, taking a step forward to adjust my tie. "I think you're beautiful too," she says with a contagious grin on her face.

"I think you mean handsome."

"I said what I said."

We finish adjusting our clothes and emerge from the closet. Pres takes a minute to tidy up her makeup, deciding that it will serve as a good excuse if anyone asks where we've been. Considering we're both flushed and look extremely satisfied, I doubt anyone will believe us.

Five minutes later, we step into the hallway. I take her hand. My eyes drift down to the closed door that used to be mine.

She notices.

"It's my mom's yoga room now," she says, with a soft sadness in her voice.

"Pres, it's okay," I tell her. "I didn't expect them to keep it the same." Even her room has been painted and remodeled since she moved out.

"They did, though," she explains. "They didn't change it for years, Hollis. They tried not to let it show how much it affected them, but they always hoped you'd come back."

My throat feels thick. I nod, brushing my thumb over hers. Plastering on a smile, I say, "We should head downstairs. Don't want to keep them waiting. We are the guests of honor, after all."

We're halfway down the stairs when Tilly comes barreling up. "Where have you been? Everyone's waiting!"

"I, uh..." Pres stumbles over her words. "Had to touch up my makeup."

Tilly rolls her eyes. "Did you touch up your husband's too? 'Cause you're both positively glowing." I sputter out a laugh. A smirk plays on her lips. "Come on."

We walk past people carrying platters of food and flowers. I've never seen so many people at the Creed house before. I thought holidays were chaotic.

Just before we reach the living room, which leads out to the deck, Tilly stops and turns. "How do you want to be introduced?"

"Introduced?" Pres raises a brow.

"Do you want the DJ to introduce you as Mr. and Mrs. Beck? Are you hyphenating? Or..."

Pres gives me a nervous smile, then answers for both of us. "Um...why don't we just skip a formal introduction, Mom? Keep this casual?"

Her eyes flick between us, sensing unresolved

tension. It's something we need to talk about, but not right now.

"Yeah, of course. Great idea!" We follow her through the open doors, step out onto the spacious deck, and then walk down to the large tent set up on the beach.

Not sure why we needed a formal announcement in the first place.

The moment we appear, everyone erupts in cheers. Music starts, and the crowd swiftly parts, revealing a dance floor.

"That was weird, right?" I murmur.

"That they all just moved like that? In sync?" she whispers with a smirk. "Yeah, totally."

Since everyone is holding back, watching instead of offering congratulations, I dip my head and say, "I guess we're supposed to dance now?"

She snorts. "Considering the way they're staring at us, I'm gonna say yes."

I take her hand, and we step onto the small dance floor. Grabbing her waist, I pull her close. Neither of us is a fan of being the center of attention, so I keep her focused on me. Smirking, I say, "Good thing you accidentally married a guy who can dance, then."

She slides her arms around my neck. "Pretty sure I married you on purpose today."

The song changes. I recognize it immediately. "My Home" by Myles Smith, but it's been slowed down, and he's singing acoustic. Perfect for a first dance. Perfect for us. Whenever I hear it on the radio, I always think of Pres.

"Did you pick this?" I ask her.

"Maybe," she answers as we sway back and forth. "I

may not have cared too much which chicken dish my mom chose, but I did have an opinion on some of the song choices."

I cup her chin and kiss her, forgetting we have an audience. The crowd whoops and hollers. We pull apart, and I try to spin her around. It's a disaster. My dancing skills are not that advanced. But we laugh, and the guests enjoy the show.

I just love seeing her smile.

When the song ends, another begins, and other couples join us on the dance floor.

About half a song in, we both look at each other. "So..." I start.

"Drinks?" she finishes.

Just as we turn, I swear I see a familiar face in the crowd—a wisp of platinum-blonde hair and a cruel smile. But then, we literally run right into Jonas and Keisha, and I forget all about it.

"You're here!" I exclaim, pulling him into a tight hug.

"Are you kidding?" he beams, giving me a hearty slap on the back. Although the wedding attire is semi-formal, he's in a heather gray suit, vest, and tie. "Wouldn't miss it for the world."

I also give Keisha a hug, who's more appropriately dressed in a flowy pink strapless dress. "Are you sure you're just not here because of all the celebrities?" I give her a knowing glance.

"There are celebrities here?" He pretends to be surprised, causing Pres to snort out a laugh. Keisha ignores her husband's antics and smiles, sincerity in her tone. "Congratulations."

"Thank you," I answer, my throat thick with emotion. I didn't doubt they would show up, but, damn, it means a lot that they're here. In a sea of strangers, it's so good to see two familiar faces.

I guess a formal introduction is necessary. "Keisha, Jonas, meet my wife, Presley."

They exchange hugs rather than handshakes, having met and talked on the phone several times now. We make small talk for a bit. They ask about the house and our honeymoon plans. I ask about their upcoming trip to Rome.

Then I notice Pres start to shift from side to side, wincing.

"What's the matter?" I ask.

"Shoes," is all she says. I look down, and peeking out of the high slit of her dress are the strappy gold heels from our first wedding night. She was barefoot for our ceremony, but when I saw her pull those out for the reception after our tryst in the closet, I damn near lost my mind.

"You know those shoes drive me crazy," I told her.

She simply smiled as she slowly wrapped those tiny gold straps around her ankle. "I know."

"Do you want me to go get you a different pair?"

She shakes her head.

I chuckle. Oh, the irony. Apparently, she's determined to tease me with those shoes on both of our wedding nights—a game I'd gladly play if I didn't know she's in pain.

I bend down so my lips brush her ear. "How about we compromise? I take those sexy shoes now, and I promise you can put them back on...later?"

It's the emphasis on the word *later* that does it. Her eyes meet mine, and her cheeks flush pink. "There's a pair of ballet flats in an overnight bag by my old bed."

I just smile and wait as she uses my arm for support and slowly removes one shoe at a time. Once she hands them over, I turn to my best friends. "Do you think you can take my barefoot bride to the bar and make sure she gets a drink?" I toss Pres a wink. "No tequila."

I'm practically on cloud nine as I climb the stairs two at a time to the deck. I might even start whistling as I walk through the double glass doors into the Creeds' living room and head upstairs.

My face breaks into a stupid grin the moment I walk into Presley's old room and see the open door to her closet, remembering how she looked pressed against that wall.

How long is one required to stay at their own wedding reception before it's considered rude? Two hours? An hour and a half?

I find the overnight bag she mentioned by the neatly made bed and drop the shoes next to it.

"Hello, Hollis."

My whole body stiffens at the sound of those two words. My back is to the door, but I already know who's standing there.

Don't turn around.

Don't turn around.

But I do, because part of me can't believe it's her.

Part of me thinks surely I'm mistaken. Maybe it's a caterer who looks or sounds like her. Or shit, maybe I've just temporarily gone insane.

I'd fucking take insanity over the sight of *her* standing in the doorway of Presley's old room in a designer coral cocktail dress and nude heels. I nearly gag as the smell of that flowery perfume she always wore wafts into the room.

She looks older, yet still in her prime—one of the perks of having a kid when you're still practically one yourself. She must be doing well for herself—or someone is—considering the diamond studs in her ears.

My lungs feel tight. My hands feel clammy.

This isn't happening.

Not today.

"What are you doing here?" My voice sounds hoarse. Weak. I hate it. "How did you even—"

"I'm a guest." She shrugs, smoothing out a nonexistent wrinkle on her skirt.

"A guest?" No. She couldn't be. They wouldn't?

That cruel smile I recognize in the crowd on the dance floor gazes back at me. "Don't worry, your precious Creeds didn't betray you." She rolls her dark brown eyes, reminding me of all the times I thanked the heavens mine were green. I may never know who my father is, but at least I can be grateful for his strong genes. "I came with someone."

"You crashed my wedding?"

She steps further into the room. I take a step back. "The record producer I cozied up to was more than happy to bring me along. Turns out his wife left him last year, and he's been feeling a little lonely ever since." She fakes a pouty frown. "Anyway, it's not like I had a choice. I wasn't invited."

"Why the hell would I invite you?"

"Because I'm your mother," she booms. "You owe me!"

My hands start to shake. "You are not my mother." I let out a pained laugh. "Pretty sure I made that abundantly clear when I took off twelve years ago."

She begins to wander around the room, glancing at

the art on the walls. She drags a finger along the dresser, even pauses to pick up one of Presley's compacts, and checks her lipstick in the mirror. I want to rip it out of her damn hand, but I can't seem to move. My feet are rooted to the floor, making me feel helpless. She doesn't even deserve to breathe the same air as my wife.

"I never really thought about you after you left, you know?" she admits with a casual wave of her arm. "I never thought you'd amount to much. Most men don't, and the ones who do usually aren't worth the hassle." She tosses the compact back onto the desk. "But then I'm scrolling through social media one day, and there you are —and with the Creeds no less."

Fucking internet. I'd gone years without social media, trying to avoid something like this, and one encounter with an asshole paparazzi is all it takes for her to find me.

"At first I was proud. I thought maybe you'd learned a thing or two from me after all." She smiles. God, she thought I married Pres for money? The thought turns my stomach. "But then, imagine my surprise when a quick internet search reveals that you are already sitting on quite the fortune. Seems like I underestimated you."

My fists clench. *You always did.*

"What do you want?" I ask through gritted teeth. "'Cause I know you're not here to celebrate my nuptials."

She folds her arms neatly across her chest and tilts her head. "Compensation."

My brow shoots up. "Compensation? What the hell for?" God, this is almost laughable. First Jace, now her.

"For the first eighteen years of your life."

"You want me to pay you back? For what? Not dumping me off with social services? Honestly, maybe I would have been better off. At least in foster care, I would've had the slightest chance of finding a parent who loved me. With you, it was never possible because the only person you could ever love is yourself."

"Is that why you came back to these people? Because you think they love you?" she scoffs, gradually closing the distance between us. Her perfume is suffocating. I hate how her presence makes me feel weak, like I'm that eight-year-old kid again, asking why Santa didn't come. *Because he only visits kids who deserve it.*

"I—" The words get lodged in my throat. A victorious grin starts to spread across her face.

"I think it's time for you to leave." I look up to see Lance standing in the doorway with Tilly.

They look pissed.

"Not until—" she starts to argue.

"No." Tilly raises her voice and steps forward. Lance reaches for her, but she bats him away. "No. I held my tongue the last time you were here, and it cost me. It cost all of us. But not today." She begins to shake her head. "I should have never let you take him that day. I should have slammed that door in your face and fought you in court, assuming you even made the effort to show.

"But I made the mistake of thinking your connection to him somehow overshadowed ours because you were his real family, and we would always be just a substitute."

Her eyes meet mine, and I see her pain. Her remorse. God, I never knew. She and Lance always seemed so confident—an endless source of positivity.

I thought they were the perfect family, and I far from it.

It was never about wanting more than what they could give. It was believing that I was worth what they were offering in the first place.

"I could go to the press," she says in a panicked rush. "I'm sure they'd love to know—" But her words are cut off by commotion in the hallway as Hendrix and Cash run in.

Their breaths are heavy, and their eyes are fixed on Lance. "You said it was an emergency. We brought the security guard, like you asked." I didn't even see him pull out his phone.

Lance motions to me and to...God, I can't even say her name. I don't ever want to say her name again.

"What the actual fuck?" Hendrix glares at her. "You have a lot of nerve showing up here."

"Come on, Hen." Cash holds him back. "Let the security guard do his job."

They step aside as an intimidatingly large man walks in. My—*she* immediately tries to bat her eyelashes at him and explain the misunderstanding that has occurred. When that gets her nowhere, she resorts to arguing. The security guard stands patiently and unmoving through her tantrum and finally threatens to call the authorities. That quickly shuts her up, and soon, she follows him out of the room without a backward glance. Cash and Hendrix follow them out.

The moment she's gone, I let out a breath I think I've been holding for twelve long years. Tilly takes a tentative step forward. "I'm so sorry, Hollis. I have no idea how—"

I hold up a hand. "It's okay," I tell her. "I knew she'd find me eventually. I just didn't expect it'd be today. Or that she'd go to such extremes. Do you know who she manipulated to get inside?"

Lance gives a sad nod. "A good friend of mine. Had his heart shattered in his divorce. He sounded so happy when he called me to ask for a plus-one. This is going to devastate him."

He won't be the first. "I'm sorry."

"Not your fault. Like you said, she would have found another way."

"About what she said," Tilly says, her voice thick and her expression hesitant. I try to remember the last thing she said before they walked in. "We do love you," she says. "We always have."

"I know." I smile. "Even back then, I think I knew, or at least wanted to. But knowing and accepting are two very different things. Growing up, anything that seemed too good to be true usually was, and I think I would have used any excuse to reinforce that belief if it meant avoiding heartache."

"I'm so sorry we didn't do more," she says.

"You did more than anyone else ever has for me. And you were right to be cautious. You had five other kids to protect. She could have bailed the second you slammed that door in her face, but she could have also tried to charge you with kidnapping, or God knows what else. She's unpredictable, especially when she's desperate for cash."

"I just wish we hadn't lost time. That you and Pres hadn't lost so much time."

I look past Tilly just as my wife rushes through the door, eyes wide and searching as she scans the room until she finds me. She lets out a relieved sigh. "I think we both needed time," I say, smiling. "Me most of all. And I love our story. I wouldn't change a thing."

Pres walks up, and I pull her into my arms, pressing a kiss to her temple. "Nothing?" She raises an eyebrow.

"Well, maybe a little less tequila. I would have liked to

remember what you looked like walking down the aisle the first time."

"Pretty sure I looked exactly like I did the second time."

"And how is that?" I ask.

"Happy."

Chapter Thirty-Eight

PRESLEY

"What if…we just stayed on our honeymoon indefinitely?" I say over my shoulder as I lazily sip coffee on the deck of our suite overlooking the ocean. The waves crash below us. There's a hint of pine in the misty ocean air, and I swear I can see every star in the sky out here where the forest meets the sea.

Hollis joins me, taking the lounger next to me. We're in matching robes, having just showered—and fucked—after a full day of hiking, followed by a couples massage and private dinner on the beach.

We've had the best honeymoon. We spent a day in Santa Cruz, riding rollercoasters and eating cotton candy. We rode the cable cars in San Francisco and bought sourdough at Boudin Bakery. We craned our necks looking at the redwoods in Muir Woods, and then we drove down Highway 1 to Big Sur, where my husband has been spoiling me at this luxury resort on a cliff.

Now you understand why I don't want to go back to real life?

"If we don't go back, you'll never be able to order that tile you love," he says tauntingly.

"Don't use my tile against me."

"Don't forget about the countertops."

I groan, remembering the beautiful veined marble. So shiny. So smooth. "Okay, now you're just being mean."

He chuckles, taking a sip of his coffee. This resort has the best coffee. I don't know what brand it is, but I'm going to find out and buy it in bulk. "You'd just get restless in a few days anyway. You'd be the one dragging me back."

He's not wrong. While I'm a big fan of rest and relaxation—self-care is important, folks—I also love my job.

"What are you smiling about?" he asks.

"Just realizing how good it feels to be actually excited to return to work. I'd forgotten what that feels like. It all just felt so hopeless after everything with Jace."

"Which wasn't your fault."

I don't know if I completely agree with that. "I'm not beating myself up over it anymore," I begin, continuing before he has a chance to argue. "And I know now it doesn't make me a failure or the shame of the family. But I do think I'm responsible for some of the blame, Hollis. I was his boss, and I let him manipulate me."

"When it comes to manipulation, I don't think you allow someone to do anything, Pres. There is no consent. I think that's what makes it truly terrifying. You don't realize you're a puppet until it's too late."

"Well, I'd say I learned my lesson and will never date an employee again, but..." I shrug, causing him to laugh.

"I do remember you saying, quite sternly in fact, that you were not my boss."

"That's right. You asked what you should call me

instead. I said my name, obviously. And you, with that cocky grin and stupidly handsome face, replied and said..." I lower my voice, trying to mimic his. "'Nah, I'll just call you wife.'"

He chuckles. "That I did. Impeccable impersonation, by the way. I didn't know I sounded like a stoned surfer from a nineties sitcom."

I bark out a laugh and shrug. "The truth hurts."

"Speaking of names," he says, turning his attention to the water glittering in the distance. His expression turns hesitant. Nervous even. "I wanted to talk to you about something."

I set my coffee cup down on the table beside me and turn in my seat to face him. "Okay."

"It's a topic I think we've purposely avoided for a while, and I think that might be my fault. When your mom brought up the question of our last name at the wedding, I know you dodged the question because you knew it made me uncomfortable."

I nod. "I didn't mind. I just don't understand why it was necessary in the first place. What about this has you so nervous? Are you afraid to ask me?"

He shakes his head. "No," he says before briefly pausing. Then he turns to me. "Pres, I don't want you to take my last name."

My mouth falls open, but no words come out. Heat starts to creep up my neck. My throat feels thick. "Oh," I say as my voice wobbles. "Okay. Yeah. That's fine."

His eyes widen. "Shit. Now I've really messed this up. I didn't mean it like that."

Tears sting my eyes. "Well, you just told me you don't want me to take your name, Hollis. How else am I supposed to take it?"

He takes my hand, closing his two large ones around it. "I don't want you to take it, because I don't want it either."

My eyes jerk up. "What?"

"Pres, my mom—we're gonna have to find something else to call her, 'cause I really hate referring to her as anything maternal. But anyway, *that woman* just crashed our wedding and demanded I pay her for keeping me alive for eighteen years. That is not the name or legacy I want to pass down to our kids." His eyes widen ever so slightly. "You know, if you want kids. I realize it isn't something we've really discussed."

"I want kids," I say with a warm smile. "Not yet, though."

"No, definitely not yet."

"And I might want to adopt."

"Yeah?" His eyes soften. "I like that idea."

We stare at each other, a small smirk tugging at his lips. "We're getting seriously off topic."

"Right." He nods, although I can tell both of us seriously want to circle back to that conversation at some point in the near future.

"All those times I called you Beck in the past. Did that bother you?"

He shakes his head. "No. Honestly, I never really thought much about it until we got married. And when we did, I knew it was something I didn't want to keep."

"So if you don't want me to take your name. What are you planning—"

"I was hoping we might take yours," he says with a hesitant shrug. "I know it's not traditional, but we're not exactly either. And I asked your parents, and they were more than—"

I throw myself into his arms. He catches me with a loud grunt. I pull back, cupping his chin with both hands. "You really want to be a Creed?"

He grins. "I thought I already was."

"Hell yeah, you are." I chuckle, but then ask, "Why the change of heart?"

His brow furrows. "What do you mean?"

"When we were walking to the showroom, and that woman referred to you as a Creed, you stiffened like it offended you."

"It didn't offend me," he explains. "It just surprised me. And then all those old insecurities started to kick in. I didn't want you to take my last name, but I wasn't sure I deserved to take yours."

"Hollis, you've been a Creed since the day you walked into that kitchen twelve years ago."

"And now I want to make it official."

I wrap my arms around his neck. "Well, you know there's only one way to do that, right?"

His brow furrows. "With a legal document signed by a judge?"

"No." My lips curve into a smile. "With ink."

"Why am I blindfolded, Pres?" Hollis groans as we walk into the tattoo studio. He's holding onto my arm, and we've been walking at a snail's pace ever since he almost ate pavement when his boot hit the curb. "I already know where we're going. You haven't exactly been subtle. And you could have at least used a different blindfold than the one we use when we're fu—"

"We're here!" I exclaim, ripping that damn blindfold off his face. His eyes adjust and then widen as he takes in everyone standing in front of us.

"Oh! Oh, shit," he mutters, realizing what he was just in the middle of saying when we walked in.

"Uh, surprise?" Hendrix does some weird jazz hands, and everyone chuckles.

"You really all showed up for this?" Hollis seems genuinely surprised. I think it's going to take some time for him to fully settle into the idea of a family.

"Of course we did," Myles says. "It's a family tradition."

"It's initiation rites," Zander adds, his arms crossed over his broad chest, revealing the tattoo he got years ago in this very studio. It took some work, but we managed to persuade them to close for the afternoon to accommodate us. It sounds bougie as hell, but it's the only way we could get Zander and Hendrix here without causing a riot.

"It's our legacy." My dad offers Hollis a hug. A swell of emotions twists my throat. "And it means a lot to me that you all started it."

"Wait." Hollis holds up a hand. "You guys started it?"

"Oh, not *us*." Hollis motions with his finger, pointing to the siblings as a whole, and then points to just one. "Cash."

"Cash?" My husband sounds like he's just been told they're remaking *The Goonies*. A little confused. Possibly excited. Maybe a little nervous.

Cash, however, just stands there in his polished gray suit, looking completely unbothered by the revelation. He glances around the room and shrugs. "I'm a sentimental motherfucker. What can I say?"

The whole room explodes in laughter.

"We still think he did it to impress Dad," Hendrix says once everyone settles down.

Cash flashes a rare smile. "Why would I need to? Pretty perfect already." Then he sighs. "It was a Father's Day present. I got it to match his, and then all you assholes had to copy me."

If he's trying to sound annoyed, he's doing a terrible job.

"So, Hollis, where's it gonna be?" Dad asks, slinging an arm over my mom's shoulder.

He looks to me, then his gaze drifts down to my arm. "I didn't think I had a choice."

"Oh, you do. This isn't a brand or anything." Myles laughs. "I have mine on my rib cage. Easier to hide that way. Makeup artists hate tattoos." He emphasizes his point by lifting his shirt to show the five letters that run vertically down the side of his rib cage.

"That must have hurt like a bitch."

"It did, in fact, suck," he confirms.

"Mine is on my collarbone," Mom says with a warm smile. "Close to my heart."

There is a chorus of awws.

"So where will it be?" Hen asks.

Hollis glances at me, and I feel that same flutter in my stomach I've been getting since I was sixteen. "I think I have an idea."

"Okay, be honest," Hollis says, his eyes glittering with amusement, as we zip down the freeway. "Exactly how much hotter am I with this tattoo?"

He grips the steering wheel and flexes his forearm. He got it in the exact spot as mine. In the exact font. God, we're one of those couples who have matching tattoos.

And I fucking love it.

"Well, right now, it's covered in a bandage and oozing blood, so I'd say not much at the moment, but check back later?"

"I'll hold you to that. In like two weeks, when I'm done shedding skin like a snake."

"Don't forget about the itching."

"What the fuck? It's gonna itch too?"

"Oh yeah." I nod. "You'll be slapping it like crazy just to get some relief...and I'll laugh and laugh."

"That doesn't sound very supportive of my suffering."

I snort. "What if I agree to rub the lotion on it for you and then maybe rub some other parts of you as well?"

His face lights up, but he keeps his eyes on the road. "Now we're talking."

He takes an exit—the wrong one—and I glance over at him with a puzzled look. "Why does it feel like I'm suddenly having a case of déjà vu?"

"I don't know." He shrugs. "I'm just driving."

Once again, instead of heading for our apartment, we go west toward Malibu. I don't bother asking if we're headed to the bar or my parents'.

I already know our destination.

We're going home.

Something warm and wonderful blossoms inside of me when I say this to myself. Home.

As an adult, I dreamed of having a space I could make my own. I could paint the walls pink or knock them down. It was mine, after all.

But for my husband, a home meant safety. Security. Love.

I'll never quite understand how much it means to him to finally have all those things, but I'm so glad I'm the one who gets to share it with him.

When we pull into the familiar circular drive, he parks, and we get out. The landscapers we hired have already been by to spruce up the front, pulling all the weeds and replacing dead plants with drought-resistant ones. The once depressing exterior now looks healthy and lush.

When we get inside, he looks around and then turns back to me. "I know there's no furniture, but I thought it might be nice to order a pizza and just..."

I smile. "Yeah, that sounds nice."

While he orders pizza—extra cheese, obviously—I walk through the kitchen and run my hands over the brown granite that will be taken out and replaced next week.

I wonder what memories were made here.

Did they roll out dough for Christmas cookies? Have a flour fight? Did a big discussion take place at this island? Maybe even an argument or two?

Whatever memories this home has, I look forward to adding our own. The perfect ones, like lazy Sundays in the winter, drinking coffee on the deck under a pile of blankets while we watch the tide come in. And even the not-so-perfect. Because there will be hard times.

Life is bound to have struggles.

But as long as we have each other, we'll weather whatever storm comes our way.

As quietly as I can manage, I slip out the sliding glass door onto the deck and pull out my phone. Smiling to myself, I type out a text.

ME

Is this still Hollis Beck's number?

A second later, three dots appear on the screen.

HOLLIS

It's Hollis Creed these days, thank you very much. Who the hell is this? Also... where are you?

My smile widens into a stupidly wide grin. Good, he's playing along.

ME

I'll give you three clues. If you guess correctly, then you'll know where to find me.

HOLLIS

This better not be some sort of weird scam to get me to send you dick pics, cause I am a happily married man.

ME

Yeah? She pretty?

HOLLIS

So pretty. But also a little displaced. You wouldn't happen to know where she is, would you?

I snort out a laugh, but quickly stifle it. I don't want him to find me quite yet.

ME

First clue: We were always more than neighbors.

HOLLIS

Patricia? I knew you had a crush on me!

ME

I swear to god, Hollis. So not funny. Also, Patricia?

HOLLIS

Had to think on the fly. Anyway, continue...

I forgive him for breaking character, and I chuck off my shoes, burying my toes in the sand.

ME

Clue number two: I tried to teach you how to surf. Emphasis on the word tried.

HOLLIS

Maybe you're just a bad teacher.

ME

And maybe you should just stick to a boogie board.

HOLLIS

Where the fuck are you, woman?!

I let out a contented sigh and smile as the sun slips behind the horizon. The sound of the waves is like the soundtrack to our love story, and we're barely through track one.

ME

Clue number three: We may have spent seven minutes in heaven, but I'd take a lifetime on the beach with you any day.

Those three dots appear and then disappear. A minute or two goes by, and then I hear the soft crunch of wet sand behind me. I don't bother turning around.

His arms slide around my waist. "Hi."

I look up at him, and he's staring down at me with those intense green eyes. "Want to go for a walk?" he asks.

"Always."

And then we walk hand in hand down the beach, knowing that if it weren't for a bit of trouble and a whole lot of love, none of this would have ever been possible.

EPILOGUE

Presley

"Oh, damn. You look nice," I exclaim as I come to a screeching halt in the middle of our bedroom. The sound of crashing waves echoes softly in the background.

We've been in our new house for about six weeks. Renos took a little longer than we anticipated. With the holidays and back orders, we ended up having to stay in our apartment for a while.

But it was worth it. The house is exactly how we imagined it. Creamy white walls. Beautiful hardwood floors throughout. Comfy couches and soft textures. Everything is understated, designed not to distract from the stunning view of the Pacific.

We walk along the shoreline almost every night.

I never want to leave.

Hollis is standing in front of the full-length mirror, adjusting a sleek black tie. It looks amazing with the trim black suit I chose for him.

My mouth practically waters.

His eyes meet mine in the mirror and spark with heat. "Jesus. Not as nice as you," he replies, abandoning his tie to pivot on his heels and face me. I watch as his gaze rakes over every inch of me. I had no idea what to pick out for this event. I decided to go with something sexy, but with a bit of an edge. The tight leather mini dress does just that and was clearly a good choice, judging by the way my husband is devouring me with his eyes right now.

He closes the distance between us and wraps an arm around my waist. "What if we just skipped this thing tonight and spent the evening peeling this dress off you instead?"

My lips twitch with amusement. "And by this *thing*, you mean the opening night of your new club?"

He nods.

"The one everyone in LA is dying to get into. The club that even top celebrities are clamoring to visit? *That thing*?"

He shrugs, lip twitching. "I mean, when you put it like that..."

I laugh. "Are you nervous, Hollis?"

"Fucking terrified."

I wrap my arms around him. "What about?"

"Running an entire club on my own. Failing miserably. Having to wear a suit every damn day again."

I try to fight the grin he's causing. He really hates suits.

"First of all, you're not alone. Is Jonas all by himself in Nashville?"

"No," he answers right away. "I'm just a phone call away. Plus, we have management staff and—" He presses his lips together, intentionally pausing. "I see your point."

"Good. You also know that fear of failing is perfectly

normal when starting something new. Especially when you care so much."

"Pretty sure I've told you that a time or two when it comes to the bar."

"You did," I agree. "And I'm glad you did. Sometimes we need a reminder. If I had let my fear and doubt consume me, it would have ruined any chances I had of righting the wrongs Jace had done under my watch."

It had been about six months since Jace broke into the bar and nearly destroyed us. Three months since he threatened and tried to extort me for money.

And he didn't get away with any of it.

Under the guidance of his lawyer, Jace took a plea deal and received a four-year prison sentence. There are days when I still look back and feel like I should have done more, noticed more.

But then I remind myself I am not responsible for his poor choices.

Unfortunately, I am responsible for the consequences of those choices, and it took a while for the bar to recoup the losses he stole from the stockroom.

"The bar is flourishing because of you."

"Because of us," I correct him. "And this club is going to do the same."

"Okay."

"As for the suits..." I run a hand down his lapel, causing him to laugh. "You are the owner, if I remember correctly. I do believe that gives you the power to make your own rules." His eyes flare like he's never even contemplated that idea. "Also, it's not every day. You hired a manager so you could spend your weekends with your wife."

His lips quirk. "Yes, and when is my wife going to hire a manager?"

"Soon." I shrug, but then give him a flirty wink. "What's the hurry when you do the work for free?"

"You just like having me around."

I shrug. "You are very pretty to look at. Plus, I love seeing the way you blush every time someone comes in and asks for a picture with Hero Hollis."

He rolls his eyes. "I really thought that would blow over."

"You clearly underestimated the power of BookTok."

"You clearly overestimate my understanding of the meaning of BookTok."

I start to adjust his tie. "Well, I'd love to explain—again—but we should probably get going. Don't want to be late to this *thing*," I say with a hint of amusement. "You and Jonas are the guests of honor after all."

He groans. "Don't remind me."

I pat his shoulder. "Don't worry. If what Hen says is true and Asher shows up, no one will care about you in the slightest."

"See, that might upset someone else, but for me, it's actually very calming. Thanks."

Smiling, I say, "Maybe we could even sneak off and celebrate privately in your office?"

He perks up. "Well, it is a pretty big deal."

"That's the spirit."

HOLLIS

There are so many people here. *Too many people.*

My hands start to get clammy. My pulse starts to race.

Something doesn't feel right.

Our driver is sitting in a line of cars, inching closer to the club.

"What's the holdup?" I lean forward, trying to get a better view from the front. "Can you see anything?"

He shakes his head. "Nothing, sir. I think there are just too many cars. Not enough parking."

Well, that appears pretty obvious.

But the question is why.

This is an invite-only event. An *exclusive,* invite-only event.

Sure, there is a lot of buzz around the opening of the club. And like Pres said, everyone in LA is clamoring to get their chance to walk through the doors, including top-name celebrities.

But we didn't publicize who was attending tonight's opening. We didn't invite the press. Doesn't mean I didn't expect a few to show up anyway, but we have protocol in place to distract them.

Because we're selling an experience, and we can't do that if there are screaming fans and flashing cameras everywhere.

"Fuck." I blow out a breath.

"Do you think someone told the press?" Pres asks.

I shake my head, scrubbing a hand down my face. "Not anyone on the list, at least," I say. "Jonas and I handpicked everyone. Not a single one of them would want this circus following them. It's why we chose them. We knew they'd want what the club had to offer."

Exclusivity. Privacy. Anonymity.

"Someone else then?"

"Maybe."

The car lurches forward, but at this pace, we're better off walking. In the mob outside, though, I'm not so sure it's worth the risk.

My phone starts to buzz, and I quickly pull it out of my pocket. Relief sweeps over me when I see Jonas's name flash across the screen.

"Hey," I answer.

But before I can say anything else, he cuts me off and says, "Where are you?"

"Stuck around the block in traffic. Where are you?"

"Also stuck in fucking traffic," he growls. "I was hoping at least one of us would be inside."

"Do you know what the hell is going on?"

"No," he answers. "But this is not the vibe we were going for, Hollis. I know there is a lot of buzz around the club, and I expected a bit of noise outside—people always show up when there's talk of celebrities—but this is insane. It looks like the merch line Keisha made me stand in at the Taylor Swift concert."

"Oh my god. It wasn't that bad," I hear her mutter.

"It was three fucking hours!"

"Why don't we get out and walk?" Pres suggests, looking out the window in hopes of catching a glimpse of the hotel.

"Are you sure?" I cast a wary glance at the crowd.

"It's either that or we sit in this car for the next hour or two."

My eyes dart from her to the sidewalk. "Okay," I agree, then I address Jonas. "Hey, we're gonna walk to the club. I'll let you know what we find out."

"Okay," he says. "We might join you if it doesn't get any better shortly."

"Sounds good."

I inform the driver that we'll be taking it from here and give him a hefty tip, feeling guilty that he'll be stuck in this traffic for the foreseeable future.

When we step out of the car, I do my best to shield Pres from the crowd, wrapping an arm around her waist as we make quick work down the street toward the club.

If anyone recognizes us, I don't pay any attention. I just keep focused on making it to our destination so I can figure out why the fuck all these people are here in the first place.

It occurs to me that I could probably ask one of them, but that would risk exposing us, and since that awkward Hero Hollis thing is still alive and well...

Yeah, no thanks.

We finally make it to the back entrance of Vine. It's where VIP guests are supposed to check in and where the bouncer meets us.

"Evening, Mr. Creed."

"Hi, Kevin. How many guests have checked in?" I ask him.

"Only a few," he replies, glancing at the list.

"Fuck. Can I see?"

Sure enough, almost every name remains unchecked.

Not that I'm surprised. The crowd outside is enough to spook even the bravest celebrities into staying in for the night.

I scan the list and let out a sigh of relief. "The family is here," I tell Pres. "Even Hen and Zander."

"They wouldn't miss this. You know that."

I swallow hard, feeling a lump in my throat. "I know."

"Come on." She takes my hand. "Let's go find them. Maybe they'll know what's going on."

"Okay," I reply, then thank Kevin and head inside.

The place is gorgeous. Brimming with elegance and old Hollywood charm, it's everything Jonas said it could be.

And more.

The only thing that's missing is the crowd.

The small groups of people wandering around make the space seem a little overwhelming. It reminds me of the one and only time I went to a school dance in middle school. I showed up early, and the boys were all huddled on one side, the girls on the other. The gym looked so much larger in the dark, like it could swallow us whole.

That's how the club looks right now, and I hate it.

My stomach twists.

This is not how tonight is supposed to go.

Pres suddenly raises her hand and waves, and I look to where she's signaling and see the rest of the Creeds huddled together. Lance looks up, his face far too serious for tonight's festivities.

"That doesn't look good," Pres comments.

"No," I agree. "Come on, let's go figure out what's wrong."

We cross what is meant to be the dance floor, but is now just an empty space in the middle of the room, to get to the rest of the family.

They greet us with hugs, but the hellos are overshadowed by something. Everyone seems tense.

"Anyone want to tell us what's going on?"

They all look at each other. Finally, Lance speaks up. "Asher's publicist went rogue. She got fed up with him refusing to make public appearances and declining interviews. Said he was ruining his career by turning himself into a hermit."

"What does that have to do with my club?"

"We're unsure if the two are connected, but given the timing, it is highly suspicious," Hen takes over. "Some pics were posted online yesterday. Then, an hour later, his publicist announced he was attending your opening."

I don't ask what kind of pics. If they were posted online, they're never the good kind. "Fucking hell."

"It gets worse."

"How much worse?" Pres asks.

"Asher's gone. He flew back to Scotland. He says he's not coming back," Zander says, pain etched in every word. "He quit the band."

A LOOK AT BOOK THREE

Scandal

A slow-burn celebrity romance where the spotlight is fake, the sparks are real, and one staged affair risks turning into something *dangerously* true.

After a scandal wrecks his career, Asher Knight—lead singer of Manic at Midnight—escapes to his family's estate in Scotland, hoping to disappear. But silence doesn't stop the noise, especially with aristocratic parents ready to mold their disgraced son back into the heir they expected.

Mercury Creed has admired Asher from afar for years. When no one else can reach him, she is sent to do the impossible—bring him home. Instead, she finds a man unraveling under the weight of legacy, expectations, and a life he no longer recognizes.

Thrown together as a carefully curated PR stunt, the two must navigate charity galas, suffocating expectations, and the dangerous intimacy of playing a role too well. What begins as a performance quickly turns into something real—something neither of them is prepared to lose.

This was only supposed to fool the press.

And falling in love was *never* part of the plan.

AVAILABLE JUNE 2026

ACKNOWLEDGMENTS

This is my twenty-second novel.

They say it never gets easier, but this is definitely the hardest book I've ever written. I can say with one hundred percent certainty that trying to write a book while also selling your house and moving is not recommended.

But these characters were also difficult. They fought me at every turn, but I think I finally worked it out.

This book, more than any other, would never have been possible without my family. My kids literally ran and got my Starbucks almost every day near the end to keep me motivated.

My husband literally packed up our whole damn house while I wrote from morning till night.

Without them, I never would have finished.

I'm so beyond grateful to Ellie, Kyla, and everyone at Love N. Books Press. They are always supportive—especially when I needed a little extra time on this one.

As always, I thank my readers—both old and new. Thank you for taking a chance on this brand-new series. Thanks for falling in love with Hen and Zara and Pres and Hollis. I hope you're ready. Asher is next!

Lots of Love,

Jenn

J.L. Berg is the USA Today bestselling author of the Ready Series and has written over a dozen other novels in the past decade. She is a California native but currently calls Virginia home.

When she's not writing, you will likely find her spending time with her family or watching Doctor Who. J.L. Berg is represented by Jill Marsal of Marsal Lyon Literary Agency, LLC

www.jlberg.com
J.L. Berg's Readers Group

www.ingramcontent.com/pod-product-compliance
Lightning Source LLC
LaVergne TN
LVHW041249110826
845146LV00005BA/1283
9798895677650